ORCHID BEACH

ORCHID BEACH

A Novel

Stuart Woods

HarperCollins*Publishers*

HarperCollins books may be purchased for educational, business, or sales promotional use. For information please write: Special Markets Department, HarperCollins Publishers, Inc., 10 East 53rd Street, New York, NY 10022.

FIRST EDITION

Designed by Elina D. Nudelman

Library of Congress Cataloging-in-Publication Data

Woods, Stuart
    Orchid Beach / Stuart Woods. — 1st ed.
        p.   cm.
    ISBN 0-06-019181-3
    I. Title.
    PS3573.064207   1998
    813'.54—dc21   98-23628

98 99 00 01 02 ❖/RRD 10 9 8 7 6 5 4 3 2 1

This book is for Carol Nelson and Harry de Polo

ORCHID
BEACH

1

Holly Barker, with the rest of the crowd, was called to her feet as the panel of officers filed into the courtroom. She was a spectator now, no longer a witness, but she wanted to be here for this.

Colonel James Bruno stood at the defense table, ramrod straight, and watched his judges with beady eyes. For the first time since his trial had begun, he was not smiling.

"Seats!" the clerk of the court called out, and all sat.

The brigadier general, who was president of the court, cleared his throat. "The following three verdicts have been reached unanimously," the general said. "As to the first charge, sexual harassment, we have reached a verdict of not guilty."

Holly's stomach shrank into a knot. She locked her knees so that they would not buckle. She knew what could only come next.

"As to the second charge, attempted rape, we have reached a verdict of not guilty," the general said. "And as to the third charge, conduct unbecoming an officer, we have reached a verdict of not guilty."

"Yes!" screamed a woman in the front row.

Holly recognized her as Colonel Bruno's wife. It was the first time she had appeared in court.

"Colonel Bruno," the general said, "you are restored to duty. This court is adjourned."

Holly made her way slowly through the crowd, ignoring the reporters who were demanding her reaction to the verdict. On her way she came abreast of the young blond lieutenant who had been the other complainant in the case. Holly found her hand and squeezed. The woman was in tears.

The cold outside air struck like a slap, reviving her, and she saw her father's car at the curb. She got in beside him.

"I'm sorry," he said. He was dressed in his master sergeant's uniform and wore the green beret of the special forces.

"You knew, didn't you?" she asked.

Hamilton Barker nodded. "It was in the cards," he said. "It was Bruno's word against yours. He's a West Pointer, and so were most of the court. They weren't going to destroy his career."

"They've destroyed mine," Holly said. She could see the gold oak leaf on her left shoulder out of the corner of her eye.

"You can request a transfer, and they can't deny it," her father said.

"Come on, Ham. They'd never let me forget it. I'd end up in some unit commanded by a classmate of Bruno's, and I'd be repeatedly passed over for promotion on some pretext or other."

Her father said nothing.

"I could get a job on a police force somewhere," she said.

"Funny you should mention that," her father replied.

They sat in a steak house near the base, the ruins of their dinner before them. The talk had been of army, Vietnam and army, and Holly had done all the listening.

She liked Ham's friend and old comrade-in-arms, Chet Marley; he was smaller and skinnier than Ham, but he had the same wiry toughness as her father, the same crow's-feet around the eyes from squinting into the distance. And he seemed very smart.

"Okay, enough of this old-soldier stuff," Marley said suddenly.

"I've got a problem, Holly, and I think you might be the person to help me solve it."

"Tell me, Chet," Holly said.

"I'm chief of a twenty-four-man force in Orchid Beach, Florida, and there's a gaping hole where the number-two man ought to be."

"Don't you believe in promoting from within?" Holly asked.

"I believe in the best man for the job," Marley said. "Or woman," he added.

"You short of good men?"

"I'm short of experienced men. Most of them are in their twenties. I've got one man who's forty and has experience, but I don't trust him."

"Don't trust him, how?" Holly asked.

"He's a politician, and I don't like politicians. He thinks he should have my job, which is okay, I guess, except he'd screw it up if he had it."

"Why don't you fire him?"

"He's never given me any real cause, and he's connected with some of the city council."

"That's bad, I guess," Holly replied. "I'm no politician, but I can see how that could be difficult to deal with."

"I'm going to retire next year, and I don't want him to have my job," Marley said. "My idea is to bring in an experienced . . . person, somebody who can take charge and be ready when I go."

Holly nodded, but said nothing.

"I know about your record from your old man," Marley said, "and I've asked around some, too, because I wouldn't take his word for anything." He grinned and cast a sideways glance at Ham Barker. "You're already running more MPs than I've got cops. I've heard about your unit citations and the level of training and performance you demand from your people, and I like what I hear."

"Thank you," she said.

"Of course, we're not the army, and things have to be handled a little different in civilian life, but I think you could get used to that."

"I'm sure I could," Holly said.

"It's a nice town, Orchid Beach. It sits on a barrier island halfway down the east coast of Florida, has a population of around twenty thousand, a lot of them retirees."

"Lots of tourists?"

"No, not really tourists. We get the same folks back, year after year, most of them to family beach houses—folks from Atlanta and Charlotte and Birmingham, and a lot of northeasterners. We've got no high-rise hotels, no casinos and only a few motels. There's a small black community and a stable blue-collar group, mostly construction workers, plumbers, electricians and a few retired military folk. We've got a low crime rate and not much of a drug problem, until recently."

"How much of a drug problem?"

"Less than in a lot of small towns, but it's there, and it has to be dealt with. We don't have the violent crime that comes with a bad drug problem."

"That's good."

"You interested?"

She certainly was. "Yes."

"I can pay you what you're making as a major," he said. "There's no PX, but we've got health insurance and a pension plan."

"What's the housing situation like?"

"Not great. Prices are going up, and cheap houses are getting knocked down and replaced with more expensive stuff."

"I live in a trailer here," Holly said.

"Bring it with you. I've got a friend runs a real nice park south of town, on the river side of the island."

"This all sounds very good," Holly said, her gloom beginning to lift. "Ham's retiring one of these days, too, and I guess he wouldn't mind moving south."

"Got any golf down there?" her father asked.

"You bet. Got a great public course and six or eight good private ones—one or two a retired master sergeant could afford to join."

Ham turned to Holly. "Chet's not a bad guy to work for," he said. "I worked for him for three years, and I didn't have to kill him."

"When can you start?" Marley asked.

"Hang on, this is all kind of quick," Holly said.

"I like decisiveness in a . . . an officer."

Holly stuck out her hand. "You're on," she said, "as soon as I can get my resignation in and turn over my command in an orderly fashion."

Ham ordered another round of drinks. "My daughter, the cop," he said, raising his glass.

"Your daughter, the cop, has hardly ever been anything else," Holly said, laughing.

They drank deeply and sat in silence for a moment. Marley seemed to want to say something, but he was having trouble.

"Was there something else, Chief?" Holly asked.

"I don't want to get into this too deep right now," he said, "but I've got a problem you need to know about up front."

"Okay, shoot."

"Somebody on my force is working for somebody besides me," he said. "I don't know who it is, and I don't know who he's working for, but I've got some suspicions about that."

"Drugs?"

"Could be. Could be more than that. Thing is, I don't have anything like an internal-affairs department, so in addition to all your other duties, you're going to have to be it. You'll come to the job without any slant on personalities or on who's doing what, and I think you can be a lot more objective than I can."

"I see."

"Does this trouble you?"

"On the contrary. It intrigues me."

Marley grinned. "Good. Like I say, I don't want to go into all this right here and now, but I promise, your first day on the job I'll brief you on everything I know. And by that time, I should know a lot more."

"Fair enough."

Marley sighed deeply. "I'm glad I got that off my chest. I was worried it might make some kind of difference to you."

"Not to worry," Holly said. She lifted her glass. "To Orchid Beach."

They all drank again.

2

Holly drove across the bridge over the sound at the north end
of the island and headed down Highway A1A onto the barrier island that contained Orchid Beach. She had already passed Mel-
bourne and Sebastian; Vero Beach lay farther south, on the next
island. It was early evening, and she had been driving all day and
the day before that, with one uncomfortable night in a cheap motel
in between. She was tired.

At first there was little to see on either side of the road; then she
began passing impressive sets of gates with the names of communities inscribed on them. At each there was a guard booth and a security officer to screen visitors. Usually, she couldn't see much of what
lay beyond the gates, but she caught an occasional glimpse of large,
expensive houses peeking through the live oaks and palms. She
rolled down her window and from the east she could hear the roll
of the surf, a pleasant sound. The soft, warm subtropical air was a
nice change from the cold weather she had left behind.

She came to the business district of the town, with rows of neat small businesses on either side of the road and the occasional motel, usually with a NO VACANCY sign out front. Business looked good. She passed restaurants and dry cleaning establishments and a great many real estate offices; then she was back in residential territory, with small subdivisions that, while less ritzy than those on the north side of town, looked prosperous and comfortable. These usually had gates, but no guards, and the houses were more visible from the road.

Then the terrain became less crowded and after another minute or two she saw a sign for Riverview Park on her right. She turned into the gates, swinging wide to allow the silver trailer behind her to pass in without uprooting a gatepost, and stopped in front of a small structure with a sign outside reading OWNER & MANAGER. She pulled over, switched off the engine, got out of her dark green Jeep Grand Cherokee and went into the building. A plump man in his sixties looked up from behind a desk and smiled.

"Bet I know who you are," he said, rising and extending his hand. "I'm Johnny Malone, I own the place."

"I'm Holly Barker," she said, shaking the hand.

"Sure you are. Chet Marley told me to expect you, and I got your check and the contract in the mail. Come on, follow me; I've got a real nice spot picked out for you." He walked out of the building, hopped into a golf cart and beckoned her to follow.

Holly drove slowly behind the cart, checking out her new neighbors. The trailers and double-wides were all well kept and were often surrounded by flowers and shrubs. Riverside Park looked like a happy place. They drove through a patch of woods, leaving the other tenants behind, and emerged onto a flat piece of ground at the edge of the Indian River, which Holly had learned was what that part of the Inland Waterway was called. Following Malone's hand signals, she backed the Airstream trailer into its space, then got out and unhitched it from her car. In a few minutes Malone had made the water, sewer, telephone and electrical connections for her, and she had the trailer leveled and braced.

"We got cable TV, if you want it," Malone said.

"I've got one of those little dishes," Holly said.

"More and more folks do," he replied. "Anything else I can do for you?"

"Not right now," she replied. "I'm sure I'll have some questions tomorrow."

Malone handed her his card. "Here's my number, and Chet Marley's home number is on the back. He said you should call him as soon as you get in."

"I'll do that," Holly replied.

Malone drove away in his golf cart, and Holly went into her trailer, switched on some lights and began tidying the things that had shifted during the drive. She was hungry, but she wanted to talk to Marley before dinner. They had talked a number of times during the five weeks it had taken her to retire from the military. She dialed his number.

"Hello?" He sounded rushed.

"Chet? It's Holly. I just got in."

"Oh, good. Everything all right for you at Riverview?"

"Sure is. I've even got a river view."

"Boy, am I glad you're here. I wanted to buy you dinner tonight, Holly, but something's come up, and I have to meet with somebody."

"That's all right. I'm kind of tired, anyway."

"It's about that internal problem I told you about."

"Anything new on that?"

"A whole lot. I'm getting close, now, and after my meeting tonight, I'm going to be ready to start knocking some heads together. Looks like there's not going to be as much for you to do as I thought."

"Well, I'm glad you've got a handle on it," she replied. "I know you've been worried."

"I sure have. Listen, you show up at the station at nine tomorrow morning, and I'll bring you up to date and get you started. I've got a boxful of uniforms for you, and we'll get you a badge and ID and a weapon issued. There's going to be a lot to do, even without the internal problem, because we're going to be a little shorthanded after I'm finished."

"That's fine," she said, "I'll see you in the morning."

They hung up. Holly went to the kitchen and found a steak and a bottle of cabernet, then she got out the stainless steel grill, set it up outside and hooked up the gas bottle, which, she noticed, seemed almost empty. She started the grill, then unstrapped her lawn furniture from the rack on the trailer, poured herself a glass of wine, put the steak on the fire and sat down to watch the sun set over the river. The water had turned purple and gold, and the sun made a big red ball as it sank through the haze. She turned the steak, sipped the wine and took it all in. Her new home was on a small inlet leading from the main river, surrounded by acres of marsh, with a little dock a few feet away. Maybe she'd buy a boat. She'd taken the money she'd saved, plus her part of the insurance money from her mother, who had died three years before, paid off the loan on the trailer, traded in her car and put the rest into treasury bills and a mutual fund. She drank her wine and took stock.

She was thirty-seven years old, with exactly twenty years in the military behind her. She'd enlisted at seventeen, been assigned to the MPs at nineteen, gotten her bachelor's degree through the University of Maryland program that operated on military bases all over the world, gone to Officer Candidate School at twenty-two and worked her way up to major and command of a company of MPs. That was when Colonel Bruno had taken a liking to her, and nothing had been the same since. What had started as a simple pass, rebuffcd, had turncd into a ycarlong campaign of would-be seduction that had ended in a nearly successful attempt to rape her. That was when she could take it no longer and had pressed charges.

Holly had known that prosecuting him would be an uphill battle, but when the young lieutenant had walked into her office and told her own story of Bruno's abuse, she had thought the corroboration of another officer would put the man in prison, or at least get him out of the military. It still stung to know how wrong she had been.

She fixed herself a salad and ate the steak absently, reflecting on the life that had brought her to Orchid Beach. What had she done wrong? Why had this happened to her? She had made a real career for herself in the army, with consistently outstanding evaluations by her superiors. She'd have made lieutenant colonel in another six months and retired after thirty years as a full colonel. As it was, she'd have only the twenty-year pension as a major, which, while it wasn't bad, wasn't what she had planned on. With a little luck, she might even have made it to brigadier general, which would have made Ham proud enough to pop—her mother, too, if she could look down from where she surely was.

She sat until well past dark, trying to limit herself to half the bottle of wine and failing, then she picked up her dishes and cleaned up the kitchen. She put a rubber cork into what was left of the bottle and pumped the air out, keeping it fresh for another time.

She took one more look out the door at the river. The moon had risen and the resulting streak of light across the water came nearly to her feet. An army brat her whole life, right now she was a civilian for the first time. Tomorrow she'd be a cop. She'd get in a run early, to work off the effects of the wine; then she'd be at her new job on the dot.

She undressed and got into bed, naked, and began to drift off. The crickets in the swamp lulled her to sleep. Chet Marley had made a good decision, she thought. She'd do him proud.

3

Holly found the municipal building half a block off the beach, parked her car in the public lot, went into the building and consulted the directory. Everything seemed neatly packaged in one four-story structure—city manager's office, council offices, tax office, city attorney, water authority and the other municipal departments, all on the upper floors. Directly ahead on the ground floor, behind a set of glass doors, was the Orchid Beach Police Department. She walked in.

A uniformed officer in what appeared to be his early twenties sat behind a broad desk, a high stool bringing him to her eye level. "Good morning," she said, "my name is Barker; I have an appointment with Chief Marley."

He blinked at her, but didn't move for a moment. "Just a minute," he said finally, then got up and walked down a row of small offices and disappeared into one. A moment later he returned, followed by an older uniformed officer.

"Morning," the officer said. He was a little over six feet, of slim build, with glossy black hair cut short. "Can I help you?"

"I have an appointment with Chief Marley," she said again.

He nodded and opened a gate in the railing that separated the public area from the squad room, where half a dozen desks sat, most of them empty. "Follow me," he said.

Holly followed the officer to the rear wall of the squad room, and into a large glass-fronted office. He sat down behind the desk and indicated with a silent gesture that she should sit opposite.

"The chief's not in," he said. "Can I help you with something?" His attitude was blank, noncommittal, not impolite.

"Chief Marley is expecting me," she said. "I'll wait."

"Who are you?" the man asked.

"My name is Holly Barker." She waited for a response but got none. "Who are you?" She kept her voice at the same level as his.

"Lieutenant Wallace," the man replied. "What did you want to see the chief about?"

Holly was a little surprised that her name didn't ring a bell with Wallace, but perhaps Chet Marley had his reasons for not spreading the word that she was coming to work that day. "I think I'd better wait for the chief and take it up with him," she said.

"Chief Marley won't be in today," Wallace said. "I'm acting chief. Maybe you'd better take it up with me."

"Acting chief?" Holly said, wrinkling her brow. "I don't understand; the chief asked me to be here at nine this morning. Why isn't he coming in?"

"That's an official matter," Wallace said.

"So is my appointment with the chief," she replied evenly.

"Do you know the chief?" Wallace asked.

"Yes."

"When did you last speak with him?"

"Last night around seven-thirty."

"In person?"

"On the phone."

"Do you know where he was at the time?"

"He was at home. I called him there."

"How long did you talk?"

"Only a couple of minutes. He asked me to come in this morning."

"For what purpose?"

"I'd rather the chief told you about that."

"The chief's not going to be able to do that."

Now Holly was growing alarmed. "What do you mean?"

"The chief took a bullet in the head last night."

Holly sat up straight. "Is he dead?"

"Not yet."

At that moment, a handsome middle-aged woman bustled breathlessly into the room, startling Holly. "Are you Miss Barker?" she asked.

"Yes," Holly replied.

"I'm so sorry to be late," the woman said. "I was at the hospital." She turned to Wallace. "Hurd, did you tell her?"

"Yeah, just now."

"I've just come from the hospital," the woman said. "I've been there since midnight."

"How is the chief?" Holly asked.

"He was in surgery most of the night; he's in the recovery room now."

"Any prognosis?"

"The doctors won't say anything, but they looked pretty grim. Oh, I'm sorry, I'm Jane Grey, the chief's assistant." She offered her hand.

Holly stood up and shook it. "Is there anything I can do?" she asked.

"I don't think so, but you and I have some things to go over. Why don't you come with me?" She turned to Wallace. "Hurd, I don't think you ought to be in the chief's office." She produced a bunch of keys, waited while Wallace left, then locked the office and beckoned to Holly.

Holly followed her to another office down the hall, as big as the chief's but crowded with filing cabinets, boxes and storage cabinets.

"Have a seat," Jane said. "This is where I live, if you can call it that."

"Tell me how the chief got shot," Holly said.

"Nobody knows exactly, but it looks like he might have tried to question somebody in a car, who pulled a gun on him. A motorist found him beside A1A around eleven last night. He was lying in front of his car, lit by the headlights. The man called 911 on his car phone, and an ambulance was there in under ten minutes. A woman I know who works in the emergency room called me, and by the time I got there he was already in surgery."

"I'd like to go and see him as soon as I can," Holly said.

"They promised they'd call me when they had some idea of how he's doing," Jane said. She seemed almost about to cry, but squared her shoulders and sat up straight. "I think the best thing you and I can do right now is get you processed and on the job." She unlocked a desk drawer and pulled out a file. "I've got all your paperwork right here; the chief signed everything before he went home last night. I do need to get some information for your ID." She turned to the computer terminal on her desk and punched a few keys.

"What would you like to know?"

"Date of birth?"

Holly told her.

"Height?"

"Five feet, eight inches."

"Weight?"

"A hundred and thirty-five pounds."

"Color of hair?"

"Light brown."

"Okay." Jane typed a command and a printer spat out a sheet of paper. "I'll need your social security number and next of kin."

Holly recited the number and gave her Ham's name and address.

"That's right, they were in the army together, weren't they?" Jane said.

"Yes, more than ten years ago. They kept in touch."

"There's another of their old army buddies living here, too—Hank Doherty. You'll have to meet him."

"My father mentioned him—he's the one with the dogs, isn't he?"

"Well . . . yes, I guess, but he's not as active in the dog-training business as he once was. Hank's . . . well, we can go into that later."

"All right."

"Okay, now documents." She began handing Holly documents to sign—health insurance, group life insurance, federal and state tax forms. "Good," Jane said, when Holly had signed everything. "You're on the payroll. Now let's get your ID done. Oh, we'd better get you in uniform for your photograph." She got up and closed the venetian blinds on the glass front of her office, then set a large cardboard box on her desk. "These are the uniforms we ordered for you, according to the sizes you gave us." She produced a khaki shirt. "Can you slip into this? I'll leave you alone, if you like."

"No, that's all right," Holly said. She slipped out of her slacks and shirt and into a uniform. Jane produced a badge from her desk drawer and pinned it on.

"Now, let's get your picture taken." She pulled down a home movie screen on one wall and produced a Polaroid camera from her bottomless desk drawers. "Just stand right there and look nice," she said, then snapped the picture. A moment later she had stuck the photograph to the computer printout and was laminating it in a desktop machine. "There," she said, looking satisfied with her work. She took a leather wallet from her desk, inserted the ID card and handed it to Holly. A gold shield was affixed to the wallet.

"Thank you, Jane."

"Now you're officially Deputy Chief Holly Barker, and nobody can do a damn thing about it. Your contract is for five years, after all."

"Might somebody want to do something about it?" Holly asked.

"You never know. Oh, one more thing," Jane said. She unlocked a heavy steel cabinet and took out a pistol with a holster and belt, a box of ammunition and an envelope. "Here's your weapon, a nine-millimeter Beretta automatic, and fifty rounds of ammunition. Sign right here." Holly signed. "You can have another weapon of your own, if you want to, but you'll need to register the serial number with me and fire a round for our ballistics records."

"Okay."

Jane opened the envelope and shook out a pair of handcuffs and two keys, then clipped them onto the pistol belt. "The chief likes everybody to have a spare handcuff key in their pocket, in case, God forbid, anybody should ever cuff you with your own handcuffs."

"Good idea."

Jane took a thick, ring-bound document from a shelf and handed it to Holly. "This is our bible," she said. "The chief has been working on it for a long time. It outlines our standard operating procedures for all personnel."

"The chief sent me a copy," Holly said. "I've read it, and I'm very impressed."

"He said he thought you might make some suggestions for revisions," Jane said.

"Not right away—maybe later."

Jane handed her a sheet of paper. "Here's a personnel roster with everybody's rank and assigned duties."

"I've seen this, too," Holly said. "I'm not sure I've memorized it yet, though."

"I believe you're all set," Jane said. "We've got an office ready for you next door. Let me show you." She led Holly into an office nearly as big as the chief's. It seemed well equipped and comfortable. "Here's the combination to your safe and your keys to your office and the building," she said, handing Holly a slip of paper and some keys. "I expect you should use the chief's car until . . . he's back at work. It's the blue, unmarked car in space one in the lot. Here are the keys."

"Thanks."

"There's a watch change at ten o'clock; we can officially introduce you then."

"Sounds good. I take it nobody but you and the chief knew I was coming?"

"That's the way the chief wanted it," she said.

"Jane, a minute ago, you said something about nobody being able to do anything about my being here. If people had known I was coming, might somebody have tried to do something about it?"

"Well," Jane said, "you never know, do you?"

"I guess not. I think I'd better see Lieutenant Wallace before the others. Will you ask him to come in here?" Holly settled herself behind her new desk and waited.

4

Two minutes passed before Hurd Wallace made his entrance. Holly stood up and stuck out her hand. "Let's start over," she said. "I'm Holly Barker, and I'm coming to work here today."

Wallace shook her hand. "Glad to meet you," he said. "Welcome aboard."

"Have a seat, and let's talk for a minute before the watch change."

Hurd did as he was asked.

Holly thought him the calmest person she had ever met. He seemed to have no reaction whatever to the news that he had been passed over for promotion, and that a strange woman was now his superior. "I know this comes as something of a surprise to you, and in a way, it is to me, too. I didn't know that there had been no announcement about my arrival."

"That was a surprise, yes," Wallace said.

"The chief hired me more than a month ago. I've been arranging my retirement from the army; I arrived in town last night."

"Anything I can do to help you settle in?"

"Thanks, but I think I'm okay. I'm at Riverview Park, in a trailer. I was already living in it off base."

"I see."

"Hurd—may I call you Hurd?"

"Of course."

"And I'm Holly to you, when we're alone, but not to the rest of the force. Hurd, I'm aware that you might have expected to get this job, and I'm sorry that things have been complicated even more by the shooting of the chief last night. I hope we're going to be able to work together smoothly."

"I'm sure we will," Wallace said.

"Before I meet the others, I'd like to be brought up to date on the shooting last night. Who's handling the investigation?"

"Bob Hurst, detective sergeant. He's our best man on homicides—that's how we're treating this."

"I'd like to talk to him as soon as possible."

"He was up all night working the crime scene and going over the chief's car. I told him to get some sleep."

"Don't wake him, but I want to talk to him at the earliest opportunity. In the meantime, tell me what you know."

"In a nutshell, a passerby found the chief lying in front of his car on the shoulder of A1A, just after eleven last night. He'd been shot once in the head, but he was still alive. Bob Hurst got there right after the ambulance arrived; I got there right after the ambulance left. The ground was dry, so there were no footprints; nothing was amiss inside the chief's car."

"Were the flashers on the chief's car running?"

"No, but the headlights were on."

"Car doors open or closed?"

"Closed and unlocked. The driver's window was down. The chief usually kept it down—he didn't like air conditioning much."

Holly looked at her Rolex, a gift from her platoon leaders on her retirement. "Okay, we'd better get out to the squad room so I can meet the others. I'd appreciate it if you'd introduce me. I'll do the rest."

"Sure, glad to."

They got to their feet and walked into the squad room, where the watch had assembled.

"Let me have your attention," Hurd said loudly. Everybody got quiet. "I want to introduce a new member of the department—Deputy Chief Holly Barker, who's starting work today. Chief Barker?"

Holly stepped forward. "Good morning. I know I'm a surprise to all of you, but Chief Marley hired me five weeks ago, and he expected to introduce me to you today, but of course, the events of last night changed that. I expect I'll get to know you all in due course, and I'm looking forward to that. There'll be no changes in assignments or duty rosters—there's a good system in place, and I don't want to change it. I know you're all good people, because Chet Marley hired you, so I come into this job with full confidence in every one of you. My first priority is going to be the solving of the chief's shooting and the apprehension of the perpetrator. I'm not going to take over the case personally, but I'll be keeping close tabs on it.

"Each of you can help in this investigation by questioning every source, every snitch you have any contact with. From what I've heard so far, that's going to be our best bet. I'm going to see what I can do to get a substantial reward offered, and maybe that will help us.

"I know you'll have a lot of questions about me. I'm going to post my résumé on the bulletin board, so that you can all read up on my background. I'll get to know you and the ropes here as fast as I can. I expect to make some mistakes. Feel free to point them out to me, I'll learn faster that way. Any questions?"

"How's the chief doing?" an officer asked.

"We're waiting for information; you'll know shortly after I do. I'm heading over to the hospital now. Any other questions?" Nobody spoke. "That's all, then."

"I'll assign somebody to ride with you," Wallace said.

"Thanks, good idea."

Jane appeared and handed her a small cell phone. "This is for you. It fits into a pouch on your belt, and the number is taped to the back of the phone."

"Thank you, Jane. I'm going to the hospital now. Call me if you hear anything before I do." She turned to Wallace. "If Detective Hurst comes in, call me and ask him to wait."

"I'll do that." He waved a young officer over. "This is Patrolman Jimmy Weathers. He'll ride with you today."

"Hi, Jimmy," Holly said, shaking his hand.

"Nice to meet you, Chief. Bob Hurst has released the chief's car, so we'll use that."

"Let's get rolling."

Holly approached the chief's car, a newish, dark blue Ford Taurus, unmarked, and walked around it slowly, looking for dents or marks. She found a couple of short, deep scratches in the paint on the hood and nothing else. She went over the interior thoroughly as well and found nothing of note.

Holly drove, and Weathers gave her directions. "How long are you on the force, Jimmy?"

"A year and a half, ma'am."

"What duties have you pulled?"

"Just patrol—on bikes and in cars."

"Motorcycles, you mean?"

"No, ma'am, bicycles. They're good for the business district and beach areas. The ground is flat, and they keep us close to the public—less intimidating than patrol cars. It was Chief Marley's idea."

"What do you want to do on the force?"

"Criminal investigation, of course. Just about everybody does."

Holly laughed. "Sure, they do." Following Weathers's directions, she pulled into the hospital emergency entrance and parked in a reserved place.

"Just put down the visor," he said. "There's a badge printed on it."

She did as he said, then got out of the car and went into the hospital, looking up surgery on the directory. They took the elevator to the fourth floor and went to the desk.

"I'm Deputy Chief of Police Barker," she said to the woman. "Can you tell me anything about Chief Marley's condition?"

"No, ma'am," the woman said, "but I can get Dr. Green for you. He did the surgery."

"Thank you."

The woman picked up the phone and paged the doctor. A moment later he stepped up to the desk.

"I'm Dr. Green. Can I help you?"

Holly introduced herself. "What is Chief Marley's condition?"

"He's still in the recovery room, on a respirator. I had hoped he would be conscious by now, but it appears that he's in a coma."

"What's the prognosis?"

"Guarded, perhaps doubtful."

"Can you describe his injuries?"

"Just one—a small-caliber bullet to the right frontal lobe."

"Did you recover the bullet?"

The doctor took a Ziploc bag from his pocket containing a chunk of lead. "I was wondering when someone was going to ask."

Holly looked at it. "Looks like thirty-two caliber," she said.

"That's what I figured."

"And nobody asked about this?"

"I understand there was a detective here during the night, but he was gone by the time I got out of surgery."

"Did he see the chief at all?"

"No."

She nodded. "I'd like to see the chief."

"He can't be disturbed yet," the doctor replied.

"I don't want to disturb him; I just want to get a look at him, with your help."

"All right, come this way."

"Jimmy, you wait here," Holly said.

The doctor led the way down the hall and through the intensive-care-unit doors. There were four beds in the room; only one was occupied. Chet Marley was surrounded by monitoring equipment, his head swathed in bandages. A nurse sat on a chair beside the bed.

"Any change?" the doctor asked her.

"No, sir, still the same."

He turned back to Holly. "Well, there he is."

Holly approached the bed and looked closely at Marley. His head was made to seem larger by the bandages, and his face was distorted by the respirator mouthpiece. She switched on a light over the bed and looked at his right cheek. "Major contusion here," she said.

The doctor looked at it. "I didn't see that before. His head was already draped when I came into the O.R."

She picked up his right hand and looked at it. There were scrapes and bruising on the knuckles. She walked around the bed and examined the left hand. Two nails were broken off to the quick, and there had been bleeding. "I need to look at his torso," she said.

"I don't want to move him to undo the gown," the doctor replied.

"Then cut it open for me."

He turned to the nurse. "Get me some scissors." The woman opened a drawer and handed him a pair, and he cut down the front of the gown and opened it.

Holly held the gown back and looked at Marley's trunk. "Big bruise on the left ribs," she said. "Some swelling down here." She pointed.

"You're right."

Holly closed the gown, and the nurse taped it closed. Holly gently pulled back the sheet and examined Marley's legs and feet. "No injuries here," she said.

"I concur," the doctor replied.

"Did you note any powder burns around the bullet wound?" she asked.

"There was some blackening; it wasn't severe."

"Thank you, Doctor." They walked out of the recovery room together. "With a wound like this, what are the chances for any kind of recovery?" she asked.

"Well, the damage was limited to the frontal lobe. Theoretically, he could make something like a full recovery, but I wouldn't want to promise that. On the other hand he could come out of this with what amounts to a prefrontal lobotomy."

"I'd like to see the chief's clothes," she said.

The doctor nodded and went to a phone. A moment later, a nurse appeared with a small trash bag and handed it to the doctor, who handed it to Holly. "Would you like to use my office?" he asked.

She nodded and followed him into the room, the nurse bringing up the rear. She emptied the trash bag onto the desk and spread out the objects. The shirt was spattered with blood and both the shirt and trousers had been cut off the chief's body. She turned them over and found dirt and grass stains on the backs of the garments. His shoes and gun belt had the same stains. "Where is his pistol?" she asked.

The nurse spoke up. "He wasn't wearing one," she said. "I had someone check the ambulance to be sure it wasn't there, and it wasn't."

"Thank you," Holly said. She unpinned the chief's badge, put it in her pocket, then stuffed the items back into the bag. "I guess that's it," she said.

The doctor led her back into the hall. Holly stopped walking before they reached the front desk. "Doctor, who are you reporting his condition to?"

"His secretary was here most of the night."

"Do you know if the chief is married?"

"I assume not. A wife would have been here by now."

"It would be a great help to my investigation if, in dealing with anybody but me, you would put the most pessimistic light on any assessments you make of his condition. And I'm not excepting other police officers."

"I'm not sure I understand," the doctor asked.

"Last night somebody tried to murder the chief. I'd like whoever did it to think he was substantially successful. If word got around that the chief was recovering, his assailant could try again. After all, the chief certainly saw who shot him and may have even known him. We don't want assassins prowling the hospital's hallways, do we?"

The doctor's eyebrows went up. "I see your point," he said.

"I think it would be a good idea if the hospital released a statement to the local press and the wire services saying that the chief has been critically wounded and may not regain consciousness, and that even if he should, the resulting brain damage would probably greatly impair his communication skills."

"I can do that," the doctor said.

Holly shook his hand. "Thank you very much. And if he should regain consciousness, I'd like not to be just the first person notified, but the *only* person." She jotted down her home and cell phone numbers, then rejoined Officer Weathers.

"How's the chief doing?" Weathers asked as they walked back to the car.

"Bad, Jimmy, bad," she replied. "Do you know where the chief was shot?"

"Yes, ma'am. I drove by there before they moved his car."

"Let's take a look at it."

5

Holly stopped by the station and took the trash bag inside. She walked into Jane Grey's office and closed the door behind her.

Jane looked up from her work. "How's the chief?" she asked, looking fearful of the answer.

"In a coma," Holly replied. "The prognosis is not good; he may never regain consciousness."

Jane's shoulders slumped. "I was afraid of that."

"How long have you worked for the chief, Jane?"

"Since he came here, eight years ago."

"You were pretty close, then."

"Yes, we were."

"Is the chief married?"

"Divorced, before he came here. The ex-wife has remarried and lives in Germany."

"Any family or close friends in Orchid Beach? Anybody who should be notified?"

"Nobody," Jane replied. "His closest friend is Hank Doherty. They were drinking buddies."

"I know about him from my father. Where does he live?"

"South on A1A, not far from your trailer park. Jimmy can show you."

Holly put the trash bag on Jane's desk. "These are the chief's clothes. Will you send somebody with them to the state crime lab?"

"Sure."

Holly produced the zippered plastic bag containing the bullet. "This, too. Please ask them to treat the ballistics as very urgent." Holly took a deep breath. "You said that everybody on the force has to submit personal weapons for ballistics?"

"That's right."

"I want this bullet checked against every one of them—official weapons, too."

Jane's eyes widened. "Do you think . . . ?"

"I don't think anything, Jane; I just want to eliminate our people as suspects."

"I know somebody in the lab. I'll get him right on it today," she replied.

"Thanks."

"Has Bob Hurst come in yet?"

"No, it'll probably be this afternoon."

"Do you know if he took charge of the chief's gun?"

"I don't know."

"When he comes in, if he has the gun, I want that to go to the lab, too. I want to know if it's been fired and if so, how many times. I want to know if anyone's prints besides the chief's are on it."

"I'll call his house and see if he has it," Jane replied.

There was a knock on the office door, and Holly opened it. A short, bald man in a short-sleeved shirt and a necktie stood there.

"Oh, Holly, this is Charlie Peterson, the chairman of the city council. Charlie, this is Deputy Chief Holly Barker."

Holly stuck out her hand. "Good to meet you, Mr. Peterson."

"Call me Charlie," the man said, shaking her hand. "Jane, when did we get a deputy chief?"

"This morning, Charlie. The chief hired her several weeks ago, but he didn't want an announcement until she got here."

"Unfortunate timing," Peterson said. "How's the chief?"

"Not good. In a coma, may not come out of it, and if he does, well, there's brain damage."

Peterson winced. "I think you and I need to sit down and talk about things," he said to Holly.

"We certainly do," Holly replied, "but right now I've got to get on top of this shooting. Will tomorrow morning be okay?"

"Sure, you do what you have to do."

"Thanks, Charlie, I'd better get going." They shook hands again and Holly left.

At Jimmy's direction, Holly pulled off A1A and onto the broad, grassy shoulder. When she set foot on the ground it was soft. "There wasn't any rain yesterday, was there?" she asked the patrolman.

"Yesterday morning, early, we had a line of thunderstorms go through. Guess we had an inch in two hours. Cleared up after that."

"Show me exactly where the car was," she said.

"Right there," Jimmy replied, pointing ahead of them. "Right in front of that real estate sign."

Holly stepped onto the pavement and walked slowly down the road, looking carefully at the wet ground. There were the tracks of two cars, one in front of the other. Beside the front set of tracks, there were bits of plaster. "Looks like Bob Hurst took a tire impression," she said, half to herself. "That's good."

She backtracked to the chief's car tracks and inspected the ground in front of where the car had rested. There were indentations, no doubt where the chief had lain after being shot. She didn't see any blood. She walked slowly around the area where the two cars had stopped but saw nothing of note. She assumed that any other evidence on the scene had already been collected by Hurst.

"Okay, Jimmy, I think that about does it," she said, getting into the car. "Jane said you could show me where Hank Doherty lives."

"Sure. Straight ahead about a mile."

Holly got the car going. "Do you know Hank Doherty?"

"Sure, everybody knows him."

"Tell me about him."

"He and the chief did a lot of drinking together."

"Where? Did they have a regular place?"

"There's a bar up the road. They were in there a lot."

"Doherty raises dogs?"

"That's right, only I don't think he does it much any more. It's a shame, too. He was a kind of wizard with dogs."

"Retired?"

"Well, chief, Hank does a lot of drinking, even when he's not with the chief. I've heard rumors he was real sick. I think he's in a lot of pain, you know? He's in a wheelchair. He doesn't have any legs. Vietnam."

"Oh." She wondered why her father had never mentioned Doherty's lack of legs.

"It's right up ahead, here," Jimmy said, pointing at a small house set only a little back from the road.

Holly pulled into the short driveway and stopped the car. A sign on the front-yard fence read DOHERTY'S DOGS. SECURITY AND OBEDIENCE TRAINING. She got out of the car and walked through the gate into an ill-tended front yard. She walked up the steps to the front porch and rang the bell. Jimmy stood next to her. Nobody came to the door. She rang the bell again, with the same result.

"He seems to be out," Holly said.

"He didn't go out, except with the chief. The chief would come by here after work, get Hank into his car and drive down the road to the Tavern, where they did their drinking. A black lady did his grocery shopping and cleaned house for him."

Holly went back to the driveway and walked toward the rear of the house. A dirty white van was parked in an alcove. A ramp led from the back door of the house to where the van was parked. She looked into the vehicle: it was fitted with hand controls for the brake and accelerator. She walked up the ramp and tried the door. It was unlocked.

"Let's take a look inside," she said. "Maybe he's passed out or something."

"I wouldn't be surprised," Jimmy said.

Holly walked through the door and found herself in a kitchen. The remains of breakfast were on a table in the center of the room. "Mr. Doherty?" she called out. "Hank?"

She started for the door on the other side of the kitchen, then stopped. As if by magic, a dog had materialized in the doorway—a Doberman pinscher, strongly muscled.

The dog emitted a low growl and its lips curled back, revealing large white fangs.

Holly stopped. "Hello, puppy," she said. She had had a dog as a little girl, but when it was hit by a car, her father had talked her out of getting another one. An army life was nomadic, and a dog was a lot of baggage.

The dog growled more loudly.

"Jimmy, back out of here," she said. "And don't run."

"Yes, ma'am," Jimmy replied.

Holly stood her ground. "Hello, puppy," she repeated.

The dog repeated its previous statement.

They seemed to be at an impasse.

6

Holly waited a moment, then got down on her knees and held out a hand, palm down. "C'mere, puppy," she cooed, as sweetly as she could. "Come see me."

The dog stopped growling but didn't move, still eyeing her suspiciously.

"Come on over here and see me, sweetheart. You're a good dog. Come on, now."

The dog made a small sound in its throat and slowly walked toward Holly. It sniffed the outstretched hand.

Holly stayed still for a moment, then stroked the dog's muzzle with the backs of her fingers. "Yes, you're a *good* dog; you're not going to eat me, are you? I certainly hope not."

Then the dog did an odd thing: it took Holly's fingers gently in its mouth and tugged.

Holly had to put out her other hand to keep from falling on her face, but the dog didn't let go. It continued pulling. Holly got to her feet and followed the dog, which backed through the kitchen door, towing her into a hallway, then dropped Holly's hand and turned toward the closed door at the end of the hall. The door was in terrible shape; it was covered in deep scratches.

"I guess you wanted to go in there," Holly said. "Just a minute, and I'll open it for you." She turned the doorknob and pulled the door open. The dog ran into the room, which was a reception area, and disappeared around the front desk into the rear part of the room. Holly followed. As she turned the corner of the desk, she stopped dead in her tracks. "Oh, Jesus," she said.

A legless man lay on his back beside an overturned wheelchair; most of his head was missing. The dog lay down beside the body and laid its head on a dead hand, making small noises in its throat.

"Shotgun," Holly said aloud to herself. She started to approach the body, but the dog lifted its head and growled. Holly stopped. "Come here, puppy. Come!" she said firmly; then she repeated herself.

The dog got to its feet and came to her. Holly stroked its face and head and scratched it behind the ears. "You're a good dog, aren't you? You tried to come and help Hank, but the door was closed. How did you get in the kitchen? Who put you there?" For a moment, she thought the dog would tell her. Holly stood up. On the counter beside her lay a leash and a chain collar. She picked up the collar and read the tag. "So your name is Daisy, is that right? You're a girl, just like me." She put the collar over the dog's head, and attached the leash to it. "I want you to come outside with me, Daisy," she said softly, tugging at the leash. It took more encouragement, but Daisy finally followed her through the kitchen and out the back door.

Jimmy was waiting beside the steps. "Everything under control?"

"Not exactly," Holly said. "Daisy, this is Jimmy. I want you to stay here with him. Jimmy, pet Daisy, and get to be friends."

Daisy allowed herself to be petted by the policeman.

"Daisy, you sit down right here."

Daisy sat down.

"Keep her here with you. I'm going back inside."

"What's going on in there? Is Hank passed out?"

"Hank is dead," Holly replied. "I'm going to phone it in, and when people start arriving, you keep Daisy here, and keep talking to her. She's very upset, and I don't think she's the kind of dog you'd want to upset any more than she already is."

"Yes, ma'am," Jimmy said.

Holly went back into the house, gingerly picked up the phone on the front desk and punched in 911. She didn't even know if the town had 911 service, but now was the time to find out.

"Orchid Beach Police," a woman's voice said. "What is your emergency?"

"This is Deputy Chief of Police Holly Barker," Holly said. She picked up a business card from a little stand on the desk and read out the address. "I've got a death by gunshot at this address," she said. "I want you to find Bob Hurst and get him out here right now, ready to work the scene. Is there a medical examiner in this town?"

"Yes, Chief, but not full time."

"Find him and get him out here, too. I'll need an ambulance later, but there's no hurry about that."

"Yes, ma'am. Have you got an ID on the body?"

"His name is Henry Doherty."

"Hank? Ohhh, I liked Hank. Is Daisy all right?"

"Daisy is all right. Now you get moving."

"Yes, ma'am."

Holly hung up and looked around the room. She hadn't noticed it before, but a pump shotgun with a short barrel lay beside the body. She didn't touch it. Apart from the dead man on the floor, the room was in good order. A desk stood in a corner, and its top was neatly arranged. She walked over and, using a pen from her pocket, poked among the papers on the desk. There was some mail—bills, mostly, but one from a Mrs. Eleanor Warner, at an Atlanta address. Holly walked around the room and looked at the rest of it. A small safe stood behind the desk, its door ajar; she'd go through that later. When she had seen the room, she walked through an open door and down another hall to a bedroom. It contained the usual furniture, except for a hospital bed with some sort of trapeze bar hanging above it. In a corner stood a pair of prosthetic legs and two canes. Apparently, Hank Doherty had not always used the wheelchair.

Out the back door was a series of kennel houses, surrounded by a chain-link fence. She was impressed with how neat everything was. Only the front yard seemed neglected. She went back into the house and then out again, via the kitchen door. Jimmy stood patiently holding Daisy's leash. She petted the dog. "Jimmy, do you think the chief's car would have some rubber gloves in it?"

"It might."

Holly took the leash from him. "See if you can find me some."

Jimmy went to the car, looked into the glove compartment and came back with the gloves.

Holly had a thought. "Did the chief carry a shotgun in his car?"

"Yes, ma'am; all the patrol cars have shotguns."

"Go see if there's one in the chief's car."

Jimmy checked the car, looked in the trunk and returned. "No, ma'am, there's no shotgun in the car."

Holly handed him Daisy's leash and went back into the house, slipping on the rubber gloves. Back in the office, she turned over the shotgun and jotted down the serial number on the back of a glove, then she called the station and asked for Jane.

"Jane here," she said.

"It's Holly. Do you have a list handy of the departmental weapons' serial numbers?"

"Right here in my computer."

"Look up the serial number of the chief's shotgun, the one he carried in his car." Holly heard the tapping of computer keys.

Jane read out the number.

"Thanks. If you need me I'm at Hank Doherty's house." She gave Jane the number, then hung up. When she turned around a man was standing in the doorway. He was in his late thirties, at least six-four and two hundred and fifty pounds, of athletic build, wearing a wash-and-wear suit.

"I'm Bob Hurst," he said.

"Holly Barker," she replied, extending a hand. "Pardon my gloves."

"Heard about you, glad to meet you."

"Same here."

"What we got?"

"Hank Doherty, apparently. Dead, shotgun to the face."

Hurst nodded, walked around the desk and took a good look. "Looks like a police weapon," he said.

"It's Chief Marley's," she replied. "I checked the serial number."

He looked at her oddly. "That's kind of weird."

"Yeah."

"I've had a walk-through. It's all in good order; nothing seems to have been stolen. The safe's open, and it doesn't seem like a robbery."

"From what I know of Hank, it could be suicide," Hurst said.

"With the chief's shotgun?"

"Well, there is that."

"Let's treat it as a homicide until we know more. You work the scene, I'll go through the desk and the safe."

"Right."

Holly went and sat behind the desk. She gave her first attention to the letter from Mrs. Eleanor Warner. It was two pages of affectionate chat, with talk of her children. Mrs. Warner was Hank's daughter.

Holly went through the bills and other mail and found nothing remarkable. Finally, she came to a bound document under a blank legal pad. The cover, apparently printed from a computer, was set in large type. It read:

DAISY
EXCELLENT WORKING BITCH

"Oh, Daisy," Holly said aloud. "Me, too."

7

Holly went through Hank Doherty's safe and found three hundred dollars and change in cash, a life insurance policy and some other personal and business documents. "I think we can discount robbery as a motive," she said to Bob Hurst, who was dusting the counter and the phone for fingerprints. "There's cash here, and nobody bothered to look."

"Right," Hurst said. "I don't hold out much hope for any relevant prints. The shotgun's been wiped clean, which means it wasn't suicide."

A man carring a medical bag entered through the front door.

"Hey, Doc," Hurst said. "Got a job for you over there."

"Is it Hank?" the doctor asked.

"Sure is. That there is Deputy Chief Barker," he said, pointing a gloved hand. "Chief, this here is Dr. Fred Harper, who passes for our M.E. around here."

Holly waved from Hank's desk. "Hey, Dr. Harper."

"How you do?" The doctor walked around the counter and into the office. "Jesus God," he said quietly.

"Yeah," Hurst replied.

The doctor knelt by the body and looked it over carefully. Finally he stood up. "I don't think I can tell you anything you don't already know," he said. "Not until I get a postmortem done, anyway."

"The ambulance is here," Hurst said. "You ready to move him?"

The doctor looked inquiringly at Holly.

"Go ahead, if you're ready," she said.

Two paramedics came into the building, loaded the corpse onto a stretcher and removed it to the ambulance.

"Let me know when you're done," Holly said to the doctor. "I'd like you to be thorough."

"I always am," the doctor said. "I'll try to get it done by the close of business, but I can't promise." He picked up his bag and left.

"I'm about done," Hurst said.

"When do you think it happened?" Holly asked.

"Last night, I reckon."

"That's what I figured, but there's the remains of breakfast on the kitchen table. Some scrambled eggs."

"Hank didn't eat a lot," Hurst replied. "That could have been last night's supper."

"We'll know for sure when the doctor is done." She indicated a chair across the desk from her. "Take a seat for a minute."

Hurst sat down, shucking off his rubber gloves.

"Give me your take on what happened here," she said.

Hurst sighed. "Somebody came in through the front door with a shotgun, used it on Hank and walked out. Simple as that."

Holly nodded. "Why was the dog in the kitchen with the door closed?"

Hurst furrowed his brow. "Good point. I can't think of any reason why Hank would shut the dog up in there."

"Maybe Hank didn't do it. Maybe his visitor did."

"Why would the dog mind a visitor, a stranger?"

"Maybe it wasn't a stranger."

"Granted. I've been around Hank and the dog, though; the dog didn't listen to anybody, unless Hank . . . "

"Gave his permission?"

"Yeah."

"Maybe the visitor asked Hank to shut the dog in the kitchen. Maybe the dog made the visitor nervous."

"Maybe," Hurst said, "but why would Hank do that? If he told Daisy to lie down and be quiet, then that's what she did. No reason for anybody to be nervous. On the other hand, anybody who was planning to shoot Hank wouldn't want Daisy in the room; she'd tear his throat out."

"She's trained that way?"

"She's trained every which way," Hurst said. "That's some dog."

"I think our perp came in through the kitchen door," Holly said. "I think Daisy went to investigate, recognized him as somebody she knew and trusted, and as he walked in here, he shut the kitchen door behind him, trapping her in there."

"Makes sense," Hurst agreed.

"The front door was unlocked when I got here, and so was the back door."

"Makes a lot of sense. Especially if it was the chief."

"You think the chief would kill Hank Doherty?"

Hurst shook his head. "No, but it wouldn't be the first time I was wrong about something like that. It's his shotgun. Daisy knew and trusted him, knew he was a friend."

"I don't think it was the chief either," Holly said, "but we've got to touch that base."

"Right."

"Tell me about last night."

"I got a call at home at eleven-fourteen; I was out there at eleven-twenty. The chief was lying on his back, lit by his car's headlights, and a man from Vero Beach was with him, trying to help. The ambulance got there at eleven twenty-three and rushed him off to the hospital. I worked the scene in a standard manner, took a tire impression from another vehicle parked in front of the chief's car. There were some footprints, but nothing good enough for an impression. The tire was a Goodyear Eagle, common rubber, no indication of the kind of car. Hurd Wallace got there right after the ambulance left, and we walked around the scene together; didn't find any other evidence."

"Did you find the chief's weapon?"

"No."

"That's a good report," Holly said. "Now tell me what you think went down, based on the evidence you found."

"Looks to me like the chief stopped a car, maybe for a traffic violation, maybe because something about it made him suspicious, and it went sour. They shot him, took his gun and went on their way."

"Simple as that?"

"Simple as that."

"You said 'they': more than one perp?"

"One, maybe two. Couldn't tell."

"You think he knew them?"

"It's possible, but there's no evidence of that."

"When you stop somebody, what usually happens?" she asked. "Does he get out of the car?"

"Not usually. They sit there and roll down the window."

"If you stopped a car with two men in it and both of them got out, what would you do?"

"I'd back off and tell them to put their hands on the car."

"Wouldn't the chief do the same?"

"Unless he knew them. I see your point."

"There was a fight," Holly said.

"I didn't see any evidence of that," Hurst said.

"The hood of the car was deeply scratched. I think the scratches were made by the chief's handcuffs, on his belt. I think somebody hit him, knocking him onto the car, and that he fought back."

"How do you figure that?"

"The chief had bruises on his face and torso, as from a fight. He had two broken fingernails on one hand. You don't get broken fingernails from hitting somebody with your fist. I think he probably grabbed hold of some clothing during the struggle."

"Why didn't he use his gun?"

"Because he knew them and didn't expect trouble."

"You're pretty sure there were two, then?"

"You knew the chief. Do you think one man could have fought with him and shot him as easily as that?"

"You're right," Hurst said, looking sheepish. "He was a pretty tough customer."

"I talked with the chief at seven-thirty last night. He told me he was on the way to meet somebody."

"Why would he have a meeting on the side of the road?" Hurst asked.

"Doesn't make much sense, does it? Maybe he was on the way to his meeting, and somebody flagged him down—somebody he knew."

"Could very well be," Hurst admitted.

"Then I think they got the shotgun out of the chief's car, came over here and killed Hank Doherty."

"Could be."

"Bob, can you think of any reason why somebody would want to kill the chief?"

Hurst shook his head. "No, I can't. I don't know of any problems he was having with anybody."

"Do you know of any investigation he was involved in that might have been dangerous?"

Hurst shook his head again. "The chief was pretty closemouthed when he was working something of his own."

"Is there anybody he might have told about it?"

"Maybe Hank Doherty," Hurst replied.

"Right," Holly said. "Okay, you go on back and write up your report. I'll take a look at it later and add anything I think is important."

"See you later, then," Hurst said, and left.

Holly picked up the letter from Hank Doherty's daughter and dialed the number on the letterhead.

"Hello?" a woman's voice said.

"Is this Mrs. Warner?" Holly asked.

"Yes."

"Is Hank Doherty your father?"

"Yes. Who is this?"

"This is Deputy Chief of Police Holly Barker, in Orchid Beach, Florida. I'm afraid I have some bad news."

8

Holly went back to the station, taking Daisy with her. The dog sat at attention in the backseat, gazing out the window; Holly thought she seemed sad, but who knew? At the station, Holly got out of the car. "Jimmy, will you stay with Daisy for a while? She seems comfortable with you, and I don't want to leave her alone in the car."

"Sure, Chief, glad to," Weathers said. "I'm comfortable with her, too."

She had hardly sat down at her desk when Jane Grey and Hurd Wallace were in her office. She gave them a rundown of the scene at Hank Doherty's place. Hurd nodded and went back to his desk; Jane sat down, practically in tears.

"What a terrible day," she said. "I just can't believe all this has happened."

"I know," Holly said. "Have you heard anything on the ballistics?"

"Oh, no. I expect it will be tomorrow, probably late in the day, before we hear anything."

"Anything from Dr. Harper yet?"

"Nothing."

"You know the number at the hospital?"

"I'll dial it for you," Jane said. When they were on the line, she handed Holly the phone.

"May I speak with Dr. Green, please? This is Deputy Chief Barker from Orchid Beach Police." There was a pause, and the doctor came on the line.

"Yes, Chief?"

"I just wondered if there had been any change in the chief's condition," Holly said.

"Not as yet; to tell you the truth, I'd be surprised if there had been. He's still in a coma. Certainly the anesthetic wore off a long time ago."

"Thanks, Doctor. Please keep me posted." She hung up.

"Anything?" Jane asked.

"Nothing yet. He's still the same. Jane, will you type up a press release and fax it to all the local media, saying that we'd like to hear from anyone who passed along the relevant part of A1A between eleven and eleven-twenty last night, who might have seen two cars at the side of the road?"

"Sure. Oh, I forgot—Charlie Peterson called. He got the city council to put up a ten-thousand-dollar reward for any information leading to arrest and conviction."

"Great, put that in the release, too, and get it out as soon as you can."

"Hank Doherty had a daughter," Jane said.

"I've already talked with her; she'll be here tomorrow. If she comes in while I'm out, find me. I'd like to talk to her."

"What's happened to Daisy?"

"She's out in the parking lot with Jimmy Weathers. I'll take her home with me tonight. I'd hate to put her in the animal shelter. She seems like such a sensitive creature."

"She's a marvel. Lots of people know her, especially around here. Hank used to bring her into the station, but he hasn't been around for months."

Holly glanced at her watch. "I think I'm going to call it a day, and so should you as soon as you get that release out."

"I will, don't worry."

The phone on Holly's desk buzzed, and she picked it up.

"Chief, Dr. Harper's on the phone for you."

"Thanks." Holly pushed the flashing button. "Doctor?"

"Evening, Chief. I'm done."

"What's the story?"

"He was killed late last night or early in the morning, say between eleven P.M. and three A.M. Death would have been instantaneous."

"Any sign of a struggle? Anything under the nails?"

"Just dirt. No injuries, except the shotgun—that was enough."

"Anything else I should know?"

"Not much. He had an alcohol level of point two two, which would not have been unusual for Hank. He had a liver the size of a watermelon, and as hard as marble, which doesn't come as a surprise. He'd have been dead in a few months anyway from cirrhosis."

"Thanks, Doctor." Holly hung up. "Nothing of use from the autopsy. Jane, do you know Hank's cleaning lady?"

"Sure, she worked for the chief, too."

"Would you give her a call and break the news to her, then ask her to go over to Hank's house and clean up his office? I wouldn't want his daughter to see it as it is."

"Of course."

Holly stood up. "I'm off. Tell the front desk to call me if anything comes in on either shooting."

Holly stopped by the manager's office on her way in and introduced Daisy to Jerry Malone. "All right if I have a dog here tonight?"

"Sure, I've got no problems with pets," Malone said. "Lots of my people have them."

Holly waved good night and drove to her trailer. Daisy hopped out and showed some interest in the area, sniffing at bushes and at the river. Holly got the dog food she had brought from Hank's and set out a dish and some water for her. Grief had not hurt the dog's appetite. The phone rang.

"Oh, God," Holly said aloud. She'd hoped she could get through the night without a call, in spite of her instructions to the front desk. She sat down on the bed and picked up the phone. "Hello?"

"Hiya, kiddo," her father said.

"Hello, Ham," Holly replied.

"So how was your first day?" he asked.

"Oh, Jesus, Ham, you're not going to believe it. Are you sitting down?"

"Yep."

"Both Chet Marley and Hank Doherty were shot last night, probably by the same person. Chet's in a coma, and Hank is dead."

There was a long silence at the other end of the phone. "Do you know who did it?" Ham asked finally.

"No, not yet. Don't know why, either."

"Tell me everything."

Holly launched into a detailed description of both crimes, finishing up with Hank's autopsy report. "And that's all I know," she said.

"What about this detective, Hurst? He any good?"

"I think he's all right, maybe a little short on imagination. Of course, he's got a new boss breathing down his neck, too, and he may be reacting to the pressure, holding back a little to avoid making a mistake."

"You think these shootings have anything to do with what Chet talked about at dinner last month?"

"I think it has everything to do with it, but as far as I know, he didn't discuss it with anybody. When I talked to him last night, he said he'd brief me this morning, tell me everything. He was going to meet somebody, and that may have been the shooter."

"I wish I could help in some way," Ham said. "Those guys were my friends."

"I know how you feel, Ham; I feel the same way, though I didn't know Chet well nor Hank at all. I'm going to bust a gut clearing this one."

"You got all the help you need?"

"I think so."

"Can you trust the help?"

"I don't know about that yet. I've hardly had time to form impressions of these people."

"Chet had a secretary, Jane. He trusted her, I think, from the way he talked about her."

"Right, she's been a big help, got me off to a good start."

"What about this guy who wanted your job?"

"Hurd Wallace. I don't know about him yet. He's a hard one to read, a real cold fish."

"You watch your back, you hear?"

"I will, Ham."

"I'm going to let you get some rest now."

"Thanks, I'm bushed."

"I love you."

"You, too." She hung up, surprised. Ham was not one for expressions of affection. She fell back onto the bed, and Daisy came and nuzzled her hand.

"Oh, Daisy." She sighed. "I could really use a beer." She struggled to sit up before she fell asleep in her clothes. She watched, puzzled, as Daisy went into the kitchen, looked around, went to the refrigerator, took the door handle in her teeth and opened the door. She stuck her muzzle inside and came out with a bottle of Heineken, holding it by the neck in her teeth, then she brought it to Holly and placed it in her hand.

Holly stared dumbly at the dog. "Wow," she said, half to herself. "You want a job, Daisy?"

9

Holly lay in a deep sleep, dreaming of nothing in particular. She was in her office and the phone rang, but before she could answer it there came a sound that didn't belong. She listened, and it came again, a short, urgent, nearly inaudible, plaintive grunt. She opened her eyes and looked around her. Daisy sat by her bed, an expression of concern on her face. She made the noise again, then stuck her nose under Holly's arm and lifted it off the bed.

Holly laughed. "And what do you want, Daisy? To go out?"

She looked at the clock, which read seven A.M. "Oh, good thing you woke me. I forgot to set the alarm." She wondered if that was why Daisy had awakened her, but dismissed the thought. "I'll bet you're hungry, aren't you?"

Daisy emitted a low, gruff woof that had an affirmative ring to it.

"Okay, okay." Holly got out of bed, threw on a robe and fed and watered Daisy, then let her out of the trailer and stood in the door and watched. The dog ranged around the little clearing, her nose to the ground one minute, in the air the next. Then she disappeared behind a bush and a minute later came bounding back to the trailer.

"You're a real lady, aren't you? Very discreet," Holly laughed, rubbing the top of her head. "Well, today, your, ah, sister is coming to take you to Atlanta, and you're going to have some very nice kids to play with." She felt a pang as she said it; she was finding Daisy good company. She took a quick shower, dressed in her uniform—in trousers, this time—and had breakfast, listening to the local news on the radio. She was pleased to hear her press release read on the air and to hear the mention of the reward for information.

At eight, she put Daisy into her Jeep and drove to the station, this time taking her inside on a leash. She had to stop half a dozen times on the way to her office for people to say hello to Daisy and pet her—a very popular dog. In her office, she told Daisy to lie down, and her instruction was immediately complied with. A moment later, Holly was startled to hear a deep growl from the dog, and she looked up to find Hurd Wallace standing in the doorway.

"Daisy! Quiet!" she commanded, and the dog put her head on the floor again and was quiet.

"We've made an arrest in the chief's shooting," Wallace said.

"What? When? Who?"

"Last night we had a call from a citizen who said he'd seen an old van parked near the spot where the shooting took place. One of our patrolmen knew the van. It belonged to two people, a man and a woman, who have been squatting on a piece of vacant land between the highway and the river, very near where the chief was shot. He went to the campsite and found these two sitting in front of a fire. The man was cleaning a weapon; it was the chief's Beretta."

"Where are they?"

"Bob Hurst is interogating them now, in room one. There's a two-way mirror, if you want to watch."

"Let's go." Holly followed Wallace down a corridor and into a small room. Two bedraggled kids in their late teens or early twenties sat at a table in the adjoining room. Bob Hurst sat opposite them, and a policewoman stood in a corner and watched.

"It's S.O.P. to have a woman present when a woman is being interrogated," Wallace said.

"I know. How long has the questioning been going on?"

"Since midnight."

"Has somebody read them their rights?"

"Yes, at the very beginning. They've signed off on that."

"Have they asked for a lawyer?"

"I suppose not, or they'd have one."

"Okay, let's listen."

The voices came through clearly over a small speaker:

"All right, let's go over this again," Hurst said.

"I told you what happened," the young man said.

"Tell me again; I want to be sure I understand. What was your van doing parked beside the road late the night before last?"

"We had been to a movie, and we had a flat, right before we got back to our camp. I changed the tire and drove on home."

"What time did you have the flat?"

"Between ten-thirty and ten forty-five."

"And what time did you drive on?"

"It took me fifteen or twenty minutes to change the tire, so I guess between ten forty-five and eleven o'clock."

"Where did you go to the movies?"

"At the multiplex on the mainland."

"What movie did you see?"

"*Air Force One,* with Harrison Ford."

"What time was the movie over?"

"Around ten o'clock, maybe a little after."

"And why did it take you forty-five minutes to make the fifteen-minute drive back to your camp?"

"We stopped at McDonald's and got some fries and a Coke. I told you that already."

"And how did you come to have the Beretta in your possession?" Hurst asked.

"I told you, our dog found it."

"Your dog has a personal interest in firearms?"

"He didn't exactly find it. I let him out early the next morning, and he wouldn't come when I called him. I found him sniffing around the fence that separates the highway from the property where we're camping. I went to take hold of his collar, and I stepped on the gun."

"How close to the fence?"

"I don't know, six or eight feet, maybe."

"Why didn't you call the police?"

"What for?"

"The gun didn't belong to you. Why didn't you turn it in to us?"

"Look, man, it was a free gun, you know? Finders keepers. I had no idea who it belonged to."

"You like guns, do you?"

"Well, yeah, I guess so."

"What other guns do you own?"

"I've got a little six-shooter, a thirty-two."

"And where is it?"

"In the van, maybe."

Wallace spoke up. "We found the thirty-two Smith & Wesson in the glove compartment of the van; it's going to the state lab this morning. They don't have a license for it, and there was a little over a gram of cocaine powder hidden under a seat."

"Tell me about when you got back to your camp, after changing the tire," Hurst said.

"We didn't go straight back to the camp. I drove down A1A and left our flat tire at a filling station to be fixed. The Texaco station."

"The station was open that late?"

"No, I left the wheel on his doorstep with a note. I went back there yesterday afternoon and picked it up. I know the guy. We buy our gas there."

"We're checking out that story right now," Wallace said.

"And what time did you get back to your camp?"

"Must have been eleven-thirty."

"They just missed the shooting," Wallace said. "Very convenient."

"Look, man," the suspect said, "I'm tired. I haven't had any sleep, and I don't know what this is about. I'm sorry I didn't turn in the gun, okay? Is it a crime not to turn in a gun you found? What's going on here?"

"Okay, I'm going to let you get some sleep, and we'll talk about this later."

"What's going on, man? This isn't about a lost gun, is it? There's something else going on."

"You tell me, Sammy," Hurst said.

"Tell you *what?*"

Hurst spoke to the policewoman. "Put them in the lockup." He got up and left the room. A moment later, he walked into the observation room, where Wallace and Holly were. "They did it," Hurst said. "I know it."

"What's the evidence?"

"Possession of the chief's weapon, tire track matching the cast I took, no alibi for the time, and the thirty-two. It's time to get the county attorney involved."

Holly turned to Wallace. "I want somebody to drive the thirty-two to the state lab in Tallahassee, wait while they do the test and phone us with the results. If they're positive, then we'll charge them."

"Right," Wallace said, then left the room.

"What about the Doherty murder?" Holly asked.

"If the thirty-two ballistics match, I'll get a confession," Hurst replied. "Then they'll cop to Hank's murder, too."

"A very neat package," Holly said. "I hope it holds together." That was no lie: she wanted this to happen, so she could clear these cases and get them off her mind.

Jane knocked and came into the room. "There's a Mrs. Warner on the phone for you."

"I'll take it in my office." She turned to Hurst. "Good job. Let's wrap this up real tight." She went to her office and picked up the phone. "Mrs. Warner?"

"Yes, Chief. We're at the airport in Atlanta, and we're leaving right now for Orchid Beach—my husband has an airplane. I wanted to know where I should go when we get there."

"What time do you expect to land?"

"About eleven-thirty or twelve."

"I'll meet you at the airport and drive you to Hank's place."

"Thank you, that's very kind of you."

"See you at eleven-thirty." Holly hung up the phone and sighed. If she could just get through this day, if it went right, then she could relax and start to get a grip on her job.

10

Holly stood in front of the little airport terminal building and watched the Bonanza taxi to a halt and kill its engine. When the prop had stopped turning she walked to the airplane and waited while the two people inside unfastened their seat belts and stepped down. She walked up to them and stuck out a hand. "Mr. and Mrs. Warner? I'm Holly Barker, deputy chief of police."

"Oh, hello," Mrs. Warner said. "I'm Eleanor, and this is Ed. We'd prefer first names. And thank you so much for meeting us."

"I'm glad to. Do you have any bags?"

Ed Warner opened a rear door of the airplane and took out two overnight bags. "We've booked a motel room locally, so that we can stay until we get this sorted out."

"This is Daisy, your dad's dog," Holly said. Daisy allowed herself to be petted but remained distant, Holly thought. "Let's get your bags into my car." She stowed the bags in the rear of her Grand Cherokee, ushered the Warners into the backseat and put Daisy up front with her.

"Have there been any developments?" Eleanor asked.

"Yes, I'm glad to say. We've arrested two people, and we expect to charge them with the shooting of the chief, if the ballistics test on their gun is positive."

"I'm sorry? The chief?"

"Forgive me, Eleanor, I haven't brought you fully up to date. Chet Marley, the police chief, was shot shortly before your father was, and your father was shot with the chief's shotgun, so we reckon that the perpetrators were the same in both cases. Right now, the evidence points to these two latter-day hippies in the chief's shooting, and when we can prove that, we might get a confession to your dad's murder, too."

"And the evidence is conclusive?" Ed asked.

"Not yet, but if the ballistics tests pan out, that will help us a lot."

"When will you know?"

"Later today, I hope." She navigated toward the bridge to the barrier island, then crossed it and turned south toward Hank Doherty's place.

"My father was so alone," Eleanor said. "We couldn't get him to move to Atlanta, and I could tell from his letters that he was drinking a lot."

"The coronor confirmed that in the postmortem examination. Hank's liver was pretty bad, and the doctor thought he wouldn't have lived more than a few months in any case. I know that's no consolation."

"It sounds as if you knew Daddy," Eleanor said. "Did you?"

"No, I've only been in town for a few days, but Hank and my father, Hamilton Barker, served together in the army; they were in Vietnam together, so I knew about him. And your dad wasn't that alone. He and Chet Marley were very close friends, spent a lot of time together. Chet hired me to come down here and be his deputy."

Holly pulled into Hank Doherty's driveway and stopped. As they got out of the car a black woman left the house by the front door.

"You must be Mr. and Mrs. Warner," she said.

"Yes, we are," Eleanor replied. "Are you Mary White?"

"Yes, ma'am. I took care of your daddy for a long time. He was a good man, and I'm going to miss him."

"Mary, will you stay with us a little longer? You could show us around the house."

"Yes, ma'am, I'd be glad to."

Holly followed the three into the house, which was much more presentable than when she had last seen it. The bloodstains had been scrubbed from the floor and walls. The Warners were taken through each room, and Eleanor packed some family photographs and some other things into boxes with Mary's help. When they had finished, they went back into Hank's office.

"Mary," Eleanor said, "there's a lot of stuff in this house, and if there's any of it you want, I'd like you to have it. We don't plan to take much back to Atlanta, so we'd just have to sell it anyway."

"Well, thank you," Mary said. "There's a lot I could use, and I expect my church could sell the rest at a tag sale they've got coming up this weekend."

"Fine, we'll pick out what we want, then you can have the rest." She turned to Holly. "Chief, is there anything here that you could make use of?"

"Thank you, Eleanor, but I live in a trailer, and it's pretty full." She looked at the computer on Hank's desk, a new-looking laptop with a compact printer next to it. "I wonder, would you like to sell the computer? That might fit into my place."

"Please let me give it to you," Eleanor said. "We've got a houseful of computer stuff, and we won't have any use for any more."

"I'd feel more comfortable if you'd let me buy it."

"All right, I'll sell it to you for a hundred dollars, not a penny more."

"Thank you. I've got to get back to work. Tell you what, why don't I loan you my car? I have a police vehicle at my disposal, and you could just leave the Jeep at the airport when you go."

"That's very, very kind of you," Eleanor said. "I think that we can remove what we want from here and put the house on the market right away. I have to make some arrangements for the cremation, but we ought to be able to fly home tomorrow night."

"Fine, keep it as long as you like." Holly called the station and

asked Jimmy Weathers to come and get her. She helped the Warners pack things until he arrived. "Well, I'll be getting along," she
said. "Please call me before you go, and let me know if there's anything I can do for you while you're here." She held out Daisy's leash
to Eleanor Warner. To her surprise, her throat was tightening, and
she was blinking a lot.

Eleanor shrank from taking the leash. "Oh, no, we can't take
Daisy back to Atlanta. We've got four kids from seven to fifteen, two
Labrador retrievers and a cat. Another dog wouldn't work at all. Do
you know anyone who'd give her a good home? Perhaps yourself?"

"Eleanor, Daisy seems to be a very special dog. I'm sure she's
quite valuable."

"I know all about Daisy," Eleanor said. "Daddy wrote me lots of
letters with all sorts of details about her. But he also said that she
wasn't good with kids, and that she was a one-man dog. Looks to me
like she's become a one-woman dog. It would be a great relief to me
if someone who likes her would take her."

Holly didn't have to think long about that. "If you'll let me buy
her," she said.

"A hundred dollars, and not a penny more." Eleanor wrote her
address on a slip of paper and gave it to Holly. "You can send me a
check for Daisy and the computer at your leisure. I'll send you a bill
of sale."

Holly felt an enormous sense of relief. Jimmy arrived and put the
computer, the printer and the operator's manuals in the trunk of
the police car, and after warm handshakes, Holly drove away, leaving her car with the Warners.

"Are they taking Daisy back to Atlanta with them?" Jimmy asked.

"Nope," Holly said, scratching Daisy behind the ear. "Daisy's staying with me. I bought her from them, along with Hank's computer."

"That's great," Jimmy said. "Nice to know Daisy will be around."

"It sure is," Holly said. She hadn't been so happy for a long time.

When they got back to the station, Jane Grey met Holly, beaming.
"The ballistics tests came back," she said. "A good match. We've got
the right people."

"That's great," Holly said, feeling vastly relieved. "Did they do the
other test I asked for?"

"I canceled it. Didn't seem to be any reason for it now. Do you want me to reinstate the request?"

"No," Holly said. "You're right, we've got our perpetrators. Tell Bob Hurst to get the county attorney over here pronto."

The first thing Holly did after that was to call Ham and tell him the news.

11

Holly picked up some groceries on the way home, avoiding an interesting-looking delicatessen that featured prepared dinners. She was determined not to get into the habit of not cooking her own meals. That way led to lazy habits and added pounds.

She fed Daisy, then mixed herself a gin and tonic, got the little satellite dish pointed in the right direction and watched the news. Nothing there to cheer her up. Dealing with Hank Doherty's daughter had worn on her more than she had expected, although she had the emotional lift of being Daisy's new owner. After the news she started the grill and made herself a fat bacon cheeseburger. Maybe, she thought as she ate it, she would have been better off bringing something home from the deli. When she had finished she switched off the grill, washed the dishes and made another drink.

Determined to keep work off her mind, she undressed, slipped into a long T-shirt and watched a pay-per-view movie beamed down to her trailer from a distant satellite, somewhere over the equator. She had another drink. She had noticed that she tended to drink a bit more when she was alone than when she was out with others.

She'd have to watch that, she thought as she leaned back in bed, switched off the light, finished her drink and tried to concentrate on the movie.

She was awakened by an unaccustomed noise, the growling of a dog. It took her a sleepy moment to remember that she, in fact, owned a dog, and that it was Daisy who was growling. It was a slight noise, down in the throat, almost as if the dog were whispering to her. Holly sat up, put her feet on the floor and listened. She thought she heard a metallic clank, but if she did, it was very faint. Daisy continued to make the noise.

Holly picked up the remote control and turned down the volume on the TV, which was playing trailers of coming attractions on satellite broadcasting. If there was someone outside the trailer, she didn't want to alert them by simply switching it off. She heard the clank again.

She leaned over and whispered in Daisy's ear, "Quiet, Daisy."

The dog was immediately silent.

"Lie down."

The dog did.

"Stay." Holly got up quietly and went to where she had draped her uniform over a chair. She dug under the trousers and came up with her pistol. "Stay," she whispered again to the dog. She walked toward the trailer door on bare feet. She didn't want to expose her presence at the door, so she stopped short and stuck her head into the doorway, straining to see through the screen. She could see nothing, but a little breeze had sprung up and was making a hissing noise in the trees.

Holly worked the action of the pistol, opened the screen door as quietly as she could and stepped out into the night, the gun at her side, her thumb on the safety. She didn't really want to shoot anybody, especially for simply trespassing, but she was worried enough to be ready to defend herself. She stepped away from the trailer, feeling the breeze around her bare legs, and walked around the perimeter of the little clearing, peering into the dark woods. She saw nothing and heard nothing.

Relieved, she started back toward the trailer, and, nearly simultaneously, two things happened. She heard a faint *whump* from somewhere nearby, and she smelled gas. Hadn't she turned off the grill? She looked over to where it should have been, but it wasn't there. A second later she saw it, standing hard against one end of the trailer. That was very peculiar, she thought, then the night sky lit up.

She looked up and saw a ball of bright red fire descending slowly from a good hundred feet in the air. She watched it, mesmerized, as it floated toward her. She was beginning to get the feeling that she might have to dodge it. A parachute flare, she said to herself. Some boater on the river in difficulties. Then she smelled the gas again. "Holy shit," she said aloud, and ran toward the trailer.

She dropped the gun and fell to her knees before the grill, as if it were some pagan altar. She twisted the knobs, but they were all in the off position. She dove behind the grill, feeling her way down the rubber hose toward the tank, and she found that she had the loose end of the hose in her fingers. She looked up; the flare was no more than fifty feet above her, seeming to home in on where she knelt. Panicked, she groped for the valve, to close the tank, but there was no valve, simply the opening through which gas was pouring, freezing her fingers.

Then she felt the gas stop coming. She leapt to her feet, grabbed a lawn chair and batted at the flare, sending it toward the perimeter of the clearing, where it hit the ground and lay there, sizzling, in the dirt. She watched, mesmerized, as it burned itself out, and she was surprised to learn that she had the pistol again, and that she was pointing it at the dying flare.

She took a deep breath and discovered that she couldn't smell gas anymore. She stepped inside the trailer and got a flashlight. Daisy was lying there, watching her intently. "Good girl," she said. "Stay." She went to the grill and switched on the flashlight. The valve from the top of the tank lay on the ground, a dent in one side of it.

It was clear to her that she was looking at a case of sabotage. Someone had removed the hose from the tank, opened it, then knocked the valve handle off so it couldn't be closed. She remembered that when she had cooked her burger, the tank had seemed nearly empty. Thank God for that, she thought. The combination of gas in the air, the parachute flare and the shrapnel from the exploding tank would have reduced her trailer to a smoking ruin, after she had burned to death in the explosion.

Her first impulse was to call the station and report the incident, but she held herself back. She sat down on the trailer's doorstep and thought about it. She would keep it to herself for the time being.

Daisy made a small noise. "Okay, Daisy, come to me," Holly said, opening the screen door.

Daisy came and leaned against her, sniffing the night air.

12

Holly was finishing a sandwich at her desk the following noon when the county attorney arrived, accompanied by a tall, slender, dark-haired man in a rumpled suit who needed a haircut. Jane made the introductions.

"Chief, this is Marty Skene, the county attorney, and the tall one is Jackson Oxenhandler, a public defender."

"Did they ask for a lawyer?" Holly asked, shaking hands with both men.

"No," Skene said, "but it seemed like a good time to do it. I want everything on the up-and-up."

"Sure," Holly said. "Mr. Oxhander . . ."

"It's Oxenhandler," the tall man said. "There was apparently some livestock in the family history."

"Oxenhandler, sorry. Have you met your clients?"

"Not yet."

"They're with Bob Hurst, right now, being questioned on another matter."

"Another matter?" Oxenhandler asked, furrowing his brow.

"The murder of Hank Doherty."

"You didn't tell me this was a double shooting," the lawyer said to the prosecutor.

"I didn't know myself until this minute."

"I want questioning ended *now*," the lawyer said, "until I've had a chance to consult with my clients."

Holly motioned toward the interrogation room. "Jane, ask Bob to come out here right now."

"What's the evidence against my clients?" Oxenhandler asked.

"Their tire tracks at the scene of the crime, possession of the victim's weapon and a positive ballistics match between the bullet taken from the chief's head and a thirty-two Smith & Wesson revolver found in the glove compartment of the accused's van."

"You go talk to your clients," Skene said, "and then maybe you'll want to discuss a plea. I'd like to wrap this up as soon as possible."

Jackson Oxenhandler nodded and walked toward the interrogation room, passing Bob Hurst along the way. He stopped at the door of the adjoining room, looked in, then went on to the door of the interrogation room. He turned back and called out, "I'd like that room kept empty while we talk." He disappeared into the interrogation room.

Holly turned to Hurst. "How'd you do with the Doherty murder?"

"They denied everything," Hurst said.

"Come into my office for a minute," Holly said, ushering him in and closing the door behind him.

Hurst took a seat. "What's up?"

"I didn't want to bring this up until now, but I'm extremely annoyed with you."

Hurst look surprised. "Why? We just broke our biggest case in years."

"When I left you, I told you to call me if there were any developments in the case. Would you call an arrest a development?"

Hurst shrugged. "Well, I was anxious to get on it when they were brought in."

"I don't give a damn how anxious you were," she said. "I come from the army, and when I give an order I expect it to be obeyed."

Hurst's ears were turning red, but he said nothing.

"*I* am the responsible officer on this case," Holly said, "not you, and if this thing should somehow blow up in our faces, I'm the one who'll have to answer for it. I'm new around here, and until I have a complete grasp of every facet of this department, I will make *every* important decision that's made in *every* case. When I've had time to learn who's an excellent officer and who's not, then maybe I'll delegate some authority, but not until then. Do you read me?"

Hurst looked down at her desktop; he was very red in the face now. "Yeah."

"What?"

"Yes, Chief," he said reluctantly.

"You bypass me again, and you'll be doing bicycle patrol up and down the beach. You read me *loud and clear?*"

"Yes, Chief."

"Good. Now get out of here." She watched his back as he left. She hadn't intended to get as angry as she had done, but his attitude had infuriated her. She went out into the hall, saw Hurd Wallace passing and called him in.

"Why didn't you call me when these arrests were made?" Holly asked.

"I did call you. I didn't learn about the arrests myself until I arrived here, half an hour before you did. I called you then, but I guess you had already left for work."

"Okay. Who did the search of the suspects' van?"

"I did."

"Did you get a warrant?"

"No, Bob got the suspects' written permission for the search."

"Thank God for that," Holly said. "I'd hate to have that weapon thrown out because of a bad search."

"So would I, but it won't happen. It was a good search, believe me."

"I believe you. Was the thirty-two dusted for prints?"

"Yes. There were none."

That brought Holly up short. "This guy shoots the chief, then wipes the gun clean and puts it back into his glove compartment for us to find?"

"I expect he planned to ditch the weapon," Hurd said.

"Then why didn't he? He had a good twenty-four hours to do it.

Why would he leave incriminating evidence in the van for us to find?"

"Because he was stupid. Remember, we found the cocaine and the chief's gun, too. He didn't even bother to ditch that."

"That was certainly stupid," Holly admitted. "Okay, that's all. You did your job, Hurd. It's not your fault Hurst didn't call me when the arrest was made."

"Chief, I can't vouch for the arrest or anything that went on in that interrogation room that I didn't see, but I promise you, it was a good search. You don't need to worry about that."

"Thanks, Hurd." She walked out of her office with him to find the prosecutor still waiting in the hall. "Is Oxenhandler still with them?"

"Yes. I'm hoping we can close the books on this one immediately. I want the community to know that we're on it."

"Me, too." She saw Oxenhandler leave the interrogation room and come toward them.

"All right, Jackson," Skene said. "Let's make this short and sweet: they plead to assault with intent to kill and take twenty-five to life. If Chief Marley dies before the judge approves the plea bargain, and I hear he might, it'll be murder, and I'll go for the death penalty. I may yet charge them in the matter of the Doherty murder."

"Sam Sweeney says his thirty-two revolver is a Colt. The gun found in his van was a Smith & Wesson."

"Well, he would say that, wouldn't he?" Skene said.

"I'll talk to them," Oxenhandler said. He walked back down the hallway and into the interrogation room.

"You think they'll plead?" Holly asked Skene.

"If they're smart. We've got them cold, and I'd like to save the county the cost of a trial."

"That would be good," Holly said. She'd be happy to see the two in jail forever.

A few minutes later Oxenhandler came out of the interrogation room. "No deal, Marty. They maintain their innocence."

"You're a fool, Jackson."

"It's not the first time I've been told that."

"I'll ask for a preliminary hearing tomorrow morning," Skene said.

"I'd like another day, Marty."

"What for?"

"Don't you think it's important for the county to show at least the appearance of fairness in a case this important?"

Skene looked like exploding but held himself in check. "All right, the day after tomorrow at ten A.M. I'll call you if that's not all right with the judge."

"Thanks, Marty," Oxenhandler said.

Skene shook Holly's hand, then Oxenhandler's, and walked out.

"He's in a big hurry, isn't he?" Oxenhandler said.

"Can you blame him?"

"Yes, but it wouldn't do any good. When did you start work here?"

"Couple of days ago. Chief Marley hired me from the military last month."

"You done a lot of criminal investigation?" the lawyer asked.

"Yes." She didn't feel like trotting out her credentials.

"You think you could put an officer on checking out the origins of the gun you found and the gun Sweeney claims to own?"

"No," she said. "We're not going to do your job for you."

Oxenhandler nodded as if he had expected that answer. "Well, good to meet you, Chief. I expect I'll see you around." He managed a small smile, shook her hand and left.

Holly watched him go. He shambled rather than walked, and he had the stoop that seemed to belong to most very tall people. He reminded her of somebody, but who? Abraham Lincoln, maybe, but he was better looking than that.

13

Holly drove the chief's car home after work. She stopped at the hospital on her way and went to the intensive care unit. Before she could ask for Dr. Green, he walked into the waiting area.

"Oh, Chief Barker," he said. "I was just going to my office to call you. Why don't you come in for a moment." He led her to his office and offered her a chair.

"Has something happened?" she asked, worried.

"Chief Marley has shown signs of regaining consciousness," the doctor said. "It's preliminary, but people in comas don't always just open their eyes and start talking. There's been some rapid eye movement and some thrashing around, too; we've had to temporarily restrain him."

"And your prognosis?"

"He could wake up at any time, or he could revert to his previous state. I should warn you that even if he does wake up, he may be unable to speak or understand you, and even if he can speak, he may not remember anything about the shooting. In fact, I would consider the odds of that happening very poor."

"I understand," Holly replied. "Who knows about this?"

"Just the shift nurses and me."

"I'd appreciate it if you'd keep it that way for the moment."

"Of course, and I'll call you if there's any change."

She thanked the doctor and left. She still hoped that Chet Marley would wake up and tell her who shot him and why, in spite of what the doctor had said.

Daisy, who had stayed in the car, began to show some animation as they approached the trailer park.

"Yes, we're going home, and you're going to get your dinner," Holly said, stroking her head. "We'll be there any minute." She pulled up at the trailer and let Daisy out of the car. Holly walked around the perimeter of the clearing, looking into the woods, but Daisy seemed unconcerned with intruders this evening. The dog ran to the trailer door and wagged her hindquarters, there not being enough tail to do the job. Holly fed her and let her out for her evening romp, then got herself a beer and the document that Hank Doherty had written about the dog he had trained.

"'Excellent Working Bitch,'" Holly read aloud. "I love that, Daisy. It describes just about every woman I knew in the army, not to mention me." It was the first time she had read the document thoroughly, and as she turned its pages her eyes widened. "Jesus," she said, "Hank should have published this somewhere." She had just closed the document when her phone rang. She got the cordless and brought it outside.

"Hello?"

"Holly, it's Eleanor Warner."

"Oh, hi, how's it going?"

"We've gotten a lot done. Everything is pretty well taken care of, so we're going home tomorrow morning."

"I'm glad it went so quickly."

"Mary is taking all of the furnishings; we're taking only those things we can get onto the airplane. We've listed the house with a broker, and now we'll just have to wait for it to sell. I've made arrangements with a local funeral parlor to take care of the cremation and ship us Daddy's ashes. I'll put them on my garden at home."

"Oh, Eleanor, you'll be glad to know that the ballistics check went well. Looks like we've got the perpetrators. They haven't confessed to Hank's murder, but as time passes, they well may."

"I'm glad you've caught them, but I don't want revenge. I'm a Christian, and that's against my beliefs. I'll try to forgive them and leave it to you and the justice system to see that they're appropriately punished."

"I think that's a good attitude to adopt," Holly said. "I've seen anger on the part of victims' families make things worse for them."

"Don't worry about us, we'll get along just fine. I want to thank you again for the use of your car. We'll leave the keys at the counter in the terminal."

"And I'll send you a check for the computer and Daisy."

"No hurry. Good-bye, now."

"Good-bye."

She sat, sipping her beer and watching Daisy patrol the property, sticking her nose here and there. There was a moment when she flushed a rabbit, scaring Daisy almost as much as the furry creature. The phone rang again.

"Hello?"

"Holly? It's Jackson Oxenhandler."

"Good evening, counselor. What can I do for you?"

He seemed somewhat embarrassed. "I was just wondering if, when this business with Sweeney and his girlfriend is over, if . . . you and I might . . . have dinner sometime."

Holly was caught completely off guard. "Well, I . . . I don't know."

"Oh, I know it would be unprofessional of us to see each other until this case is resolved, but I thought perhaps . . ." His words trailed off.

"I have to agree with your ethical perceptions," Holly said. "Tell you what, why don't you call me when the case is over, and we'll see?"

"That's good enough for me," Oxenhandler said. "And it might be sooner than you think. Good night, Holly."

"Good night," she said, and hung up. Daisy came over, sat down and rested her head on Holly's knee, gazing up at her adoringly. "You're a good girl, Daisy," Holly said, "and the only girlfriend I have to talk to. Are you a good listener? Well, I've just had a call from a gentlemen of short acquaintance who'd like me to go out with him, just as soon as he's finished defending the people who shot my boss. Does that seem weird to you? Does to me. I'm not sure just how I feel about that. Police officers don't much like defendants' lawyers, but . . . I think I might be able to get past that."

Daisy said nothing, but Holly thought she had somehow given her blessing. Holly went back to reading about Daisy.

14

Holly entered the courtroom and took a seat in the front row, near the county attorney's table. She had only rarely been to civilian court proceedings, and she wanted to be here for this one as much for the experience as for the outcome, of which she was certain. In spite of what she felt was strong evidence, she had a queasy feeling that she could not explain, and she hoped that by witnessing this process, she could dispel it.

The clerk of the court stood and said, "This court is called to order, Judge Sandra Wheeler presiding. All rise." The judge, an attractive woman of around Holly's age, took the bench and called the court to order. She nodded to Marty Skene, and he stood.

"Your Honor, we're here for a preliminary hearing in the matter of the State of Florida v. Samuel Sweeney and Tanya Cooper, on a charge of assault with intent to kill."

"Call your first witness," the judge said.

Skene called Bob Hurst to the stand. Hurst identified himself by name and rank. Skene questioned him on his arrival at the scene of the shooting of Chet Marley and on the investigative procedures he used. Hurst testified to the chief's missing weapon and to the impressions of tires taken at the scene.

Next, Skene called the police officer who had arrested Sweeney and Cooper, and he testified to the finding of the missing weapon in their possession. "What was the caliber and make of the weapon?" Skene asked.

"It was a nine-millimeter Beretta automatic pistol."

"Did you investigate the ownership of this pistol?"

"Yes, I did."

"And what did you learn?"

"The serial number of the pistol showed that the weapon was the property of the City of Orchid Beach, and that it had been issued to Chester Marley."

"Did you then arrest Sweeney and Cooper and impound their vehicle?"

"Yes, I did."

"Your witness," Skene said to Oxenhandler.

The lawyer approached the witness stand. "Officer, when you came upon Mr. Sweeney and Ms. Cooper, what were they doing?"

"They were sitting in front of a campfire, and Sweeney was cleaning the Beretta pistol."

"Did Sweeney make any effort to conceal the pistol?"

"Ah . . . no."

"Were the headlights of your car on as you approached their campsite?"

"Yes."

"So they would have had ample warning that someone was coming?"

"I guess so."

"And yet Sweeney made no effort to hide the gun."

"No."

"No further questions."

Skene called Hurd Wallace to the stand, and the lieutenant identified himself by name and rank. "Lieutenant Wallace, did you, after the arrest of Sweeney and Cooper, come to conduct a search of their vehicle?"

"I did."

"Was this a lawful search?"

"Yes, Detective Hurst had obtained written permission from Sweeney for the search."

"Did you come to search the glove compartment?"

"I did."

"And what did you find there?"

"A small pistol."

"Could you describe the pistol?"

"It was a thirty-two-caliber Smith & Wesson revolver with a four-inch barrel."

"Did you conduct ballistics tests on this pistol for the purpose of comparing a bullet from this gun to the bullet removed from Chief Marley's head?"

"The pistol was sent to the state crime lab for that purpose."

"And did the lab issue a report?"

Wallace produced a sheet of paper. "Yes. The lab found that the bullet removed from Chief Marley's head was fired from the revolver found in Sweeney's van."

Skene handed the ballistics report to the clerk. "Entered as evidence. No further questions."

"No questions, Your Honor," Oxenhandler said.

"Recall Detective Robert Hurst," Skene said, and Hurst took the stand again and was reminded that he was still under oath. "Detective Hurst, in your investigations, did you learn that Sweeney's van had a connection with the crime scene, and if so, how?"

"Yes, I learned that the tread on the right rear tire of the van matched the plaster impression I had taken at the crime scene."

"Did you interrogate Sweeney and Cooper subsequent to that time?"

"Yes."

"Did Sweeney admit ownership of a gun, and if so, what kind?"

"Yes, he admitted ownership of a thirty-two-caliber revolver."

"No further questions."

Oxenhandler stood. "Detective, during your questioning of Mr.

Sweeney and Ms. Cooper, did you mention to them the make of pistol found in their van?"

"I'm not sure whether I did," Hurst replied. "I told them that we had found a thirty-two revolver in the van, and Sweeney admitted to owning a pistol of the same description."

"But the description did not include the name of the maker?"

"I'm not sure that it did."

"Thank you, no further questions."

Skene stood. "Your Honor, I have no further witnesses."

"Mr. Oxenhandler, do you wish to call any witnesses?"

"Yes, Your Honor, I wish to call Samuel Sweeney."

Sweeney was sworn. He was now clean-shaven and barbered, and his clothes looked new.

"Mr. Sweeney, how long have you resided at the campsite off highway A1A?"

"A little over two weeks."

Oxenhandler took Sweeney through his account of his activities on the evening of the chief's shooting. "So you were not at your camp between the hours of eleven and eleven-thirty P.M.?"

"No, I was not."

"Mr. Sweeney, do you own a pistol?"

"Yes, I own a *Colt* thirty-two-caliber pistol with a two-inch barrel."

"When Detective Hurst asked you if you owned a pistol, and you affirmed that you did, was the Colt pistol the one to which you were referring?"

"Yes, it was."

"Do you own a thirty-two Smith & Wesson pistol?"

"No, I do not."

"I have no further questions of Mr. Sweeney, Your Honor, but in trial I can produce witnesses confirming his presence on that evening at both the movie theater and the gas station where he left his tire to be repaired. I can also produce a witness who can testify that he changed a tire on or near the spot where Chief Marley was shot, only a few minutes before that event occurred."

"Any questions for Mr. Sweeney, Mr. Skene?" the judge asked.

"Not at this time, Your Honor."

"Any other witnesses, Mr. Oxenhandler?"

"One, Your Honor. Call Mr. Everett Schwartz."

A man sitting near Holly in the front row of the courtroom got up, took the stand and was sworn.

"Mr. Schwartz, how do you earn your living?"

"I'm a gun dealer. I have a shop in Jacksonville, and on weekends I often attend gun shows, where I buy and sell weapons."

"Do you recognize the gentleman sitting at the defense table?"

"I do."

"Have you ever sold him a gun?"

"Yes."

"What kind of gun?"

"A thirty-two-caliber Colt revolver with a two-inch barrel, nickel plated."

"When and where did you make this sale?"

"Four weeks ago, at a gun sale in Jacksonville."

"Can you substantiate this sale?"

Schwartz produced two sheets of paper. "Here are a copy of the bill of sale and a copy of the federal form that Mr. Sweeney filled out and signed."

Oxenhandler handed the papers to the clerk. "Entered in evidence. I have no further questions." He returned to his seat.

The judge turned to Skene. "Any questions, Mr. Skene?"

"No, Your Honor," Skene replied.

"Any further witnesses, Mr. Oxenhandler?"

"Your Honor, may counsel approach the bench?"

She nodded.

Holly watched as the two lawyers went to the bench and had a spirited conversation that went on for perhaps three minutes. Oxenhandler was calm and insistent, while Skene seemed outraged.

"Step back," the judge said finally, and the two attorneys stood near their respective tables.

"Do you have a motion, Mr. Oxenhandler?" the judge asked.

"Move for dismissal of all charges," the lawyer replied.

"Mr. Skene?" the judge said.

"The state does not oppose the motion, Your Honor, but reserves the right to bring these charges again at a later date."

The judge said, "Motion granted, charges are dismissed. Mr. Sweeney, Ms. Cooper, you are free to go."

"Your Honor," Oxenhandler said, "will you restore Mr. Sweeney's van and possessions?"

"So ordered," the judge said. "Court is adjourned."

Holly sat on the bench, unmoving, astounded. So what, if Sweeney owned a different gun? That didn't mean he didn't own more than one. She stood up and intercepted Skene as he walked down the aisle. "Marty, what happened?"

"I'll call you later," he said, looking furious. "We'll need to talk."

Holly moved down the aisle and left the courtroom. Hurd Wallace and Bob Hurst were standing in the hallway outside, talking animatedly. They attempted to question Skene, but he brushed them off and stalked from the building. She started toward Wallace and Hurst, but stopped when someone took her arm from behind. She turned to find Jackson Oxenhandler towering over her.

"May I speak to you for a moment in private?" he asked.

She followed him to an unpopulated corner of the hallway. "What happened in there?"

"I explained to the judge that a search of records showed that the thirty-two Smith & Wesson revolver is registered to Amanda Smith Wallace, who is the ex-wife of Hurd Wallace."

Holly's mouth dropped open.

"Your mouth is open," Oxenhandler said.

Holly closed it, but she was unable to say anything.

"I disclosed this at the bench, rather than in open court, to avoid publicly embarrassing the department. I trust you'll take the appropriate steps."

Holly nodded.

Oxenhandler smiled a little. "I'll call you for dinner," he said, then walked away.

Holly walked to where Wallace and Hurst were standing. "Back at the station, in my office, *now*," she said.

15

Holly followed the two officers into her office and closed the door, trying her best not to slam it. She sat down at her desk. "Does either of you know what happened in the courtroom?"

"No," they said simultaneously.

"Hurd, when you searched the van and found the pistol, did you recognize it?"

"Recognize it? I don't know what you mean. It wasn't the first Smith & Wesson I've seen."

"Hurd, that gun is registered to your ex-wife."

Wallace's composure did not change, but he appeared to be thinking hard. Hurst turned and looked at him in amazement. "Chief," Wallace said, "I need a moment to find a file."

"A file?" Holly asked. "What does a file have to do with this?"

"If you'll give me just a moment, Chief." Wallace maintained an icy calm.

"All right," Holly said. Wallace got up and left the office. Holly turned to Hurst. "Do you have anything to say about this?"

Hurst shook his head. "No, Chief. I'm as flabbergasted as you are. In fact, I'm having trouble believing this."

Hurd Wallace returned holding a manila file, but before he could speak, the desk officer knocked on the door and opened it.

"Excuse me, Chief, but Sweeney is here wanting his van. What should I do about it?"

"Give him the van and anything else we have of his, except the drugs."

The young man nodded and closed the door.

"We've still got grounds for arrest on a drug possession charge," Hurst said.

"We can't do it," Holly replied. "Right now, the department is under suspicion of having planted that gun in the van. If we charge him with possession, his lawyer will say we planted that, too. We're in no position to move. We have to let him go."

"I guess you're right," Hurst said.

"All right, Hurd, I'm waiting," Holly said.

Wallace handed her the file. "This is a report of a burglary at my ex-wife's house nearly three months ago."

Holly opened the file and began to scan it.

"You'll note that nearly five hundred dollars in cash was taken, and . . . "

"And a Smith & Wesson thirty-two," Holly said, reading from the file. Her shoulders slumped. "Thank God."

"I reckon Sweeney bought the gun off whoever stole it, or whoever he sold it to," Wallace said.

"Sweeney's been in town less than three weeks."

"The gun could have changed hands half a dozen times. He could have bought it at any time after he arrived."

"We'd never make *that* stick," Holly said. "Who brought the van to the station?" she asked.

"It was towed in; that's policy."

"Where was it left?"

"In the parking lot outside. We don't have any secure garage space."

"Was it locked?"

"Yes," Hurst answered, "and I was given the keys. I gave them to Hurd for his search."

"Hurd, was the van locked when you got to it?"

"Yes."

"So the van was in the parking lot for how long before you found the gun?"

"From shortly after midnight until around eight-thirty A.M., when I arrived."

"Is the parking lot lighted at night?"

"Poorly."

Hurst spoke up. "The van is from the late seventies. Anybody with a coat hanger could have opened it in thirty seconds. The question is, who would gain by planting the gun?"

"Whoever shot Chet Marley," Holly replied. "That seems pretty straightforward."

Hurd Wallace was shaking his head. "I think it's much more likely that Sweeney bought the gun locally, and that he's our man."

"He didn't behave like a guilty man," Holly said. "Oxenhandler brought that out in court this morning. When he was approached by an officer, he made no attempt to hide the chief's gun. He didn't run, he didn't resist. He didn't behave like a drifter who had shot the chief of police twenty-four hours before." She turned to Hurst. "Bob, did Sweeney give up anything at all during your interrogation?"

Hurst shook his head. "No, he was solid."

"And the question of the make of the gun didn't come up?"

"No, I don't think it did."

"Did you bring up the Doherty murder at all?"

"Not until late in the interrogation. I was trying to get him to cop to the chief's shooting before I got into that."

"Well," Holly said, "I can't fault anybody's conduct in all this; it was handled by the book. I'll call Marty Skene and tell him what we know. He's very pissed off, and we need to defuse him right now before he starts making charges. You two return to your duties."

The two men left her office, and Holly called Marty Skene. "I know you're angry about this, and I am, too, but we're both going to have to sit on it." She told him about the burglary report. "Wallace and Hurst think that Sweeney bought the gun locally and used it on the chief, and I have to say that's the most plausible explanation."

"Maybe so," Skene said, sounding placated, "but you're going to have to face the possibility that somebody in your department planted that gun in the van."

"I know that, believe me, and I intend to pursue it, but I'll have to do so quietly. Was anybody from the local press at the hearing this morning?"

"Yes, their regular court reporter."

"We'll have to see how they play this. Maybe they'll think Schwartz's testimony torpedoed your case."

"Maybe, but I wouldn't count on it. You'd better be prepared to answer questions."

"I'll keep that in mind." She said good-bye and hung up. Her phone buzzed immediately. "Hello?"

"Chief, Evelyn Martin, the court reporter for the local paper, is on the line."

"Tell her I'll call her back." She hung up and let her mind range over the problem. Finally, she got up and went into Jane Grey's office and closed the door. "Jane," she said, "do you know anything about the relationship between Hurd Wallace and his ex-wife?"

"Just that she hates his guts," Jane replied. "Their divorce went to trial, and she behaved like a madwoman."

"So it wouldn't be likely that she'd support him in some story he'd made up."

"Not at all likely."

"Do you remember anything about a burglary at her house a while back?"

"Seems like I do; she lost some money and a gun, but they didn't take the TV or stereo or any jewelry. She came in and made a report for insurance purposes, I believe." Jane smiled wickedly. "I think Hurd's lucky her gun was stolen. She might have used it on him."

Holly went back to her desk and called the reporter. She wasn't looking forward to the conversation.

"First of all, Chief, welcome to Orchid Beach."

"Thank you, Ms. Martin."

"Tell me, what was all that at the judge's bench this morning?"

"I was no more privy to that than you were," Holly replied.

"Did you think you had the right man in Chief Marley's shooting?"

"We did, but the fact that Sweeney owned a different gun didn't help us."

"You think Sweeney's innocent?"

"I wouldn't hazard an opinion on that. Let's just say that we don't have enough evidence at this point to say conclusively that he did it or didn't do it. Anything else? I've got a busy day ahead of me."

"Any news on the chief's condition?"

"Unchanged."

"Do you think that he will ever be able to help in the investigation of who shot him?"

"That seems very unlikely. We'll just have to solve the shooting with good police work."

"Sometime I'd like to sit down and interview you for the paper."

"Maybe later, but I think you can understand how full my days are right now."

"I'll call you in a few weeks."

"That would be a better time. Good-bye." Holly hung up. She felt that Sweeney was probably innocent, but before she could be at peace with that, she was going to have to talk to him herself.

16

Holly drove south on A1A and slowed at the spot where Chet Marley had been found. There was a good fifteen yards of thick sod between the road and a chain-link fence closing off the property beyond. Whoever shot Chet had thrown his gun over that fence, but why? Why not steal it, or better, just leave it where it lay? She drove along for another hundred yards until she saw a break in the fence, where it had been peeled back. There were tire tracks across the grass and leading into the brush. She turned and drove through the gap. Daisy sniffed the air through her open window.

The ground was bumpy, and the brush dense on each side of the track. It looked as though there had once been a road or driveway that was now disused, except for Sam Sweeney's van, which appeared ahead, pulled off the track to the right. Holly stopped behind the van and got out. "Daisy, you stay," she said.

She walked past the van, and her nostrils were assaulted with the odor of human feces. Sweeney had apparently not been a Boy Scout; he had never learned to dig a latrine. She pushed through a stand of palmetto and came into a clearing, shaded by live oaks and bay trees. Sweeney and the girl were sitting at the campfire, roasting hot dogs on sticks. Sweeney got to his feet.

"What now?" he said.

"I want to talk to you," Holly replied.

"Sure," Sweeney said. The girl went on cooking the hot dogs.

"Show me your Colt thirty-two," she said.

"I don't have it," he replied. "The cops must have took it when they searched the van."

"Where was the thirty-two in the van?"

"In the glove compartment."

"You have any other firearms?"

"No, ma'am," he said, shaking his head. "Just the one, and I don't have that one no more."

"You'd be wise not to replace it," Holly said.

"Maybe you're right."

"I heard your testimony in the courtroom. Did you leave anything out?"

"No, ma'am. I answered all the questions they asked me."

"What about the questions they didn't ask you?"

He looked at her narrowly. "What do you mean?"

"Come on, Sam—you were all over this area that night. You had a flat where the chief was later shot, you were camped here, you drove up and down A1A all the time. What did you see that nobody asked you about?"

"I didn't, ah, see anything," he replied.

"All right, then what did you hear?"

He looked at the grass under his feet.

"Come on, Sam, this is off the record, just between you and me."

"I reckon we got back here five minutes before it happened," he said.

"Go on."

"I heard them talking. They sounded angry."

"How many?"

"Two, maybe three. I couldn't see nothing. You see how dense that brush is," he said, pointing toward the road.

He was right about that, Holly thought. The brush between

where they stood and the road, some fifty feet away, was virtually a wall. "What were they saying?"

"I couldn't make any of it out, but it was angry. Both sides of the conversation was real mad. Then I heard the shot."

"What did you do?"

"I didn't do nothing. I wasn't about to stick my nose in something where there was shooting going on."

"Then what happened?"

"I heard something hitting the brush and then fall to the ground. I don't know why, but my first thought was a hand grenade. I kept waiting for something to explode."

"That was the Beretta?"

"Yeah, I guess so. I didn't find it until the next day. Whoever threw it really let go. He'd have to clear that brush. If it had landed in the brush, you'd have needed a chain saw to get at it."

"After you found it, did you check the clip? Had it been fired?"

"No, ma'am. I mean I checked the clip, and it was full. There wasn't one in the chamber."

"How many shots did you hear?"

"Just the one."

"You know enough about guns to guess what it was?"

"Not really. Anyway, you don't have to guess. It had to be that Smith & Wesson thirty-two."

He was right about that. "Did you hear a car drive away?"

"Yeah, I heard the doors slam . . . "

"How many doors?"

"Two. I guess that means there was two of them."

"I guess so. What did the car sound like?"

"Like a car—not a truck. Like a regular car. Kind of sporty, maybe. You know how some of them sporty cars sound?"

"Like a Ferrari or something?"

"Nah, I'd know that sound. Like something that wanted to be a Ferrari, you know? Something cheaper."

"Which way did it go?"

"I reckon it made a U-turn and went north."

"What are your plans, Sam?"

"Plans? I ain't got no plans. I'm just hangin'."

Holly shook her head. "No. I want you out of here."

"Out of the campsite?"

"Not just that. Out of Orchid, out of the county."

"How come?"

"You want to be busted on the cocaine charge? Nobody planted that."

"I, uh, see your point," he said.

"I want you gone before dark," she said.

"Yes, ma'am, and thank you for not busting me on the drugs. They was just recreational, only for my own use, you know; I wasn't dealing nothing."

"Fine, just pack it up and go," she said.

"Can I check back with you to see if you find my Colt thirty-two?"

"Sam, you're pressing your luck."

He held up his hands in front of him. "Yes, ma'am, I get the picture. We'll be on our way just as soon as we can get our stuff in the van."

"That's the idea," Holly said. "Good luck."

"Thank you, ma'am."

Holly walked back to the car, where Daisy was looking anxiously out the window. "I'm back," she said to the dog. "No need to worry. We'll go home and get you some dinner."

The mention of dinner got a favorable reaction.

When Holly got back to her trailer, there was a car in her parking spot. Daisy made a low noise in her throat. Holly drew her gun.

17

The car was a Toyota Camry, late eighties, before the new design came along. She was impressed by its condition—no dents or rust, clean, polished. Daisy was still making the noise; she preceded Holly around the corner of the trailer.

"Easy there," Jackson Oxenhandler was saying, holding out his hands toward the dog, as if to fend her off.

"Daisy, stop," Holly said. Daisy stopped, but she continued to growl.

"I'm not a burglar," the lawyer said to the dog. "Look," he said, holding up a large paper bag, "I brought dinner."

"Daisy, he's all right. Good dog," Holly said. Daisy stopped growling, walked over to Oxenhandler and sniffed the bag.

"Good dog," Oxenhandler said. He offered her the back of his hand to sniff. "Doesn't smell as good as the bag, does it?"

"Who invited you to dinner?" Holly asked.

"Nobody. I'm inviting you." He held up the bag again. "You like barbecue?"

Holly's stomach woke up and growled, as if on cue. "I like *good* barbecue," she said.

"This is the best," Oxenhandler said, pointing at the bag. "Pit-roasted, hand-basted, from an extremely attractive pig."

"How come you're so anxious to go out with me?" she asked.

"Because I find you overwhelmingly attractive," he replied.

"That's hard to argue with, I guess."

He held up the bag again. "It's *really* good barbecue."

Holly's mouth watered. "I accept," she said, then smiled.

"That took a long time," he said.

"What?"

"That smile. First one I've seen on you."

"First one I've worn since I came to this town," she said. "You want a beer?"

"Sure."

She motioned him off her doorstep, unlocked the trailer door and motioned Daisy inside. "Daisy, bring the gentleman a beer," she said. Daisy disappeared and came back half a minute with a Heineken in her jaws, surrendering it to Oxenhandler.

"That," he said, "is a *very* valuable dog."

"I'd like a beer, too, Daisy," Holly said, and the dog brought her one.

"Did she close the refrigerator door?" he asked.

"You bet." Holly reached inside the trailer, got an opener and cracked both bottles. She dragged up a couple of folding chairs and they sat and watched the Indian River.

"Hope this isn't too much of a shock," he said. "I mean, I hope I'm not being too persistent."

"I like persistence in a man," she replied. Involuntarily, she thought of Colonel James Bruno, then dismissed him from her mind. "Up to a point."

"Point taken. You hungry yet?"

"Let's finish our beer."

"Good idea. I hear you're an army brat."

"Brat, filly and . . . older filly. Grew up in it, joined it, stayed twenty years."

"You don't look old enough to have done anything for twenty years."

"I'm thirty-eight and a half, if you're fishing. How old are you?"

"Forty-one."

"How long you been practicing law?"

"Six years."

She frowned. "You have trouble getting out of law school?"

"I had trouble getting in," he replied. "Once in, I did okay."

"What did you do before?"

"I was a cop in Miami."

"What kind of cop?"

"Street, uniformed. I wasn't suited to it."

"How long did it take you to figure that out?"

"Oh, about eight years. They finally made it clear to me."

"Who did?"

"All the other cops, especially my superiors."

"What were your shortcomings as a police officer?"

"Do I have to?"

"Yes."

"I was too sensitive. I tended to feel for the people I arrested. I tended not to feel for most of the cops I knew."

"How so?"

"Too many of them were unnecessarily violent, on the take. I saw them hurt people, lie to their superiors, perjure themselves in court."

"What percentage of all cops were like that?"

"I don't know, maybe fifteen, twenty percent of the ones I knew. Trouble was, those were the ones I seemed to get partnered with or put to work for."

"So you left and went to law school?"

"First I testified against my partner; after that it was easy to leave."

"I'll bet. What did your partner do?"

"He beat a man to death with a baton."

"And you saw it happen?"

"I was driving. He told me to stop alongside a guy walking along the street. I stopped. My partner got out and started hitting the guy in the head. By the time I got there, the guy's brains were on the sidewalk. I asked my partner why he'd done it, and he said the guy hadn't paid off. He'd apparently been taking a cut of the guy's drug sales."

"What did you do? Immediately, I mean."

"I arrested him, cuffed him, threw him in the back of the patrol car, took him down to the station and booked him. A crowd gathered at the booking desk—a crowd of cops. The shift was changing."

"What did they do?"

"They locked *me* up."

"On what charge?"

"Murder, of course; my partner fingered me for the killing."

"Jesus."

"Yeah, it wasn't much fun."

"And how did you get out of that mess?"

"Fortunately, a lawyer—a public defender—saw them lock me up and called Internal Affairs. I've had a soft spot for public defenders ever since. IA got there before somebody killed me. Fortunately, also, there was a witness to the event on the street—a teenaged Cuban girl. She backed me up, and eventually, after nearly a year on administrative leave, I testified, and my partner got a life sentence."

"What kind of life sentence?"

"The kind that makes parole possible after ten years."

"And how long ago was this?"

"Twelve years ago. He's out."

"Any idea where he is?"

"He's in Miami, working for a security company run by an ex-cop. Cops take care of their own, you know."

"They didn't take care of you."

"I wasn't one of their own, and they knew it."

They were quiet for a little while.

"I'm hungry," Holly said. "You want another beer?"

"Yeah, thanks."

She gave him some dishes and napkins, then got them both another beer.

"How come you left the army after twenty? Why didn't you stay for the whole thirty?"

"I decided my career was pretty much at an end."

"How come?"

"I accused my commanding officer of attempted rape and sexual harrassment. He was acquitted at the court-martial."

"He really tried to rape you?"

"He tried real hard. It all started with his asking me out. When I wouldn't go, the . . . remarks began, and that degenerated into grabbing. I asked him to stop; he wouldn't. Finally, one day, he grabbed me and I hit him. I hit pretty good. That's when he started tearing my clothes off."

"You fought him off?"

"I got a knee into his crotch, and he seemed to lose interest."

"So you turned him in?"

"Not until I found out he'd been giving a young lieutenant in the outfit a hard time. I figured, with the two of us to testify, we'd have a case. I was wrong."

"He got off scot-free."

"He did."

"Looks like you and I are sort of black sheep, doesn't it?" he said.

"You could say that." They plunged into the barbecue. It was sensational. "This is sensational barbecue," she said. "Best I've ever had."

"I know a guy," he replied.

"So tell me about law school."

"I applied at a dozen places, all out of state. They all liked my academic record—I had a degree from Florida State—but they didn't like the idea of a thirty-two-year-old first-year law student. I finally got into the University of Georgia Law School, after I hinted that I might sue for age discrimination if I didn't get in."

"How'd you do?"

"Third in my class; edited the law review."

"So how come you're not practicing corporate law in some glass tower somewhere?"

He smiled sadly. "I like criminals. I mean, I understand them, somehow—what makes them do what they do. It makes it easier to defend them. You know, I don't think I've ever defended an innocent man until today. And, of course, ol' Sam possessed an unlicensed weapon and some drugs, so I guess he wasn't innocent, after all."

"I just said good-bye to Sam," she said. "Right before I got home."

"He's going somewhere?"

"At my suggestion. We don't need him around here."

"I can see it's going to be tough to make a living in Orchid with you around."

She laughed. The phone rang. She got up and went into the trailer. "Hello?"

"Ms. . . . Chief Barker?"

"Yes."

"It's Dr. Green, at the hospital."

"Yes, Dr. Green?" She had the awful feeling that Chet Marley was dead.

"Chester Marley is awake," he said.

"I'm on my way," she replied, then hung up.

18

Holly started to change out of her uniform. "I've got to go to the hospital," she called through the open door. "Can you give me a lift to the airport? My car's there."

"Sure, glad to. Something to do with Chet Marley?"

She came out of the trailer, buttoning her blouse. "Sort of."

"Okay," he said. They got into his car and drove off. Daisy sat in the backseat.

Holly was quiet, wondering what was going to happen next. Probably, Chet wouldn't be able to talk. Never mind, at least she could let him know she was on the job.

"I hope Chet hasn't died?" Oxenhandler said.

"No."

"Why are you being so closemouthed about his condition?"

"Somebody tried to kill him," she said. "They could try again."

"They? There was more than one?"

"Didn't Sam Sweeney tell you that?"

"No, he didn't. He told me he knew nothing about it. Did he tell you different?"

"He said he heard the shot but didn't see anything. He thought there were two people."

Oxenhandler drove along quietly for a while. "Something stinks in your police department," he said.

"How long have you thought that?"

"A while. Chet said something to me once."

"I didn't even know you knew him. What did he say?"

"It's a small town; everybody knows everybody. I had a few beers with him once, about three weeks ago. We were talking about the town. I said it was a nice town. He said it was going to be nicer before he was through being a cop. I asked how it could be any nicer, and he said it could have a better police department, and he was working on that."

"He was," Holly said. "That's what got him shot."

"You know who did it?"

"No, but I'm going to find out."

"Good," he said. He drove to the main entrance to the hospital and stopped.

"I've got to pick up my car at the airport," she said.

"You go on in and see Chet. I'll stay here with Daisy, and we'll pick up your car later."

"Okay. Daisy, stay here with Jackson and be a good girl." She got out of the car and ran up the steps to the hospital, then took the elevator to the surgical floor and went to intensive care. Dr. Green was waiting for her. "How is he?" she asked.

"Come take a look," the doctor said. He led her into the ward. Chet Marley's bed had been cranked into a sitting position, and he was taking soup from a nurse. He turned and looked her way.

"Holly!" he said, and he sounded weak.

"Hey, Chet," she said, taking his hand. "How you feeling?"

"Kind of tired. Am I in the base hospital?"

"No, Chet, you're back in Orchid Beach."

Chet thought about that for a moment. "You got here kind of quick, didn't you?" he asked.

"No, some time has passed since we last met. You've been hurt."

He put his hand to the bandage on his head. "What happened?"

"Somebody shot you."

"Who?"

"I was hoping you could tell me."

Chet shook his head. "Last thing I remember, you and Ham and I were having dinner. I hired you, didn't I?"

"That's right, Chet, and I came to work a few days ago. You were hurt before we could talk."

He pushed the soup away. "Boy, I'm tired," he said. "None of this makes any sense."

Dr. Green spoke up. "We'd better let him get some sleep. You can talk more tomorrow."

"Yeah," Chet said, closing his eyes. The nurse lowered the bed, and he seemed to drift off.

Holly left the ward with the doctor. "Is he going to be all right?"

"Except for his memory loss, he seems to be recovering."

"Is he going to get any of his memory back?"

"Hard to say. He seems perfectly aware of everything up until a few weeks ago, but as you saw, he remembers nothing about the shooting. That could come back to him, if the relevant brain tissue hasn't been destroyed, but I can't promise you it will. Come back tomorrow morning, and let's see how he's doing then."

"All right. Thank you for calling me, Doctor, and let's keep this quiet."

"Of course. I'll see that contact with him is limited. The nurses already know they're not supposed to talk about him."

"See you tomorrow," Holly said, shaking his hand. She took the elevator downstairs and walked out to the car. Daisy was in the front seat now, her head in Jackson's lap.

"I see you two are getting along," Holly said. "Backseat, Daisy." Daisy jumped into the backseat.

"We did fine," Jackson replied. "She's very nice when she's not threatening to tear my throat out. I hope she doesn't sleep with you."

"She does," Holly lied.

"Oh. How's Chet?"

"Can you keep your mouth shut?"

"It's one of the things lawyers do best. If we talked, the world would tremble." He started the car and headed for the airport.

"He's awake and talking."

"That's great! Who shot him?"

"He doesn't remember that part—nothing, in fact, since our last meeting, when he hired me."

"That's bad news," Jackson said. "Is his memory going to improve?"

"Nobody knows. I'll come back to see him tomorrow and see how he's doing."

"Do you really think they might try again?"

"If they thought he could identify them, they'd have to."

"Has it ever occurred to you," Jackson said, "that they might find it convenient for you to be dead?"

"Yes," she said. "Somebody had a go at me very recently." She told him about the incident with the gas bottle and the parachute flare. "But I can take care of myself," she said finally.

"I hope you won't mind if I help," he said.

"And how would you do that?"

"I'll just keep an eye on you, mostly in the evenings."

She was surprised at how much the offer pleased her. "I think I could get used to that," she said.

"Who do you suspect in the department?" he asked, changing the subject.

"I don't know who to suspect. When you told me about the gun in the van, I thought I had Hurd Wallace cold, but it turns out that his ex-wife's place was burgled three months ago. She reported the gun stolen at that time. The most plausible scenario I have right now is that your client bought the gun from whoever stole it."

"You know that's not the case," he said.

"How do I know that?"

"Because whoever shot Chet killed Hank Doherty. Sammy didn't even know who Doherty was, let alone have a motive for killing him."

"Why do you think the same people killed Hank?"

"I hear things. I heard he was killed with the chief's shotgun."

"You heard right."

"Well, we know Chet didn't kill him, don't we?"

"That's what I think."

"So Sam Sweeney is out of it."

"Yes, he is. Frankly, I was afraid somebody might kill him, once he was identified as a suspect. That's why I ran him out of town; it would be easy to hang it on a dead guy."

"Good move."

"I wonder where Sam's Colt thirty-two is?" she said.

"In a killer's pocket, probably." He drove up to the airport terminal and stopped. "I'll follow you home," he said.

"Don't bother, I'll be all right."

"Are you armed?"

"No."

"I'll follow you." He bent down and kissed her.

She kissed him back, and she liked it. "Whatever you say, counselor," she whispered.

19

Holly slept alone, though Jackson Oxenhandler had made it clear he would have preferred it otherwise, and she wasn't so sure that she wouldn't have preferred it, too. It had been a long time, she reflected. As soon as word had gotten out on the base about her intention to charge Colonel James Bruno, half the men on the base had stopped speaking to her, except when absolutely necessary, and those she found attractive among the other half had stopped asking her out.

She had just waked up when the phone rang. "Hello?"

"It's Dr. Green. I'm sorry to call you so early, but I thought you'd want to know right away."

"Know what?"

"The supervisor in intensive care called me a minute ago. Chester Marley is back in a coma."

"But I thought he was doing so well."

"So did I, but they were unable to wake him this morning. I can't offer you any sort of prognosis; we'll just have to wait and see what happens."

"Thank you for letting me know, Doctor," she said, then hung up. This was depressing news. Even if Chet had been unable to remember the shooting, he could have filled her in on his earlier suspicions. The phone rang again. "Hello?"

"It's Jackson. Did you sleep well?"

"Like a stone."

"I'm sorry to hear it."

She laughed. "Bad news," she said. "The doctor just called, and Chet is back in a coma."

"I hear that happens sometimes."

"It's depressing."

"I can see how it might be. Dinner tonight?"

"Can I call you later? I don't know what the day holds."

"Sure." He gave her his office and home numbers.

"Talk to you later." She hung up and started her day.

She was in the office by eight-thirty, and at nine Charlie Peterson, of the City Council, knocked on her door. "Good morning."

"Good morning," she said, remembering that she had been supposed to call him. "I'm sorry I haven't gotten back to you, but it's been extremely busy around here."

"Yeah, I heard. We've got a council meeting at ten; I think you should come up and meet everybody."

"Sure, I'll be glad to."

"It's room 404."

"See you at ten." She walked next door to Jane Grey's office. "Jane, will you make a copy of my contract, please? I think the city council might like to see it."

"I expect they already have," she said. "The council chairman, John Westover, asked for a copy yesterday. I couldn't think of any reason not to give it to him."

"You did the right thing," Holly said. She sat down. "Tell me about this Westover."

"He's a power, locally—owns a car dealership, a printing company, a fast-food franchise and a funeral home, among other things."

"What's he like?"

"Professionally jovial," Jane said. "He's a car salesman at heart, I think. Wants everybody to like him. Takes the council seriously, though. He's said to have a real good grasp of the city's finances, and he manages them well. The city is well run, and property taxes are under control, so he keeps getting elected."

"Who's the mayor?"

"John is, for all practical purposes. There's no mayor, just a city manager, Ted Michaels, and he jumps when John Westover hollers."

"What about the rest of the council?"

"There's only five, and they're elected at large, not from districts. Charlie Peterson is the only one with any gumption. The others vote yes when John Westover clears his throat."

"I think I get the picture," Holly said. She went back to her office.

At ten o'clock, she went up to the city council chambers and was asked by a receptionist to take a seat in a waiting room. She leafed through a magazine for a few minutes, then the door to the chambers opened and a large, pink-faced man with a crew cut smiled at her and shook her hand.

"I'm John Westover," he said. "Sorry to keep you waiting. We had some business to get out of the way. Come on in."

Everybody stood up.

"I guess you already know Charlie Peterson. The others are, left to right, Frank Hessian, Howard Goldman and Irma Taggert."

Holly shook all their hands and took an offered seat at their conference table.

"First, let me welcome you to Orchid Beach," Westover said.

"Thank you," Holly replied.

"We're a little in the dark about your hiring, so I wonder if you'd just tell us how it came about?"

"I'd be glad to," Holly said. She explained her military background briefly. "Chief Marley and my father, Hamilton Barker, are old friends from the army. The chief came up to see us and offered me the deputy chief's job."

"What did he know about your background?" Westover asked.

"Everything there was to know," Holly replied. "The chief is a careful man; he did his homework."

"I'm sure he did. Now, I've read your contract, and I'd like to know how much negotiation was involved."

"There was none," Holly said.

"I beg your pardon?"

"Chief Marley made me an offer and I accepted it. He sent me a contract, I read it and signed it without any changes."

"You're a very trusting person, Miss Barker," the woman councillor, Irma Taggert, said.

"It was a good offer and a well-drawn contract," Holly replied. "From what I've learned about Chief Marley's work habits, it was typical of the way he does things."

"God knows, the chief does things his own way," Frank Goldman said.

"I think the organization and training of his department speak for themselves," Holly said.

"Perhaps you could tell us something about your background in the military and law enforcement."

"I'd be glad to. I joined the army out of high school and after basic training was assigned to the military police. I earned a degree in criminology from the University of Maryland, was accepted into Officer Candidate School, commissioned and assigned as a platoon leader in an MP company. Over the years I was promoted regularly and rose to the rank of major, in command of an MP company with a complement of a hundred or so men and women, a job that I held at retirement."

"Did you have any civilian law-enforcement training?"

"I attended four courses at the FBI Academy at Quantico Marine Base, where I trained in criminal investigation and law-enforcement management. The other, nonmilitary trainees were officers and chiefs of police from cities all over the country."

"I see. And why did you choose to retire from the military?"

Holly took a deep breath: best to be frank about it. "I and another female officer charged the provost marshal on our base with sexual harassment and attempted rape. Although we both testified against him, a court-martial failed to convict him. I believed that his acquittal might damage my chances for promotion, and it was at that time—on the same day, actually—that I met Chet Marley, and he offered me the job in Orchid Beach. It seemed a fine opportunity, and I took it."

"Holly," John Westbrook said, "may I call you Holly?"

"Of course. I'd like it if you all would."

"Holly, we've had some discussion this morning, and I believe it's fair to say that it was the sense of our meeting that we appoint an acting chief while Chet Marley is incapacitated."

Holly said nothing.

"What I mean is, we feel that a person who is more familiar with the way the department is organized, and more familiar with the territory in Orchid Beach, would be a better choice for this position. We'd like you to stay on, of course, but we feel that Lieutenant Hurd Wallace is the natural choice for the position."

Charlie Peterson spoke up. "Not all of us feel that way, John," he said, and Frank Goldman nodded vigorously in agreement.

"All right, then," Westover said, reddening, "a majority of us feel that way."

"Mr. Westover . . . "

"John, please."

"Of course, John. I believe you've had an opportunity to read my contract."

"Well, I did take a quick look at it."

"Then I'm sure you know that it specifies that, in any circumstance when Chief Marley is unable to perform his duties, I automatically become acting chief."

"Well, now, I don't know about that," Westover said.

"Holly," Irma Taggert said, leaning forward, "we don't want to be sticklers over legal matters here, we're just doing what we believe is best for our little city."

"Of course you are, Irma," Holly said, "and I feel I have that same obligation."

"I'm so glad," Taggert said, looking relieved.

"I believe that I have an obligation to live up to the terms of my contract, and that the city has the same obligation. It's my understanding that the city charter gives Chet Marley the authority to hire and fire in his department and to appoint his own choices in supervisory and executive positions. Chief Marley told me that he considered Hurd Wallace for the position and decided against him. Now he has made his choice, and my intention is to carry out his wishes to the best of my ability."

"Young lady," Irma Taggert spat, "do you realize that we could fire you out of hand this minute and appoint whoever we want to your job?"

Holly felt her hackles rising, and she couldn't resist the impulse to fire back. Charlie Peterson saved her from herself.

"Irma, I'm the lawyer here, so let me give you the city's legal position in a nutshell. Deputy Chief Barker has a five-year contract properly approved and executed by the relevant authority, Chief Marley. If we were to fire her, she would be entitled, at the very least, to every penny specified in her contract, plus health insurance and pension contributions. It's my considered opinion that, if we fired her, she could also bring an action against the city for unlawful dismissal and sex discrimination and that she would probably get both compensatory and punitive damages."

"Just tell me this, Charlie Peterson," Taggert shot back. "Why hasn't she arrested the person who shot Chet Marley?"

Holly held up both hands. "Please, ladies and gentlemen," she said. "I don't want to be a bone of contention in this council, so just let me state my position, and then I'll leave you to get on with your deliberations."

"Please do," Charlie Peterson said.

"I've been hired to do a job here. It's one I'm well qualified for and one I intend to do. If I ever feel that I can't handle it for any reason, I'll come to you and resign, I promise you that. With regard to the shooting of Chief Marley, I can tell you that every resource of this department is being deployed to find and arrest the perpetrator. I would remind you that, if I resigned today, the same people would still be investigating that crime. Now, if you have any questions of me, about my background or my intentions, I'll be glad to answer them right now."

There was silence for a while, finally broken by John Westover. "Holly, welcome aboard," he said. "If any of us can be of any help to you, please don't hesitate to ask."

Holly smiled sweetly. "Thank you all so much."

20

Back at her desk, Holly called in Hurd Wallace and Bob Hurst. "I want to bring you up to date on something," she said. "I interviewed Sam Sweeney yesterday, and he eventually admitted that he heard the shot that hit Chief Marley, a single shot."

Hurst spoke up. "I went over all that very thoroughly with him several times, and he didn't tell me that."

"Maybe he felt less threatened after having been released," Holly said. "He also told me that he heard heated arguing before the shot was fired, from two or three men, and that, after the shot was fired, he heard two car doors slam, indicating two perps. He said the car—not a truck or large vehicle—made a U-turn and drove north on A1A."

"What else did he say?"

"That was it. I thought you should both have his information for your investigation."

"Thanks, Chief," Hurst said, but he was looking embarrassed for not having produced it himself.

"Is anybody getting anything?"

"Not a thing," Wallace said. "I've interviewed every street officer, and there's just nothing."

Hurst spoke up. "I think the reason for that is that this was some sort of isolated incident, not connected to any other criminal activitiy that our snitches might know about. Everything points to it being a stopping of a vehicle that went wrong—speeding, drunk driving, broken taillight, suspicious activity—something like that."

Holly didn't believe that for a moment, but then she knew a little more than Hurst did. "That would seem to cover the events," she said. "Except for the fact of Hank Doherty's murder."

Neither of the men said anything.

"Whoever shot the chief took his shotgun from his car, went straight to Hank Doherty's and killed him."

"We don't know that," Wallace said.

"Can you think of any other scenario that works?"

"You're right, Chief," Hurst said. "She's right, Hurd; the two shootings are connected by the shotgun."

"Anything new on the chief's condition?" Wallace asked, changing the subject.

Holly quickly decided to tell them. "The chief woke up yesterday and started talking."

Two sets of eyebrows went up. "Did he say who shot him? Anything at all?" Hurst asked.

"He remembered nothing about the incident or anything that had occurred for a good five weeks before it. His last memory was of meeting with me, on the occasion when he hired me to come here."

"Any chance he'll regain some of that memory?" Wallace asked.

"The news gets worse, I'm afraid. He went to sleep while I was there, and this morning, the nurses couldn't wake him. He's back in a coma, and the doctor can't offer any real prognosis."

Wallace nodded. "For a minute there I thought we'd had a break."

"So did I," Holly said, "but we're going to have to solve this crime without the chief's help. The odds of his waking up and remembering everything have gotten a lot worse. Although the doctor hasn't actually said so, my feeling was that he didn't expect him to recover." She watched the two men carefully for their reactions, and they were what she would have expected—sadness and worry on the part of Hurst, and the usual lack of emotion on the part of Wallace.

"Where do we go from here?" Hurst asked.

"We start again from the beginning," Holly said. "I want you to visit the crime scene again and, this time, work both sides of the road. When they made the U-turn, they could have thrown something out. Check out Hank Doherty's again, too; see if we missed anything."

"I'll talk to Sweeney again, too," Hurst said, sounding annoyed that the man hadn't given up all his information the first time around.

"I think Mr. Sweeney has left us," Holly said. "Anyway, he told me that was his intention."

"You know where?"

"Where does a guy like Sweeney go? Anywhere, I should think."

"I could get the state police to put out a watch for him."

"What for? We can't charge him with anything, and I really believe he's told us all he knows."

Hurst shrugged. "I guess you're right."

"Tell you what you can do," Holly said. "Put out a bulletin on Sweeney's Colt thirty-two—the serial number will be on the receipt that guy Schwartz produced in court; the county attorney will have that. Maybe somebody sold it and we can trace it back."

"I'll do that," Wallace said.

"Good. Now let's all get back to work."

The two officers left, and Holly, mindful of what the council had said about her lack of knowledge of the town, decided to see more of it. She went next door to Jane Grey's office. "I'll be on patrol for a while," she said. "Let the dispatcher know I'm in the car, okay?"

"Sure. How'd it go with the council?"

Holly closed the door. "They had voted, three to two, to make Hurd acting chief," she said. "But Charlie Peterson, who I didn't know was a lawyer, read them the riot act about my contract, and they calmed down and accepted the situation."

"Hurd's close to John Westover," Jane said. "That's where that came from. And the other councilman to vote against Westover would have been Howard Goldman, I think."

"I think you're right."

"Howard's sometimes the swing vote; he goes with Westover most of the time, but occasionally opposes him."

"Good to know," Holly said. "I got the impression that Irma Taggert is solid with Westover."

"That's right, and she's a prig, as well. She's always wanting to shut down the movie house if something racy is running. Even Westover won't go with her on that."

"What about the other guy?"

"Frank Hessian? He's a cipher. Rarely says anything to anybody, doesn't make waves."

"How'd he get elected?"

"He's a nice man, and everybody knows it. He's a veterinarian. Everybody takes their pets to him."

"Okay, I'll see you later." Holly left the station and decided to drive north on A1A. She hadn't seen much of the high-rent district yet, and she wanted a look at it.

21

Holly drove north on A1A, with Daisy in the front seat beside her. Gradually, the town gave way to a kind of suburbia, studded with the gates of upscale subdivisions. She turned into the first one she came to. There was a guardhouse, empty, and a keypad-operated gate, open. She drove down a typical upper-middle-class street, lined with roomy but unpretentious houses on half-acre lots. There were a pair of tennis courts at the end of the block, apparently serving the whole neighborhood. At a T junction, a cross street ran parallel with the beach, and the houses on the ocean were larger and sited on more land. Visits to two more such subdivisions revealed a similar layout. Daisy lost interest, curled up and went to sleep.

As she drove north the subdivisions grew in size, and one or two of them had an actual guard posted in the gatehouse, who waved her in when they saw her police uniform. In these neighborhoods, the lots were an acre or more and the houses more elaborate, some with white columns out front and circular driveways. Here the tennis courts were behind individual houses, and the beach houses were well into the million-dollar bracket, she reckoned.

She continued north and came to a state park, which turned out to be nothing more than a beach with a parking lot and rest rooms. Back on the road, the subdivisions were becoming more spectacular. She visited one, the reason for which seemed to be polo, and there were actually people on horseback swinging mallets at balls. "We're in the two-million-dollar category now," she said aloud to herself.

She drove all the way up to the Sebastian Inlet, where the river emptied into the sea under a large bridge; then she turned around and started south toward town. Now she visited subdivisions on the river side of the islands, most of which had marinas and golf courses, sometimes more than one. She thought of her father and how he loved his golf. She had played with him a lot and enjoyed it, but she had been working too hard to have the time to play often. Nothing had changed in that regard.

Now she came to a subdivision that was different from the others in several respects. It was larger, if the length of the twenty-foot-high hedge along the road was any indication; there was more than a mile of it before and after the main gate. Behind the guardhouse, she saw as she turned off the road, the interior of the development was shielded from the main road by an equally high hedge. The place was visually sealed off from the rest of Orchid Beach. There was a live guard at work, too, and this one was armed, the first time she'd seen that. She pulled to a stop next to the guardhouse. Ahead of her was an electrically operated wrought-iron barrier, and a few feet beyond that, steel claws erupted from the pavement. Anybody attempting to crash the gate would quickly lose all his tires to that contraption.

"Good afternoon," she said to the guard.

He nodded, but didn't say anything.

"I'm Deputy Chief Holly Barker from the Orchid Beach Police Department," she said. "I'd like to take a look around inside. I'm new and just getting to know the territory."

"Sorry, miss," he said, avoiding using her rank. "Residents only."

"I don't think you understand," she said. "I'm a police officer, and this development is in my jurisdiction."

"Sorry, no one is allowed inside without a resident's sticker or an employee's badge."

"Who is your chief?" she asked.

"Captain Noble," he said.

"Get him on the phone."

The man looked at her for a moment. He was large, muscular and very fit looking. His uniform fit him like a glove, and he looked capable of handling anything that might come along. He picked up a phone and, turning his back on Holly, spoke into it, then hung up. "Captain Noble will come down and speak to you," he said. "Pull right over there and park your car." He indicated a parking spot a few yards away.

Holly parked her car and got out, stretching her legs. Daisy sat up and looked around, then lay down and curled up again. Nothing happened. She waited five minutes, then walked over to the guardhouse. "So where is he?"

"On his way, miss."

As she was about to turn away, she glanced down and through the open door, saw an Armalite assault rifle in a rack under the countertop where the guard sat. She was about to mention it when the exit gate opened. A white Range Rover pulled out, made a U-turn and stopped at the guardhouse. On each front door of the vehicle was painted a symbol, a palmetto plant.

"You're Deputy Chief Barker?" the driver asked.

"That's right," Holly replied.

"I'm Barney Noble," the man said, smiling and sticking his hand out the window. "I run the security operation at Palmetto Gardens."

Holly shook the hand, which was hard and cool. "Good to meet you. I was just driving around, getting to know the area, and I thought I'd take a look at Palmetto Gardens. Little did I know," she said, indicating the guard.

Barney Noble grinned. "I run a pretty tight ship," he said. "Hop in, and I'll show you around."

"Just a minute," she said. Holly walked over to her car and said to Daisy. "Stay, Daisy. Guard the car." She made sure the car was well ventilated, then she walked back to the Range Rover and got in. The gate ahead of them opened, the steel claws retracted into the pavement and the car moved forward.

"Welcome to Orchid," Noble said. "I'd heard you'd arrived in town."

"Yes, just last weekend."

"How's Chet Marley doing?"

"Not well," she said. "He's still in a coma."

"I heard he came out of it," Noble said.

That was interesting to Holly. How did he know that? "For a few minutes, then he went under again."

"Sorry to hear it. Chet's a good man. We played a little poker once in a while."

They had passed the barrier hedge now, and the landscape opened up in a wonderful way. They were driving along the shore of a large lake on one side of the road and a golf course on the other.

"This is beautiful," Holly said.

"Just between you and me, it's the most beautiful real estate development in Florida, and I've seen most of them in my line of work."

"Why have I never heard of it?" she asked.

"The folks who live here like to lead a quiet life. They're among the richer people in this country—CEOs of large corporations, heads of conglomerates, billionaires of every stripe. It's a private club, really; we don't advertise for customers. It's all word of mouth among friends. You'd recognize a lot of the names of the members, but I'm not allowed to mention them."

"What sort of security force do you have?"

"I've got fifteen men—twelve usually on duty or on call—there's always somebody on vacation or out sick or something."

"Are they all armed?" she asked.

"All armed and very well trained to use their weapons," he replied. "We've got our own firing range back in the woods there." He waved a hand vaguely to his right.

They passed what looked like the business district of a tiny village—grocery, drugstore, news shop, dry cleaner, doctor, dentist.

"We've got just about everything we need here," Noble said. "None of our members ever has to go to town." He slowed and pointed at a low building. "That's my bailiwick right there. It's like a small-town police station, really. We've got a small lockup and the usual equipment."

"Does that include assault weapons?"

"Of course," he said.

"I assume everything is properly licensed."

"Sure. Florida as a state is pretty liberal about gun ownership, and we're licensed by the state as a private security service."

They drove through the village, and homes began to appear on both sides of the road, at widely separated intervals—or rather, gates began to appear. The houses were nearly invisible behind lush tropical plantings.

"How long has this place been in business?" Holly asked.

"A little over twenty years," Noble replied. "The first five was mostly the construction of the village and the infrastructure, which is considerable. We've got our own water and sewage treatment plants and a backup generating system that pops on if there's a power failure. None of our members ever goes more than five seconds without electrical power, even in a hurricane."

They passed a house under construction; it was huge.

"Is that representative of the size of the houses in this place?" Holly asked.

"Sure is. There's nothing under ten thousand square feet here."

They passed the Palmetto Gardens Country Club, with a club-house that was large and comfortable looking.

"We've got three eighteen-hole courses here," Noble said. "Every one of them the equal of anything in the country."

"For how many members?" she asked.

"That's confidential, but let's just say that our people don't like to reserve tee times. They like to walk out there and play, so we keep it uncrowded."

"My dad is a big golfer," she said. "He's a senior master sergeant in the army, stationed in North Carolina."

"Does he ever get down this way?"

"He plans to."

"Tell him to call me, and I'll give him a round here. Certain employees are allowed to use the facilities."

"That's very kind of you," she said, meaning it. "Ham would love that."

"Ham? Ham Barker?"

"That's right."

"Sorry, I didn't get the connection. I did a tour with him in Vietnam."

"No kidding. That's three people he knows here, then."

"Yeah, except two of them ... I heard about Hank Doherty. That's a tough way to go when you've been through what he has."

"Did you serve with Hank and Chet, too?"

"I knew them both in the army, but we were never in the same outfit, like Ham and me. How is the old fart?"

"He's got his thirty in; he'll be retiring one of these days. Did you know my mother?"

Noble shook his head. "There weren't any wives where we were."

They passed a sign saying AIRFIELD.

"You've got a landing strip here, too?"

"Six thousand feet of it. We can take anything up to and including a Gulfstream V. All of our people arrive and depart by private aircraft. We've got the only instrument landing system in the country at a private airport. When our foreign members arrive, we arrange to have customs and immigration here to clear them, so they can fly directly here, nonstop, from any airport anywhere. It's a great convenience not to have to stop at a port of entry to clear."

"These people have their own little world here, don't they?"

"Now you've got the picture. These guys work like slaves most of the time; they're glad to get down here for a little golf or tennis and some R and R."

They could see the Indian River now, and a marina with some large motor yachts.

"Some of them come by sea, now and then," Noble said.

"I've never seen anything like this," Holly replied.

"Neither has anybody else," Noble said.

"I was surprised to be denied entry to part of my jurisdiction."

"Sorry about that, but you have to remember that this is private property. Legally you couldn't come in without a search warrant, but if ever you want in, just give me a call and I'll tell the gate man you're coming."

"Thanks. You should warn your people, though, that if we have an emergency or a crime out here, my people are not going to wait at the gate."

Noble laughed. "Well, we're what you might call a crime-free area," he said. "We've never had so much as a burglary, so I don't think we'll be needing the services of the Orchid Beach PD anytime soon."

"Tell me," Holly said, "why does such a crime-free development need a security force of fifteen, armed with automatic weapons?"

Noble laughed. "Let's just say our people like us to err on the side of caution. You have to understand the mind-set with people at this level: most of them have bodyguards, armored limousines and elaborate security precautions at their other homes. You never know when somebody is going to try to kidnap some corporate executive, as happened in New Jersey a few years ago. Remember the oil company president who was taken and died of a gunshot wound?"

"Yes, I read about that."

"That case and the Unabomber made a *big* difference in the way corporate America looked at personal security. A lot of boards of directors insisted that their top execs beef up their protection."

They had completed a huge circle now and were approaching the gate. Noble pulled the Range Rover up to her car, stopped and held out his hand. "You let me know when Ham visits, and I'll get him on the course."

"Thanks, Barney," Holly said, shaking his hand. "I'll call when you least expect it." She got out of the vehicle and went to her car, profoundly impressed with what she had seen. It was a dream world for a privileged few—and their security force. She wondered what would happen if one of these people murdered another. She'd probably never even hear about it, she reckoned.

22

Holly worked seven days a week for her first two weeks on the job. She concentrated on getting to know her force by name and assignment, and on getting to know their experience and capabilities. There were four women on the force, none of them on the street; she rotated them onto patrols and decided that the next four vacancies she had would go to women applicants. She discussed this with Hurd Wallace, who nodded and said little. She was becoming accustomed to his reptilian stillness and his reticent manner, and she began to know that he had a good grasp of the department. He was a capable man, and she wondered why Chet Marley had been reluctant to promote him further. Chet occasionally showed signs of coming out of his coma, but always regressed.

Late in her third week, on Friday afternoon, she had a phone call.

"Holly Barker," she said.

"It's Jackson."

She had been dreading this. She wanted to see him, but was reluctant to do so.

"You were supposed to call me two weeks ago," he said.

"Jackson, I'm sorry. Look, let me lay my cards on the table. I feel that I'm under the gun here. The city council has already told me they'd prefer to have somebody else in this job, and I don't want to give them anything to use against me. I think they might frown on a police officer seeing somebody who's on the opposite side in the courtroom."

"Do you really think that's a legitimate concern?"

"No, but it's a concern."

"Let me ask you straight out, Holly: do you have any interest in me?"

"Yes, I do," she said without hesitation. "But I don't know what to do about it. I don't think we should be seen together in restaurants and at the movies, not until I've got my feet firmly on the ground here and have more political support."

"That's prudent, and I understand completely."

"I'm relieved to hear it," she said.

"I think the solution to our problem is not to appear together in public."

"Thank you for understanding."

"I think the immediate solution is for me to cook you dinner at my house tonight."

She laughed. "Well, I guess that's not too public. Can I bring Daisy?"

"Do you go *anywhere* without that dog?"

"That remains to be seen."

"Here's what you do: When you leave your trailer park, turn right and drive three point three miles south—I measured it—then turn left into a dirt driveway. There's no sign, not even a mailbox. Follow that road to its end, and you're there. Seven o'clock?"

"Okay, you're on." She hung up and sighed. Her resolve had vanished at the first opportunity.

Holly missed the driveway and had to turn around and hunt for it. It was no wonder: the narrow dirt road was nearly overgrown on both sides, and branches scraped against her car as she drove. Daisy was sniffing the air.

"Smell the ocean, Daisy? It's got to be down here somewhere." It was. By the time she came to the house, she could hear the surf. The house appeared to be fairly old and was neatly painted white, with green hurricane shutters. Jackson Oxenhandler was standing on the porch, waiting for her.

"You're fashionably late," he called as she got out of her car, walked up the stairs and presented her lips for a light kiss.

"My mother brought me up not to appear too eager," Holly replied. "What a nice place."

"Come on inside," Jackson said. He led her into a large room that seemed to cover most of the first floor, along with a kitchen, separated from the living room by only a counter.

"Wait a minute," she said, stopping and looking around her. "How does a public defender who wears unpressed suits and drives a fifteen-year-old car afford a place like this in Orchid, and right on the beach?"

"You're a suspicious person," Jackson said.

"Occupational hazard."

"Well, I'm only occasionally a public defender. A decent litigator gets paid fairly well in Orchid, and occasionally I get a plum. This place was a plum. Come have a look out front." He led her out onto a broad front porch overlooking dunes that led down to the sea, less than a hundred yards away.

"This is just perfect," she said. "Tell me about the plum."

"I defended a rather well-off citrus grower who was stopped by the cops for speeding, and who turned out to have twenty kilos of cocaine in his trunk, which came as something of a surprise to him."

"Did you get him off?"

"Of course. He was innocent. One of his fruit pickers had used his car to transport the goods when the boss was out of town. The owner returned unexpectedly, before the man had a chance to transfer the dope. It took me nearly a year to get him off, and he ran up quite a legal bill. I took this property in exchange for services, then I saw something in the paper about an old Florida farmhouse that was about to be torn down and was being offered practically free to anyone who would move it. I took a look at it, paid a hundred bucks for it, had it sawn in half, moved down here and reassembled. A couple of hundred grand later, it is as you see it. I had to get a mortgage, but it was quite a bargain."

"It's just grand," she said. "How'd you ever get the house down that driveway?"

"There was no driveway when I moved it, just open land. I planted all that foliage you drove through. Things grow fast around here. Take a rocking chair, and I'll get you a drink. What would you like?"

"You decide," she said, plopping down in a chair. Daisy curled up at her feet.

Jackson went away, and Holly took in the sky and ocean before her. The setting sun lit the huge cumulus clouds and turned them pink, and the blue water reflected the color. Jackson was back in a couple of minutes with a cocktail shaker and two glasses.

He strained a clear, green-tinted liquid into the glasses and handed her one. "Your continued good health," he said, raising a glass.

"And yours," she replied, sipping the lime-flavored cocktail. "What is this?"

"Vodka gimlet," he said. "Vodka and Rose's Sweetened Lime Juice, shaken very cold."

"Delicious," she said. "What did you mean, my *continued* good health?"

"You're healthy—I'd like to see you remain that way."

"Do you have some reason to believe I might not?"

"To tell you the truth, after your story about the gas bottle and the flare, I've half expected to hear that something had happened to you. That would have explained why you didn't call, and anyway, I figured that nothing short of hospitalization would have stopped you."

She laughed. "I did have to stop myself," she said.

"If you're worried about what the city council thinks about us, don't."

"Why not?"

"Let's take them one at a time: Charlie Peterson is a sweet guy and couldn't care less; Howard Goldman is a *mensch;* you know what that means?"

"Yiddish for a sweet guy?"

"Right. Frank Hessian, the vet, is just indifferent, couldn't care less."

"What about John Westover and Irma Taggert?"

"They're the least of your worries, since they've been screwing each other for years, unbeknownst to his wife and her husband."

"You're kidding! Westover and that prim lady?"

"She's apparently not so prim. Guy I know walked into Westover's office at the car dealership one day and interrupted John and Irma in the middle of a quickie."

Holly nearly choked on her drink. "I don't believe it."

"Believe it."

From somewhere inside the house, a single chime rang.

"Excuse me a minute," Jackson said. He set down his drink, got up and went into the house. It was becoming a little chilly, so Holly followed, bringing their drinks. To her surprise, he went to an umbrella stand beside the back door and retrieved from it a pump shotgun, a riot gun with an eighteen-and-a-half-inch barrel, the kind the police use. He pumped the shotgun once, held it behind him, opened the door a couple of inches and peered down the driveway.

"What's going on?" Holly asked, alarmed.

"Visitors," Jackson said. "Are you armed?"

"In my handbag."

"Get it, please."

23

Holly set down the drinks, got the Beretta from her handbag and went and stood behind Jackson, straining to see past him. "Who is it?" she asked.

"Looks like a light-colored truck of some sort," he replied. "Hard to tell much, it's getting dark."

"Who's in it?"

"Can't see anybody."

"Is it coming toward us?"

"No, just sitting. I can hear the engine idling."

Holly changed positions and saw the dim outline of the vehicle. "Maybe it's not a truck," she said. "Maybe it's an SUV, something like my Grand Cherokee."

"Or a Ford Explorer," he said.

"What's going on, Jackson?"

"My guess it's somebody who's interested in the lack of continuing good health of one of us."

"So who's after you?"

"You remember, I told you about my ex-partner?"

"Oh, yeah."

"He's not the kind to forget."

"And you think whoever this is could be after me, instead?"

"That's why the Beretta was in your bag, wasn't it?"

"It's department policy for officers to go armed when off duty—increases police coverage. But yeah," she admitted, "I had that in mind, too."

The vehicle continued to sit there, idling.

"They know I'm here," she said. "They can see my car."

"Maybe that's why they're still sitting there," he said. "They know somebody else is here, not necessarily you."

"Glad to be of service."

"Nice having police protection."

She pinched his backside. "Any time."

The vehicle reversed back down the driveway and disappeared. A moment later, the chime rang again. Jackson waited for a minute, then closed the door, put the safety on the shotgun and returned it to the unbrella stand, where the barrel barely peeked out. "I hope you meant that," he said.

"What?"

"The pinch."

"Oh, I meant that. That chime is kind of a car bell, then?"

"Yeah, it offers notice of visitors."

Holly returned the Beretta to her bag.

"How about some dinner?" he asked.

"You bet. What are we having?"

"My famous crab cakes." He walked toward the kitchen, switching on lights.

"Famous to whom?"

"To them that has eaten them." He took several items from the fridge and began to put together their dinner.

Holly watched with interest. She was a good, plain cook, but Jackson had obviously had a lot more practice. He had half-prepared everything in advance, and in twenty minutes they were sitting at the table consuming a very fine dinner.

"Your cue," he said.

"Oh, terrific crab cakes," she said.

"The best you've ever had?"

"Absolutely."

"Good guest. Like the wine?"

"It's perfect, what is it?"

"Robert Mondavi Reserve Chardonnay, '94, one of the best of the vintage, which is said to be the best ever for California chardonnays."

"I believe you," she said, sipping her wine. "So, how come you're still single, Jackson?"

"Just lucky, I guess."

"That's *my* line."

"We'll share it."

"Never married?"

"Nope. You?"

"Nope."

"How do you feel about that?"

"I don't know. When I was in the army I wasn't much interested in being married to an army man. Too many complications—transfers, assignments, et cetera. And being married to a civilian would have been even worse."

"And now that you're out of the army?"

"I don't know. I haven't had time to think about it."

"I've had all the time in the world to think about it, but I haven't, much."

"Is there a shortage of single women in Orchid?"

"Not really. I've managed to stay reasonably busy in the evenings. Am I the first guy to hit on you?"

"You hitting on me?"

"You betcha."

"Yeah, you're the first. Well, I did catch our esteemed city council president looking at my tits a couple of times."

"I don't blame him," Jackson said. "Considering that the alternative tits were Irma Taggert's."

"Oh, he would have looked anyway," she said smugly.

"Don't be smug."

"I'm smug about only a few things," she said.

"What else?"

"I'm a very good pistol shot. I'm smug about that."

"Great. What else?"

"You'll have to figure that out for yourself."

"I can't wait." He got up and took their plates to the kitchen. "You want some dessert?"

"What've you got?"

"I've got freshly made apple pie, à la mode."

"I'll have the pie, hold the à la mode."

"Smart girl," he said. Shortly he returned with two plates, one à la mode.

"I'm not as skinny as you are," she said. "A girl has to watch her figure."

"Don't worry, John Westover and I will do that for you."

"That's a load off my mind."

They finished their dessert and Jackson produced two cups of espresso. They sat on the sofa before a fire, drank their coffee and watched it get dark outside. When they had finished, Jackson took her face in his hands and kissed her for some time.

"You taste like espresso," she said while he moved his kisses to her neck.

"You taste like girl," he replied, moving down. "Everywhere, so far."

"That's good."

"You smell good, too," he said, pushing his prominent nose between her breasts.

"I bathe."

"You do a good job." He began working on her buttons.

"If you keep that up, you're going to have to make love to me," she said.

He didn't stop. Now he had unhooked her bra and had a breast in his hand. "Shall I throw you over my shoulder and take you upstairs?"

"I'm still ambulatory," she said, standing up and removing her blouse and bra. "But not for much longer. My knees are getting weak."

He held her against him and kissed her some more, taking her buttocks in his big hands and pulling her toward him. Then he took her hand. "This way," he said, leading her through the living room and up a flight of stairs to a large bedroom with a large bed, both of them shedding clothes along the way. Daisy followed, her claws clicking on the hardwood floors.

"Lie down, Daisy," Holly said. "Time to go to sleep."

Daisy lay down and rested her head on her paws, watching them.

"Good dog," Jackson said, struggling with Holly's jeans.

"I hope to god you've got a condom," she said as he laid her on the soft bed, "because I foolishly didn't bring anything."

"Not to worry," he said.

And she didn't.

24

Holly heard the surf before she opened her eyes. Then she sat straight up in bed. Work! She fell back. Saturday, thank God. She reached for Jackson as she had done several times during the night, but he was not there.

Daisy came and nuzzled her, poking her nose under Holly's arm and lifting so that she could get underneath.

Holly heard the rattle of pots from downstairs, so she got up, washed her face, took Jackson's terry-cloth robe from a hook on the back of the door and padded barefoot downstairs. Jackson was scrambling eggs.

"Good afternoon," he said.

"Afternoon? What time is it?"

"Just past ten. That's afternoon for me."

"You're not working today, are you?" she asked.

"Nope. I'm spending the day with you."

"Good call," she said, wrapping her arms around his waist from behind.

He turned and embraced her. "You feel better on this side of me."

"Mmmm," she agreed.

"Dog food under the sink," he said. "I was hoping Daisy would be here for breakfast."

Holly fed the dog and let her out.

"Eggs are ready," Jackson called. He put the eggs, with bacon, toast and orange juice, on the table, then set down a pot of freshly made coffee. "Hope you're hungry."

"You bet," she said, digging in.

"You're a girl with a healthy appetite."

"I'm not a girl, but you're right about the appetite."

"You're a girl to me."

"I'll take that in the best possible light," she said.

"What do you normally do in the mornings?"

"I run, then I work. Normally. What do you do?"

"The writer Max Shulman once said that exercise destroys the tissues; I've never forgotten that."

"You don't enjoy exercise?"

"Not for its own sake. I enjoy tennis, golf and sex."

"I'm acquainted with your enjoyment of the latter," she laughed.

"I reckon we burned a lot of calories last night. I'll think of that as the moral equivalent of my morning run."

"That's the kind of slippery thinking a lawyer can get away with," she said, "but not a police officer. On the other hand, maybe I could skip the run today."

"We could always burn some more calories," he said.

She laughed. "Mind if I finish breakfast?"

"Not if you hurry."

"Jackson, the car or truck or whatever it was last night—could it have been a Range Rover?"

Jackson thought about that. "Let's see, a Range Rover looks kind of square from the front, doesn't it?"

"Yeah, I think so."

"Maybe it could have been, I don't know. Could have been anything big—pickup, SUV, whatever. Why a Range Rover?"

"What do you know about a real estate development called Palmetto Gardens?"

"That's easy: almost nothing, which is what most people know about it. I know it's a superprivate, superexclusive retreat for the super-rich. When they were building the place they hired local contractors to do the basic work—roads, sewers, electrical and phone—and locals seem to do all the basic work on the houses—foundations, framing, roofing. But they bring in their own construction people for the finishing work. There was stuff in the papers about that early on; there was some resentment that more local jobs weren't being created, but their public relations people came back with some very detailed answers about what the development was doing for the community at large—number of jobs, money spent in the town, their contribution to the tax base. It was very impressive, and it pretty much squelched any opposition. The city council backed them up, too."

"Have you ever been inside the place?"

"No, and neither has anybody else I know."

"I have."

"You *have?*"

"Yeah. I was driving around a couple of weeks ago, getting to know the geography and the neighborhoods, but when I tried to drive in there I got stopped cold."

"Well, it is private property, I guess."

"Yeah, but the head of security came out and gave me a tour of the place."

"What was the place like?"

"Like you'd imagine a superexpensive place would be: a lot of facilities for apparently only a few people. What heaven would be like, if it had been designed by a real estate developer."

"Oh, I remember, too, that the local real estate agencies were pretty pissed off not to get a piece of the action on property sales. They don't work with local agents at all. But what has all this got to do with Range Rovers?"

"The head of security, a guy named Noble, was driving one, and I saw a couple more while I was there. The security force drives them."

"Noble? What's his first name?"

"Barney."

"Uh-oh."

"Huh?"

"You remember, I told you my ex-partner, the ex-convict, now works for a Miami security outfit?"

"Yeah."

"It's called Craig and Noble. Jack Craig is a former Miami police captain. Barney Noble is, or was, his partner."

"You think that means something?"

"Let's see, what could it mean? That maybe my ex-partner sent Barney Noble up here, under cover, to off me?"

"I guess not."

"I think it's just a coincidence. I've never even met Noble, or anybody else from that place, come to think of it."

"What's your ex-partner's name?"

"Elwood Mosely, a.k.a. 'Cracker.' I never heard him called anything else."

"Description?"

"Six-two, two-twenty-five, bright red hair, pale complexion." He thought for a moment. "Ugly."

"You think he could be around here?"

"Who knows? After last night, maybe."

"I could pull his photograph out of the system and have a watch put out for him."

"That's just the sort of thing that could backfire on you with the council—doing favors for a . . . what am I to you?"

"A lover."

"That's the word I was looking for."

"You're a citizen. Write me a letter on your law firm letterhead saying that you've had previous difficulties with the guy, and you've heard he may be in town, and could we keep an eye out for him."

"Okay, I can do that."

"Can I use your phone? I usually call my dad on Saturday mornings. I'll use a credit card."

"Sure, and don't worry about the charges; I've got the ten-cents-a-minute deal."

Jackson cleared the table while Holly sat on the living-room sofa and used the phone on the coffee table. She dialed Ham's number and waited. It rang and rang, but there was no answer.

Jackson came and sat down beside her. "Nobody home?"

"Apparently not, but it's strange—Ham has an answering machine that picks up on the third ring, but it didn't pick up."

"Probably he's out somewhere and his machine is broken."

"I guess so," she said. "I'll try him again later."

Jackson kissed her on the ear. "How about burning a few calories?" he breathed, loosening the tie on her robe and finding a breast.

She turned toward him and let the robe fall open. "You're a regular maniac for exercise, aren't you?"

"You betcha," he said, pulling her down on the sofa.

25

They showered together, then went for a walk on the beach. It was warm and breezy, and Daisy seemed to go berserk, running at top speed, disappearing into the dunes, then tearing across the beach and running into the surf. Jackson found a stick, and Daisy loved chasing it.

"Where are you from?" she asked.

"A small town in Georgia called Delano."

"Where's that?"

"About forty miles east of Columbus."

"That's funny, I was born in Columbus—or rather, at Fort Benning. I grew up on half a dozen military bases, from Fort Bragg to Mannheim, in Germany."

"I grew up in Delano."

"Your folks still there?"

"Both dead, Mom eight years ago, Dad six. He didn't take much interest in living after she went."

"My mom's gone, too, but Ham had the army to keep him going."

"Dad was a lawyer, but he didn't love it enough for it to keep him going. A month after she died, he closed the office, and after that, he hardly left the house. Not even golf could keep him interested, and he had always been an enthusiastic golfer."

"My dad, too. Just loves it. Barney Noble told me to bring him out to Palmetto Gardens to play sometime. Oh, I forgot to tell you, they knew each other in the army—they served in the same outfit in Vietnam."

"Connections, connections," Jackson said absently. "I belong to the Dunes Club; tell your dad I'll take him there when he visits." He looked at her. "You said you play?"

"Yeah, but it's been almost a year."

"You got clubs?"

"Yeah. Ham gave them to me for Christmas last year, I think hoping to get me out on the course more, but I was always working."

"You want to play this afternoon?"

"Sure, why not? You know, this is the first day I haven't worked since I got here."

"You got a handle on the job yet?"

"Pretty much. Chet had the department superbly organized. What I have to do mostly is not screw it up. What I haven't got a handle on is these shootings."

"You sound discouraged."

"I'm at a dead end. The department has done the job it was supposed to, but we just don't have anything to go on."

"You have no idea why somebody might want to kill Chet and Hank?"

She looked at him closely. "This doesn't go any further."

"Right."

"When Chet hired me he intimated that he had a serious problem that he would brief me on when I arrived in town. Wouldn't say more than that. Then, the evening I arrived, we talked on the phone, and he told me that he was meeting somebody, and he'd have a lot to tell me the following morning, when I reported for work."

"He didn't give you any idea what it was about?"

She shook her head. "Not much. Part of the problem was that

there was somebody in the department who was working both sides of the street. He said he had an idea, but he didn't tell me."

"You have any idea now?"

"No, not really. It could be anybody."

"Have you told anybody on the force—anybody at all in Orchid—about this?"

"No."

"Good."

"I'm afraid I'll tell the wrong person. I've been all through Chet's office, looking for some notes or something, but there was nothing." She looked at Jackson. "I wonder if he could have left something with his lawyer, just in case."

"He didn't do that," Jackson replied.

"How do you know?

"Because I'm his lawyer."

"Why didn't you tell me that before?"

"It didn't come up. Mind you, all I've ever done for him was to close the sale of his house a couple of years ago, and draw up his will."

"When did he make the will?"

"He signed it about ten days before he was shot."

"You think he thought his life was in danger?"

"He didn't give any indication of that, but who knows? It was pretty simple and straightforward. He left everything . . ." Jackson stopped. "I'm sorry. That, of course, is a client-attorney confidence."

"Did Chet have any family you know of? I haven't been able to discover any."

"No."

"I see. You'd have thought that if Chet was worried enough to make a will, he'd have told somebody else what was going on, or at least, left some evidence with somebody."

"Maybe he did," Jackson said.

"You got any ideas?"

"It could only have been Hank Doherty."

"Of course. That has to be the motive for Hank's murder."

"Did you go through Hank's place?"

"With a fine-toothed comb. I went through his desk and his safe myself. The safe was open."

"So, somebody shoots Chet, then thinks, holy shit, he might have told Hank Doherty something, so he goes over there and kills Hank."

"And finds whatever Chet gave him, which is why I didn't find it."

"And you're sure it couldn't still be there?"

"Don't see how it could be. The house has been cleaned out. Hank's daughter took some memorabilia, and his housemaid took the rest. Her church sold some of it at a tag sale the following weekend."

"So everything is now scattered."

"Irretrievably, I would think."

"Did you search Chet's house?"

Holly stopped walking. "No. It wasn't a crime scene, so it just didn't occur to me. Boy, am I stupid!"

"I've got a key."

"Then let's get over there," she said, starting for the house.

"Hang on," he said, catching her wrist. "I don't know that I'd go out there in broad daylight. You never know who's watching. Let's wait until tonight."

"Okay, I guess it can wait until then."

"Besides, you and I have a golf date."

Holly did some stretching, then took a couple of practice swings and addressed the ball. She tried to relax and make an easy swing. There was the sound of a metal driver striking the ball, and she looked up to see it going high and straight down the fairway.

"Very nice," Jackson said. "That's a good two hundred and ten yards." He stepped up to the ball, went through his routine and swung mightily.

"That's a good two hundred and fifty yards," Holly said. "Trouble is, it's in the trees. Take a mulligan."

Jackson made a grumbling sound.

"And don't hit it so hard this time."

He swung again; this time his slice was gentler. The ball landed ten yards beyond Holly's but to the right of the fairway. They got into the cart and started driving.

For seventeen holes, they remained more or less even, trading the lead hole by hole. They were tied going into the eighteenth, and they both had good drives, but Holly's second shot went into a bunker, while Jackson made the green in two. It took Holly two strokes to get out of the sand, and she three-putted, for a double bogey. Jackson parred the hole.

Jackson totted up their scores. "You had a ninety-one, I had an eighty-nine."

Holly thought she had never seen a man so relieved, but she couldn't resist puncturing his balloon. "What's your handicap?" she asked.

"Twelve."

"Mine's fifteen. You owe me three strokes."

His face fell. "It's rude to beat your host, you know."

"I know, and I'm *so* sorry."

"No, you're not."

"I know. I lied."

They both burst out laughing.

"Come on," he said. "Let's get some dinner, then we'll go out to Chet's house."

26

They drove north on A1A from the center of the town and turned onto the North Bridge, one of two serving the barrier island. Daisy sat in the rear seat, calmly looking out the window. Before they reached the mainland, Jackson turned off at an exit.

"It's on Egret Island," he said, pointing ahead. "It's a beautiful place, the sort of property that would have made a very expensive development, but it was bought up in the late thirties by people who built fairly modest houses on fairly small lots. Some of them have been renovated and enlarged, and it's getting to the point where waterfront property is rare enough that people are buying two houses, tearing them down and building a large one."

They were driving down a fairly ordinary middle-class residential road, with two or three larger, more expensive houses among them, brightly lit in the darkness.

"Chet's place is right down at the tip of the island," Jackson said. "By the way, a couple of your officers, Hurd Wallace and Bob Hurst, live out here—or at least, Wallace's ex-wife does. She got the place in the divorce."

The road narrowed, and the houses on either side disappeared. Holly saw a FOR SALE sign offering thirty acres.

"As you can see, the land along here has never been built on. A local guy put together several small parcels some years back, and I think he hopes to get a lot of money for it from some developer who wants to put in a gated subdivision. He wanted Chet's property, too, but the old lady who owned it took a liking to Chet, and he got a real deal. And, until a subdivision gets built, he has a lot of seclusion out here."

The road was ending up ahead, and Jackson turned left into a driveway marked by a mailbox. "The house is just around this bend," he said, following the road and passing through an open gate. They emerged into a clearing, and a small frame house ahead was illuminated by their headlights. When Jackson switched off the lights, it was very dark outside. He reached into the glove compartment and took out a flashlight. "Come on," he said.

They left the car and walked up a flagstone path to the house, with Daisy going on ahead. "This must be very pretty in the daytime," Holly said.

"It is. Chet could fish off a little dock right behind the house."

Holly stopped him. "Let's walk around the house before we go in. Can I have the flashlight?" He handed it over, and Holly began a very slow walk around the place, playing the flashlight carefully over each window. She paused for a long time at the back door, then continued her walk. "There," she said finally, pointing the light at the middle of a window. She pushed a bush aside and got close to it.

"What?" Jackson asked.

Holly pointed at the spot where the two sashes met. "This window has been jimmied," she said, "and the intruder split a little piece off the wood right here. He pushed some sort of thin blade between the sashes and pushed the lock open." She pointed at some smudges on the glass, rubbed a finger over them, then rubbed her fingers together. "Talcum powder," she said. "He used rubber gloves. Some brands have talcum on them to make them easier to put on."

They continued to the front door, and Jackson opened it with his key and flipped a switch. Two lamps came on. They were standing in a good-sized living room. A desk in a corner helped create a small office area. There was a sofa and a pair of chairs in front of the fireplace, and another corner held a round dining table and six chairs.

"I expect that's where poker got played," Holly said. The room was extremely neat and tidy. "I'd half expected the place to be trashed," she said. "Looks like our intruder was very neat."

"Or his cleaning lady came in behind them," Jackson said. "Chet shared one with Hank Doherty."

"I met her," Holly said, "and I've got her number in my notebook, I think." She dug her notebook out of her bag and found the number. "Let's phone her before we start looking." She sat down at Marley's desk, picked up the phone and dialed the number.

"Shouldn't you be careful about obscuring fingerprints?" Jackson asked.

"There won't be any fingerprints; he was wearing rubber gloves, remember?"

"Right."

"Hello, is this Mary White?"

"Yes," the woman replied.

"This is Deputy Chief Holly Barker. We met out at Hank Doherty's house a while back."

"That's right, I remember."

"Ms. White, I understand that you worked for Chief Marley as well as Mr. Doherty, is that right?"

"That's right. I'm still going out to his place once a week to dust, while he's in the hospital."

"That's good. Do you remember when Chief Marley and Mr. Doherty were shot?"

"Sure, I do."

"After that night, when was the first time you went to Chief Marley's house?"

"Let's see, it would have been two days later."

"Did you let yourself in with your own key?"

"That's right."

"Did you notice anything unusual about the place that day? Had anything been disturbed?"

"Well . . . it was just a little messier than it usually was. Chief Marley is a very neat man. I mean, it wasn't *real* messy, just a little bit. Things that were stacked up on his desk were a little bit messed up, but I straightened them. And there were two beer cans on the big table in the living room, half full. First time I ever found a beer can in the house. The chief would clean up after himself and his poker friends after they were there."

"I see. Ms. White, I'm out at the chief's house right now. Do you know if he had some special place in the house to hide valuables? A safe, or a lockbox, maybe a hidden place?"

"No, I don't believe he did, except for that little box next to his desk. It's one of those safe things that's supposed to be fireproof, you know?"

Holly looked around and saw the box on the floor, against the wall. "I see it," she said. "Is that the only place you can think of?"

"Well, I don't think the chief had much in the way of valuables, except for his guns and fishing stuff and the TV. I guess those were the only things somebody might want to take."

"Thank you, Ms. White," she said. "You've been a big help."

"Glad to do it," the woman said, then hung up.

"Fire safe," Holly said, picking up the box and placing it on the desk. She reached to open it, and the hinged lid came off in her hands. "And somebody's used a crowbar on it." She removed the contents and spread them out on the desk. "Insurance policies, warranties on some electronics, checkbook, just ordinary stuff."

"No notes or other papers?" Jackson asked, rifling through the files.

"Nope, not that I can see." Holly opened the checkbook and went quickly through the ledger. "Nothing unusual here, just the regular bills he paid, and a few checks made out to cash." She picked up the files and papers and returned them to the box, then she started going through the desk drawers. They were very neat and contained nothing out of the ordinary. "Okay, let's go through the whole house, every room, every closet and cupboard. Look for another lockbox or a loose board—any place he might hide something."

"Shall we split up?" Jackson said. "I'll take the bedroom, you take the kitchen."

"Okay, but let's both go through the living room, first." The two of them searched the room carefully, looking under furniture, under the rugs, behind everything. Holly checked the gun and fishing racks, but found nothing. Jackson went into the bedroom, and Holly took the kitchen. She went through every cupboard, checking every can for a false top and emptying cereal boxes. She searched the refrigerator and freezer, opening packages wrapped in foil and checking frozen food packages for signs of being opened.

Jackson came in from the bedroom. "Nothing in there, how you doing here?"

"Zip," Holly said.

"Looks like if there was something here or at Hank Doherty's, whoever was looking must have found it."

"His notebook," Holly said.

"What about it?"

"There isn't one. Every cop is trained to keep a notebook; you never know when you might have to testify in court about the details of some incident. There's no notebook here, and there was no notebook in the personal effects the hospital gave me."

"So the shooters took it."

"Yeah. I reckon that after they shot Chet, they took his notebook from his pocket and the shotgun from his car; then they went to Hank Doherty's house, killed him and searched the place. It was fairly neat when I got there. Then they came here and turned over Chet's place, taking some care to keep it neat. They'd have had the whole night to do it. Any panic they felt would have passed, so they took their time, even had a beer."

"And left no traces, no prints."

"Real pros," Holly said.

"No mistakes?"

"Not so far. And if they don't make one soon, we're never going to clear these crimes."

"You ready to go home?" he asked.

"Whose home?"

"Mine. I'm not letting you go until Monday."

Holly glanced at her watch. "Let me try Ham again first. By the time we get home it will be past his bedtime." She called from the phone on the desk, using her credit card. This time the phone rang only once; there followed an electronic shriek and a recorded message. "This number has been permanently disconnected at the request of the customer. There is no forwarding number."

"I must have dialed wrong," she said. She made the call again and got the same message. "I don't understand," she said, hanging up.

"Maybe your dad moved," Jackson said.

"Without telling me? And without leaving a forwarding phone number? That would be very unlike him."

"Is there somewhere else he might be?"

"Not that I can think of."

"A woman? Maybe he's got a new girlfriend, and he moved in with her."

"That's possible, I suppose. Well, I can call him at his base office on Monday and find out what's going on."

"Good idea. Let's get out of here."

They locked up and got back into Jackson's car.

"I need to stop by my trailer to pick up a few things," Holly said. "I hadn't planned to make a weekend of it."

"Sure," Jackson said.

It was after midnight now, and with no traffic they made good time to Riverview Park. As they got out of the car, Daisy jumped out in a hurry, nearly knocking Holly down.

"Daisy?" she called. "What's wrong?"

Daisy had her nose to the ground, running along the path to the trailer. Now her hackles were up, and she was standing at the door, sniffing, staring at it as if she could see through it, a low growl coming from her throat.

Holly put a finger to her lips and raised a hand for Jackson to stand still. She dug the Beretta out of her bag and walked quickly up the path, her keys in her left hand, the pistol at shoulder height. She put an ear to the trailer door and listened. Then the door swung open.

27

Holly nearly fell into the trailer, with Daisy snarling, trying to get past her. "Freeze!" she shouted, getting the gun out in front of her.

"Okay, I'm freezing!" a man's voice called from the darkness inside. "Get hold of that dog, will you?"

Holly dropped her left hand and got hold of Daisy's collar, but she kept the gun pointed into the trailer.

"Jesus, Holly," the man said. "Are you going to shoot me?"

The voice was familiar. "Ham?" she called out.

"Right. Is that dog going to eat me?"

"Daisy, back!" Holly said. She pointed to the walkway. "Sit!"

Jackson was there now. "What's going on?" he demanded.

"Jackson, I'd like you to meet my father. Ham, this is Jackson Oxenhandler."

Ham turned on a light and looked at the two of them. "How you doin'?" he said, offering Jackson his hand.

"Good to meet you," Jackson replied.

Holly turned to the dog. "Daisy, come. It's all right."

The dog walked warily into the trailer, her hackles still up.

"Daisy, this is Ham; he's good, good. Ham, hold out your hand, palm down."

"Am I going to get it back?" Ham asked.

"Just do it."

Ham held out a hand. Daisy sniffed at it, tasted it.

"Good dog," Holly said. "Ham is good, and you're a good dog. Don't eat Ham."

"Thanks a lot," Ham said. "I thought that was his next move."

"It's a she," Holly said. "What on earth are you doing here? I've been trying to call you today, and a recorded message said your phone had been disconnected. Didn't you pay your bill?"

"I moved," Ham said.

"Where did you move?"

"Here. My truck's parked down by the gate. There didn't seem to be enough room for it by the trailer."

"Let's all sit down," Holly said. "Anybody want a beer?"

"You talked me into it," Ham said.

"Nothing for me," Jackson said.

Holly got Ham a beer and sat down. The three of them and Daisy made the trailer seem crowded. "Okay, Ham, let's have it."

"I'm a civilian," Ham said. "I am officially a retired military person."

"Congratulations," Holly said. "Why didn't you tell me you were coming?"

"I thought it would be a nice surprise."

"Well, it is. I'm glad to see you. What are your plans?"

"Orchid Beach sounds like a nice place," he said. "Chet said there was some golf to be had."

"Well, I'm delighted to hear it," Holly said. "You just picked up and drove down here? Why so sudden?"

"Look, Chet Marley and Hank Doherty are the two best friends I've ever had. It pisses me off when somebody shoots one and murders the other one. I thought I'd give you a hand finding out who did it—and killing the bastards."

Holly turned to Jackson. "Everybody's a detective—first you and now him." She nodded at Ham.

"Unless you've already killed them," Ham said.

"Whoa, there, Sarge," Holly said. "I'm not going to kill anybody, and neither are you."

"Well, is anybody going to do *anything* about this?"

"I'm working on it," she said. "It's not an easy one."

"Tell me everything," Ham said. "I'm all ears. Start with how Chet is."

"Still in a coma, and nobody knows if he's ever going to come out of it."

"Shit."

"Yeah."

"All right, start at the beginning," Ham said.

"Now?" Holly looked at her watch. "It's one o'clock in the morning, and you've been driving all day. Tomorrow will be soon enough."

"Aw, c'mon, Holly, tell me about it."

"Here's how we're going to do this, Ham: you're sleeping here, and I'm going to Jackson's house."

Ham's eyes narrowed, and he looked back and forth at the two of them.

"Now, don't start, Ham," Holly said. "I've been a big girl for a long time, and I'll decide where I sleep."

Jackson looked at Ham and shrugged.

Ham rolled his eyes. "Whatever you say, darlin'."

Holly looked down at his bag. "I see you've got your stuff. You get some sleep, and tomorrow morning, you come down to Jackson's place, and we'll all have breakfast, and I'll fill you in."

"Okay, what time?"

She looked at Jackson. "Ten o'clock?"

Jackson nodded.

"Hell, that's practically afternoon," Ham said.

"If you get hungry earlier, just root around in my galley." She gave him directions to Jackson's.

"Okay, ten o'clock."

Holly got a small duffel and stuffed some clean clothes and underwear into it. When Ham wasn't looking she dug her diaphragm out of a drawer and stuck it under the clothes. "All right," she said, "let's go. The sheets are pretty clean, Ham; don't get them any dirtier. If the phone rings, let the answering machine get it. The station knows to call my cell phone first if they need me."

"Okay, then," Ham said. "See you in the morning." He glared at Jackson. "You be nice to her."

"Ham, shut up!" Holly said.

"Don't worry," Jackson replied, "I'll take good care of her. See you at breakfast."

They left the trailer and got into Jackson's car.

"Jesus, what a shock!" Holly said.

"Aren't you glad to see him?"

"Sure, I am, but I would have liked a little notice. What am I going to do with him? We can't both sleep in the trailer. I'd kill him the first day."

"Listen, you can go right on bunking with me until we can find him a place."

She reached over and patted his thigh. "What a sweet offer," she said.

"He seems like a nice guy," Jackson said. "But he talks about killing a lot."

"He's done a lot of that in his time. You're lucky he didn't kill you with a single blow," Holly replied. "He's been trained to do that, you know."

"I'll make it a point to be *real* nice to him."

"And me, too."

"Especially you."

28

Holly woke up at nine forty-five and reached for Jackson, who wasn't there. She struggled out of bed, threw on some clothes, brushed her teeth and her hair and went downstairs. Jackson and Ham were drinking coffee over the remains of a large breakfast. Daisy was leaning against Ham, looking up at him with adoring eyes.

"What time did you get here?" she asked Ham.

Ham shrugged. "I don't know,"

"Eight forty-five," Jackson said. "I tried not to wake you."

"I got hungry," Ham said, "and I didn't want any of that health food crap you eat, so I came on down here and made Jackson scramble me some eggs."

"You want something?" Jackson asked.

"I'll toast myself a bagel," she replied.

"I've brought Ham up to date on what's happened," Jackson said while Holly made her breakfast.

"Jesus, what a mess!" Ham chimed in. "Now I see why you haven't found the bastards."

"Thanks for the vote of confidence," Holly said. "Now, Ham, it's important that you don't go sticking your nose into this."

"Why the hell not? Sounds like you could use the help."

"Ham, I'm running a police department, here, and the city council is watching me like a hawk. I can't have some gung-ho military type, bent on revenge, messing with my investigation."

"What investigation? From what Jackson tells me, you're about investigated out. You don't have a damn thing to go on."

"Ham, how would you like to spend your first few weeks in Orchid Beach in a cell?"

"What?"

"You ever hear of interfering with a police investigation? Obstruction of justice?"

"You wouldn't do that to your old man."

"Try me. I'm not having you under my feet, and I mean it." She took a bite of her bagel.

"All right," Ham said sullenly, "I'll stay out of your way."

"I'm talking about work, now, not personal."

"Well, I certainly don't seem to be standing in your way personally," he said, glancing sharply at Jackson. "I didn't slow you down last night, did I?"

"Ham, I am a woman in my prime, and you are a crusty, interfering old fart, and I don't want to hear another word about sex."

Ham turned crimson. "Jesus, who said anything about sex?"

"You did."

"I did *not*."

Jackson broke in. "Is it always like this?"

"Only when he starts bitching about my private life," Holly said. "He's never approved of a single man I've known."

Ham pointed at Jackson. "I approve of *him*," he said.

Holly blinked. "You do?"

"We've been talking for a while, and I reckon I know a lot about him by now."

Jackson spoke up. "Where I was born, education, hobbies, past sexual experience, time as a cop, my legal practice, how much money I make. Considerably more than *you* know about me."

"Ham, you can really be a pain in the ass sometimes," she said.

Ham held up a finger. "It's a father's right to know something about the man who's screwing his daughter."

"*HAM!*" she screamed.

Jackson broke up and started clearing the table. "I'm out of this," he said. "You two can fight it out."

"All right, all right," Ham said placatingly. "I guess I know enough for now. I'll ask him the rest when he comes to me and asks for your hand."

"Arrrrrrghhhhh!!!" she yelled, throwing up her hands in exasperation.

"Oh," Ham said, "on a different subject, you had a phone call at the crack of dawn this morning. He dug a slip of paper out of his pocket and handed it to her. "Guy named Paul Green."

"Doesn't ring a bell," Holly said, looking at the number. "Oh, it's the hospital. Dr. Green. Maybe he's got some news about Chet." She went to the sofa, dialed the number and asked for Dr. Green.

"I'll put you through to his home," the operator said.

He answered on the first ring. "Green."

"Dr. Green, it's Holly Barker. You left a message for me."

"Oh, Chief Barker, I'm sorry to have called so early. I seem to have woken up the gentleman who answered."

"That's all right, he's my father."

"I called with bad news, I'm afraid."

Holly's stomach tensed. "What's happened?"

"Chief Marley arrested at six-twenty this morning. The team worked on him for nearly half an hour, and I came in, too, but we weren't able to revive him. Official time of death was six forty-five. I'm very sorry."

"Oh, God," Holly said. "Did he ever regain consciousness at all?"

"I'm afraid not. Is there anything I can do?"

"No, Doctor. Thank you for calling me immediately. I'll make the announcement through the department, and someone will be in touch with the hospital about the arrangements." She hung up. Jackson and Ham were standing there, looking at her.

"Is is Chet?" Ham asked.

Holly nodded. "He died at six forty-five this morning."

"Shit and goddamnit!" Ham spat, stomping his foot. "He deserved better than that."

"He sure did," Holly said. The two men sat down, silent. Nobody spoke for a couple of minutes. "I'd better call the station," Holly said. She called in, dictated a short press release and told the operator to post it on the bulletin board and fax it to the local media. "And post a notice that we'll have a departmental meeting tomorrow morning, at the change of shift. I want everybody there." She called Hurd Wallace and Jane Grey and gave them the news. Jane burst into tears; it took Holly several minutes to calm her down. Wallace said almost nothing.

Jackson took the phone. "I'll make the arrangements," he said. "I'm his executor."

"What are we going to do about burial?" Holly asked. "He didn't have anybody."

"He had us," Jackson said. "He left instructions that he wanted his body cremated as quickly and cheaply as possible, and that he didn't want a service." He got the phone book and called a funeral director.

"You want some more coffee, Ham?"

"I'm going to take a walk on the beach," Ham replied. "Come on, Daisy." The dog got up and followed him outside.

An hour later they were all back at the table.

"I've got some things to tell you," Jackson said. "The funeral parlor is picking up Chet's body today. He'll be cremated tomorrow. Chet wanted his ashes scattered on the river behind his house, and we can do that whenever you like."

"Is that it?" Ham asked.

"No, there's more," Jackson said. "Now that Chet is gone, I can tell you about the terms of his will. It's pretty simple, really: he had a fifty-thousand-dollar insurance policy, which increased to a hundred thousand in the event of being killed in the line of duty, which he was. He instructed that his debts be paid and that the remaining cash in his accounts, along with the insurance, should be divided between Hank Doherty and Jane Grey. He left his house and his personal possessions to Hank. Hank, of course, predeceased him, and in that event, Ham, Hank's share of the estate goes to you."

"To me?" Ham asked incredulously.

"He didn't have anybody else, just you and Hank. It's what he wanted."

"I think that's wonderful," Holly said. "That will make your retirement more comfortable." She turned to Jackson. "What did he have in the way of debt?"

"He had mortgage insurance, which pays off that balance, so the house is free and clear, except for a home improvement loan of about ten thousand dollars. Apart from that, there's a few thousand in credit card debt and his monthly bills to close out, and that's it. On the asset side, he had some money in mutual funds—thirty or forty thousand, I think."

"I don't believe it," Ham said.

"Well," Holly replied, "your housing problem is solved."

"I don't see why you can't move into the house today, Ham," Jackson said. "It's very nicely furnished. All you'll need is some groceries. There's a small boat, too, tied up at Chet's dock. And if you decide you don't want to live in the house, there's a ready buyer waiting in the wings."

"It's a nice place, Ham," Holly said. "You'll like it."

"I expect I will," Ham said sadly.

29

Holly and Jackson led the way, followed by Ham and Daisy in Ham's truck. She thought the place very pretty in the afternoon light; the property was nicely planted, something she hadn't noticed in the dark. Everybody got out and walked around the house with Ham. The boat was there, tied to the little dock. It was a seventeen-foot Boston Whaler with a forty-horsepower outboard engine, ideal for skimming up and down the quiet waters of the Indian River. Jackson unlocked the house and they went inside.

"Hey, this is nice," Ham said. "Chet made himself real comfortable." He walked over and looked at the guns and the fishing rods in their racks. "Nice gear, too."

"There's only one bedroom," Holly said. "Over there." She pointed.

Ham walked through the place. "It's just wonderful," he said, and his voice cracked.

"Jackson," Holly said, "why don't you and I start getting Ham's stuff off his truck?" They went outside, leaving Ham alone. "I'm so glad Chet did this," she said. "Ham's in there crying right now, and I haven't seen him do that since Mom died."

"Let's unload all this stuff from the truck," Jackson said, "and give him a minute." He got up onto the pickup, folded back the tarp and started handing Holly boxes. A few minutes later, Ham came out, seeming recovered, and helped them carry things in. They began emptying boxes.

Holly went to the chest of drawers in the bedroom and started packing Chet's things into some of the empty boxes. That done, she began helping with the other things. When she came to Ham's shotgun, she unzipped the sheepskin case and set the weapon in an empty slot in Chet's gun rack. While doing that, something caught her eye. There were three pistols in the rack: an army .45 automatic, a .38 police special and a smaller revolver. It was the smaller gun that got her attention: there was a trace of talcum powder clinging to it.

She went into the kitchen and came back with a pair of dishwashing gloves and a zippered plastic bag. She put on the gloves and gingerly lifted the revolver off the rack by its trigger guard. It was a Colt .32.

"What have you got there?" Jackson asked.

"Jackson, do you remember this pistol being here last night when we were searching the place?"

"I didn't pay much attention to the guns," he said.

"Neither did I, and I searched the rack for a piece of paper tucked away."

"Why does the pistol interest you?"

"Because I think it belongs to your client, Sammy."

Jackson looked closely at the weapon. "So when they searched the house, they not only took something, they left something."

"Looks that way."

"What a weird thing to do."

"They hid it in plain sight," she said. "I guess they figured nobody but Chet would ever know the difference, and that he wasn't coming home. I only noticed it because it had some talcum powder on it."

"Maybe it'll have some fingerprints on it," Jackson said.

"They haven't left a print anywhere else; I doubt they'll start with this." She handed it to him. "I guess you'd better send it to your client, if you ever hear from him again."

"You don't have any further need of it in your investigation?"

"Nope. It's not material."

Jackson walked out into the backyard and threw the pistol as far out into the river as he could, then he came back. "That's the last of that," he said. "Well, looks like we've gotten just about everything unpacked. Ham, you want to go out for some dinner with us?"

"Thanks, Jackson, but I think I'll pick up some groceries and just be by myself tonight; get used to the place."

"Okay, Ham," Holly said, and kissed him on the cheek. "Have a good evening in your new place, and we'll talk tomorrow."

They got into Jackon's car and drove away. "I hope he's going to be okay out here by himself," she said.

"He looks pretty self-sufficient to me," Jackson replied.

"Yes, he is that."

The following morning she sat down in Jane Grey's office. "Jane, I've got some good news for you: Chet had some insurance, and he left half of it to you. It's fifty thousand dollars."

Tears welled up in Jane's eyes, and she seemed unable to speak.

Holly patted her on the shoulder, then went back to her office to collect her thoughts. Ten minutes later she walked into the squad room and yelled for everybody's attention. The room was packed with officers and clerical workers, and as she began to speak, she saw John Westover walk in.

"I guess you've all heard by now that Chief Marley died yesterday," she said. "I've learned that he requested that his body be cremated and his ashes scattered on the river next to his house. That's being taken care of today. He also had requested that there be no funeral or service, so I guess this meeting will be the closest thing to a memorial service that he'll have. Anybody have any questions or want to say anything?"

A young officer at the back of the room spoke up. "Did the chief die without ever waking up?"

"He woke up for a short while a couple of weeks ago, then slipped back into the coma. I talked with him briefly, and he wasn't able to remember anything about the shooting or anything else that would help the investigation."

A young female officer raised her hand. "I think we ought to have some sort of memorial for the chief around here," she said.

"Stacy," Holly replied, "that's an excellent idea. Why don't you take charge of that? Ask around and see if anybody has a good idea of what sort of memorial it should be, and then you can take up a collection. I'll start it with a hundred dollars, and the rest of you can give whatever you feel you can manage."

John Westwood spoke up. "I think I can persuade the council to contribute a thousand dollars to such a memorial."

"Then we're off to a good start," Holly said. "Jimmy," she called to Weathers, "will you go stand guard at the door while you listen? I don't want anybody coming in here while I'm talking about this."

"Yes, ma'am."

"I'm going to bring you all up to date on our investigation so far, because I think that's the best way to get every man's and woman's maximum contribution to solving these two murders. I don't want you to discuss any of this with anybody who's not in this room right now—not your wives, girlfriends or boyfriends, not anybody. Here's what I've surmised from what we've learned: it appears the chief met with someone who was supposed to give him some information on an investigation he was conducting himself. We don't know what the investigation was about. There was a fight, some blows were exchanged, and the chief was shot. He may have tried to draw his weapon, because one of his murderers—we think there were two—threw his pistol over a fence into the brush, where it was recovered the next day.

"The chief was shot with a thirty-two Smith & Wesson that had been stolen from the house of Lieutenant Wallace's ex-wife some time before and probably sold on the street, maybe more than once. The murderers then took the chief's notebook and the shotgun from his car, went to Hank Doherty's house, somehow got his dog, Daisy, locked in the kitchen, then shot Hank with the shotgun. They searched the place, then they went to the chief's house and searched that.

"The murderer was clearly not the man we first arrested for the crime. He owned a thirty-two of a different make." She turned to Bob Hurst. "Bob, you have anything to add to that?"

"No, chief," Hurst said. "That about sums it up."

"Any questions?"

Jimmy Weathers raised his hand. "What were they searching for at the two houses?"

"I think they believed that the chief had made some notes on the investigation he was conducting. They were looking for the notes, and that's why they took his notebook. Any other questions?"

Nobody spoke.

"All right, now you all know as much as anybody about what's happened. I want each of you to talk to every snitch, every source, everybody you can think of, and pick up as much information as you can. This is going to be a tough one to crack, and you just might be able to supply us with the break we need to make arrests.

"Chet Marley was a fine police chief. He has left us a well-organized and well-trained department to work with. Let's use it to find his killers. That's all."

The meeting broke up, the shift changed, and John Westover came to Holly's office, closed the door and sat down.

"Holly, you're still acting chief for the time being, but we have to go through a formal process in order to replace Chet."

"I'd imagined you would have to," Holly said.

"The city charter requires us to advertise the position for a month and to receive and consider applications from qualified applicants. I expect you want the job."

"Yes, I do."

"I imagine Hurd Wallace will apply, too, and I'm sure we'll have some out-of-town applicants, but you and Hurd, with your experience of the department, are probably going to be the front runners. Chet's confidence in you will be taken into account, as well. I'll send down an application form, and I'd like to get it back as soon as you can complete it."

"Of course, John. There's something I should tell you. Jackson Oxenhandler, who is Chet's lawyer and the executor of his estate, told me yesterday about Chet's will. He left some insurance money to Jane Grey and everything else to Hank Doherty. In the event of Hank's predeceasing him, which of course happened, Hank's share was to go to my father, Hamilton Barker, who was in the army with

Chet and Hank. My father has just retired from the military, and he arrived in Orchid on Saturday night. He has, at Mr. Oxenhandler's suggestion, moved into Chet's house. I wanted you to hear about this from me."

"Thank you for telling me, Holly. I'll go see Hurd now and let you get on with your work."

"I'll see you later."

Westover left, and Holly sat, thinking about the hiring process ahead. She knew it had to be done, but she wasn't looking forward to having it hanging over her head.

Daisy came and put her head in Holly's lap.

"Good girl," Holly said. "Nice to have your support."

30

Palmetto Gardens had only one listed phone number; apparently all calls went through a switchboard. Holly asked for security, then asked for Barney Noble.

"Who's calling?" a young male voice asked.

"Chief Holly Barker, of the Orchid Beach PD."

"I'll patch you through to his house."

There was a click and one ring.

"Barney Noble."

"Hey, Barney, it's Holly Barker. How you doing?"

"Good, Holly, and you?"

"Can't complain."

"When's Ham coming down?"

"That's why I called you. He's here for the duration, retired last week."

"No kidding? About time. When's he going to play some golf with me?"

"The sooner, the better, he says."

"How about this afternoon?"

"Perfect. Mind if I tag along?"

"You play?"

"I'm my father's daughter."

"Sure, you come ahead. Two o'clock?"

"Sounds good."

"I'll meet you at the front gate. Park where you did last time."

"See you at two." She hung up and turned to her father. They were in Jackson's living room. "We're on for two. Better wear your best golf duds, it's a fancy place."

Ham frowned. "Shit, you mean I can't wear my combat fatigues?"

"You'd be shot on sight. Don't wear those awful plaid Bermuda shorts, either."

"You're limiting my options."

"That's the idea."

Jackson spoke up. "Why wasn't I invited?"

"You want Barney Noble to know where you are? He might call Cracker Mosely and tell him."

"You've got a point," Jackson said.

"You can baby-sit Daisy."

"Or her me."

"That's more like it, come to think."

Holly pulled into the parking space at two sharp. Barney Noble was already there, waiting for them in his white Range Rover with the little green palmetto on the door. He got out to greet them.

"Hello, Holly. Jesus, Ham, it's been a while, hasn't it?"

Ham shook his hand and grinned. "Must've been, what, '73?"

"I reckon. Come on, let's get your clubs in my car."

Holly and Ham transfered their clubs to the Range Rover, then got in. The security gate opened, and the tire-buster spikes retracted.

"That's some arrangement there," Ham said. "You expecting armored personnel carriers?"

"Nah," Barney replied. "Our board of directors is fond of overkill. Makes the members feel safe. It's not like anybody ever tried to bust in here. Holly, did you know your old man was the toughest, meanest noncom in 'Nam?"

"That's what he keeps telling me," Holly replied.

"You're both full of shit," Ham said pleasantly.

"You ever miss 'Nam, Ham?"

"Not for a minute."

"I do, sometimes. You know what I miss?" They hit a large pot-hole. Barney swore. "That was supposed to have been fixed yesterday," he said. He picked up a handheld radio and said, "Base."

"Base," a tinny voice said.

"This is Noble. Call maintenance and tell them to put down their comic books and get down to Gull Drive at Live Oak and fix that pothole. If a member's car hits that I'll never hear the end of it."

"Roger, Chief," the voice said.

Noble put down the radio. "Sorry about that. Where was I?"

"I forget," Ham said, looking out the window at the golf course.

"Well, never mind, here we are." He pulled into the drive of the country club building and parked. Immediately a man in a large golf cart drove up, took their clubs out of the Range Rover and stowed them in the cart. He drove them to the first tee, where two carts were waiting.

"You two ride together," Holly said. "You've got a lot of catching up to do." She told the man to put her clubs in the other cart.

"What are you playing with, Ham?" Noble asked, peering at Ham's clubs.

"Callaways."

"The stainless steel ones?"

"Yep."

"Tell you what: I'll play your clubs, and you play mine. They're the new Callaway irons, the tungsten-titanium ones." He gave Barney a brief lecture on the clubs.

Holly teed off first, sending a long straight drive down the middle of the fairway. The two men drove next, landing within ten yards ahead of her ball. Holly got into her cart and followed Noble down the fairway. They were all on the green in two, and all three parred the hole.

As they played along, Holly realized that, for the first time, she could see many of the houses, which backed up onto the course. They were grandiose in scale, but seemed well designed, and the properties were beautifully landscaped.

Just beyond the ninth green was a little outdoor bar, and they sat down for a few minutes and had a beer. Holly thought it was a nice convenience, even if she had never had a beer in the middle of a golf game. What caught her attention was that the barman had a pronounced bulge under the left arm of his tight, white jacket.

"This is some place, Barney," Ham said, looking around. "How long you been here?"

"Since shortly before the place opened. I'm a partner in a security service in Miami, and we were approached about providing services up here. In the end, they hired me to put together their own force, and I liked it up here, so I stayed. I've still got my share of the Miami outfit, though, and it does real well. You ready to play on?"

They drove from the tenth tee and continued their game. By the time they had finished the three of them were in a dead heat, when the handicaps were figured in. Barney drove them up to the clubhouse and led them into the pro shop. The place was large and had many displays of equipment.

"We stock only the finest stuff," Barney said. "What did you think of the new Callaways?"

"I thought they were sensational," Ham replied. "I played over my head today."

"You want a set? Everything here is half price."

"You sure? Wouldn't that get you in trouble with your board?"

"Not a bit. It's a funny thing: very rich people don't like to pay retail for *anything*, so we make it cheap for them in the pro shop and the restaurant, while charging them an arm and a leg for just about everything else. Come on, let's pick you out a set. How about you, Holly?"

"No, thanks, Barney. I'm well fixed for clubs." Holly tagged along while Ham chose his irons and a set of the titanium woods, plus a new bag and a couple of dozen balls. He paid with a credit card, and Barney instructed the shop manager to have the new clubs put into Holly's car at the front gate, along with his old ones.

Barney took Ham and Holly upstairs to the grill room, where they feasted on cheeseburgers. It was Holly's first glimpse of some of the members, though there were no more than a couple of dozen of them in the large room. She thought they looked foreign, even the ones who weren't Hispanic or Asian. She thought she heard two men speaking Arabic, but she wasn't sure.

"Is it always this crowded, Barney?" she asked.

He laughed. "This is pretty typical. We never have a strain on the facilities."

"Barney," she said, "so far, I've seen three armed men—the guy who drove us in the cart, the bartender at the ninth hole and the golf shop manager. Is that usual?"

"You have a sharp eye," Barney said. "A lot of our employees are trained and licensed to carry firearms. Makes for a nice extension to our security force, and the members like it that way."

"Whatever you say." Holly dug into her cheeseburger, which was as good as she'd ever had.

Driving home, Ham said, "I saw at least three more armed men around that place, and I don't buy Barney's explanation. What's the point?"

"I don't know," Holly said, "but when I get time I'm going to look into it."

"Something I didn't tell you about Barney Noble," Ham said.

"What's that?"

"Lieutenants didn't live long in Barney's platoon. He lost three while I was in the company, and there were rumors that they'd been fragged. Barney never denied it."

Holly knew that *fragged* meant killed by their own men.

"Barney didn't like taking orders from shavetails just out of OCS," Ham said. "None of them was a West Pointer; something would have been done about that."

"Nothing was ever done, then?"

"Barney was transferred to headquarters and given a desk job halfway through his tour. When he was up for promotion to master sergeant, he was passed over."

"Weren't there any witnesses to all this?"

"If there were, they kept their mouths shut. None of them was going to cross Barney."

"I can see why."

"Did you notice, when we said good-bye, he didn't ask us to play again?"

"Yeah, I did."

"Why do you think he asked us in the first place? He could have made an excuse when you called him."

"I think he wanted us to see what a nice, quiet, unthreatening place Palmetto Gardens is."

"He didn't like it much when you brought up the people who were packing."

"No, he didn't, did he?" Holly grinned.

"You be careful with him, honey," Ham said.

"I will."

31

On Sunday afternoon Holly, Jackson and Ham took Chet Marley's whaler out into the river. Ham unscrewed the top on the urn that contained Chet's remains and, as Holly drove slowly south from the dock, scattered the ashes on the river. Nobody said anything for a while, and Ham sat with his face in his hands for a couple of minutes. Finally he looked up.

"Well, that's done," Ham said, taking the wheel from Holly. "Let's do some sightseeing." He put the throttle forward and they sped down the river, making almost no wake, past sailboats and motor yachts—every kind of pleasure craft.

Holly looked up and was alarmed to see a business jet descending at a sharp angle, flying unbelievably low. It disappeared behind a stand of tall pines, and she tensed, waiting for the explosion and fireball. She had seen a jet fighter crash once, and she didn't want to repeat the experience. To her surprise, nothing happened.

"That was pretty scary," Ham said, reducing speed.

"It's the Palmetto Gardens airfield," Holly said. "I had forgotten about it. I was waiting for the crash."

"Me, too," Ham said. "That was a pretty good-sized jet."

"They can apparently take anything short of a 747."

"That's got to be the entrance to their marina," Jackson said, pointing at an inlet. "There's no marker for it, but it can't be anything else, given the location of the airport."

"Let's have a look at it," Holly said. "Turn in there, Ham, and go slow."

Ham throttled back nearly to idle and turned into the inlet.

"Water looks pretty deep here," Jackson said.

Holly pointed to a group of masts rising above the low trees. "Got some pretty big boats in here, huh?"

"One of them has a satellite dish," Ham said, pointing. "Probably a satphone. When we're around this bend, we ought to be able to see the marina."

As they were starting around the bend in the inlet, another boat suddenly appeared, going in the opposite direction. It was an open boat of about twenty-five feet, and a large spotlight was mounted on a thick mast next to a couple of radio antennae and a radar housing. A loudspeaker blasted across the water.

"Stop," a metallic voice said.

Ham took the whaler out of gear and drifted. The larger boat came alongside, carrying two uniformed security guards. They were both wearing sidearms, and the one who wasn't driving was carrying an assault rifle.

"This is private property," the rifle bearer said, looking them over. "Turn your boat around." He wasn't actually pointing the weapon at them, but he appeared to be ready to do so.

"Sorry," Ham called out. "What is this place?"

"I told you, pal, it's private property," the man replied. "Now turn that thing around or I'll sink it for you."

"Isn't this part of the intracoastal waterway?" Jackson asked. "Isn't this a public right of way?"

The man put down the assault rifle, picked up a boat hook, extended it to its full length and used it to hook the bow cleat on the whaler. "Okay," he said to his companion. The man gunned the engine, spinning the whaler around, nearly dumping its occupants overboard.

Ham put the engine into forward gear to ease the strain on the cleat, but they were being towed at a good ten knots, and water from the bigger boat's wake was coming over the bows of the whaler in rhythmic waves, soaking its three passengers. When they were back in the river, the guard released the whaler, and the boat's driver spun his craft around and headed back into the inlet at high speed, creating a wake that nearly swamped the whaler.

"You son of a bitch!" Ham yelled.

Holly was bailing water out of the whaler. "You think maybe we're not welcome in there?"

"Could be," Jackson said.

"I'd like to go back in there with a shotgun," Ham said.

"Now, Ham, don't come over all military on me," Holly said. "They just overreacted to our presence."

Ham headed back toward Egret Island at high speed, the wind drying their clothes. When they were alongside the dock, he leapt out and headed for the house, Holly chasing him.

"What are you doing?" she yelled after him.

"I'm going to call Barney Noble and tell him what I think of his son-of-a-bitch security guards!" he yelled over his shoulder.

She caught up with him as he was lifting the phone. "Ham, don't do that, please."

"And why the hell not?"

"I don't want Barney to think we were snooping around Palmetto Gardens."

"Well, that's what we were doing, wasn't it?"

"Yes, but I don't want Barney to know it. I'm interested in that place, but I've got to move carefully. I've got an interview with the city council coming up, and I don't want any complaints lodged."

Ham slammed down the phone. "Well, shit."

"Why don't you have a beer and get your blood pressure down, Ham? I don't want you stroking out on me."

Ham went into the kitchen, found a bottle of bourbon and poured himself a double over ice. "You want one?" he asked Holly and Jackson, who had caught up with them.

"It's a little early for me," Holly said. "A little early for you, too, come to that."

"That place is like a goddamned foreign military base, right here on American soil," Ham said. He tossed back half the bourbon. "And it burns my ass."

"Ham, I'm going to look into it, all right? But I don't want to lose my job while I'm at it."

"I don't know why you're so goddamned worried about your job," Ham said. "You're retired military; you've got a pension." He sank the rest of the bourbon but didn't pour another.

"I *like* my job," Holly said, "and I haven't gotten to the time of my life when all I want to do is fish and play golf."

Ham was becoming calmer, now. "Yeah, I guess I can understand that."

"Also, I'd like to find out who killed Chet Marley and Hank Doherty, and my chances are a lot better if I'm running the police department."

"I'm sorry, Holly," he said, putting an arm around her. "I'm just not used to being pushed around."

"I don't know why not," Holly said, laughing. "That's all the army did for the past thirty years, was push you around."

"Well, I'll tell you, sweetie," Ham said, "I did a lot of pushing myself."

"Yeah, I guess you did, Ham."

"I'm going to watch the game," he said. "Anybody want to join me?"

"Not me," Holly said. "I'm going to sit out back for a while and watch the boats go by."

"I'll join you," Jackson said.

"You don't wan't to watch the game with me?" Ham asked.

"She's prettier than you are," Jackson said, nodding at Holly. "I'd rather watch her." He took her hand and led her outside.

They took off their shoes, sat down on the dock and let their feet dangle in the water.

"Well," Jackson said, "that's my introduction to Palmetto Gardens, and I didn't like it much."

"Yeah, those folks have got *way* too much security. Barney Noble says the members feel better with the overkill, but it doesn't make any sense to me. The members are supposed to be corporate CEO types, not banana republic dictators."

"That airplane had a foreign registration number," Jackson said.

"What country?"

"I don't know, and I can't remember the letters, but all U.S. aircraft have registration numbers starting with *N*."

"Noble told me that they had some sort of special customs and immigrations deal, where their members can fly in directly from any foreign airport."

"That's unusual," Jackson said. "Normally, when an aircraft enters the U.S. from another country, it has to land at a port of entry—an international airport—where the airplane is subject to search and the crew's and passengers' documents are examined. That's what I've had to do when I fly back from the Bahamas. I land at Fort Pierce, clear customs and immigration, then fly to Orchid airport."

"You fly?"

"I've got a license, but I don't own an airplane. I belong to a flying club out at the airport, and I can rent their machines."

"Why don't we go have a look at Palmetto Gardens from the air?"

"You think they'll shoot us down?"

"Let's find out."

32

Jackson used a card with a magnetic strip to open the security gate at Orchid Beach Airport. This was Holly's third trip there, but now they drove past the terminal building with its tower and stopped a quarter of a mile down the runway at a low, concrete-block building with a windsock on top. A number of light aircraft were parked outside. Jackson led the way in.

"Hey, Doris," he said to the woman behind the high desk. "Is 123 Tango Foxtrot available for a couple of hours?"

"You're in luck, Jackson, we had a cancellation." She put the keys and a printed document on the desk for him to sign.

"Doris, this is Holly Barker, our new chief of police."

"Acting chief," Holly corrected.

"Well, hey there, honey," Doris said, standing up and offering her hand. She was a buxom woman, pushing fifty, in tight pants with a pile of peroxided hair on her head. "Welcome to Orchid. I was real sorry to hear about Chief Marley's death. Anything new on that?"

"Nothing so far, but we're working on it," Holly said.

"He was a nice man. Say, can I interest you in some flying lessons?"

"You might be able to a little further down the road, when I get my feet on the ground," Holly replied.

"We're about getting your feet *off* the ground," Doris said.

Holly laughed and looked over Jackson's shoulder.

"This is a document," he said, "which commits my entire net worth to the flying club if I bend the airplane, and makes Doris my sole heir if I kill myself in it."

Doris laughed. "How else can I ever retire?" she asked. "The way Jackson flies, it's only a matter of time."

"I'm beginning to reconsider this trip," Holly said.

"Oh, he'll get you back alive, honey," Doris said. "I taught him all he knows about flying."

"And most of what I know about life," Jackson laughed. He picked up the keys and a clipboard. "Let's get out of here."

Holly followed him outside to a yellow-and-white airplane. "I've never been up in one of these," she said.

"A Cessna?"

"In anything smaller than one of Delta's jets, except for army helicopters."

"This is a Cessna 172, the most popular airplane ever built," Jackson said. "Come on, we'll preflight her together."

She followed him around the airplane while he wiggled things, peered into holes and checked the oil and fuel. "How much experience have you had at this?" she asked.

"I've got nearly five hundred hours," he replied. "I'm working on my instrument rating right now, and I ought to have that soon, then maybe I'll buy a good used airplane."

"Five hundred hours sounds like a lot," she said, seeking reassurance.

"Not really. A couple of thousand is more like a lot." He helped her into the airplane and showed her how the seat belt worked.

"Have you ever carried a passenger?"

"Oh, sure. The airplane is a great seduction tool: by the time you get them back down, they're so grateful to still be alive, they just fall right into bed with you."

"Let's see if it works," Holly said.

Jackson climbed into the little airplane, switched on the ignition, pumped something, and turned the key and the engine started. He picked up a checklist from the floor and talked himself through it, flipping switches and adjusting controls; then he handed Holly a headset and showed her how to wear it. Five minutes later, they had been cleared for takeoff and were rolling down the runway. The airport was on the mainland, and as they climbed they could see the barrier island stretched out before them a few miles away. Jackson turned right, headed for the middle of the island, and when he reached it, turned north, flying at two thousand feet.

"How low can we fly?" Holly asked, hearing her own voice clearly over the headset.

"A thousand feet AGL—that's above ground level—in built-up areas. Since Orchid is about twelve feet above sea level, that means about a thousand feet." He pulled back the throttle and began a descent. "There's Palmetto Gardens up ahead," he said, pointing. "See the golf courses?"

"Got it," Holly said.

"Jesus, look at the length of that runway," he said, pointing at the airfield.

"Barney said it was six thousand feet."

"That's longer than the Orchid airport. We're at a thousand feet, now."

Holly looked around. "It runs from A1A to the river," she said, "and a long way north and south. It's a lot bigger than I thought."

Jackson circled over the development. "Huge houses," he said. "They must be on at least five acres each." A foursome of golfers was looking up at the airplane.

"Uh-oh," Holly said, pointing out her side.

Jackson turned the airplane in that direction, dipping a wing. A white Range Rover had stopped and the driver had gotten out and was looking up at them. He reached into the vehicle and came out with a pair of binoculars. "Okay, let's see if he shoots at us," Jackson laughed.

"Are we invading some kind of private airspace?" Holly asked.

"Of course not. They may have themselves an exclusive club down there, but up here belongs to everybody."

"Fly on north, and let's get away from that security guard. Look, that's a hell of a big greenhouse. They must grow a lot of their own plants."

"Looks like they grow their own vegetables, too," Jackson said. "And there are some stables and a riding ring." He pointed. "What do you suppose that is?"

Holly followed his finger and found a two-story building with a forest of antennae on its roof. "Looks like a NASA substation," she said. "I count four dishes of varying sizes and there are at least a dozen other kinds of antennas. And look at that giant dish in back of the building. That thing must have a diameter of at least fifteen feet."

"I visited CNN headquarters in Atlanta, once," Jackson said. "They had dishes like that."

"Okay, we're at the northern extremity; let's turn and fly south again," Holly said.

Jackson turned the airplane and headed back for the golf courses, which were at the center of the development. The Range Rover was on the move again, headed toward the airport. "There's the runway up ahead," he said. "Let's do a touch-and-go."

"Are you nuts?" Holly demanded.

"Aw come on, what can they do about it? You think they've got antiaircraft missiles?"

"I wouldn't be surprised," Holly said.

He had the nose of the airplane down, now, and the runway loomed large in the windshield. The word PRIVATE had been painted in huge letters in the middle of the asphalt.

"Jesus," Holly said. "I don't want to do this."

"Nothing to it," Jackson said as they crossed the threshold. The wheels of the little airplane touched down softly.

"Oh, shit!" Holly yelled, pointing ahead. A white Range Rover had pulled onto the middle of the runway and had stopped. A man in a uniform was standing beside it with his hands up, motioning them to stop.

Jackson pushed the throttle to the firewall and the airplane accelerated. The Range Rover seemed to be rushing toward them. He held the airplane on the ground until it picked up speed, then yanked back on the yoke.

Holly had just enough time to see the security guard throw himself to the ground before she covered her eyes. Jackson banked sharply to the right, and she looked back over her shoulder to see another Range Rover arrive and Barney Noble get out. "Oh, shit, it's Barney! I hope he didn't recognize me!"

Jackson was laughing maniacally. "Not a chance!" he yelled. He turned left and headed for the beach side of the island. He tuned in a radio freqency, picked up a microphone and said, "Orchid Flying Club, November 123 Tango Foxtrot."

"This is Orchid," a husky female voice replied.

"Doris, you might get a phone call this afternoon, asking about who's flying the airplane."

"Tango Foxtrot, have you been buzzing the nude beach again?"

"Not yet. Just tell anybody who calls that the airplane was stolen by some joyrider."

"That ain't far off the truth," Doris said. "You bring that thing back in one piece."

"Over and out," Jackson said. "Boy, that was fun. Now let's buzz the nude beach."

"What nude beach?" Holly asked.

"Oh, I forgot, the police aren't supposed to know about that," he laughed. He turned out over the water, then descended another five hundred feet. "We can legally fly lower over the water. Here come the naked people!"

Holly looked out and saw a couple of dozen people disporting themselves on the sand and in the surf. They were, indeed, naked. "What on earth is a place like Orchid doing with a nude beach?" Holly asked as they whizzed past the bathers, who were grabbing for towels and making obscene gestures.

"Well, it's not exactly an *official* nude beach," Jackson said. "There are just a few adjoining property owners who have a few friends over now and then."

"Sounds like you're well acquainted with the spot," Holly said.

"One hears things," Jackson said, grinning. "Don't worry, they're outside the city limits, so you won't have to arrest them. Look, there's my place. Uh-oh, what's that?" He was pointing to the parking area outside his house.

"Looks like a pickup truck," Holly said. "A white one."

"And somebody getting out," Jackson said. He banked out over the water and turned back toward the house.

"What's that flashing light on your roof?" Holly asked.

"That's the strobe attached to my burglar alarm," Jackson said. "It means that whoever that was has broken into the house. Hang on. The tide's out, so I'm going to put this thing down on the beach." He made another turn and lined up for landing.

Holly groaned and braced herself against the instrument panel. The wet sand was rushing at them.

33

Jackson set the little airplane down on the sand, cut the engine and simultaneously stood on the brakes. The airplane ground to a halt on the firm beach. "Come on," he yelled, hopping out of the airplane. He sprinted across the beach toward the house. As they approached, the electronic siren of the burglar alarm became louder.

Holly grabbed her handbag and followed. "Jackson, stop!"

He kept running, but he had reached dry, soft sand now, and that slowed him down.

Holly used her last few yards of hard sand to catch up. "Stop, goddamnit!" she hollered.

Jackson plowed on.

Holly slung the strap of her bag over her head and tackled Jackson, bringing him down. "Hold it right here!" she yelled.

"What the hell are you doing?" he demanded, trying to get to his feet.

Holly dug her gun out of her bag. "This part is *my* job. You stay behind me!" She started across the dunes toward the house, with Jackson running behind her. As she hit the back porch she threw down her bag and struggled with the glass sliding doors.

Jackson reached the porch and came up with his key. "Hang on," he yelled, unlocking the door. "Now go!"

Holly slid open the door and stepped into the house, pistol out in front of her in both hands, finger on the trigger guard. A tinny voice was screaming, over and over, "Unauthorized entry in progress! Vacate the premises at once! The police are on the way!"

Jackson stepped inside and disarmed the alarm with the keypad beside the door. The voice and siren went silent.

Holly listened for sounds of someone inside the house. Nothing. The front door stood open, and she heard the truck start up and its tires spit gravel. "Come on!" she yelled. "Get your shotgun!" She ran out of the house and down the stairs. The rear of the truck was just disappearing behind some foliage, and she kept running. As she reached the driveway, she caught one more glimpse of it way ahead as it turned right and headed toward Orchid.

Jackson caught up to her and stopped, the shotgun in his hands. "Did you get the plate number?"

"No, all I saw was a big 'Ford' stamped into the tailgate. It was a Florida plate, though." She turned and ran for the house. By the time Jackson got there, she was on the phone, dialing 911.

"Orchid Beach Police, what is your emergency?" the operator asked.

"This is Chief Barker. I interrupted a burglary in progress south of town. The suspect is a white male in a white Ford pickup truck, Florida plates, I didn't get the number, heading north on A1A near the south end of town. Intercept and detain; approach with caution, he may be armed."

"Got it, Chief."

"Call me on my cell phone with any sightings."

"Roger."

Holly hung up. "We may get him yet."

"Let's pursue him," Jackson said. "He hasn't got that much of a start."

"He's a mile away by now, maybe two, and my car doesn't have a siren or a light; let's let the patrol cars handle it." She went out onto the porch and picked up her bag, still panting from her run. She took deep breaths and let her adrenaline production get back to normal.

When she came back inside, Jackson was sitting on the couch, getting his breath. The phone rang. "Hello," he said. "Yes, the code is three-six-six-nine. The burglar has gone and the police are already here. Thanks." He hung up. "That was the alarm company. They might have been a little quicker to call."

"What do you think the guy was looking for?" Holly asked.

"I don't know. Let me have a look around." Jackson checked his home office. "He's been through my desk, and there's a file drawer open."

"Anything missing?"

Jackson went through the files, then checked his desk drawers. "Nothing," he said.

"I guess we interrupted him before he could get any farther."

"Maybe so."

"Have you ever had a burglary out here?" she asked.

"I had an attempt more than a year ago. The alarm went off, and by the time the cops got here whoever set it off was gone. They figured the alarm scared him off."

"How come you've got a strobe light on top of your house, connected to the burglar alarm?"

"Just an idea I had," he said. "After the alarm went off that time, I thought, suppose I'm walking on the beach and the alarm goes off? I might not hear it over the surf, so I installed the light."

"Good idea," she said. "It worked."

"Even if not in the manner I imagined."

Holly's cell phone rang, and she dug it out of her bag. "Chief Barker."

"Chief, it's Jimmy Weathers. I'm duty officer today. No sign of your white pickup anywhere on A1A, south or north. We're checking side streets now."

"Good, Jimmy, keep it up and call me when you know something."

"Yes, ma'am."

Holly hung up. "Maybe he was looking for you," she said.

Jackson sat bolt upright. "Shit, the airplane! Come on!" He sprinted out of the house and across the dunes, with Holly close behind. The airplane was where they had left it, but the incoming tide was over its wheels. Jackson ran to it, opened the luggage compartment and got out a T-shaped bar. "Come help me," he yelled.

Holly ran to him as he reached under the water and attached the bar to the nosewheel. Holly grabbed one side of the T and pulled with all her strength. For a moment, nothing happened; then, with the two of them pulling like oxen, the airplane began to move. They towed it well free of the surf.

"We've got to fly it out of here now," Jackson said, "or pretty soon, all we'll have left to roll on is soft, dry sand." He hopped into the airplane. Holly got into the other seat, and Jackson got the engine started. "No time for a runup," Jackson said, shoving the throttle forward. The airplane started to roll, slowly at first, then faster. Soon they were back in the air. They got their headsets on.

"Let's look for the pickup," Holly said.

"Why didn't I think of that?"

"Fly right up A1A. It won't be on the highway, but you can look out your side, and I'll look out mine."

"Right."

Holly looked out over the passing subdivisions. "Can you make this thing fly slower?" she asked.

"Okay." Jackson lowered the flaps and reduced power. "Okay, that's seventy-five knots. I don't want to go any slower. The controls are mushy enough as it is."

"Well, don't stall it," Holly said. "Hey, I've got a white pickup over here." She pointed. "No, I've got two."

"I've got one over here, too, parked in front of a house."

"Here's another one. I'm beginning to get the feeling there are an awful lot of white pickups around here."

"Your father drives one," Jackson said.

"Oh, the hell with it, this isn't doing any good. Let's go back to the airport."

"Right," Jackson said. He went back to cruise power and retracted the flaps. "Here," he said, taking his hands off the yoke. "You fly it."

Holly grabbed the yoke on her side. "Are you nuts? I've never flown an airplane."

"It's not quantum physics, just keep her straight and level."

Holly held on to the yoke tightly.

"Take your hands off for a second," he said.

Holly removed her hands; the airplane continued to fly straight and level.

"See? You don't need to strangle the yoke. You can fly her with a couple of fingers." He reached over and adjusted something on the panel in front of Holly. "That's your compass," he said. "Now turn left to two hundred seventy degrees. Just turn the yoke."

Holly turned left, overshot 270, then corrected.

"We're already at traffic pattern altitude, which is a thousand feet AGL. See the field? Twelve o'clock and five miles?"

Holly looked out over the nose of the airplane. "Yes! I see the runway!"

"Very good. You see we're approaching the runway at a forty-five-degree angle?"

"Yes."

"When we're one mile out, you'll turn parallel to the runway; that's called the downwind leg. I'll announce our presence to the tower." He called the tower and got clearance to land. "Okay, start your turn now. Just keep parallel to the runway."

Holly made the turn.

"Now we're going to put in a notch of flaps and reduce power," Jackson said, performing the tasks. "When we get to the end of the runway, let the airplane descend to seven hundred and fifty feet."

Holly did as she was told.

Jackson added another notch of flaps. "Now make a ninety-degree turn toward the runway, and descend to five hundred feet." He reduced power further. When she had reached five hundred feet, he said, "Now turn for the runway, and you're on final approach. Just point at the runway numbers." He kept his hand on the throttle.

Holly watched the numbers come closer.

"Use the rudder pedals to help you stay on the center line. Now, start pulling back on the yoke. That's called flaring. Further, further." He helped her a little. "Get the nose up. Don't want the nose-wheel to touch first."

Holly pulled back on the yoke, steering desperately with her feet to keep on the center line. The main wheels touched down with a little squeak.

"Now ease the yoke forward."

She did so, and the nosewheel touched down.

"Excellent landing. Now steer with your feet. Use your toes for brakes, and make the first right turn and follow the yellow line to the flying club."

Holly taxied to the club and parked the airplane where Jackson indicated. "Did I really land the thing all by myself?"

"All by yourself. Fun, huh?"

"A *lot* of fun. I want to learn how to do this."

"Doris will be so pleased. Either she or her boyfriend, Fred, will be delighted to sign you up as a student."

They got out of the airplane, tied it down and went inside.

Doris looked up. "I had a phone call about you," she said.

"Who was it?"

"Wouldn't give a name. I hung up on him."

"Good girl. Don't worry, I don't think they'll be reporting me to the FAA."

The phone in Holly's bag rang, and she dug it out. "Chief Barker."

"It's Jimmy, Chief. We've stopped three white Ford pickups, none of them with a single male occupant."

"Did you take names and license numbers?"

"Sure did."

"I'll check them tomorrow," she said. "I think you can cancel the alert now."

"Yes, ma'am."

She hung up. "Nothing," she said.

"We better get back to the house," Jackson said. "It's unlocked."

"You know," Holly said as they got into the car, "there may be something to what you said about flying as a seduction tool."

"Yeah," Jackson replied, "I think I can feel it working."

"You, too? Let's get home. Daisy can stay with Ham tonight."

34

The middle of the following week, Holly had her job interview with the city council. She was ushered into the meeting room and reintroduced to all the councilmen, which was unnecessary, since she had long since learned their names.

John Westover did the initial talking. "I don't believe you've met Ted Michaels, our city manager," he said, indicating a chubby man in his middle thirties sitting at the end of the table.

Holly shook his hand. "Good to meet you, Ted."

"Sorry I haven't been in to introduce myself, but I've been on vacation," Michaels said.

"Ted doesn't have a vote in these proceedings, but we respect his opinion, and we're glad to have it," Westover said. "Now, Holly, we've received a number of applications, and we've interviewed three other people for the job of chief, including Hurd Wallace and two out-of-towners. You will be our final interviewee before we make a decision on who to hire. Hurd Wallace has told us that, if he is hired as chief, he will retain you as deputy chief. Should we give him the job, would you stay on in that capacity?"

This was a question Holly had not been expecting. "John, I don't think I can give you an answer to that question. I've never discussed that possibility with Hurd, and, of course, I've never worked for him. I suppose I'll just have to cross that bridge if I come to it."

"Fair enough," Westover said. "Now let me present the other side of the coin: if we hire you as chief, will you retain Hurd Wallace as your deputy?"

This one Holly had been expecting. "John, since I've been on the job, Hurd has conducted himself properly and has shown himself to be a competent police officer. I haven't decided if I would need a deputy chief—Chet Marley operated without one for years—but if I decide that I do, Hurd would certainly be a prominent candidate for the job."

"Would you agree that, since you are new in Orchid Beach, it might be very useful to have a deputy who knew the town well, as opposed to an outsider?"

"I think that any chief of police would be well advised to promote from within whenever someone within is well qualified."

"I seem to be having trouble getting a commitment from you on this, Holly."

"If I am named chief, I expect to have the authority to hire and fire all the personnel under my command, within budget constraints. Chet Marley had that authority, and I don't think I would accept the job under conditions that were less favorable than those in Chet's contract, except that I would not expect to begin the job at Chet's most recent salary."

Charlie Peterson interrupted. "Hurd made more or less the same statement in his interview, I believe."

"Yes," Westover muttered. "Tell me, do you anticipate that you would make any changes in the department, if you were hired?"

"Very few," Holly said. "I have noticed that there are only five women including me among thirty-six officers, and I think the balance might be somewhat redressed, given female applicants with the proper qualifications."

"Are you suggesting using affirmative action guidelines?" Frank Hessian asked.

"No. In a field of applicants I would hire the best person. If I had two equally qualified candidates and one was female, I would tend to hire the female, for purposes of balance."

Everybody thought about that for a minute, and no one objected.

"Anyone else have any questions?" Westover asked.

"Under what circumstances would you fire an officer?" Howard Goldman asked.

"For cause," Holly said, "to include criminal activity, brutality with suspects or members of the public, consorting with criminals, a pattern of spousal abuse, abuse of authority, and, of course, incompetence. There might well be other reasons."

"Would you have any hesitation to arrest one of your own officers who had committed a crime?"

"None whatever. I believe that police officers have a special obligation to behave within the law."

"Good," Goldman said

Frank Hessian spoke up. "Would you oppose unionization of your department?"

"I would do everything I could, within my budget, to make a union unnecessary. If officers are decently paid and well treated, and ours are, I don't think the question will arise. In general, I would prefer to deal with individuals instead of a union, particularly in a department of our size."

There was a brief silence, then Irma Taggert spoke up. "Do you think the personal behavior of a police officer should be above reproach?"

A little warning bell rang inside Holly's head. "That goes without saying," Holly replied. Taggert was about to continue, but Holly interrupted her. "Of course, there is a very wide range of opinion as to what constitutes behavior worthy of reproach. Generally speaking, I would adhere to the same standard that I would require of the officers under my command, as I mentioned earlier, in answer to Howard's question."

Irma Taggert pressed on. "Do you feel that it is proper for a female police officer to publicly consort with a man?"

Holly frowned. "Is there a dictionary available?"

Ted Michaels went to a bookcase, found a dictionary and handed it to Holly.

Holly looked up the word. "'Consort: Keep company; associate; harmonize.'" She looked up at Taggert. "Yes, I do think it is proper."

"That's not exactly what I had in mind," Taggert said.

"What, exactly, did you have in mind, Irma? And please be direct." Holly smiled a little.

"I mean that it has come to our . . . my attention that you, an unmarried woman, are living with a man."

"I live with a dog named Daisy," Holly said.

"All right, sleeping at his house from time to time."

Charlie Peterson spoke up. "Now wait a minute, Irma . . . "

Holly held up a hand. "It's all right, Charlie. Irma, I will tell you that I am a grown woman, and I conduct myself by my own ideas of proper behavior, ideas formed in a happy home with good parents and in the Baptist Church, with which I do not always agree. Unless you wish to make a formal charge of misconduct, that is all I have to say on that subject."

Taggert was about to reply, but Charlie Peterson would not be stopped this time. "Irma, your comments are improper and irrelevant to these proceedings," he said. "Unless you have relevant questions to ask, it's time for you to be quiet."

Taggert clamped her jaw shut and turned red.

John Westover spoke up again. "Holly, are you aware that there is a city ordinance against landing an aircraft on our beaches?"

"I am aware of that, John. I think you may be referring to such a landing last Sunday afternoon."

"I am."

"The landing took place about a mile outside the city limits."

"Oh," Westover said, glaring at Irma Taggert.

"I was flying just off the beach at low altitude with a friend at the controls when I observed what appeared to be a burglary in progress. We landed on the beach and investigated, rousting the burglar, who fled in a white truck. I called in a bulletin on the truck, then we took off from the beach and searched further for the vehicle from the air. As it turned out, there were too many white trucks in town for the search to be successful."

"I understand," Westover said. "I'm sorry, I didn't mean to criticize."

"Thank you, John. I should tell you that I was sufficiently impressed with the aerial search experience to think that, at some time in the future, it might be a good idea to investigate the possibility of having a police aircraft, if the need exists, and if such a program could be cost effective."

"Interesting idea," Charlie Peterson said. "I have a question, Holly. What do you think of Orchid Beach and your department so far?"

"I think Orchid Beach is an extraordinarily good place to live and work, and I think that the department I have joined is extremely well organized and trained. My father has retired from the army and has come to live here, and that gives me a family again, which I had begun to miss. I want very much to continue in the chief's job, and I hope for your favorable action on my application."

"Thank you, Holly," John Westover said. "I think that concludes the interview. We expect to make an early decision, and we'll be in touch."

"Thank you, John. Thank you all." Holly stood up and left. Alone in the hallway, she stopped and leaned against a wall for support. Her heart was thumping, and she had begun to perspire.

35

Holly was sitting at her desk half an hour later when she looked up and saw John Westover and Charlie Peterson enter the squad room and walk toward her office. They'd made a decision, she thought. The two men stopped a dozen feet from her door, talked for a minute, then separated. John Westover went down the hall toward Hurd Wallace's office, and Charlie Peterson headed for her door. Uh-oh, she said to herself, the chairman of the council is going to see Hurd, and Charlie is going to break the news to me. This doesn't look good. She waved Peterson into her office.

Peterson took a chair. "Well, Holly," he said, "we've spent the last hour rehashing all the applicants, reviewing qualifications and discussing the interviews. As John said, it came down to you or Hurd Wallace. John is in Hurd's office, now, to tell him of our decision."

Holly took a deep breath and said nothing. In the moment that passed, she decided to resign from the department rather than work for Wallace, and she realized that she had not given a thought to what she would do afterwards. Maybe she'd go to law school.

"The discussion was . . . vigorous," Charlie said. "Ted Michaels weighed in at some length with his opinion, and it was clear that we were divided. Frank Hessian was the swing vote, and I think what bore the most weight with him was the opinion that Chet Marley had, in effect, expressed when he hired you."

Holly let out the breath in a whoosh.

"The job is yours, and on your terms. There's a twenty percent salary hike, and you'll have the same insurance and retirement benefits that Chet Marley had. In essence, we'll present his contract to you for signing, with only the salary changed."

"Thank you, Charlie," Holly breathed, trying to quiet her heart. "I'm grateful to all of you. It's a great vote of confidence."

"It was not a unanimous vote of confidence, I'm afraid. I think you probably guessed that Irma Taggert was going to vote against you, and after considerable hemming and hawing, John Westover voted for Hurd, too, though he said he was very impressed with you. John and I thought it would be best that he tell Hurd of our decision."

"I understand," Holly said.

"One more thing," Peterson said. "While your contract gives you the authority to hire and fire, we voted unanimously that the offer of the contract be made conditional on your accepting Hurd Wallace as deputy chief, on terms identical to your present contract, and with immediate effect."

"Is John telling Hurd that right now?"

"Yes."

"I would have preferred to tell him myself, but I accept the condition," Holly said.

"I'm glad. We all feel that Hurd is a good man, even if he is a little, well, hard to read at times."

"We've gotten along well so far, and I'm sure we'll continue to," Holly said.

Peterson stood up. "Congratulations. We'll have a contract for you to sign before the day is out." They shook hands, and Peterson left.

Holly saw John Westover leave with him, and she got up and went to Hurd Wallace's office and sat down. It was important that she start on the right foot with him.

Wallace looked at her with his usual lack of expression.

Holly wondered if he had been born missing some facial muscles.

"I expect John Westover has told you of the council's decisions," she said.

"Yes, he has," Wallace said tonelessly.

"I want you to know that I'm happy to have you as deputy chief; you've worked hard, and you deserve the job."

"But apparently not the chief's job," Wallace said.

"That was their decision. Can you live with that?"

"Yes, I can."

Holly stood up, took off her deputy chief's badge, removed the smaller badge from her ID wallet and placed them on his desk. She held out her hand. "I look forward to working with you, Hurd."

Wallace stood up and shook her hand. "Thank you," he said. "I'm sure we'll continue to work well together."

Holly went to Jane Grey's office. "Jane, will you type up a notice for the squad room bulletin board that the council has appointed me chief of police and Hurd Wallace deputy chief?"

Jane broke into a broad smile, came around her desk and hugged Holly. "Congratulations," she said. "They did the right thing. Shall I send out a press release?"

"I think that should probably come from John Westover."

"You're right. I'll remind his secretary when I see her in the cafeteria at lunchtime."

"No, don't press it, please."

"As you wish."

Holly went back to her office, opened her desk drawer, took out Chet Marley's chief's badge and pinned it to her uniform, then pinned his smaller badge in her ID wallet. She called Jackson Oxenhandler.

"Hello?"

"Suppose I buy you and Ham a celebratory dinner at the Ocean Grill in Vero Beach tonight?"

"You got the job?"

"I did."

"What about Hurd Wallace?"

"I'll tell you everything tonight."

"See you then."

She hung up and called her father. She was looking forward to giving him the news.

Holly was working at her desk when one of her female officers knocked on her door. "Come in, Sara," she said, "and sit down."

Sara Rodriguez, who was small and dark, perched on the edge of the chair across from Holly. "Congratulations on getting the job as chief," she said.

"Thank you, Sara. What can I do for you?"

"Chief, you know the picture you posted on the bulletin board?"

"Yes."

"I saw the guy this afternoon."

"Where?"

Sara got up and went to the large map of Orchid Beach on Holly's wall. She pointed at a street. "I was driving down this road on patrol, and I turned in right here so that I could turn around. It's the trade entrance to Palmetto Gardens, where deliveries get made and the construction vehicles go in."

"I see. And where was this man?"

"He was in the guardhouse there, wearing a uniform. He tried to chat me up."

"You're sure it was the same man as in the photograph?"

"Yes, ma'am. There could only be one face like that."

"Thank you, Sara. Good job. And keep this to yourself, will you?"

"Yes, ma'am." The young woman got up and left.

Holly went to the bulletin board and took down Cracker Mosely's photograph, then she had an idea. She went into Jane Grey's office. "Jane, there's something I'd like you to do."

"Just name it, Chief."

"I'd like you to find out—if you don't already know—what state agency licenses private security services. Then I'd like you to call them and request a list of all the licensed security guards with Orchid Beach addresses."

"No problem."

"One other thing. Ask them if they license these people to carry firearms, and if they don't, who does? I want a list of everybody who lives at Palmetto Gardens who's licensed to carry a weapon, and who's licensed to carry a concealed weapon, if that requires a special license."

"I'll get right on it," Jane said.

Holly was getting ready to leave for the day when Jane came into her office and handed her three sheets of paper. "Here's everything you asked for," she said, then left.

Holly spread out the papers and looked at them. "Good God," she said aloud.

36

They were shown to a table overlooking the ocean and ordered drinks. Holly contained her news for the moment. When the drinks came, Jackson and Ham raised their glasses.

"To the new chief of police of the Orchid Beach Police Department," Jackson said.

"Hear, hear," Ham echoed, grinning.

"Thank you, gentlemen. I suppose this calls for a speech."

"No, it doesn't," Ham said. He squeezed her hand. "I'm sure proud of you, though."

"Me, too," Jackson said. "Tell us how the interview went."

"It was pretty straightforward until the subject came around to you," Holly said.

"Me?"

"Irma Taggert evidently has a pretty good network of spies around town. She'd nailed you and me as living together, which I denied, and she knew about our landing on the beach on Sunday."

Jackson whistled. "I've underestimated our Irma," he said. "I'll try not to do that again."

"Who's Irma Taggert?" Ham asked.

"A prune who sits on the city council," Jackson replied. "How did you handle her, Holly?"

"I pretty much told her it was none of her business, then Charlie Peterson weighed in and shut her up. She put John Westover up to asking about the airplane and bringing up a city ordinance about not landing on beaches. I told him we were outside the city limits and why we landed. He actually apologized for raising the question and gave Irma a look that fried her makeup."

"Wish I'd been there to see that," Jackson said.

"Charlie came down and told me I had the job by a three-to-two vote, and that they were making Hurd Wallace deputy chief. That's okay. I can live with that."

"So you're home free, then?"

"I'm not going to be home free while Irma Taggert and John Westover are on the council. Why don't you run against one of them next election?"

"Now there's a thought," Jackson said. "I couldn't beat John, but I bet I could beat Irma."

"You're prettier, too," Holly said.

"I'm afraid I can't disagree with you."

"Listen, I have more news. Cracker Mosely has been spotted in Orchid. Guess where?"

"Under a rock?"

"More or less. He's a security guard at Palmetto Gardens."

"I don't know that I'm all that surprised," Jackson said. "After all, he worked for Craig and Noble in Miami. He must have come north with Barney."

"There's more," she said, taking the papers from her purse. "Just on a whim, I asked Jane Grey to get me a list of all the state-licensed security guards in Orchid. There are thirty-seven, and nearly half of them work at Palmetto Gardens. I also asked her to get me a list of everybody licensed to carry a weapon in Orchid. There are nearly three hundred people, and *one hundred and two* of them work at Palmetto Gardens." She handed him the lists.

"Jesus," Jackson said, "they've practically got a private army there, haven't they?" He was looking at the lists. "Uh-oh," he said.

"What?"

"This list of the security guards at Palmetto Gardens—sixteen of them, counting Barney."

"What about them?"

He tapped his finger down the list. "I know four of them besides Cracker and Barney. They were all kicked off the Miami police force because of felony convictions, three of them in the same racial beating. All four of them did time."

"That means their police records have been doctored, like Cracker's, or they wouldn't have been licensed by the state."

"And those are just the ones I know," Barney said, checking off their names. "God knows how many of them I *don't* know. Wait a minute, I recognize another name: Eduardo Flores. He was on the Tampa force and was convicted of assaulting a series of motorists he'd stopped for traffic violations. It was a famous case six or seven years ago."

"So that's half Barney's security force who are convicted felons."

"And all of them convicted of *violent* crimes."

"I'd be willing to bet the rest have records, too, records that have been scrubbed."

"I wouldn't take that bet," Jackson said. He handed Holly back the lists. "You should take this to the state attorney general's office tomorrow. Blow it wide open."

Holly shook her head. "Not yet. There's a reason that people like this are carrying guns around that place, and I'm going to find out what it is. I'll bet it's bigger than falsifying state records; otherwise, why wouldn't Barney just hire guys who were clean? Why go to all the trouble and risk of altering records?"

"Let's look at the menus," Jackson said. "Here comes our waitress."

They sat drinking coffee over the remains of their dessert.

"All right, let's go through what we know so far about Palmetto Gardens," Holly said. "One, the place is sealed off. They don't want the locals taking Sunday drives through the place. Two, at least half the security force are convicted felons, and there must be a reason. Three, the club members are solicited privately, not by the usual advertising that sells lots and houses in ritzy developments. What are the membership requirements, besides great wealth? And four, if they don't want anybody visiting the place, what are they hiding? Is there something there that, if seen by outsiders, would tip them to something unusual going on?"

"Well, on our brief overflight, we did see that building with all the antennas. They must have some extraordinary communications equipment. I mean, they're not just trying to get good TV reception with that really big dish."

"You know, I'd really like to fly over there again," Holly said.

"I've got a better idea," Jackson said. "I know a guy who does aerial mapping. He's got a big, slow airplane with a camera in the belly that takes overlapping landscape photographs. You must have seen that one at the municipal building of the whole island?"

"I thought that was taken by satellite," Holly said.

"No, he took that series, and since he flies low, he can get as much detail as a spy satellite can. Two or three passes over the place, and we'd have some really nice snapshots."

"Jackson, if you'll spring for that, I'll get you reimbursed from departmental funds, if we find something. How much will it cost?"

"I'm not sure, but certainly not more than a couple of grand. I'll tell him I've got a client who's interested in building a similar development. He'll buy that."

"Listen," Ham said, "I'll spring for the money. I'm flush."

"You're on, Ham," Holly said.

"I know a guy at the FBI office in Miami," Jackson said. "He's in charge of the organized-crime division in the city. You want to get him involved?"

"Let's wait until we know more. I don't want him to think I'm crazy."

"Okay, let me know when."

"What we really need is somebody on the inside at Palmetto Gardens," Holly said. "Somebody who's in and out of there all the time, who could look around without calling attention to himself."

Jackson thought about that. "I don't know anybody," he said.

"There must be at least *some* locals who deal with those people. They can't *completely* cut themselves off from the outside."

"You wouldn't think so, would you?"

Ham spoke up. "I got an idea," he said. "Why don't I call Barney and tell him I'm looking for a job, that I'm bored with retirement."

"Yeah, sure," Holly said. "He's going to hire the father of the chief of police? If there's something illegal going on there, you'd be the last person he'd hire."

"Well, maybe that would tell us something—if he wouldn't hire me, I mean."

"Ham, I appreciate the thought, but let's just assume that he wouldn't hire you, all right? If you called him, he'd just think I'd put you up to it. It's important that Barney doesn't think we're too interested in the place."

"I see your point," Ham said. "I wish there was *something* I could do to help."

"If I can think of anything, I'll let you know," Holly said. "Really, I will." Like hell I will, she thought.

"Like hell you will," Ham said.

37

Holly stood in the entrance hall of the municipal building, just outside the doors of her department, and looked at the large aerial photograph of Orchid Beach. She reckoned it must be many years old, because Palmetto Gardens simply did not exist. Prominent properties and developments were labeled, but the only thing named on what was now the development was a road that ran from the northern end of the island to just where Palmetto Gardens now stood. The road was called Jungle Trail.

Holly went upstairs to the county planning commission and introduced herself to the director, a woman named Jean Silver. "What I'm looking for," she said, "is a map that shows the current state of development on the north end of the barrier island."

"That's easy," the woman said, going to a wide drawer and extracting a map.

"Can I borrow this?" Holly asked, looking at the large sheet of paper.

"You can have that copy," Silver replied. "Interdepartmental courtesy."

"Thank you very much." Holly went back to her office, closed the door and spread out the map. Apparently, Palmetto Gardens didn't exist for the planning commission, either: it was shown as nothing more than an empty parcel of land, whereas other developments had maps of roads and lot divisions. She picked up the phone and called Jean Silver.

"Yes?"

"Jean, it's Holly Barker."

"What can I do for you, Holly?"

"I was just looking at the map you gave me, and I noticed that, with all the north-end developments, streets and lots are outlined."

"That's right. We include everything in developments where the city or county has built roads or installed sewer and water lines."

"I notice that one place, Palmetto Gardens, is shown as just an empty space."

"That's correct. It's a completely private development, which has made no demands for city services. In fact, they petitioned, early on, to have the whole of their acreage removed from the city limits, but the city council didn't buy it because of the tax situation. If they'd been outside the city limits, they wouldn't be paying property taxes, which, I suppose, was their intent. They also petitioned to be removed from the oversight of this department for planning purposes, and the council gave them that. That's why there are no roads or lots marked on the map; they built their own. It's officially none of our business what they do out there."

"I see there's a road called Jungle Trail along the river."

"Right. It starts up at the north end of the island next to the Sebastian Inlet and runs nearly all the way to the south bridge. I think that when the council cut Palmetto Gardens out of the planning authority's jurisdiction, they didn't realize they were giving them the right to close that part of the road on their property to outsiders. There was a lot of anger about it, because that road was practically a city park, and, in fact, the rest of it has now been given that status, even though it crosses a lot of private property. Jungle Trail is a big favorite with bike riders and hikers."

"I see. Thanks for the information. 'Bye." Holly hung up.

There was a knock on her door.

"Come in."

Jane Grey stuck her head in. "The telephone man is here to put in your private line," she said.

"Oh, good, tell him to come ahead." Holly had ordered the line at her own expense, because she felt uncomfortable talking to Jackson over departmental lines.

A man wearing a tool belt and carrying a telephone came in. "Hi, I'm Al," he said, and went to work.

Holly was still looking at the map. "Al," she said, "did you ever do any work on the phones out at Palmetto Gardens?"

"I worked on putting in their basic service a long time ago," he said.

"What do you mean by basic service?"

"Well, it's like when you do an office building: you run in the lines they've ordered to a central box, then they complete the installation. They'll buy a phone system from somebody like Lucent or Panasonic, and the supplier's people will run all the lines and extensions."

"And that's what you did at Palmetto Gardens?"

"Well, yeah, but it was pretty elaborate. They ordered something like two thousand lines."

"That many?"

"Well, you figure they have a few hundred houses, and what with fax machines and computers they might have, say, four lines each. Then you've got all the common lines—the clubhouse, shops, maintenance, security, all that. It adds up. In the case of Palmetto Gardens, the company had to open a new prefix, just for them. Nobody had ever asked for two thousand lines before. It's like they built a small town, from scratch." He screwed something together and placed the new phone on her desk. "There you are. All hooked up."

"Thanks, Al."

He went on his way.

Holly called Jackson. "Okay, I've got a private line." She gave him the number.

"Does this mean I can talk dirty on the phone now?"

"Certainly not, you pervert."

"Then what's the point of having a private line?"

"Oh, all right, you can talk dirty."

"Wish I could, but I'm due in court," he said.

"Promises, promises. See you tonight."

"Oh, I talked to my buddy at the airport. He's shooting our pictures today, and for only twelve hundred bucks."

"A bargain. See you tonight." She hung up, called Ham and gave him the number. "How's Daisy?"

"She's okay. I think she misses you, though."

"I'll come out there and get her later this afternoon," Holly said.

"Maybe I'll get a dog of my own."

"Good idea."

"This one is kind of spooky."

"How so?"

"Well, she brought me a beer yesterday."

"She does that. You just say, 'Daisy, bring me a beer.'"

"I didn't say anything, she just did it."

"Maybe you looked thirsty."

"Probably."

"See you later." Holly hung up and looked at the map again. Maybe it was time she saw Jungle Trail.

38

Holly drove out A1A to Sebastian Inlet, and took a left on an unpaved road marked JUNGLE TRAIL. The road ran along the northern end of the island for a mile or so, then curved south along the shores of the Indian River. Soon the river was obscured by heavy foliage; the road wasn't called Jungle Trail for nothing.

She drove slowly down the dirt lane, occasionally passing a jogger or someone on a bike. There were sometimes views of the river, or, looking east, pasture land or citrus groves. She crossed small bridges over creeks leading to the river. She passed a number of developments to her left and an occasional golf course or stable. The air was warm and muggy, with any breeze captured by the trees. Then, after several miles, she drove around a sharp bend and came hard up against a high chain-link gate. A large sign read:

PALMETTO GARDENS
PRIVATE PROPERTY
STRICTLY NO TRESPASSING
ARMED RESPONSE!!!

She got out and looked. The gate was set into a ten-foot chain-link fence, and along its top was a double roll of not ordinary barbed wire, but razor wire. She peered through the fence and saw, perhaps a dozen feet away, another, equally high fence, trimmed in the razor wire, and this fence had signs saying DANGER—HIGH VOLT-AGE. The ground between the fences had been denuded of vegetation and run over with what appeared to be a shallow harrow, leaving long, unbroken grooves in the dirt. Whoever breached the first fence faced electrocution at the second, and if he chickened out between the two, he would leave sharply defined footprints behind for some passing security officer to see.

Holly walked along the fence toward the river, but gradually, the vegetation made progress difficult, then impossible. The double fence went as far as she could see. She went back to the car and looked at the planning commission map. Jungle Trail ran through Palmetto Gardens and out the other side; she assumed that an identical fence closed off the south side, as well. There was nowhere to go but back, so she turned around and drove north on the trail. Back on A1A, she took the north bridge to Egret Island and Ham's new house.

She picked up the microphone of the police radio she had had installed and called dispatch.

"Yes, Chief?"

"I'm done for the day. You can reach me on my cell phone."

"Roger, Chief. There was a message for you."

"Shoot."

"Call Jackson."

"Thanks, over and out."

She dialed Jackson's office number on her car phone.

"Oxenhandler."

"Hey, it's me."

"Hi. I'm going to have the photographs in an hour or so. He's dropping them off at the office."

"Why don't you bring them out to Ham's?"

"Okay. What time?"

"Whenever you finish work. Bring some steaks, too, and a decent bottle of wine. All Ham ever has is beer and bourbon."

"Will do."

As Holly drove up to Ham's house, Daisy bounded out to meet her, making yelping noises and laying her head onto Holly's body, which was Daisy's version of a hug. Holly knelt next to her and let the dog lick her face. "Hi, there, girl," she cooed. "Yes, I'm glad to see you, too." Daisy had spent several days with Ham.

Ham came out of the house. "That dog has really missed you," he said.

"I've missed her, too."

"I guess you two have really bonded. She wasn't exactly unhappy with me, but it always seemed like there was something I was supposed to do or say that I wasn't doing or saying."

"I won't leave her for so long again," Holly said, rubbing the dog's flanks and accepting the outpouring of affection. "Got a beer in there?"

"Sure, come on in."

"Jackson is coming over and bringing some steaks; I hope that's all right."

"Sure, I'll be glad to see him." Ham got them both a beer from the fridge. "You know, I haven't spent this much time alone for a long, long time—maybe never—and I'm really enjoying it. All I've done is read and watch sports on the satellite."

"That's all you ever did anyway, isn't it?"

"Well, I worked, didn't I? You forget I was in the army?"

"Why haven't you played golf?"

"I haven't had anybody to play with. You and Jackson have been so busy."

"I'll play with you this weekend, then."

They sat down and watched Tiger Woods sink a forty-foot putt on TV.

"Holy shit," Ham said.

Jackson arrived at half past six, loaded with groceries and a cardboard tube. "I'm starving," he said. "Can we eat before we do anything else?"

Ham warmed up the grill and put on the steaks Jackson had brought.

"Oh, Ham," Jackson said, "I've got something for you." He handed Ham a sheet of paper. "It's your application for the Dunes Country Club. The committee meets later this week, so fill it out and I'll get it over there tomorrow."

"That's fast work," Ham said, finding a pen and going to work on the form.

"Glad to do it."

They finished dinner and cleared the table, then Jackson opened the cardboard tube he had brought. "Get me some transparent tape and some thumbtacks," he said. He pinned rolls of photographic paper to the dining table and taped the seams. "Okay," he said, "there you have it: Palmetto Gardens."

Holly pointed to where Jungle Trail met the fence. "I was here this afternoon," she said. "There's a double fence here with a plowed strip in between and signs about high voltage." She pointed elsewhere on the photographs. "Look, it goes all the way around. In front, the wire is obscured by the high hedges."

"Here's the building with all the antennas," Jackson said, pointing.

"What are these buildings here?" Holly asked, pointing to a series of parallel structures.

"Looks like housing of some sort—for staff, maybe."

"You think all the employees live on the place?"

"I don't know, but I've never met anybody who worked there, so maybe."

"What do you suppose they do for R and R?" Ham asked.

"They've got an airfield. Maybe they fly them to Disney World or something," Jackson offered.

"Hey, look at this," Ham said, pointing.

"Looks like vegetation," Holly said.

"That's not vegetation, it's camouflage netting."

"Are you sure?" Holly asked, peering at it.

"You think I've never see that stuff? I lived under it for two years, in 'Nam. I've seen a lot of it in photographs, too. Look, here's another patch, and another." There were half a dozen patches, scattered over the area, and two more near the airfield.

"What would they be covering up with camouflage netting?" Holly asked.

"Antiaircraft-gun emplacements?" Ham offered. "Ground-to-air missiles?"

"Come on, Ham, we're not in Vietnam. It must be something else."

"What else would you need to hide from overflights?" Ham asked. "That netting doesn't work if you're on the ground, you know."

Jackson spoke up. "Does it strike anybody that this place looks more like a military installation than anything else?"

"Yeah," Ham said. "I mean, there's lots of big houses and the golf courses, but if you don't count those, it looks military to me."

"Look," Jackson said, pointing. "Radar at the airfield. Orchid Beach Airport doesn't have radar."

"Ham," Holly said, "if you had to take Palmetto Gardens, how would you do it?"

Ham looked at the photographs again for a moment. "I'd chopper in a regiment of airborne, take the airfield and overwhelm the rest of the place in a hurry."

"How would you do it if you were the cops, instead of the military?"

Ham shook his head. "I wouldn't," he said.

39

Holly started the next day by asking Jane Grey to run all the employees of Palmetto Gardens who were licensed to carry firearms through the state's criminal records section.

A couple of hours later, Jane came into her office. "Not one of them had anything on his record more serious than a juvenile offense or a speeding ticket," she said.

To Holly, that meant one of two things: either they had screened every applicant for a record and discarded those who had one, or they had cleaned up the records of some of their employees. There was no way to judge, from the state's records, which was the case. And, if they had done some record scrubbing, there was no way to determine for which employees, except the five that Jackson knew about. There was another way, though.

"I've got a lot on my plate today, Holly. Is there anything else you need?"

"No, Jane, and thanks. You get back to work."

Holly turned to her computer and logged on to the national crime computer, in Washington. One by one, she entered the names from the list she had run through the state computer, printing out individual files. It took her a couple of hours, but when she was done, she was astonished at the results.

Holly picked up her private line and called Jackson. "Can we meet at Ham's?" she asked.

"What's up? Why don't we go to my house?"

"Just meet me there as soon as you can."

"I'll see you around six."

She called Ham and told him they were coming.

"You young people sure like it here," Ham said, as Jackson arrived. "Holly's already here."

"What's going on?" Jackson asked her.

"I didn't want to meet at your place or mine, because I thought there was an outside chance that one or both of them had been bugged."

"By whom?"

"I don't know. Maybe I'm just feeling paranoid."

"Tell me about it."

Holly took the stack of criminal records from her briefcase and laid them on the dining table. "This morning I ran all the gun-toting employees of Palmetto Gardens through the state crime computer. They were all clean. This afternoon I ran them through the national crime computer. Of a hundred and two, seventy-one had criminal records, lots of them for serious crimes."

"That many?" Jackson said, sitting down.

"That many."

"And all of them clean with the state?"

"All of them."

"Jesus Christ."

"I guess they couldn't fix the FBI records."

"I guess not," he said.

"I don't know what to do, Jackson," Holly said. "There's something going on at Palmetto Gardens, but I just don't have the resources to figure it out."

"Maybe it's time for the feds," Jackson said.

"Maybe so, but I'd like to feel them out informally, if I can."

"Like I told you, I know an agent in the Miami office; he's in the organized crime division."

"Let's talk to him."

Jackson dug an address book from his pocket, looked up his friend, and looked at his watch. "He's probably on the way home from work. I've got a cell-phone number." He dialed it. "Harry? It's Jackson Oxenhandler. Yeah, pretty good, how about you? Listen, Harry, can you call me right back from a land line? Yeah, here's the number." Jackson gave it to him and hung up.

"What's his name?" Holly asked.

"Harry Crisp. He'll call us back soon. If you're worried about bugging, I thought a land line would be better."

"What are you . . ." The phone interrupted her.

Jackson picked it up. "Thanks, Harry. Listen, I'm in Orchid Beach with the local chief of police, a lady named Holly Barker. She's stumbled onto something extraordinary that I think you ought to know about, and I don't think we should talk about it on the phone. Could she and I come to Miami to see you? Where? What are you doing there? Well, great. Yeah, I'm buying, and I'll put you up for the night. You got a pencil? I'll give you directions." He dictated directions from A1A. "See you later." Jackson hung up. "He was at a filling in Fort Pierce, less than an hour away. He's coming up here for dinner."

"Great," Holly said.

"I'll make some spaghetti," Ham said, and headed for the kitchen.

Jackson looked at Holly. "What's the matter? You look worried."

"I just hope I'm not making an ass of myself," Holly said.

40

Harry Crisp looked less like an FBI agent than Holly had imagined. He was fairly tall and skinny, and wore horn-rimmed glasses. She thought he looked more like a bank loan officer than a lawman. He shook everybody's hand and sat down to dinner, declining wine.

"So what's up, Jackson?" he asked, twirling spaghetti on his fork. "What's so mysterious we needed a land line?"

"We're just being careful, Harry," Jackson said. "Holly is beginning to worry that there might be bugs at both our houses, and . . . well, maybe we're just paranoid."

"Paranoid about what?"

"Holly, you tell him."

Holly put down her fork. "Orchid Beach has a lot of upscale residential developments—houses, tennis courts, golf courses, polo, the works."

"I'm familiar with the type of thing," Crisp said.

"We've got one that's unusual."

"How so?" Crisp asked, munching.

"Well, it's on a good fifteen hundred acres, but it's only got a couple of hundred houses, and it appears to be already fairly fully developed."

"Sounds expensive," Crisp said.

"Extremely," Holly replied. "It's also got three eighteen-hole golf courses and its own six-thousand-foot airfield."

"For two hundred households?" Crisp asked.

"That's it. And the airfield gets a lot of international traffic. They have some sort of deal with customs and immigration to clear arrivals on the spot."

"A *private* airport of entry? I've never heard of anything like that."

"Neither have I," Jackson said.

"Tell me more."

"The place is surrounded by a ten-foot-high double fence with razor wire on top, and the inner fence is electrified."

"Security conscious, huh?"

Ham spoke up. "We tried to get a look at their marina the other day, and they threatened us with automatic weapons and threw us out in a hurry."

"Touchy."

"You could say that."

"There's more," Holly said. "The place is nearly completely cut off from any local services, except maybe the food supply. It has an electricity generating plant, its own water and sewage system, and the houses were built by labor imported from somewhere else. Only the basic infrastructure was built by locals."

Crisp finished his dinner and pushed his plate away. "What else?"

Ham got up and started clearing the table.

"The employees seem all to live on the grounds," Jackson said. "No locals were hired. We estimate there's housing for four hundred employees."

"They've got two thousand telephone lines and a communications center you won't believe," Holly said, bringing out the aerial photographs and spreading them out on the table.

"How the hell did you get this?" Crisp asked. "This looks like a sat-shot."

"Old-fashioned aerial photography," Jackson replied. "Friend of mine does it for a living."

Holly pointed out the building with the antennae.

"Anybody got a magnifying glass?" Crisp asked.

Holly found one on Ham's desk and handed it to him.

Crisp peered closely at the communications equipment. "I'll tell you something," he said. "This is more stuff than the bureau has on its roof in Miami."

"Check this out," Holly said, pointing at place after place. "We think this is all camouflage netting."

"Covering what?"

"Use your imagination."

"That's asking a lot of an FBI man," Jackson said.

"I'll do my best," Crisp said. "Okay, I give up. What could be under there?"

"Ham is ex-army. He says maybe antiaircraft guns or even ground-to-air missiles."

"Whoa," Crisp said. "Let's try to keep both feet on the ground, here."

"Harry," Jackson said, "everything about this place defies the imagination."

"Yeah," Holly said. "State licensing records show that a hundred and two employees, including a security force of fifteen, have licenses to carry weapons."

"That's a lot," Crisp said.

"Jackson recognized five of the names on the security force as having criminal records, but when we checked the state computer, they were all showing as clean."

"Everybody makes mistakes," Crisp said.

"There's more," Holly said. "Today, I ran all one hundred and two gun-toters through the state computer, and they all came up clean. Then I ran the same names through your national computer, and seventy-one of them turned up with convictions ranging over most of the spectrum of criminal activity." She placed the files on the table.

Crisp looked at a few of them, then looked up at Holly. "That's unbelievable," he said. "You've got a very serious problem at the state level. Have you reported this to Tallahassee?"

"No, only the three of us know about what we've told you."

"Thank God for that," Crisp said. "For Christ's sake, don't tell anybody else."

"Don't worry," Holly replied.

"Is there anything else you want to tell me?"

"Ham knew the Palmetto Gardens head of security in the army. His name is Barney Noble."

"I know that name. Doesn't he have a security company in Miami?"

"Right," Jackson replied, "Craig and Noble. I think all the security guards have come out of there."

"And they're armed to the teeth," Holly said. "I've seen assault rifles, and a lot of the regular support staff—waiters, groundskeepers and the like—are packing."

"I'm going to have to talk to some of my people about this," Crisp said. "Can I call you at your office, Holly?"

"Not on the regular departmental line," Holly replied. She wrote down her private number. "On this line."

"Are you worried about somebody in your department?"

"Yes. My predecessor, Chet Marley, thought somebody was dealing with somebody outside, but I never found out who or what. He was shot the night I arrived in town, along with a friend of his that he might have told about this. They're both dead."

"And you think this is connected to Palmetto Gardens?"

"I can't prove it. What do you think is going on here, Harry?"

"Well, it's highly suspicious, of course, to have what amounts to a private army to protect two hundred houses and a golf course, but that's probably not criminal."

"Altering the state's criminal records is," Jackson said.

"It's certainly probable cause for me to get involved," Harry replied. "It was a very smart move, Holly, to run those records and compare them with the national computer. If you hadn't done that, I'd probably have to tell you to call me when somebody at Palmetto Gardens commits a crime."

"What can you do with what we've got, Harry?"

"If I bring half a dozen people up here, is there somewhere we can all meet without attracting attention?"

"My house," Jackson said, "but bring somebody who can sweep it for bugs." He drew Crisp a map.

Crisp looked at his watch. "I'm going to drive back to Miami tonight and try to set up a meeting with my agent in charge tomorrow morning. Is there an airport here?"

"Yeah," Jackson said, "but I don't think you want a lot of suits getting off a big airplane out there. Be inconspicuous."

"Thanks, Jackson," Crisp said sarcastically. "I'll try to keep that in mind. Holly, can I have these photographs and records?"

"Sure, but I'll want them back."

"I'll have copies made and return the originals," he said. He stood up. "I've got a long drive, and I've got to pick up my stuff from a motel in Fort Pierce. I'd better get going."

"Thanks for coming," Holly said. "I feel like I'm in over my head, here, and I could sure use some help figuring this thing out."

"I think I can get you what you need, Holly," Crisp said.

"And try not to get her killed while you're doing it," Jackson said.

"Jackson, your overwhelming confidence in your government never ceases to amaze me," Crisp replied, gathering up the photographs and records.

Jackson laughed aloud.

"Be seeing you," Harry Crisp said, then left.

41

Holly had begun going through the departmental personnel files, something she had been putting off. She wanted to read up on the backgrounds of all her people to get a mental picture of who everybody was. She started with Hurd Wallace's file.

Hurd had been born in Orlando, had attended Florida State, majoring in business, had served a hitch in the Marine Corps and had joined the Orlando force after his discharge. Three years before, Chet Marley had hired him as a sergeant, then promoted him to lieutenant two years after that. She was wondering why Chet had hired him, promoted him, then came to distrust him. He had expressed annoyance about Hurd's having political connections, and she assumed that meant John Westover. Her intercom line rang.

"Yes?"

"Chief, there's a Mr. Barney Noble to see you."

Holly looked through her glass wall and across the squad room to the front desk. Noble was standing there, in civilian clothes, gazing at her. "Send him in," Holly said, wondering what the hell this was about.

Barney ambled in, shook her hand and took a seat. "So, Holly, how's the new job going?"

"It's going okay, Barney," she said, smiling. "Right now, I'm pretty much just plowing through paperwork. I expect you know about that."

"Part of the job, I guess."

"How are things out at Palmetto Gardens?" she asked.

"Humming along," he replied. "I had kind of a surprise this morning, though."

"What was that?"

"Friend of mine up in Tallahassee called and said that the Orchid Beach PD had requested a criminal records check on over a hundred of our employees. What was that all about?" He was looking serious now.

"Just a routine thing," Holly replied. She was glad he didn't know she had run his people though the national computer as well.

"C'mon, Holly, don't hand me that. What the hell are you looking for?" His face had turned pink.

"Take it easy, Barney, and I'll explain." She was thinking fast now—this had to be good.

"Please do that."

"One of the things I think helps keep the peace is to keep a close watch on firearms in the community. Last week, with that in mind, I requested from the state licensing authority a list of every citizen of Orchid Beach who held a license to carry weapons. I have to tell you, I was *very* surprised to find that of the three hundred or so licensed individuals, a hundred and two of them had addresses at Palmetto Gardens."

"I can explain that," Barney said. He started to, but Holly held up a hand.

"Let me finish. I assumed that there were so many gun-toters out there because of what you had told me about your members liking overkill when it comes to security."

"That's right."

"I accept that; I don't have any problem with that."

"Then why did you run criminal records checks on all those people?"

"Barney, I'm running a criminal records check on every person in Orchid Beach who has a firearms license, to make sure he's entitled to one. Your people just got checked first, that's all."

"Sorry, I don't understand what you hope to accomplish by checking three hundred people like that."

"I'll tell you. I've already discovered eighteen people in town who had felony convictions *after* they got the gun license, and I'm only halfway through the list," she lied. "I'm going to have those licenses pulled and, if I can, confiscate the weapons."

Barney started to speak, but Holly interrupted him again.

"I'm also going to check that, among the people with licenses, *all* their guns are licensed. By the way, you'll be happy to know that none of your people had a conviction of any sort, and they all hold their licenses legally."

Barney seemed to relax a little. "Well, of course they do; I ran checks on all of them when I hired them."

"Good. Now what you might do is to tell them all that I'm going to check out their individual weapons, to make sure they're legal. I'm not having any unlicensed assault weapons or machine guns in my jurisdiction."

"Tell you what," Barney said enthusiastically, "why don't you let me do that for you with my people? I'll check them out individually and make sure everything is kosher."

"Why, thank you, Barney, I'd really appreciate that. You'd be taking care of a third of our work for us."

"No problem, I'm glad to do it," Barney said. "Say, I really enjoyed the golf with you and Ham. How's he doing?"

"He's doing really well," Holly replied. "He's moved into a nice place, and he's reading and watching sports on TV a lot. He's joining a golf club, too."

"That's great news," Barney said. He got to his feet. "Well, I'd better get going."

Holly had an idea. Now that she had reassured him, she wanted to stick a burr under his saddle. "Hang on a minute, Barney," she said. "Sit down. There's something I was going to call you about that's troubled me, and we might as well talk about it now."

"Sure," he said. "What's up?"

"You've got a man on your security force named Mosely, haven't you?"

"Sure, Cracker Mosely. Good man. You got a problem with him? I'd like to know about it, if you have."

"I'm just a little confused," Holly said. "When I ran Mosely through the records check, he was clean."

"Well, sure he was. He's one of mine, and mine are all clean."

Holly thought Noble was looking uncomfortable again.

"The problem is, I've come across some information that your man Mosely did time in state prison for manslaughter one."

"That's news to me," Noble said, flustered.

"I can see how it would be," Holly said, "after I ran him through the computer, and he came up clean. I expect it's just some problem at the state level. Everybody makes mistakes."

"Yeah, I guess so."

"But you see my problem, Barney. If Mosely has a felony conviction, he shouldn't be working as a security guard, and he shouldn't be carrying weapons. I'm going to have to have those licenses."

Suddenly, Barney Noble looked like a cornered rat, and Holly was enjoying it.

"On my desk today, Barney," she said, trying to sound regretful.

Barney seemed unable to speak.

"Or I'll have to come get them," she said.

"I'm sure this is just some kind of mix-up," Barney said.

"I sure hope so, Barney."

"I'm going to check into this right now, and if what you say is true, you'll have the licenses. Can I have until noon tomorrow?"

"Sure, Barney, if you need the time."

"Uh, if I turn in Mosely's licenses, are there going to be any charges against him?"

"I can't really say, Barney, until I've talked to the county attorney. But speaking for myself, I don't see any reason to pursue it. As long as I get the licenses."

Barney stood up.

"And as long as Mosely doesn't carry a gun. I mean, you can put him to work maintaining the golf course, or something, but I wouldn't want to find out he was still working security."

"I'll get back to you," Barney replied.

"I'll walk you out," she said. "I was just going to lunch."

Holly followed him through the squad room and out to the parking lot, where they shook hands and said good-bye. As Barney got into his car, she fired a parting shot. "Oh, Barney," she said sweetly, "I'd like for Mosely to bring in the licenses himself." She didn't wait for a reaction; she smiled and waved as he drove away.

As Barney stopped for traffic on the street, she noticed something she hadn't seen before. On the back of his Palmetto Gardens Range Rover was a small sticker that read WESTOVER MOTORS.

That was very interesting, she thought. She wondered how long it would be before she got a call from John Westover.

42

Holly didn't have to wait long. When she got back from lunch, John Westover was sitting in her office. "Hey, John, how are you?" she asked.

Westover got up and shook her hand, but he didn't look happy. "I'm good, Holly? You?"

"Just fine, thanks." She sat down behind her desk. "To what do I owe the pleasure?"

"Holly, there's something we have to talk about," Westover replied.

"Shoot."

"Let me begin at the beginning."

"All right."

"Some years ago when the Palmetto Gardens people were looking for land here . . . "

"Oh, this is about Palmetto Gardens?"

"Please let me finish."

"Sorry, John, go right ahead."

"When they were looking for land, they came to the council with

214

a number of proposals that sort of set them apart from other developers, things they wanted that other developers never seem to think about."

"What sort of things?"

"Well, at first, they wanted to incorporate as their own town. We explained to them that we wouldn't do that, because that would put them outside our tax base. Then they wanted some other things that were all aimed at making them as separate as possible."

"What sort of things?" Holly asked again, continuing to play dumb. She wanted Westover to have to spell it out.

"For instance, they let us know up front that they weren't going to hire much local labor, that they would be mostly bringing in their own people."

"But that wouldn't be so good for Orchid, would it, John?"

"Normally, no, but the taxes on such a large and expensively developed parcel of land more than made up for that."

"I see, it was the money."

"Well, of course it was the money," Westover said irritably. "That one development accounts for a very healthy percentage of our income from local property taxes."

"I understand, John."

"They even brought in their own construction workers, which didn't sit well with local builders, I can tell you, and there were other things we don't need to go into right now."

"What things?"

"I just said, I don't want to go into all of them now," Westover said heatedly.

"Sorry, go ahead, John."

"Well, the whole thing has worked out brilliantly for Orchid Beach," Westover said.

"Yes, I've seen the Westover Motors stickers on the vehicles from out there."

"Damnit, Holly, I'm not talking about me, I'm talking about the community as a whole, and how we benefit from having them out there."

"How does the community benefit, apart from the tax revenues?" Holly asked.

"In many ways."

"Such as?"

Westover was sweating now. "Holly, you're just going to have to take my word for it."

"I'm glad to do that, John," she replied.

"Now, as I say, the Palmetto Gardens people want to be as separate as possible, and that works very well for the community, too."

"You already said that, John."

"Now I understand that the question of the licensing of a security guard has arisen."

"You spoke to Barney Noble, then?"

"Yes, he called me an hour ago."

"I see. Go on."

"Well, as you might understand, Barney is upset that we're trying to deprive him of one of his valued people, and I really don't think that we should be sticking our noses into his operation out there."

"I see, John. Tell me, did Barney explain to you who this man is and why I have a problem with him?"

"I didn't ask any questions," Westover said quickly, holding up his hands. "It's really not necessary for me to know about it."

"I think you need to know about this individual, John," Holly said, continuing over his protests. "Mr. Elwood Mosely, a.k.a. Cracker Mosely, has a record going back to his teens, when he was convicted of vandalism and cruelty to animals. I don't know if you're aware of this, but you've got to do something *really* cruel to animals to attract the attention of the authorities."

"Holly, I . . . "

"Please listen to me, John. Mr. Mosely joined the Miami Police Department, and soon he was running a protection racket for drug dealers. They'd give him a cut of their take, and Mr. Mosely would spread the money around, keeping some for himself, of course, thus removing these drug dealers from the attention of the police. Then one day one of these dealers failed to give Mr. Mosely his cut, so Mr. Mosely, when he saw the man, jumped out of his police car and, in broad daylight, in front of witnesses, beat the man to death. Mr. Mosely's own partner arrested him, and Mr. Mosely was convicted of manslaughter, a serious crime, and sent to prison."

Westover had turned pale now. He was mopping the sweat from his face with a large handkerchief, but he didn't interrupt.

"Now, John, perhaps you don't know that a convicted felon may not be licensed as a security guard in the state of Florida; neither may he be licensed to carry a weapon. But, because of some anomaly in the state's record keeping, Mr. Mosely now holds both those licenses. This means that a convicted killer is wearing a badge and carrying a gun in our lovely community, and, John"—Holly leaned forward and rested her hands on her desk—*"I'm not going to have it."*

"Oh, Jesus," Westover said, his shoulders slumping.

"So," Holly continued, "I think you'd better call Barney Noble back and tell him that if Mr. Mosely isn't in this office by noon tomorrow to surrender those licences, I'm going to come out to Palmetto Gardens and get him."

"Holly . . . "

"I hope I've made myself perfectly clear on this, John, and if I haven't, then I suggest you call an urgent meeting of the city council, and I'll explain it to them."

"All right, all right," Westover said, defeated. He stood up and walked out of her office without another word, mopping the back of his neck with his handkerchief.

Holly watched him go with some satisfaction. She had known that she was going to butt heads with him eventually, and she was glad that she had been on such solid ground when it had happened.

The private line on her desk rang, and she picked it up. "Holly Barker."

"Holly, it's Harry Crisp."

"Hey, Harry, what's up?"

"You've got the bureau's attention. I'm coming up there with some people later today; we should be at Jackson's place by eight o'clock tonight."

"I'm glad to hear it, Harry," she said. "Are you bringing somebody who can sweep Jackson's house and my trailer for electronic surveillance?"

"I am, and he's very good, believe me."

"I believe you. Do you need any help from me? Do you have someplace to stay?"

"I'm staying at Jackson's, and we've booked the others into various motels around town, so as not to attract attention."

"Harry, I had one other thought."

"Go ahead."

"That communications building. I have a hunch that it's at the heart of whatever is going on out there. Do you know anybody at the National Security Agency?" Holly knew that the agency existed to monitor communications around the world.

"I'm way ahead of you. I've put in a request for analysis of their transmissions, but I don't know whether they're going to give us what we want or even how long it will take to find out if they will or won't."

"Okay, I'll leave the red tape to you."

"Will you call Jackson and tell him we're on the way, and that I expect dinner for six hungry feds?"

"I sure will, and don't worry, he's a wonderful cook."

"Yeah, sure."

"No kidding. See you around eight." Holly hung up the phone with hope in her heart.

43

Holly worked late on the personnel files, then went home, changed, fed Daisy and went to Jackson's house. In addition to Jackson's car there were two gray vans parked outside. Inside, Harry Crisp was talking on Jackson's phone, five young men sat around the living room watching TV and reading magazines, and Jackson was on the back porch, grilling steaks. She gave Harry a wave and went out back.

Jackson flipped over some steaks. "You're just in time," he said. "These guys are hungry, and if I kept them waiting any longer, they'd be eating Daisy."

Daisy looked up at the mention of her name.

"Don't worry, sweetheart, nobody's going to eat you," Holly said.

Daisy sat down and watched the steaks closely, as if they might bolt at any moment.

"How long have they been here?" Holly asked.

"Nearly an hour. Harry has been on the phone for all of that. What with the long-distance charges and the steaks, they're going to break me." Jackson started forking the steaks onto a large platter.

"His guy swept the place and your trailer; I gave him the key. No bugs."

"That's good."

"Let's eat," he said. He walked into the house, showed Harry the food and called everybody to the table.

Harry hung up the phone. "Holly, how are you?"

"Okay, Harry."

"Oh, these are my agents—Bill, Joe, Jim, Ed and Arnie."

"Hey, guys."

Everybody waved; a couple of them shook her hand. They sat down and fell on the food.

Daisy curled up on the rug a few feet away.

"What kind of dog is that?" Bill asked.

"Doberman pinscher, name of Daisy."

"Girl dog?"

"Bitch is the word."

"Funny, she looks very nice. Does she do anything besides sleep?"

"Daisy, get me a beer," Holly said.

Daisy got up, went to the fridge and brought Holly a beer.

"What, she doesn't open it?" Bill asked.

"That's my kind of dog," Arnie said.

"She'll chew your leg off at the hip, too, if she's asked nicely," Holly said.

"Sorry if I said anything to offend you, Daisy," Bill said contritely.

"Anything new since yesterday?" Harry asked.

"Yeah," she replied. "You'll like this, Jackson. I'm pulling Cracker Mosely's security-guard and gun licenses. I told Barney to have them on my desk by noon tomorrow, or I'd come out there and get them."

"Why'd you do that?" Jackson asked.

"He showed up at my office and demanded to know why I was running criminal records checks on his people; he apparently got a call from his contact at the state level. I concocted a story that satisfied him, but he was annoying me, so I built a little fire under Cracker. Then he called John Westover and bitched about it to him, and John came down to my office and asked me to change my mind."

"What'd you say to that?"

"I pretty much told him to go fuck himself. He didn't have a leg to stand on. Did you know that he sells Palmetto Gardens their vehicles, including the Range Rovers?"

"Doesn't surprise me," Jackson said.

"I want to get inside Palmetto Gardens," Harry said.

"Yeah? How you going to do that?" Jackson asked.

"I don't know. I was hoping you and Holly would have a suggestion."

"They don't use any local help that I've been able to learn about," Holly said. "They seem to do all their own maintenence."

"You know anybody who's ever been in there?"

"Yeah, *I* have. Barney Noble gave me a superficial tour of the place, and I played golf out there with him once. I didn't see anything out of the ordinary, except that some of the help were wearing guns under their jackets."

"Tell me about the security you saw when you were there."

"There are two gates, main and service. Both of them have steel barriers and tire spikes that are operated by the guard on duty from his booth. The guards wear sidearms and have assault rifles in their booths. Barney showed me security headquarters, but I didn't go inside. He told me they had a lockup there, said it was like a small-town police station. That's about it."

"What do you think would happen if I went to the front gate, flashed my badge and said that I wanted to look around?"

"You'd be told that it was private property, and Barney would probably come to the gate and tell you you'd need a search warrant. He might give you the same tour he gave me."

"Oh."

"Why would you want him to know the feds were interested?"

"I wouldn't. I'm just exploring possibilities."

Jackson spoke up. "Might be nice to know who the owners are of the airplanes that fly in and out of there."

"Good idea. Could the local tower give us that?"

"I doubt it, since they don't land at Orchid airport," Jackson said. "Air Traffic Control would have the registration numbers from the flight plans in their computer—Miami Center would be the place to call. They could also tell you where the flights originate."

"Jim, you get onto that first thing tomorrow," Harry said.

"Right," Jim replied.

"Bill, you talk to customs and immigration. See if you can interview whoever they send to the Palmetto Gardens airfield when flights come in. I want to know *everything* about the people who're flying in there."

"Right," Bill said.

"I could fly you over the place for a look, if you like," Jackson said.

Harry shook his head. "I don't think I'd see anything that isn't in your aerial photographs. Besides, they've seen two low overflights already; we don't want to make them nervous. Bill, while you're talking to customs, find out if any boats have come into the Palmetto Gardens marina from out of the country."

"Okay," Bill replied.

"Arnie, I want you somewhere near the service gate out there. I want a description of every vehicle that comes and goes—food deliveries, plumbers, whatever."

"Okay," Arnie said.

"What can I do to help, Harry?" Holly asked.

"Well, you can't put any of your people on this," Harry said. "Not while you think you've got a mole in your department."

"Good point. I've got complete freedom of movement myself, though."

"First thing I want to know is does this Mosely guy show up with his licenses," Harry said. "If he doesn't, that'll give you an excuse to go out there with a warrant. Then, if we want to get in there again, we could bust some more of Noble's guys. How many of them showed up in the national computer?"

"All of them," Holly said. "Barney's security force is a regular rogue's gallery."

"That would rattle whoever controls the place," Harry said. "If we bust their whole security force, that would get their attention."

"I could have already done that," Holly said, "but that's not going to tell us what's going on out there."

"Could you check your local records for the names of the owners of the houses at Palmetto Gardens?" Harry asked.

"I can do that," Holly replied

"That might give us a list of the members, then we could do background checks on them."

"Good idea."

"If Mosely comes in tomorrow, I'd like to get a good look at him. Can you arrange that?"

"Sure."

"Without anyone knowing who I am?"

"Sure, I can handle that."

"Suppose you question Mosely about something, anything, and I listen in. Maybe Mosely is a way into that place."

"I've got an idea," Holly said. "Let's do it this way." She outlined the idea that had just come to her. "It might not work, but it wouldn't hurt to try."

44

At eleven o'clock the phone on Holly's desk rang. She let it ring a couple of times, then picked it up and said, "Holly Barker. Hold on a minute, will you?" Then she pressed the hold button. She knew it was Barney Noble, and she wanted him to sweat a little.

"Hello?" she said finally.

"It's Barney."

"Hi, Barney," she said brightly. "Sorry to keep you waiting."

"Mosely will be in your office at eleven-thirty with his licenses," Barney said. "I want your assurance that you won't charge him with anything."

"Barney," Holly said, "I'm not giving you any assurances about anything. I run this department, not you, and if you ever try to go over my head with the city council again, you're going to find out just how hard I can make your life."

"Don't threaten me, Holly."

"I'll threaten you all I like," she said. "How would you like me to have all your people's gun licenses pulled and then come out there and confiscate all your firearms? I can do that, you know, and you can't do a goddamned thing about it."

Barney was suddenly placating. "Now, Holly, let's not get into a pissing match here."

"We won't have any problem, Barney, as long as you understand that *you* are operating in *my* jurisdiction, and not the other way around." She didn't know quite why she was pushing him so hard, but every instinct in her body told her to do it.

"All right, all right," Barney said. "Mosely will be there in half an hour. How long are you going to keep him there?"

"As long as I want to," Holly said, then hung up. She called Harry Crisp's cell phone.

"Yes?" Crisp said.

"Come now."

"Right with you."

Two minutes later Crisp walked into the police station, gave his name and asked for Holly.

Holly's intercom rang. "Put Mr. Crisp into interview two," she said. She hung up and watched as Harry was led down the hallway.

At eleven-thirty, her intercom rang again. "Yes?"

"A Mr. Mosely to see you."

"Put him in interview one," she said. Now she got her first look at Mosely. He was just as big as Jackson had said, and just as ugly. She let him wait ten minutes, then stood up. "Come on, Daisy," she said, "let's you and I interview Cracker Mosely." She picked up a file folder, put the dog on a leash and walked down the hallway toward the interview rooms. She opened the door of number two. Harry Crisp was sitting quietly at the two-way mirror, looking at Mosely. "The volume control is right there, Harry."

"Got it," Crisp replied. "He's mean-looking, isn't he?"

"You bet."

"I'll shoot him through the glass if he gives you a hard time."

"I don't think that will be necessary," Holly said. She opened the door to interview room one and was nearly dragged off her feet by Daisy, who had her front paws on the table, trying to reach Mosely. "Daisy! Back off! Back off!"

It was the first time that Daisy had not obeyed her instantly. It took her the better part of a minute to get the dog calmed down. When she was satisfied that the dog was completely under her control again, she unhooked the leash and took a seat.

Mosely was staring at the dog, fear on his face. "Put him back on the leash," he said. "I don't want to have to kill that dog."

"Tell you the truth, Cracker, my money would be on the dog, and I'd give long odds."

Daisy made a rumbling noise in her throat, imitating Holly's tone.

"Stay, Daisy. Guard!"

Daisy moved from a prone to a sitting position, staring intently at Mosely.

Holly was intrigued by Daisy's reaction to Mosely, but she didn't make a point of it. "Let's have the licenses," she said, without further ado.

Mosely shoved an envelope across the table.

Holly opened it and examined the two pieces of paper; the gun license had been laminated. "Good," she said, looking up at Mosely and smiling a little. "Now all I have to decide is whether to send you back to prison."

Mosely's jaw dropped. "Barney said that wasn't an issue."

"Gee, I don't know where Barney got that idea," Holly said. "As far as I'm concerned you're all mine, if I want you."

"I don't get it," Mosely said. "I applied for the licenses, and they were issued."

"Yeah," Holly said, opening her file folder, "I have copies of your applications right here. Both of them ask the question, 'Have you ever been convicted of any crime?' And your answer, on both applications, was no."

"That's what I was told to put," Mosely said.

"Told by whom?"

Mosely looked away. "A friend advised me."

"Well, Cracker, when Barney advised you to lie on your application, he advised you to commit a felony."

"What?"

Holly shoved the gun application across the desk. "Look right down at the bottom there. It says, 'I swear, under penalty of perjury, that all the statements I have made in this application are true.' Perjury is a serious crime, Cracker; it'll get you five years, easy. And of course, when you perjured yourself, you violated your parole. And you've still got, what, ten, twelve years left on your sentence?"

Mosely's mouth was working. "I want a lawyer," he said.

"Nah, you don't want a lawyer, Cracker. I haven't read you your rights yet, and you were a cop long enough to know that until I read you your rights, whatever you tell me doesn't count."

"What do you want?" Cracker demanded.

"Ah," Holly said. "Now you're getting the picture."

45

Holly sat and waited, staring at Mosely. Daisy made the noise in her throat again, as if urging him to speak. Mosely looked back and forth between Holly and Daisy.

"Tell me," he said. "Tell me what you want to know."

"Everything," Holly replied.

"Everything? What do you mean, everything?"

"Tell me what you do for a living, Cracker."

"I'm a security guard. Well, I was, until today."

"And what did you guard?"

"Palmetto Gardens. It wasn't a big deal. I just kept out intruders, except we didn't really have any."

"How long you been doing this work, Cracker?" she asked.

"Nearly a year."

"What kind of training did you have?"

"Not much. Barney just told me what to do."

"And what did he tell you to do?"

"To guard the place—you know, gate duty, patrol duty."

"When you were on patrol, what did you patrol?"

"The whole place."

"Give me a rundown on your typical day patrolling," she said.

"Well, I'd go on shift, say the morning shift. I'd drive around to each house, go up the driveway. Sometimes I'd get out of the car and walk the property. I'd drive to the clubhouse and take a walk around, checking out things."

"What about the special buildings?"

"What do you mean, special?"

"How about the building with all the antennas?"

"Oh, we didn't go out there. They have their own security."

"What are they protecting?"

"What do you mean?"

"What goes on there that they need their own security?"

"I don't know, really. The place is called the com center, so I assume it's for communications."

"Communications with whom?"

"Jesus, I don't know. They don't tell me that stuff."

"Who is Barney's boss?"

"The general manager, Mr. Diego, I guess."

"What's his first name?"

"I don't know. Barney just calls him Diego."

"What does he look like?"

"About forty-five, I'd guess; five-ten, a hundred and seventy-five, black hair going gray, has a mustache. He's Mexican or something, has a light accent."

"I want to know his first name, Cracker."

"Wait a minute, let me think. That's his first name, Diego. His last name is something like . . . Romeo."

"A Spanish name?"

"Yeah."

"Come on, think."

"I'm trying. It's Ramos, or Ramero, or something like that. Ramirez! That's it, Ramirez."

"Diego Ramirez—good boy, Cracker. Now who else works for Ramirez?"

"Well, everybody—the club manager, the shop managers, the people in the accounting office, the maintenance manager, the airport manager—they all report to him."

"Where is the accounting office located?"

"It's in the village, next door to the security station."

"And who runs that?"

"A woman named Miriam something . . . uh, like Talbot."

"Is that it, Talbot?"

"Yeah, I think so."

"Description?"

"Late thirties, early forties, five-six, a hundred and forty, mousy hair, not pretty."

"What kind of vehicles are driven by the staff?"

"Security drives white Range Rovers, maintenance drives Ford vans and pickups, all white, with the green palmetto thing on the doors."

"Where are they serviced?"

"In town. We take them to Westover Motors when they need something."

"Any vehicles there now?"

"I'm taking Barney's Range Rover in when I leave here."

"What for?"

"Regular service. We get it back tomorrow. Barney's a stickler for regular maintenance."

"Where do you live, Cracker?"

"I have a room in the staff quarters."

"How many of the staff live on the place?"

"All of them."

"What do you do for entertainment?"

"They fly us to Miami. Everybody works seven days on and four off. Palmetto Gardens owns a refurbished DC-3 for flying staff back and forth."

"Which airport in Miami do they fly into?"

"Opa Locka."

"Tell me the names of some of the members of Palmetto Gardens."

Cracker looked blank. "I don't think I know any of them."

"How do they refer to them among the security people?"

"By addresses. I've never heard any names used."

"What do these people look like?"

"Rich. All kinds of nationalities. There's some Europeans and some Hispanics and some Americans. There's a couple of Arabs, too, I think. It's not like I ever have a conversation with any of them."

"Do they have wives and children?"

"Women, most of them. I've only seen a few kids—that's less common."

"How many members?"

"There's two hundred and eight houses; I guess a member a house."

"How many employees, total, on the place?"

"Something over six hundred, I think. Half of them are domestics. "

"Six hundred employees are living on the place?"

"No, the domestics are local."

"How do they get in and out of the place?"

"They drive or take the bus to the service gate; there's a parking lot for them there. Then they walk or are driven in vans to their work."

"How do they hire the domestics?"

"I don't know. I guess they run ads. The pay is good, so there's not much turnover. There's an employment office in Orchid."

"What sort of arms do you have at the security station?"

"We all carry nine-millimeter automatics, then there's a supply of AR fifteens."

"Anything heavier than that?"

"Not at the station."

"Elsewhere?"

Mosely suddenly looked uncomfortable.

"Come on, Cracker, or I'll be talking to your parole officer."

"There's some stuff scattered around the place. I don't know exactly what."

"You've got to do better than that, Cracker."

"I've never been close to it, but there are some . . . places around the property."

"Are they camouflaged?"

Cracker looked surprised. "How did you know that?"

"We're talking about what *you* know, Cracker."

"Yeah, they've got netting over them."

"Who mans them?"

"There are certain employees who're trained for that, a couple of dozen, I think. If there's an alarm, they go to their positions."

"What kind of an alarm?"

"There's a siren on a pole at the security office. If we get three blasts, we're to go to our preassigned positions."

"What's your position?"

"Backup at the front gate, unless I'm already on service-gate duty."

"What are they afraid of out there, Cracker?"

"I don't know, exactly, but I know that they don't want *anybody* from the outside there, unless they're invited and escorted."

"What kind of aircraft land at the airfield?"

"Corporate jets, mostly, and some support airplanes that bring in stuff."

"What sort of stuff?"

"Equipment, parts, special foods, whatever's needed. The DC-3 and a Cessna Caravan do that work."

"Is there any special security at the airfield?"

"Yeah, there's a couple of those camouflaged places."

Holly couldn't think of anything else to ask him. "Stay here a minute," she said. "Guard, Daisy."

"You're leaving me with that dog?" Cracker asked, worried.

"She won't hurt you unless you move." Holly left the room and went next door. Harry Crisp was gone. She went back to the other room. Cracker had not moved. "Okay, Cracker, I'm going to let you go. If Barney wants to know why you were here so long, tell him I kept you waiting. If you tell him about our conversation, I'll know, and I'll have you back in prison before nightfall, you understand?"

"I understand," he said. "I'm not going to jail for Barney."

"Good, now get going." She followed him to the squad room and watched as he walked out.

Hurd Wallace approached. "Who was that guy?"

"Just an interview," Holly said. "Nothing important."

46

Holly went straight to Jackson's house after work. One of the two FBI vans was parked outside. Harry Crisp was on the phone, as usual, when she walked in, and Jackson was having a beer with Bill and Joe. Harry waved and covered up the phone. "Be with you in a minute."

Holly fed Daisy and got herself a beer, returning to the living room as Harry finished his call. "What happened to you today?" she asked. "I came in there to see if you had any more questions, but you had gone."

"Sorry, when I heard that Cracker was driving Barney's Range Rover I went out there to see if I could bug it, but I didn't have the right equipment." Harry waved at the other people. "Let's all sit down for a minute," he said.

Everybody gathered at the dining table.

"I just want to tell you all where we are," Harry said. "First of all, Holly did a brilliant job of interrogating Cracker Mosely this morning. She got a hell of a lot of information that would have taken us a week to get. Thanks, Holly."

"You're very welcome."

"Let's see." Harry consulted a list. "I talked with a guy from the National Security Agency this morning. They were already aware of the transmissions coming out of Palmetto Dunes."

"They've been listening in?" Holly asked.

"They did for a while, starting a couple of years ago, but they'd assigned it a lower priority for the past year."

"Why? What was coming out of there?"

"Commodity trades."

"I don't understand."

"They were dispatching sell and buy orders for futures on soybeans, wheat, pork bellies, everything you'd find at a commodities exchange, but they were doing it on a worldwide basis."

"Well," Holly said, "that doesn't make any sense at all to me. I thought those things were handled through brokers."

"What they've got there *is* a brokerage. There's something odd about it, though."

"What's that?"

"They're using a Chinese telecomunications satellite to move their information."

"I'm afraid I don't understand that, either," Holly said.

"Neither does the NSA. Their earlier scans were handled routinely by lower-level personnel. All they did was to listen in; they didn't do any analysis. Now they're going to take another look at the transmissions and see if there is any change in what's coming out of there. They'll also do an analysis of the information."

"I still don't understand it," Holly said, "but maybe that'll help somehow."

"Sounds like your old man's idea of the antiaircraft emplacements wasn't all that far-fetched," Harry said. "Though, for the life of me, I just can't believe that anyone on the Florida coast would start shooting at airplanes."

"Who would do something like that?"

"It doesn't make any sense as a security precaution. It might make more sense if they intended to use that kind of weaponry to buy some time."

"Time for what?" Jackson asked.

"Time to evacuate. From what Cracker had to say in his interview with Holly, it sounds like they have a plan to hold the place just long enough for some aircraft to get out of there. I mean, they can't get into a shooting war with the outside and expect to win, can they?"

"They could sure hold off my department for a while, though," Holly said.

"I think that's what they're counting on. In a pinch, they can get out of there before reinforcements arrive. Your dad's right; they couldn't hold out against a military assault, but cops with small arms couldn't take the place."

"Have you found out anything else so far?" Jackson asked.

"We've had a report from Miami Center on the aircraft in and out of there. They've had airplanes with registrations from Saudi Arabia, Mexico, Canada, Japan and, mostly, from the United States. We ran down the U.S. tail numbers and nearly eighty percent of them were owned by a charter service out of Miami, which is owned by a Delaware corporation, which is owned by a Luxembourg company. Wheels within wheels."

"Spooky," Holly said.

"We checked out Diego Ramirez, the general manager of the place, too. He's Panamanian, a former colonel in Manuel Noriega's palace guard. He got out before the invasion and has been living quietly in Miami. No criminal record in this country, and his immigration status is okay."

Holly spoke up. "I checked out the property ownership this afternoon, but the results were disappointing."

"Dummy ownership, I'll bet," Harry said.

"Not even that. Every house is owned by the Palmetto Gardens Corporation. But, of course, that's a Cayman Island corporation. Here's a list of the directors." She handed him a sheet of paper. "The only one I recognize is Ramirez. You might check out the others."

"Good work, Holly."

"I've been thinking about this," Harry said, "about what sort of people could own and operate this place. It seems to be operated without regard for profit, which is strange, and if the members are taking up the slack, then it has got to be the most expensive club in the world to belong to. Rich people, even billionaires, didn't get that way by flushing money down the kind of toilet that Palmetto Gardens seems to be, so that leaves just two other candidates for ownership that I can think of—governments or drug cartels. The presence of Diego Ramirez there, given the recent history of Panama, makes me lean in favor of the drug cartels, or maybe a combination of governments and the cartels."

"That makes sense," Jackson said. "Even if you got Bill Gates, Ted Turner and the Sultan of Brunei together, with all their money they would expect a return on investment, or, at the very least, some kind of value for money. With only a couple of hundred houses there, the expense per house has got to be staggering."

Harry continued. "We're going to bug Barney Noble's Range Rover tonight, come hell or high water," he said. "It's at Westover Motors, still outside in the rear parking lot; apparently, it gets serviced first thing in the morning. Arnie is out on Jungle Trail, scanning their VHF radio frequencies, all their handheld radios, and he'll record what he can get there. Once the frequencies are identified, which should be easy, we can jam them, if we have to go in there."

"Don't you need a court order to bug Barney's car?" Holly asked.

Harry shook his head. "Between you and me, Holly, this is just to get information; we'll never use it in court, so the hell with a warrant. It's quick and dirty, but it'll work. Oh, one more thing—I'm trying to get a female agent into Palmetto Gardens as a domestic worker. There's an ad in the local paper and a hiring office on the mainland. We're flying up a woman who'll try to get an interview tomorrow morning."

"That's a great idea," Holly said. "We really need somebody inside."

"Well, there's always Cracker," Harry said. "I think you scared him shitless this morning, and I don't think he'll spill to Barney, do you?"

"I sure hope not. I've got him by the short and curlies. I didn't lie to him about that. I know who his parole officer is."

Bill spoke up. "I learned something this afternoon," he said. "I don't know how important it is."

"Tell us," Harry said.

"I tracked down the people who were in charge of most of the infrastructure work at Palmetto Gardens, a construction company called Jones and Jones, in Vero Beach."

"And?"

"We went over a map of the place, while he showed me what he had done out there. The only really unusual thing was at the communications center."

"What?"

"He put in a basement and a sub-basement, fully waterproofed and insulated."

"A sub-basement? In Florida? It's probably full of the Indian River by now."

"He said it was *fully* waterproofed," Bob said.

"Got any ideas what it's for?"

"It's all heavily reinforced, superdense concrete. I reckon it's either a bomb shelter or a vault."

"Now, *that's* interesting," Bob said. "Anybody else?"

Holly spoke up. "Well, I learned something from Cracker this morning that I didn't expect to."

"What's that?"

"I think he killed Hank Doherty, maybe Chet Marley, too. Or, at least, he was one of the killers."

"The dog?" Harry asked.

"Daisy."

"She went nuts, didn't she?"

"She sure did. Whoever killed Hank got him to lock Daisy in the kitchen first, but Daisy sure remembered him."

47

The next morning, Holly was back at her desk. She and Harry Crisp had agreed that she should keep something like regular office hours so that, if anyone were keeping tabs on her, she would appear to be doing nothing out of the ordinary. She was working her way through the stack of personnel files when Hurd Wallace rapped at her door.

"Morning, Hurd," Holly said. "Come in and have a seat."

"Morning," he said, sitting down.

"What's up?"

"I feel sort of out of the loop," Wallace said.

"What loop is that?"

"Well, I'm beginning to get the impression that you know something about Chet Marley's murder that I don't."

"What makes you think that?"

"You seem to be doing a lot of investigative work these days that I'm cut out of," Wallace said.

"Such as?"

"You're making trips to the county planning office and looking up documents there; you've had Barney Noble in here, and he didn't look happy; and then you interrogated that guy yesterday, the one whose picture you had up on the bulletin board a while back."

"All that is true, I guess."

"What's it all about, Holly?"

"Well, it's no big thing, Hurd. I found out that this guy, who is one of Barney's security guards, has a criminal record and shouldn't be licensed for security work or to carry a gun."

"And what did you do about it?"

"Barney promised me he'd take him off security work, so I haven't done anything, except talk to him."

"Why'd you sic the dog on him?"

"How'd you know about the dog?"

"She made a lot of noise."

"I didn't sic her onto the guy. She just didn't like him, I guess. I don't know why."

Hurd nodded.

"What's the problem, Hurd? What's on your mind?"

"Tell you the truth, I get the very strong impression that you don't trust me to do my job. Ever since you got here, we've hardly talked about anything, and I guess we didn't have to, until I got the deputy chief's job. But now I figure I ought to know everything that's going on."

Holly felt cornered. Wallace was right; she didn't trust him, but she hadn't meant for him to know that. "I'm sorry I've given you that impression," she said.

"You know, if Chet had confided in me about what he was working on, we would probably have already made an arrest in his killing. And now you're working on something you're keeping from me. What happens if *you* end up dead? Where is the department then?"

"Hurd, you have a very good point there."

"It doesn't seem to be doing me very much good, Holly. Are you going to bring me in on this or shut me out?"

"There isn't anything to shut you out of, Hurd. Ask me questions, and I'll give you answers."

"Do you have some particular interest in Palmetto Gardens?"

"What do you know about that place, Hurd?"

"Just what everybody else knows: practically nothing. What do you know about it?"

"Just about what you know," she lied. "You think we ought to know more about it?"

"I certainly do."

"Why?"

"I know it doesn't come as a surprise to you that we have what amounts to a city-state, right here in our jurisdiction—that they don't allow us to patrol out there, that we can't even enter the place unless we're escorted. Doesn't that bother you?"

"It did until I visited the place," Holly said.

Wallace came close to changing his expression. "You visited the place?"

"I've been out there a couple of times. Barney Noble gave me the five-cent tour, and he invited my father and me to play golf out there once. He and my dad served in the army together."

"What's it like out there?"

Holly told him about her two visits.

"I don't like the idea of the security people having automatic weapons," he said.

"Neither do I, much," Holly replied, "but there's nothing we can do about it."

Wallace shrugged. "We could make a stink at the state level about the licenses being issued."

"The automatic weapons licenses?"

"Couldn't hurt."

"You think we could get the licenses pulled?"

"Maybe. I know some people."

"We'd need more than personal contacts, Hurd. If the licenses were canceled, Barney would request a hearing and get it. He'd be able to say that none of his people had ever fired one in anger."

"And we'd be able to say that they've no need for more firepower than we have in our department."

"I don't know what that would get us, except to alert Barney Noble that we have more than a passing interest in what he's doing out there."

"Would that be a bad thing?" Wallace asked. "It might rattle him a little."

"What's the purpose of rattling him?"

"To let him know that we take an interest in what goes on on our turf."

"I think I've already let him know that, with this Cracker Mosely thing."

"What's Cracker Mosely?"

"The man I interrogated yesterday."

"Who is he?"

"He's an ex-cop out of Miami. He killed a drug dealer with his baton and did time for it." Holly wanted to see where Wallace would go with that information.

He wrinkled his brow, a major use of facial expression for him. "And yet he got licensed for security work?"

"And to carry a gun."

"How'd that happen?"

"A computer check showed no criminal record."

"Well, that's a major lapse, isn't it?"

"I thought so."

"Have you called anybody at state records to find out why?"

"Not yet."

"Why not?"

Holly shrugged. "I just want to let it ride for a while and see what happens."

"While you're letting it ride, I'd like to run records checks on all the security people out there."

"How? We don't even have their names," Holly said.

"I could run a check on security-guard licenses issued in Orchid and cross-check that against the Palmetto Gardens addresses."

Now Holly was stuck. So far she hadn't told him anything that Barney Noble didn't already know, but this was new territory. She took a deep breath. "I've already done that, Hurd."

"So you have a list of the security people?"

"Yep."

Wallace shook his head. "You might have told me that a few minutes ago and saved me all these questions."

"I wanted to see what questions you'd ask, Hurd."

"Well, my next question is, does anybody else with a criminal record belong to the Palmetto Gardens security department?"

Wallace was now only a step from where Holly's curiosity had taken her, and she saw that it would cost her nothing to make it easier for him.

"Well, yes and no," she said.

There was a tiny ripple of anger across Wallace's placid face.

Holly held up a hand. "There are a hundred and two people at Palmetto Gardens who are licensed to carry weapons."

"A hundred and two?"

"That's right. Only fifteen of them are security guards, in the formal sense."

"Have you checked to see if any of them has a criminal record, like Mosely?"

"None of them shows a criminal record in the state computer system."

"Yeah, but neither did Mosely."

Holly took a deep breath and let it all out. "Seventy-one of them show up in the national crime computer as having criminal records."

Wallace stared blankly at her for a moment while he digested that information.

"What do you think I ought to do, Hurd?" Holly asked.

"I think you ought to call the fucking FBI," he said. "Right now," he said, pointing. "There's the phone."

Holly laughed. She would have thought Wallace incapable of such an outburst.

"Let me tell you my problem, Hurd," she said. There was no point in holding this back any longer. "Chet Marley thought there was someone in this department who was working with . . . somebody outside this department."

Wallace's mouth dropped open. "And you thought it was *me?*"

"I thought it was a possibility," Holly said. "The same possibility applies to everybody else in the department." Then Wallace did something Holly thought she would never see. He burst out laughing.

48

After work, Holly drove out to Jackson's house, with Hurd Wallace following in his own car. She looked in her rearview mirror from time to time, wondering if she were doing the right thing. Hurd, she admitted to herself, had been her prime suspect, and she had not gotten used to the idea that he might be on her side of this thing. She had made the decision, late in the afternoon, to bring him inside the investigation, and she had made it on little more than some newly informed intuition.

She turned into Jackson's driveway, drove down the narrow lane and parked next to one of the FBI vans. It appeared that the whole team would be present. She waved Hurd inside and came upon a scene that was, by now, all too familiar. Harry Crisp was on the phone, the agents were drinking beer and watching sports on television and Jackson was out back, grilling something. She stuck her head outside and told him there'd be one more for dinner.

Harry hung up the phone. "Who's this?" he asked, clearly uncomfortable with the new face.

"Harry," Holly said, "this is my deputy chief, Hurd Wallace." She introduced all the other team members.

"Forgive me, Holly," Harry said, "but I'm a little confused at this turn of events. Isn't this the guy . . . "

"Yeah, he is, or rather, he was. I'm satisfied that he's not my mole, and I want him brought fully into this."

"I understand your suspicions," Wallace said, "but I assure you, I've never given any departmental information to anyone on the outside. I just want to help."

"Okay," Harry said, waving him to a chair. "Have a seat. Looks like dinner is ready."

Jackson came in with a huge platter of grilled fish and set it on the table. Nobody said grace.

When the food had been consumed and the dishes stacked, Harry got down to business.

"Okay," he said, "let's start with our black bag job. Bill and Jim went over the fence at Westover Motors last night and nearly got eaten by a very large German shepherd."

There was laughter around the table.

"We tranquilized the thing," Bill said. "I expect he felt a little woozy this morning, but we removed the dart, so nobody will be the wiser, except the dog, and he's too hung over to talk."

"Then they got the bug installed, and it was a good job," Harry said. "We've got a recorder on the frequency, and we check it every few hours. Same with the walkie-talkie frequencies that Palmetto Gardens is using." The driveway chime rang, and Harry stopped. "That'll be Rita," he said.

"Who's Rita?" Jackson asked.

"You're about to find out." Harry stood up and walked to the door in time to meet a young woman at the door. She was no more than five-two, slim but shapely, with big, curly hair, dressed in tight jeans and a sweater.

"Jackson, Holly, Hurd, this is Rita Morales, from our office."

Everybody waved, and so did Rita. They made room for her at the table.

"You eat?" Harry asked.

"McDonald's," she replied. "Smells better here."

"No more McDonald's," Jackson said. "The best grub in town is at my house."

"How'd it go today?" Harry asked.

"I'm hired. I start tomorrow morning. I have to be at the service gate at seven."

"Do you know where you'll be working?"

She shook her head, making her curly hair shake. "They wouldn't say. Said I'd be assigned somewhere tomorrow morning, and it wouldn't necessarily be the same assignment every day. They put me through a kind of indoctrination this afternoon at the employment office, along with three other women."

"What kind of indoctrination?"

"Everything is strict: we wear a uniform, we don't speak unless spoken to, we don't hobnob with any other employees. We can't make or receive phone calls, and no cellulars are allowed; they said we'd be searched."

"Don't take a badge or a gun in there," Harry said.

"No kidding, Harry? I thought I'd wear an FBI jacket and body armor."

"All right, all right, I just don't want you to get your—"

"Tit in a wringer?" She turned to Holly. "You see what a woman has to put up with in the Bureau?" she said. "They're all Neanderthals."

"Don't put words in my mouth, Rita," Harry said. "What else?"

"That's about it. You've finally turned me into a domestic servant, Harry. What's next? Turning tricks?"

Harry turned red. "Rita, I wouldn't send you in there if anybody else could do it."

"Well, that's a ringing endorsement of my abilities," she replied.

"Jesus, I just can't win with you, can I, Rita?"

"No, Harry, you can't." She turned to Holly again. "The director himself assigned me to keep Harry as humble as possible. It isn't easy."

"All right, I've got some news," Harry said, anxious to change the subject. "I heard from my guy at the NSA again today. They're monitoring Palmetto Gardens again, and guess what?"

"Okay, what, Harry?" Rita asked.

"The last time they monitored the place all they got was commodity trades. This time, they got exactly the same thing."

"This is news?" Bill asked.

"No, you don't understand," Harry said. "They got *exactly* the same thing—the same trades."

"Why would they make the same trades over and over?" Bill asked.

"The trades are on a loop. They're playing a tape over and over."

"Sorry," Bill said, "I still don't get it. You're saying that they've got this satellite station set up just to play a tape on a loop?"

"That's what it sounds like, but that's not all that's happening," Harry said. "The NSA processed the transmissions, and they're getting microbursts between the trades."

"What's a microburst?" Jackson asked.

"You know what a microdot is?"

"You mean, when they photograph a page and reduce it to the size of a dot?"

"Exactly. A microburst is the audio equivalent of a microdot. You take a string of words or a message, and you speed it up, I don't know, a thousand times, or something, and what you get is a microburst of sound. It's received . . . wherever it's received, and it's slowed down again so the message can be heard."

"So what are the microbursts saying?"

"We don't know. They're encoded."

"Isn't that what the NSA does? Break codes?"

"Yeah, but it's a lot more complex than it used to be. Now that everybody has got computers, codes can be constructed that are much, much more sophisticated than, say, the Enigma codes the Germans used in World War Two. And, of course, they can be changed daily, with a few keyboard entries on the computer. The government is trying to limit the development of codes, or to make the encoders include a key that guys like us can use to break them."

"But Palmetto Gardens isn't giving us any keys, are they?" Bill asked.

"Right. So it's going to take time to break down these microbursts and see what they mean. All we've got right now is meaningless strings of numbers."

Holly spoke up. "What are you getting from the bug in Barney's car?"

"Chitchat, mostly. One good piece of news: Cracker Mosely seems to be scared enough of you not to tell Barney everything you asked him yesterday. Barney questioned him closely, and all he said was that you threatened to call his parole officer if he continued to do security work. Barney has made him a radio operator."

"That puts Cracker right in the middle of the security office, instead of out in a patrol car, doesn't it?" she asked.

"That's right, Holly."

"So the next step is to pick up Cracker again the first chance we get and really turn him."

"Good thinking."

"I can't have my people pick him up, though. We've still got our mole."

"We're surveilling both gates," Harry said. "Anybody sees Cracker—and we'll give you a photograph—call me, and we'll get him alone for a few minutes and threaten him beyond his wildest nightmares."

"Good," Holly said.

"Yeah," Jackson echoed, "real good. And at some point, I hope to get an opportunity to tell him that I was the one who put you onto him."

"I'll see if I can arrange that," Harry said.

49

Rita Morales showed up at the service gate to Palmetto Gardens at six forty-five the following morning in the rusting 1978 Impala the Bureau had furnished her. She was wearing old, baggy khakis and a South Beach sweatshirt, faded and full of holes. She parked her car, walked up to the security shack and rapped sharply on the glass. The guard, who had been dozing, nearly had a heart attack.

"Hey," she said in a pronounced Cuban-American accent, "I'm here for the cleaning work."

The guard got hold of himself and picked up a clipboard. "Name?"

"Rita."

"Rita what?"

"Garcia."

"Yeah, okay," he said, checking her off. "The bus will be here in a few minutes. Just wait in the parking lot."

Rita walked back to the parking lot, where other women were gathering, most of them being dropped off by relatives. Time to go to work, she thought. She approached an ample woman who had gotten out of a pickup truck. "Buenos días," she said, and continued in Spanish. "I'm Rita. This is my first day. What sort of work is it?"

"It's cleaning work," the woman said. "I'm Carla."

"Yeah, Carla, I know about the cleaning. I mean, is it a good place to work?"

"It doesn't get any better around here," the woman said. "The pay is twice what you'd get working some lady's house, but you have to work hard. They fire you if they catch you grabbing a smoke or loafing."

"That's okay, I guess. I don't mind working hard if the money is good. What sort of places you been working in there?"

"I've worked everywhere at one time or another. I've cleaned houses, I've cleaned shops, I've cleaned the country club."

"Where will they start me out?" Rita asked.

"You never can tell. You're just a number to these people. They don't care about your name, or anything. It's just 'Hey you, clean that house.' They'll drop you off with a partner, and the two of you will do the place. You get half an hour for lunch. You bring lunch?"

"No," Rita replied. "Nobody told me."

"Tell you what, you stick with me today. I've got enough food for the two of us. I'll show you the ropes."

"Thanks," Rita said. She turned to see a white school bus drive out of the gate and stop in the parking lot. The workers started to get on.

"You just sit next to me," Carla said, "and they'll put us together. That's how they do it."

Rita gave her name to a man with a clipboard, who checked off her name, compared her face to a Polaroid photograph that had been taken when she applied for the job and gave her a polyester jump suit and a security pass, which had her name and photograph on it. She sat down next to Carla.

"You should change now," Carla said, "and leave your clothes on the bus. It will pick us up later."

Rita went to the back of the bus, took a seat, changed clothes, aware of the driver's eyes in the rearview mirror, and returned to her seat next to Carla in the middle of the bus.

"If we're lucky, we'll get office space to clean," Carla said. "That's why I sit in the middle of the bus. The people up front get the houses, where you have to do laundry and clean up after parties and all that. The people in the back get the shops."

"Thanks," Rita said. "I'm lucky I met you."

"You sure are," Carla replied, patting her on the knee.

The bus stopped half a dozen times to let off people. Finally, it drew to another stop, and a security guard got on. "You two," he said, pointing to Carla and Rita. "Come with me."

The two women got off the bus, and it drove away, leaving them with the guard at the side of the road. Rita could not see any buildings.

"Hands on top of your head," the man said.

Rita followed Carla's example and allowed herself to be searched. The guard got a good grope of her breasts and leered at her. She tried to appear demure.

"Get in the car," he said, pointing to a Range Rover.

Rita opened her mouth to ask where they were going, but Carla grabbed her arm and shook her head. She kept quiet, as the Range Rover drove down a thickly wooded lane for a quarter of a mile and pulled into a parking lot. Rita's heart leapt. Ahead of her she saw a huge satellite dish, and to her left was a two-story building with very narrow windows. It looked like a cross between an office building and a jail, she thought.

"Everybody out," the guard said. He led the two women through the front door of the building and into a small reception room. A hard-looking man in civilian clothes checked their names on a list and looked carefully at their ID cards, comparing their faces to their photographs. That done, they were buzzed through an opaque glass door and into a hallway. "You cleaned here before, didn't you?" the guard said to Carla.

"Yes, sir," she replied.

"You know the drill, then. You tell the new babe here what to do. I want you done in two hours."

"Yes, sir," Carla said. She turned to Rita. "Come with me." She led the way down the hall to a utility closet and handed Rita a roll of plastic trash bags. "There's offices up and down this hallway," she said. "You start at this end, and I'll start at the other. Empty all the trash cans and shredders into the bags and bring them back here to the closet. I'll show you where to put them then."

"Shredders?"

"Shredding machines, for papers, you know?"

"Okay," Rita said. She went to the nearest door, which was open, and rapped on the jamb. "Cleaning lady," she said.

A man was working at a desk; he waved her in.

Rita found the wastebasket, emptied it, then went to a shredder, which sat on top of a plastic bin. She removed the top, set it on the floor and empted the bin into her bag. "Thank you," she said, smiling.

The man didn't even look up, just waved.

She repeated the process up and down the hallways. The offices were all identical—a steel desk, a filing cabinet, a chair, a wastebasket and a shredder. Each had a phone on the desk; some had copying machines. There was nothing on the walls of any of the offices, no pictures, no diplomas, no calendars, nothing. She went back to the utility closet and Carla showed her to an outside door with large plastic garbage cans outside. They dumped the trash bags, then each got a vacuum cleaner, and they vacuumed the offices and the hallway.

"Now, upstairs," Carla said. She led the way up the staircase through a door and into a large room that appeared to cover the whole of the second floor, with a row of offices along one side.

Rita's mouth fell open, and she closed it quickly, heading for the nearest wastebasket. The room was full of desks, each with a computer terminal. At the rear, reaching across the width of the room, was a row of large computers. She reflected that the computer room at the Miami field office of the FBI was a third the size of this. As she emptied each wastebasket she glanced at the computer screen on the desk. There was no time to read anything, but she saw, on various screens, spreadsheets, documents being written, columns of figures, and, on one desk, a full-color Mercator projection map of the world with red dots placed on at least two dozen spots around the globe. What appeared to be satellites were superimposed on the map. She noted the absence on every screen of anything resembling a market tape running. No commodities were being traded here.

Rita and Carla took out the trash bags, then returned with the vacuum cleaners. As Rita pushed hers around the floor, she began looking at the men at the desks. Each of them wore a telephone headset and a pistol in a holster. When they had finished vacuuming, Carla gave her a dust cloth, and they went from desk to desk, office to office, wiping down every surface. Each room was nearly identical to the ones downstairs—same furniture, same lack of anything personal on the desks or the walls. The windows were no more than six inches wide and tinted green. Carla estimated that the glass in each was at least two inches thick.

As they left the second floor, Rita noticed a bulletin board with work schedules posted on it, but she could get only the briefest of glances at it.

They returned to the ground floor. Rita turned a corner and came up against a steel door. Next to it was a keypad and a glass surface with the outline of a hand drawn on it. A sign on the door read, ACCESS TO THE LOWER LEVELS IS BY AUTHORIZED PERSONNEL ONLY. ARMED RESPONSE.

Rita and Carla were picked up on time and taken to the country club, where they cleaned the men's locker room, but Rita saw nothing out of the ordinary there, except for four or five men carrying weapons. They had their lunch outside, and Rita gently pumped Carla for information about what she had seen while cleaning there. At three o'clock, the bus returned the workers to the parking lot, searching each of them as they got off.

Rita drove away in her terrible old car, checking her mirrors and driving an erratic pattern to be sure she wasn't followed. Finally she allowed herself a deep breath and a smile. She had gotten away with it.

50

Holly sat at Jackson's dining table and listened to Rita's report. Ham had joined the group, and was intent on what she had to say. Harry Crisp was thrilled at his agent's prompt success, and kept saying how lucky she had been.

"Doesn't sound like luck to me, Harry," Holly said.

"Thank you, Holly," Rita said, smiling at her.

"I don't mean to belittle what you've done, Rita," Harry said. "But I do think you were awfully lucky to get into the com center your first day out."

"Harry," Holly said, "Rita manipulated her way into that building—there wasn't a lot of luck involved. Can't you give the woman credit?"

"I'll do better than that," Harry said. "Rita, I'm giving you a pay grade promotion, just as soon as we get back to the office."

"Thank you, Harry," Rita said sweetly.

"We interrupted you; go on."

"The upstairs looked like the back room of a big bank, or a brokerage house. Everybody had a computer terminal and a phone headset, and they were all talking at once, like at a stockbroker's. There was almost no paper upstairs. Everything is done on the computers, I guess, and they've got major capacity, more than we've got in Miami. These guys work like machines, and they only work six hours a day."

"How do you know that?" Harry asked.

"I saw the work schedule on a bulletin board. There are shifts from six A.M. to noon, noon to six, and six to midnight. That's all I had time to see."

"Were there any women in evidence?"

"Just Carla and me. Everybody else was a guy."

"What else did you see?"

"When we came downstairs I came to the end of a hallway and found a big steel door with a security keypad and a palm-print analyzer and a sign saying they'd shoot any unauthorized entrant."

"That squares with what the construction guy had to say about the basement he built," Harry said.

"The place is like a fortress," Rita said. "Thick walls, armored glass in small windows, air conditioners on the roof, not out back, where they might be accessible to tampering. Did I mention that all the computer operators were armed?"

"Weird," Holly said. "Armed computer operators."

"That doesn't make any sense," Harry said, "unless they're trained to make some sort of last stand."

"Like Waco?" Holly asked.

"Don't say that word," Harry said with a shudder. "I was there."

Holly shook her head. "You can't *pay* people to do a Waco, they've got to be motivated by some cause."

"Maybe," Rita said, "they're trained to hold the building until everything in it can be destroyed."

"Now, that makes sense," Harry said. "The only other building you were inside was the country club?"

"Yes, but only the men's locker room," Rita said.

"Anything unusual there?"

"It was a locker room, Harry. There were a lot of dirty towels. I found out about the other buildings from Carla, though. She's worked there for three years, and she's cleaned every building on the place at one time or another."

"And what did she have to say?"

"All the other buildings are normal, except the com center and the security office. They've apparently got a real arsenal at the security office, too—lots of weapons. Oh, and all the houses have big walk-in safes, concealed, usually in a library. At least, it sounds like all of them—Carla has seen three."

"Did you get any chance to see what we think might be gun emplacements?"

Rita shook her head. "I only saw what I could see from the bus, which was houses, the country club, and the village shops."

"All right," Harry said, "what have we got here in the nature of a crime?"

"We've got the tampering with state criminal records and probably perjury on seventy-one license applications," Holly said.

"That's state stuff. What have we got that could justify my going into that place with a SWAT team?"

Everybody thought for a minute.

"What about communications?" Holly asked.

"What do you mean, communications?"

"There must be licenses required for some of that stuff they've got out there."

"Good point," Harry said. "Bill, you check with the Federal Communications Commission and see if there's anything we can hang a criminal charge on."

"Right," Bill replied.

"What else? Anybody?"

Ham spoke up. "If they've got anything in the way of heavy weapons in those camouflaged spots, wouldn't that be a federal crime?"

"Yes, it would, if it's heavy enough," Harry said.

Holly spoke up. "Harry, I think these people are too slick to overtly violate some federal statute. What they're doing is covert, and unless the NSA can do some code breaking, the only way you're going to find out what they're doing is to go in there. So, what I think you should be looking for is not grounds for a SWAT bust, but probable cause for a federal search warrant."

"I'm afraid you're right," Harry said, "and I haven't heard anything from the NSA today."

Bill spoke up. "I've got something I'd like you to hear from the bug in Barney Noble's car," he said. "There was a lot of ordinary chitchat that is of no interest, but then this happened." He set a tape machine on the table and turned it on. There was the sound of the car running, then slowing, then the squeak of brakes and the sound of a car door opening and closing. "Rear door," Bill said. "Somebody got into the backseat, and you can barely hear him talk."

"What's happening?" Barney Noble's voice said.

There was a mumbled reply.

"She doing anything unusual?"

"Nah," the voice said. "Routine stuff."

There was the sound of paper crackling, and Noble spoke again. "Here's this week's money. Call me if anything comes up."

"Okay," the voice said, then the rear door opened and closed again.

"He must be talking about you, Holly," Harry said. "It's got to be one of your people. Did you recognize the voice?"

"No. Play it again, Bill."

Holly listened carefully to the tape. "Hurd? You recognize anybody?"

Wallace shook his head. "It's too faint. It could be anybody. Is there any way to enhance it, Bill?"

"Yeah, but I'll have to send it to Miami," Bill replied.

"Do that," Harry said. "And next time, bug the backseat, too."

"Yeah," Bill said.

"Rita, how thoroughly were you searched?" Harry asked.

"Thoroughly enough to get groped, but not all *that* thoroughly. I had already changed out of my clothes into a jumpsuit, and that didn't have any pockets."

"Did you keep the jumpsuit?"

"Yeah, they told me to."

"Bill, take a look at the garment and see if you can hide some bugs in it for Rita to take in."

"Okay."

Rita shook her head. "That's not the best way, Harry."

"What have you got in mind?"

"Well, nobody looked up my ass with a flashlight, or up anywhere else."

"I think I see your point," Harry said.

"Bill," Rita said, "do you think you can find a canister of some sort, say four inches long by an inch in diameter?"

"Probably."

"Would that hold some bugs?"

"Four, maybe half a dozen."

"No sharp corners, okay?"

"Sure, Rita."

Rita looked around the table. "I'll shoot anybody who smirks," she said.

51

Ham Barker got into bed and turned on the TV, but he couldn't concentrate on any program, and when he switched it off, he couldn't sleep, either. He had listened to what was said at the meeting with Harry Crisp, and he was intrigued. He was also a little annoyed at how everybody seemed to be tiptoeing around the Palmetto Gardens problem, instead of *doing* something about it. "Fucking feds," he said aloud to himself. If this had been an army problem, it would already have been solved. He lay there thinking for a few minutes, then he got out of bed, got into a bathing suit and a T-shirt, and slipped into some Top-Siders, no socks.

He walked around the cabin, picking up things, looking at them and putting them down again. Then he got a large, zippered plastic bag and started collecting what he needed. He found a waterproof flashlight and taped over most of the lens, leaving an open area about half an inch in diameter, and added that to his bag. He dug a black nylon warmup suit out of his closet, rolled it into a small, tight wad and put it into the plastic bag, along with a pair of black sneakers. Then he went to his tackle box and lifted out the plastic tray that covered the bottom. Under that were two things that he had stolen from the army: one was his standard-issue special forces knife, which was still razor sharp; the other was a small black .22-caliber pistol with a silencer attached that had been issued to him for a mission in Vietnam by a CIA field agent. When, after the job had successfully been completed, the CIA man had asked for the weapon back, Ham had told him to go fuck himself. He had never thought that he would actually need it, but he liked it so much that he'd have been willing to fight the agent for it, which hadn't been necessary. The man had laughed and told him to keep it. He put the knife and the pistol into the plastic bag, along with a spare clip.

Ham took the gear down to his dock and tossed it into the whaler. Then he got an electric trolling motor from the back porch, clamped it to the stern of the whaler and attached it to the boat's battery with alligator clips. He fastened his rubber diving belt around his waist, minus the weights, got into the whaler, started the engine and headed out into the Indian River, accelerating to around fifteen knots. There was a moon, occasionally covered by clouds, but it was bright enough to light his way down the waterway.

Twenty minutes of running brought him within half a mile of the entrance to the Palmetto Gardens marina. He cut the outboard, pulled it out of the water and switched on the nearly silent trolling motor. He sat on the bottom of the boat to keep a low profile, and moving silently along at around two knots, he soon reached several acres of marsh just north of the marina entrance. A little creek provided an opening in the marsh grass, and he turned into it, peering ahead into the darkness, heading toward the riverbank. After perhaps three minutes, the bow of the whaler touched the mud, and Ham switched off the trolling motor.

He sat silently in the bottom of the boat and listened for five minutes by his illuminated wristwatch. His eyes were well accustomed to the darkness, now, and he could see that he was perhaps thirty feet from dry ground. He kicked off his Top-Siders and stepped into the water, feeling out the soft mud with his bare feet. He pushed the whaler into the marsh grass, which was a good two feet tall, shucked off his T-shirt, got his plastic bag and waded slowly toward the land. It was another twenty feet to the brush, and he covered it quickly.

He sat down on the ground, his back to the dense thicket, and listened again for another five minutes. Once, he heard a vehicle in the distance, but it was driving at a steady speed and soon passed by.

He grabbed some leaves and cleaned the sticky river mud off his feet; then he dressed in the black warmup suit and sneakers, fastened the rubber belt around him, slipped his knife into the scabbard, worked the action of the small pistol and stuck it into his belt, slipping the spare clip into a zippered pocket. Finally, he pulled the jacket's hood around his head and tied it loosely, so as not to interfere with his hearing.

He walked silently along the thick brush bordering the marsh, occasionally using his hooded light for a second or two, until he found a small break in the vegetation. He pushed his way through for a good fifteen feet and emerged in a stand of pine trees that was well clear of any brush. The schmucks hadn't bothered with a fence along the river, he chuckled to himself. They had thought the dense brush would be enough. He walked along the edge of the clearing until his flashlight picked up a hint of a trail no more than a foot wide. Deer came this way, he reckoned, and if the ground was mined or, more likely, had security sensors, the deer were not setting them off. Neither would he, on this trail.

He emerged from the trees at the rear of a large, well-lit house, where there was a party going on, to judge from the noise. He found a window and peeked in. Fifteen or twenty people were standing or lying around a large room, and loud music was pounding against the walls. At least half of the people were naked. Ham watched with interest as various couples did various things to each other while the others watched and cheered them on. Tearing himself away, he moved to the north, toward the chain-link fence Holly had told him about.

Keeping to the edge of the pines, he walked north for ten minutes until the fence loomed high above him. Following the inside of the fence, he walked in a generally easterly direction until he came to a gate, which was secured with a chain and a padlock. Looking through the wire, he saw that this was one of not two, but three fences, and the middle one had the warning of high voltage.

Ham found a wire leading from the middle fence through the inner one and then into the ground along the inner fence. He followed the fence along until he came to where the wire emerged from the ground. It ran to a small wooden shed that was not locked. He opened the door and switched on his flashlight. The wire ran to an ordinary car battery, a large one. This was clearly a backup for the security system.

He left the shed and, working from his memory of Jackson's aerial photographs, walked south for a few minutes. He knew he was in the right place when he saw the huge satellite dish peeking up over the shrubbery. The com center was dark, except for a single light burning in what seemed to be an entrance hall. He could see a man at a desk, reading a magazine by the light of a lamp.

Ham circled the building until he came to a large live oak tree. He found footholds and climbed into its branches, one of which ran close to the top of the two-story building. He shinnied out the limb as far as he dared, then stopped. He could see three large lumps on the roof: two of them were air conditioning units and the other appeared to be a vented metal box of about the same size. He backed his way to the trunk of the tree and slowly climbed down.

There was one more place he wanted to see, and it was no more than a hundred yards from the com center, if he recalled the aerial photographs correctly. Watching for any sign of security measures, he walked silently to the southwest, in and out of shrubbery and trees. He crossed the lawn of another large house, this one dark, and went on for another fifty yards before stopping.

Ham looked around. It could be in either direction. Suddenly, he stood stock-still. Although he was in an area that appeared to be deserted, hairs were standing up on the back of his neck. He could almost smell somebody in the area. In fact, he realized, he did smell something. It was cigarette smoke, and he didn't know from which direction it came. He stood frozen, his eyes open wide. Afraid to use the flashlight, he turned his head from right to left. Then he saw it. Not ten feet from where he stood, the end of a cigarette glowed in the dark. Then it grew brighter and revealed a head.

Ham did not move, afraid of appearing in the man's peripheral vision. They were too far apart for the knife, so Ham slowly eased the pistol from his belt and waited. A minute passed, then two. Finally, the man dropped the cigarette and ground it out with his foot. He appeared to be dressed in camouflage fatigues.

The man moved forward a few steps and vanished. Ham blinked. Where had he gone? As quietly as he could, he walked to the tree the man had been leaning against, stood behind it and surveyed the ground on the other side of it. Perhaps twelve feet ahead, he saw a dim light on the ground. He walked very slowly toward it, keeping an eye out for the man, and stopped a pace away, looking down.

What he was looking at, he realized, was a light shining through netting. Silently, Ham lay down on the ground and put his face against the netting. He could see the light now, and it illuminated the inside of a hole in the ground. He saw a man's foot and then a steel ammunition box. Shifting slightly, he was able to see more. The man was wearing a headset attached to a small cassette player or radio. He was sitting on a camp stool next to a heavy automatic weapon, the barrel of which protruded through the camouflage netting. Ham reckoned the ammo was larger than fifty caliber. There was nothing else to see here. He backed away from the netting, got to his feet and disappeared into the nearby woods.

Half an hour later, he was back in the water, pushing the whaler out into the creek. Half an hour after that, he was back home, with a story to tell.

52

Rita turned up on time for work at Palmetto Gardens, her second day on the job. She hooked up with Carla, and this time they were assigned to clean shops. She looked longingly at the security building—that was most where she wanted to plant one of her bugs, but instead, she was put to work in a jewelry store across the street.

She was surprised by the elaborate nature of the merchandise in the shop's cases. As she sprayed the glass top of a counter and wiped it clean, she gazed at a diamond necklace that would not have been embarrassed to be in a showcase at Tiffany's in New York. Counting the stones quickly, she estimated that the necklace contained at least twenty carats of diamonds, none of them small.

Carla sent her to clean the office, and she disturbed a man who was taking still more jewelry out of a large safe. As he closed the steel door she caught sight of two stacks of cash on the top shelf. Apparently, the shop's customers didn't bother with credit cards or checks.

The two women cleaned two more shops, then broke for lunch. They sat on a bench outside and ate their sandwiches, chatting idly about Carla's children and grandchildren.

"What's in there?" Rita asked, nodding at the security station.

"Security guards," Carla said.

"You ever clean in there?"

"Sure, a bunch of times."

"They got a toilet?"

"Yeah, I've cleaned it."

"I'll be right back," Rita said. She got up, walked across the street, carrying her cleaning supplies, and walked through the front door.

A young man sat on a stool at a high desk. "We already got cleaning people in here today," he said.

"I know," Carla replied. "I just want to use your bathroom, is that okay?"

"Yeah, I guess so," the man said. He pointed. "It's right down the hall, there. It's coed, so you better lock the door."

Rita walked down the hall and into a small bathroom. Quickly, she retrieved the canister that Bob had given her, removed the bugs, and put them under a rag in the plastic carrier that contained her cleaning supplies. She left the bathroom and looked around. Dead ahead of her was a communications station, and a large, red-haired, mean-looking man sat at it, reading a gun magazine. He looked up and stared at her, smiling, until she walked away. Apart from that, there was only the hallway; there was nowhere to place a bug. She went back to the front door. "Thanks," she said to the man at the desk, then left the building.

Well, shit, she thought to herself. That was a waste of effort. She had four bugs and nowhere to plant them. Then her luck changed. A truck came down the street and stopped in front of the security station. Two men got out, went to the rear and started to remove a steel desk from the back of the truck. Rita got up and walked across the street, carrying her plastic carryall.

"You guys need a hand?" she asked.

"Nah, we got it," one of the men replied. They set the desk on the ground.

"Wait a minute," she said, "Let me give it a wipe." She grabbed a spray container and a rag from her carryall and palmed a bug.

"Don't worry about it," the man said, waving her off.

"It's filthy," Rita said, spraying cleaning fluid all over the desktop. "Where's it been, in the warehouse?"

"C'mon, lady, you're holding us up," the man said.

Rita began wiping the desktop clean, while with her other hand she gripped the edge of the desk. Just for a moment, she got the hand all the way under the desktop, and the magnetic bug took hold. "There you go," she said. She went back to her bench and watched them move the desk into the building.

Then her heart stopped. In order to get the desk through the front door of the building, the two men had turned the desk on its side. There, in plain view, was the bug she had planted. The security officer at the desk came to the door to help get the desk through, and as they wrestled it through the door, his face was within a foot of the bug. Finally they disappeared inside, and she could no longer see the desk.

"Let's get back to work," Rita said to Carla. For the first time, Rita began to think about how she might get out of Palmetto Gardens, if she had to. She thought about it as they cleaned the next shop, and she came up with absolutely nothing. There was nothing to do but finish the day's work and hope no one had seen the bug on the desk.

At three o'clock, Rita and Carla got back on the bus. It was not until that moment that it occurred to Rita that, at the service gate, she would be searched again. And she still had three bugs. She couldn't leave them in the carryall, because somebody else might get it the next day and discover the bugs.

"You got any Kleenex?" Rita asked Carla as they reached the back gate and started to get off the bus.

Carla rummaged in her carryall and found a box of tissues.

Rita got the three bugs from under the rag and concealed them in her hand, grabbing a couple of tissues from the box. They lined up to be searched, and while one guard took the carryalls and set them aside, another body-searched each of the women. Rita hung back as the searches continued, and when her turn came, she managed a large sneeze. She blew her nose loudly into the tissues, then wadded them up around the three bugs. "Excuse me," she said to the guard, wiping her nose again with the tissues. He showed no interest in inspecting the damp mess in her hand. Rita walked across the parking lot to where she had left her car. All the other women were driving away. She had her hand on the door handle when someone's heavy hand landed on her shoulder and spun her around.

The man who had been sitting at the radio in the security office now had her by the throat. He began dragging her toward the guard shack.

Rita thought fast. Her FBI ID, her gun and her cell phone were hidden under the spare tire in the trunk of her car. As she struggled, she let the Kleenex in her hand fall to the ground, she hoped unnoticed.

Mosely cuffed her across the face and, stunned, she was dragged into a waiting Range Rover.

53

Harry Crisp looked at his wristwatch, then at the group around him at the table. "Rita should be here by now," he said. "She got off at three."

Holly spoke up. "Did we get anything from any of the bugs she took in there?" She turned and looked at the front door as it opened. Bill walked in. "Hey, everybody," he said. "Where's Rita?"

"She's not here yet," Harry replied. "Did any of the bugs go live?"

"They were all live when she took them in," Bill said. "I got a few words on one of them, then it seemed to go dead. We've picked up some car noise on at least one of the others, but no voice."

"What words did you get on one of them?"

"Two men talking, then they stopped, went quiet."

"They found the bug, then?"

"Could be."

"Bill, get on the radio and get somebody to check the parking lot at the service gate at Palmetto Gardens," Harry said. "I want to know if her car is still there."

"Right away."

Harry turned back to the group. "If the bugs don't work, then we're going to need another excuse for a search warrant."

Ham raised a finger. "Maybe I can help."

Everybody turned and looked at him.

"How?" Holly said, looking at him narrowly.

"Well, I was in there last night, and I saw a few things."

"What?" Holly said.

Harry spoke up. "Tell me what you're talking about, Ham."

"I just thought I'd take a look around," Ham said.

"Ham . . ." Holly began, but Harry held up a hand to quiet her.

"How did you get in?" Harry asked.

"I went in through the marsh next to the marina entrance, then I took a walk."

"Somebody get the aerial photographs," Harry said. They were laid on Jackson's dining table, and Harry spread them out. "Show me," he said.

Ham stood up and pointed. "I took my boat in here about three this morning, then waded ashore. They're depending on about fifteen feet of thick brush for a fence back there, and it ain't working." He began to give them an account of his reconnaissance.

"I don't believe this," Holly said. "You're completely crazy."

"Well, everybody just seemed to be dying to know what was in there, so I thought I'd take a look," her father replied.

"Go on, Ham," Harry said.

Ham pointed to the photographs again. "I got a look inside a house right here. A regular orgy going on in there."

"Anybody see you?"

"Nope. Then I worked my way over to the chain-link fence, right here," Ham said. "Turns out there's three fences. The middle one is hot."

"Three fences," Holly repeated tonelessly.

"Yep. I went over to the com center, right here, which seemed to be shut down for the night, except for one man inside the front door. Had a look on the roof, too. The air conditioners are up there and what looks like either a self-contained generator or maybe a battery backup."

"For the computers," Jackson said. "I guess it would be bad if all of them went down at once, in a power failure."

"But they've got a big generator that cuts in if the power fails for five seconds," Holly said. "Barney Noble told me that."

"Five seconds without power is forever to a computer," Jackson said. "They'd want a battery backup, even if it's only good for long enough to let them save the data they're working on and shut the things down."

"What else did you see, Ham?" Harry asked.

"There's a gun emplacement right here," Ham said, pointing. "I saw a heavy automatic weapon—not something I recognized either. Might be Chinese or something. Bigger than fifty caliber. It would sure play hell with a helicopter. One guy manning it, and he didn't look too vigilant. I could have killed him three or four times."

"If I can tell a federal judge that an informant has told me there are illegally imported weapons in there, that might get me a warrant," Harry said.

Bob came back. "Rita's car isn't in the parking lot," he said.

Harry went into his briefcase, came up with a sheet of paper and handed it to Holly. "This is a description of her car. Can you put out an APB on it? I'm worried."

"Sure, I can." Holly made the call from Jackson's office, then came back. "You think they caught her placing the bug?"

"It's a better possibility than I want to think about," Harry said.

"I think we ought to let Barney Noble know we know she's missing," Holly said.

"What? You're going to call him up and ask if he's got our agent?"

Holly got out her notebook, looked up the number for Palmetto Gardens and dialed it. "Security office," she said to the operator.

"Security," a man's voice said.

"Barney Noble," Holly said.

A moment later, Barney came on the line.

"Barney, it's Holly Barker. How are you?"

"Pretty good, Holly. What's up? I was just on my way home to dinner."

"Barney, we just had a call from a Mrs. Garcia, whose daughter works out there as a domestic. The girl didn't come home after work, and she's worried. You folks heard anything about her?"

"Hang on, I'll check," Barney said. He didn't cover the phone. "One of you guys hand me the checkout roster for the service gate," he said. There was a shuffling of paper. "Here we go," he said. "Is she Rita Garcia?"

"That's the one."

"She checked out at the service gate with the other cleaning women just after three o'clock this afternoon."

"Do you check them out one by one?"

"Yeah, we do a body search to be sure they haven't lifted anything from one of the houses, and then they're checked off the list. She left, all right—no doubt about it."

"Okay, Barney. Would you do me a favor?"

"Sure."

"Would you call me if she doesn't show up for work tomorrow morning?"

"Be glad to. I'll alert the man on the gate to look for her."

"Thanks. Good night."

"Good night."

Holly hung up. "He says she checked out just after three this afternoon."

"Sure, she did," Harry said. "I've got another reason for a search warrant now. Jackson, can I use your office phone? I want to call a judge of my acquaintance."

"Sure, help yourself."

Harry disappeared into Jackson's office and closed the door behind him.

"Ham," Holly said, "what the fuck do you mean going into that place?"

Ham shrugged and grinned.

"Those guys could have *you* right now."

"No, they couldn't," Ham replied. "They don't have anybody could take me."

Holly rolled her eyes and sighed.

Harry came back. "The judge is thinking about it," he said. "He'll call me back later."

"If we're going in there, we're going to need a lot more help," Holly pointed out.

"Yeah, but I can't request the manpower until I've got a search warrant."

"Jesus, Harry, if Rita is missing and presumed in there, what more does the judge need?"

"I think he just wants to see if she turns up on her own. He knows what a big effort this would be, and he wants to be sure his warrant stands up on appeal."

"So what do we do now?" Holly asked.

"We wait," Harry replied.

54

Holly was wakened from a deep sleep by the telephone. She reached over Jackson's inert form and picked it up. "Hello?" She listened for a moment. "Where?" she asked. "Have you ordered any equipment?" She listened. "I'll be there as soon as I can."

Holly got out of bed and looked at the clock: just after one A.M.

"What?" Jackson mumbled.

"Go back to sleep, baby," she said, kissing him on the cheek. She got into a robe and padded down the hall to the guest room where Harry Crisp was sleeping.

Harry's light was on, and he was sitting on the edge of the bed, rubbing his eyes. "Was that call what I hope it wasn't?"

"I'm afraid so. Some mullet fishermen found the car up next to the north bridge. They're trying to get it out now."

"Give me five minutes," Harry said, heading for the bathroom.

Holly got dressed quickly and met Harry downstairs. On the way, Harry was quiet. At the north end of the island Holly headed for the bridge, but turned off the road before reaching it, into a roadside park with a few picnic tables and a boat ramp. Two police cars were parked beside the ramp, their headlights illuminating the area, and a large wrecker had backed down it to the water's edge. A man in a diving suit emerged from the water.

"Okay!" he yelled. "It's hooked on." He came and stood next to Holly while the wrecker winched the car up the ramp. "Looks like somebody just drove it right down the ramp," he said. "It was only a couple of feet underwater."

The car came backing out of the river. When it was securely on the ramp, the wrecker drove forward a few yards until the car rested on dry ground. There seemed to be nothing wrong with it, except that it was wet.

Holly and Harry looked inside the car, opened the doors, checked the backseat. Holly took the keys from the ignition. "Let's have a look at the trunk," she said. She walked to the rear of the car, found the right key, and unlocked the trunk. "Oh, Jesus," she said.

Harry stood next to her. "The bastards!" he said.

Rita's naked body lay on top of the spare tire. Her gun, her ID and her cell phone were scattered around her.

Harry took out his phone and punched in a number. "This is Crisp," he said. "Who's the duty officer? Put me through to him. . . . Warren, it's Harry Crisp," he said. "I've got a dead agent in Orchid Beach. It's Rita Morales. I want you to get hold of the best pathologist in the Miami area and fly him up here immediately. He'll be met at Orchid Beach Airport and brought to the local hospital. I want the most thorough possible postmortem." He broke the connection.

"I'll call an ambulance," Holly said.

Harry began talking on the trip back, his voice low and sad. "She came over from Cuba on a raft when she was eight years old," he said. "She nearly died of thirst before they were picked up by a pleasure boat and brought to Miami. Her mother did die, but her father made it. He'd been a lawyer in Havana before Castro. She got a law degree from the University of Virginia and joined the Bureau right out of school. She was first in her class at the academy. She was only twenty-six, but she was as smart an investigator as I've ever worked with. She had a real future with us. She was ambitious, and she wasn't afraid to take chances. That could be what got her killed."

"It wasn't your fault, Harry," Holly said quietly.

"I know it wasn't, in my head," he said, "but in my gut, I know it was."

"She was qualified for the job. You trusted her judgment. In the circumstances, it was the right call."

"I know it was," Harry said. "But sometimes the right call can rise up and bite you on the ass. And it hurts like hell."

Back at the house, Jackson scrambled them some eggs, and they ate disconsolately. It was just after nine when the call came for Harry. He took it in Jackson's office and left the door open. He listened, nodding. "Thank you for coming up here, Doctor," he said finally, then hung up. He came back to the table and sat down heavily. "Cause of death was blunt force trauma to the head, probably from fists. Ligature marks on both wrists and ankles. All her ribs were broken, massive internal injuries. First, they raped her . . . every orifice."

"Was the doctor able to collect any sperm samples?" Holly asked.

Harry nodded. "The samples will be in the Washington by noon. The lab will pull out all the stops—we don't lose an agent all that often."

They were quiet for a while.

"Maybe you'd better call the judge," Holly said.

Harry nodded and stood up. "I've got to call Rita's father first," he said. He went to Jackson's office and closed the door behind him.

Holly and Jackson drank coffee, saying nothing.

Half an hour passed, and Harry came out of the office and sat down. "Jackson," he said, "I need a place to marshal my people. A big place—warehouse, theater, something."

"What time of day?"

"After dark, until morning."

"The community college has a gymnasium that's also used as an auditorium. It's separated from the rest of the school by a stand of woods, and there's a big parking lot."

"You know anybody there?"

Jackson wrote down a name and handed it to Harry. "That's the president," he said.

Harry went back into Jackson's office and closed the door.

The phone rang, and Holly picked it up.

"Chief, it's the dispatcher. You had a call from a Barney Noble."

Holly dialed the number and asked for Barney.

"Hi, Holly. You asked me to call if Rita Garcia didn't show up for work this morning. She didn't. We called her home number, but there was no answer."

She wanted to scream at him, but instead, she said, "Thanks, Barney."

"Has her mother heard anything?" Noble asked.

"No."

"Let me know if you hear anything. Maintenance will want to find a substitute if she's not coming back."

"I'll let you know, Barney." She hung up. "I wish I could just go out there and shoot him right now."

"I'd help," Jackson said.

Harry finally came out of the office. "Okay," he said, "we're set. I've got over three hundred men coming—FBI, DEA, ATF—every federal agent we could muster. They'll be arriving at the community college after dark in vans and cars, and they'll be heavily equipped." He sat down. "Holly, there's not going to be a lot in this for you—not even Barney Noble."

"I had a feeling," Holly said.

"Killing an FBI agent is a federal crime. I want him for that. If we can't put together the evidence to support the charge, then you can have him on the falsification-of-records business, and you can have whoever did the work for him at the capitol, if the state doesn't take it away from you."

"What I want most is the murderers of Chet Marley and Hank Doherty," Holly said. "Can I have that, if you take Barney?"

"Sure, you can. I'll talk to the federal prosecutor for you."

"I'm going to have to get a confession, or somebody to finger them, so I'll need interrogation time."

"You'll have it, I promise. In the meantime, I think you'd better go to work, keep everything as normal as you possibly can. You and Jackson can come out to the gym tonight around nine. I'll leave word with the sentries that you're to be admitted. I want your input on how we go about this. Ham's, too, of course. He's the only one with any hard information about what we're up against."

"Sure," Holly replied.

Harry looked out over the sea, and he seemed far away. "This is not going to be an easy one," he said.

55

Holly went into the office like a good girl, but her heart wasn't in it. She was sad and angry and having a hard time with both emotions. Finally, for something to keep her busy, she picked up the personnel files and began to plow through them, concentrating as hard as she could.

There was a rap at the door, and she looked up. Bob Hurst, the homicide detective, was standing in her doorway. "Morning, Bob," she said.

Hurst looked red-faced, angry. "Why didn't you call me on the homicide last night?" he demanded.

"Sorry, Bob," she said. "I had it covered."

"Don't you think that when an FBI agent gets killed in this jurisdiction that I ought to be on it?" he demanded.

"As a matter of fact," she said, "nobody from this department is on it. It's a federal matter, and the FBI are handling it."

"Even when it's on our turf?"

"The United States of America is their turf, Bob, and when an FBI agent gets killed, the FBI investigates."

"What was the FBI doing up here, anyway?"

"They wouldn't tell me—some sort of investigation, I guess. They asked me to put out an APB for their missing agent yesterday, and I did. Apparently, she was working out at Palmetto Gardens on something. She checked out of there at three yesterday afternoon and disappeared. A fisherman found her car early this morning, and I called the agent in charge and went out there with him, as a courtesy."

"How was she killed?"

"The FBI handled the autopsy; they didn't share the results with me."

Hurst looked at the floor.

"Bob, if it had been my call, I would have involved you, but it wasn't."

"Yeah, well, I'm sorry if I got huffy. You think this has anything to do with Marley and Doherty?"

Holly wrinkled her brow. "That hadn't occurred to me. Why do you connect the two incidents?"

He shrugged. "I don't know. You think anybody at Palmetto Gardens had anything to do with the woman?"

He's fishing, Holly thought. "I talked to Barney Noble. He checked his lists and said she left work around three P.M. with all the other domestic help. I've no reason to doubt him. If you want my take on this, she went for a drink somewhere after work and met the wrong guy."

"You don't think it was connected with what she was investigating?"

"I don't know what she was investigating, so I can't make that judgment."

"Thanks, Chief," he said, and went back to his desk.

Holly sat, wondering why Hurst had done that. He'd surely heard from the two patrolmen last night that the corpse was that of an FBI agent, and he'd know that another agent had been present and had ordered the autopsy. She dug Hurst's personnel file out of the pile and opened it. She'd been through it a few days before, but she wanted a closer look now.

There was a new document in the file, one that hadn't been there the last time Holly had seen it. Bob Hurst had gotten married, and he had filled out a form requesting that his new wife be added to his health insurance. The box requiring her name before the marriage read "Linda Tomkins Wallace" and her address before the marriage had been on Egret Island, where Hurst also lived. Nobody had mentioned it to Holly, but Bob Hurst had married Hurd Wallace's ex-wife. She thought about that for a moment. Something was gnawing at her memory, but she was tired, and she couldn't bring it into her frontal lobe. Never mind, it would come to her.

She put down the file, picked up the next one and began reading. Then she stopped. There, staring at her from the file, was something so obvious that she was dazed. She went to the ladies' room and splashed cold water on her face, staring at herself in the mirror, realizing how naive she had been.

Holly told Jane Grey that she was going to do some patrolling and left the station, taking Daisy with her. The dog sat in the front seat of the jeep and stuck her nose into the wind through the partly open window. She was so enthusiastic about the experience that Holly was afraid to open the window more than three or four inches for fear Daisy would lean out too far and fall out of the car. Holly drove north aimlessly, thinking about what she had discovered and what it could mean and wondering why she hadn't read those personnel files sooner. At the north end of the island, wanting to remain alone with her thoughts, she turned onto Jungle Trail and drove slowly along its deserted length, coming to a halt a few yards from the back gate to Palmetto Gardens.

"Stay, Daisy," she said and got out of the car, leaving the motor running to keep the interior cool. She paced up and down beside the car, taking deep breaths and trying to calm herself, while Daisy poked her nose through the partly opened car window and watched her. This wasn't what Holly had expected at all. She leaned against a tree. First, Hurd Wallace had seemed like the bad guy, then had turned out not to be—or was he? And now . . . She jumped as she realized somebody was standing only a few feet away from her.

"Well," he said, "good afternoon, Chief."

Holly looked at the gun in Cracker Mosely's hand; it was pointed at her chest. "Why are you pointing a weapon at me, Mosely?" she asked. Her heart was pounding.

"Why, you're trespassing, don't you know that? You're on Palmetto Gardens property."

"No, I'm not. Point that gun somewhere else." Holly realized that she was alone in a secluded spot with Mosely, and that Daisy couldn't get to her. A trickle of cold fear ran down her bowels.

Mosely walked quickly toward her and pressed his pistol up under her chin. He removed her own weapon from its holster and threw it away. Behind him, Daisy was going crazy, trying to get out of the car. "Shut the dog up," Mosely said.

"Daisy! Quiet!" she said. Daisy stopped growling, but she was jumping back and forth from the front seat to the rear, trying to find a way out of the closed car.

"Good," Mosely said. He drew back his empty hand and backhanded her, knocking her to the ground, then he put his knee in her back and cuffed her hands behind her with her own handcuffs. He turned her over and sat astride her. "Well, now, it's just you and me, isn't it?" he said, grinning. "I've been waiting for the chance to be alone with you, baby."

"Cracker, do you want to go back to prison?" she asked, trying to control her fear. "I can arrange that, you know."

"You're all through arranging things for me," Mosely said, starting to unbutton her uniform shirt.

"Don't do this, Cracker. You can still stay a free man."

"You bet your ass I can," he said, yanking her shirt open. He moved down, unbuckling her gun belt and unzipping her pants. Soon he had them off. Holly was now exposed, except for her underwear. He stood up and started taking off his own clothes. He holstered his gun and tossed the gun belt a few feet away. "I'm going to give you some of what I gave little Rita," he said. "She loved every minute of it, believe me. She enjoyed Barney, too. We gave her a real ride."

Holly started trying to get to her feet, but Mosely kicked her in the chest with his bare foot, and she went down. Daisy went nuts again, but this time Mosely didn't seem to notice. He was fondling his penis, which was responding. He came back toward Holly.

Holly waited until he was at the right distance and kicked at his genitals, but instead, her heel caught him on his muscular thigh.

He jumped on top of her, pinning her bare legs under his body, then sat astride of her again. "You're going to pay for that one," he said, beginning to fondle his penis again. He reached down with his other hand, took hold of her bra and yanked it off her, then he did the same with her panties.

Holly was now wearing nothing but her open shirt and the handcuffs. She struggled, but now he was rubbing his penis around her face, trying to force open her mouth. Holly looked over his shoulder at Daisy. Something had happened. She still had her head out the window, struggling to get her body through the narrow gap. But the window had gone down maybe an inch. In her frenzy, Daisy had somehow put a paw on the electric window switch. Do it again, Daisy, Holly prayed to the dog.

"You don't want it in the mouth, huh?" Mosely said. "Well, we can save that for later, when you don't have so much fight in you." He rolled her over onto her stomach, staying astride of her.

Now she was completely helpless. His weight on her legs kept her from moving them, and she couldn't get any leverage to attack him with her cuffed hands. Mosely was rubbing his penis up and down her buttocks. He parted them with his hands and was now probing for her anus. Holly gritted her teeth and held her breath, helpless. She could stand this, she thought; she could stand this and live to kill this man.

Then, suddenly, Mosely screamed and was off her, rolling in the dirt.

Holly tried to get to her feet. She could see that the car window was open, and Daisy was out. She moved forward on her knees, pressed her forehead against the car door, stood up and turned around. Daisy was on Mosely's back, and her teeth were buried in the nape of his neck. The dog held on gamely while Mosely tried to get his hands on her throat and hit at her with his fists. He was on his feet, now, trying to swing Daisy against a tree. Holly moved. She ran up to him from behind and, aiming well, kicked him in the balls as hard as she possibly could, throwing herself to the ground in the process.

Mosely fell down and continued to struggle with Daisy. He tried to get to his feet again, but this time, Holly was in front of him and swung a kick into his solar plexus, sending him down again. Still, he struggled.

He was going to be too strong for both of them, Holly thought. She looked around for her gun, but he had thrown it away. His gun, still in its holster, was on the ground behind him. She aimed a swift kick at his nose, splattering blood everywhere, then ran around his writhing body and found the holster. There was no way she could get at it while on her feet. She knelt, but that wasn't working, either. She lay down on the ground beside the holster and groped for the weapon.

Mosely stood up and swung around, bashing Daisy against a tree trunk. This time, the dog let go of him and fell on the ground, stunned. Mosely looked surprised to be free, then he looked at Holly and saw what she was trying to do. He came at her, naked and awesome, blood streaming from his nose down his body.

Holly rolled across the holster, finding the butt of the pistol with her left hand on the way. She would have one shot, nearly blind, and then he would be on her. She rolled over again to increase the distance between them, then, half guessing where he was, she pointed the gun away from her body and pulled the trigger. It was a double-action pistol; it did not need to be cocked. The gun roared, and over her shoulder, she saw the bullet strike him in the right shoulder, spinning him around and sending him to the ground. She got her head against a tree and struggled to her feet.

Mosely was on one knee now, trying to get up, making animal noises.

Holly ran around him and, standing close to him, watching his face over her shoulder, pulled the trigger again. The bullet entered Mosely's forehead, and the back of his head exploded. He fell backwards and lay, inert, on the ground.

Afraid to let herself relax, afraid that others from Palmetto Gardens would hear the shots and come running, Holly ran to her empty trousers, sat on the ground next to them and began rummaging for her spare handcuff key. It took her a moment to root it out and another moment to get free, then she went to Daisy.

The dog got unsteadily to her feet. Holly held her head in her hands and talked to her. "You're fine, girl, and he's dead; he can't hurt us any more." Then she became conscious that she was still very vulnerable, naked and without Daisy to protect her. She got into her pants and shoes, buttoned her shirt and got her gun belt on again. With Mosely's pistol in her hand, she searched the woods for her own gun, found it, holstered it, then tossed Mosely's weapon into the car. She opened the door, and Daisy jumped into the car.

Holly got into the still-running vehicle, yanked it into reverse and raced backward until she found a spot to turn around. Finally headed back down Jungle Trail toward A1A, she used the speed dialer on her car phone to call the station and ask for Hurd Wallace.

"Deputy Chief Wallace," he said.

"Hurd, it's Holly."

"You sound winded. Are you all right?"

"I'm all right. Listen to me: out on Jungle Trail, near the north gate to Palmetto Gardens, Cracker Mosely attacked me, but I managed to shoot him. He's dead. Get out there and work the scene. Photograph everything, then call an ambulance and get the body out of here. Clean up the scene. Do it all as quietly as you can, and don't say anything to anybody about it. You got that?"

"Holly, we can't just let a shooting go," Wallace said.

"We're not letting it go. I'm reporting it to the police, right?"

"Right, I guess so."

"Register the body at the hospital as a John Doe. I don't want anybody to know he's dead."

"All right."

"Do you know where the community college gymnasium is?"

"Yes."

"Meet me there at sundown, but don't try to enter the gym or even the parking lot; just wait for me on the road. I'll fill you in then."

"Are you all right, Holly?"

"I'll be fine."

"Okay, I'll get out to Jungle Trail right now."

"And, for God's sake, don't let anybody, and I mean *anybody*, know where you're going. And when you get out here, watch out for Mosely's people. There may be more of them around."

"I'm on my way."

Holly drove toward Riverside Park and her trailer. She had to get cleaned up. She didn't want anybody to know what had happened to her. She thought about Rita Morales and realized how lucky she had been.

"Daisy," she said, rubbing the dog's head, "you are a wonderful human being."

56

Holly got changed and fed Daisy. She still had a couple of hours before dark. She drove north on A1A and turned into Jungle Trail. Maybe Hurd was still there. She drove rapidly along, then came around a corner and saw a police car and an ambulance. The body was being loaded, and Hurd had a garbage bag in his hand. Holly parked off the road to allow the ambulance to pass, then got out of the car and approached Hurd.

"Are you sure you're all right?" Hurd asked.

"I'm fine, thanks."

"What happened here, Holly? I found your underwear. Were you raped?"

"Almost," she said, then she gave him a terse account of what had happened while, at her insistence, he took notes.

She went to the car, got Mosely's gun and handed it to Hurd. "This is what I shot him with."

Hurd took the gun, released the clip and looked at the ammunition. "Hollowpoints," he said. "That accounts for the condition of the body."

"Did anybody show up here from Palmetto Gardens?" she asked.

"I was here for about fifteen minutes alone before the ambulance came," he replied. "A Range Rover drove up to the gate from the inside, sat there for a minute, then left. Nobody got out."

"Did they see your car?"

"I don't think so," Hurd said. "It was parked where it is now, out of the way." He pointed. "And the brush would have made Mosely's body hard to see."

"I wonder what Mosely was doing out here," Holly said. "He certainly wasn't looking for me, because nobody knew I would be here. I didn't know myself until I arrived."

"He was wearing sweatclothes and sneakers," Hurd replied. "Maybe he was jogging along the outside of the fence."

Holly realized that she had not even thought about what kind of clothes he was wearing. "Maybe so. But who would wear a gun while jogging?"

"Somebody who hoped to shoot something," Hurd said. "There are deer and other wildife out here. Maybe Mosely just liked to kill things."

"It wouldn't surprise me to learn that," she said. "Tell me, did you let *anyone* know you were coming out here?"

"No, you said not to."

"Good. There's something else I have to ask you about, Hurd. I'm sorry if it seems like prying."

"Shoot."

"Did Bob Hurst have anything to do with your divorce?"

"What do you mean?"

"I mean, was he having an affair with your wife?"

Hurd shook his head. "I don't believe he was. They started seeing each other after we separated. He told me that himself. Our house was just down the street from his, and we had socialized a little while I was still married. Bob had been divorced some years ago. He was lonely, I guess. I wasn't suprised that he and Linda got married."

"So, after Bob started seeing your wife, he would have had access to her house?"

"Yes, I suppose so. I had moved out, into an apartment, and like I said, he lived just down the street. Why are you asking about this?"

"Because I think Hurst stole the Smith & Wesson thirty-two from her house, the one Chet Marley was killed with."

"That makes some kind of sense, I guess. It was Bob who filed the burglary report for Linda."

"A smart move," Holly said. "Let me ask you this: remember the tape we heard of the bug in Barney Noble's car?"

"Yeah."

"You think that could have been Hurst in the backseat?"

"I honestly don't know. It was impossible to identify a voice from what we heard. Wasn't the FBI going to try to clean up the tape and improve the quality?"

"Yes, but I don't know if it's been done yet. I haven't heard anything."

"I think we ought to go talk to Bob Hurst," Hurd said, looking at his watch. "He might still be at the station."

"We don't really have anything on him yet. The tape isn't good enough, unless the FBI can work wonders with it."

"He doesn't know how good the tape is," Hurd said.

"You've got a point. Let's go."

As they walked into the police station, Bob Hurst was walking out.

"Got a minute, Bob?" Holly asked.

Hurst looked at his watch. "My wife's expecting me for dinner."

"You're going to be late," Holly said. She led Hurst to interrogation room one, with Hurd Wallace bringing up the rear, and closed the door behind them. "Sit down," she said.

Hurst looked at Holly and Hurd. "What's this about?" he asked.

"Put your gun and your badge on the table," Holly said.

"I asked you a question."

"And I gave you an order."

Reluctantly, Hurst did as he was told. Hurd put the two items into his pocket, and they all sat down.

"Consider that I have read you your rights," Holly said.

Hurst now looked worried.

"Bob, this is the one and only chance you're going to have to help yourself," Holly said.

Hurst watched as Hurd set a tape recorder on the table.

"Before we turn on the machine, I need to tell you three things. First, the FBI has had a bug in Barney Noble's car for some time, now; second, we know you stole the Smith & Wesson thirty-two from Linda's house; and third, Cracker Mosely has confessed." Mosely had confessed only to raping Rita Morales, but Hurst didn't know that.

"Confessed to what?" Hurst said.

"It's over, Bob. We've got you on tape taking money from Barney Noble to rat out the department."

Hurst didn't deny it. "What did Cracker tell you?" he asked.

"You have to tell us everything right now, or face . . . well, you know what you'll have to face."

Hurst began to sweat. "Jesus, I just got married," he said.

Holly said nothing.

"I talk, I walk," Hurst said.

Holly still didn't speak.

"Look, I didn't kill anybody! I can give you who did, but I have to walk!"

"We may be able to help you," Holly said.

"I want a guarantee. I was there. I didn't have a choice. But I didn't kill anybody."

"If that's the truth, and you testify against them, tell us everything, and I mean *everything*, then I'll recommend to the prosecutor that you walk." She turned to Hurd and nodded.

Hurd turned on the recorder.

"I am Chief of Police Holly Barker," she said into the microphone. "Deputy Chief Hurd Wallace is present." She gave the date and time. "Detective Robert Hurst is present for interrogation. Detective Hurst, have you been apprised of your Miranda rights?"

"Yes," Hurst said.

"Do you wish to have an attorney present during this interrogation?"

"No," Hurst replied.

"Start at the beginning. Tell us everything," Holly said.

Hurst took a couple of deep breaths. "I first met Barney Noble at Hank Doherty's house at a poker game last May. Hank, Barney,

Chet Marley, Cracker Mosely and I were present. It was the first time I had met Mosely, too. My car was in the shop, and Chet had given me a ride. When we were through playing, Barney offered me a ride home, and I accepted. We stopped at a hotel bar for a nightcap.

"Talk got around to money. I had lost a couple of hundred bucks, mostly to Barney, and I couldn't really afford it. Barney gave me back my money and said he might be able to send some off-duty work my way. I had gotten soaked in a divorce and was pretty hard up, what with the alimony, and I said sure, I'd like that. Barney explained to me about Palmetto Gardens and how private the members wanted to keep it, and he said that it was important for him to know if my department ever had any interest in the place. All he wanted, he said, was a little advance warning. He offered me two hundred a week for that, and I agreed, and he drove me home. He gave me two hundred that night.

"A few weeks passed. I met with Barney once a week and told him I hadn't heard anything, and he'd give me the two hundred. Then, all of a sudden, he tells me he wants me to follow Chet Marley when he's off duty. I didn't want to do that, but Barney pressed me and reminded me that I had been signing receipts for the money he'd given me. So I started to follow Chet. Turns out, he was meeting with a guy, some kind of accountant, who was working at Palmetto Gardens. I saw them talking in a bar twice, on successive nights. When my meeting day with Barney came around, he got pretty excited when I told him about it. Next thing I knew, the guy was gone. Barney said he'd been transferred to his security company in Miami. I figured the guy was dead.

"Chet went to see Barney about it, but Barney gave him a line, and, I guess, Chet couldn't prove anything. I'm still following Chet at nights, and he's driving around Palmetto Gardens, sizing the place up, and at the next poker game, he starts pumping Barney about the place. Barney didn't like it. Next day, Barney calls me and says Chet's meeting with somebody else from Palmetto Gardens. I followed Chet, as usual, but he lost me. This happened two, three nights in a row. I don't know how he did it, but I just couldn't stay with him. I reported this back to Barney, and he told me to keep trying, and he'd work it from his end.

"Pretty soon, it becomes clear to me that Barney knows more about the department and the way it's run than I'm telling him. I ask him how he knows this stuff, but he won't tell me. I go on for a few months, meeting with Barney every week, telling him stuff I'm finding out, but he already seems to know what I'm telling him. It's like he's using me just to check out his other information.

"Then one night I'm meeting with Barney and Mosely at a gas station on A1A, and Chet Marley drives by. We hop into Barney's car and follow him. Barney figures if I can't stay with Chet, then he can. We're in Barney's personal car, a Lincoln, instead of the usual Range Rover. So we're following Chet south on A1A. Then Chet pulls over and when we pass, he flags us down.

"Oh, I forgot to say that Barney had asked me to get him a clean gun. I didn't know why he wanted it, and I didn't want to know, but he asked me for a gun. I gave him the thirty-two I had taken from Linda's place. Barney turns his car around, and we pull over, nose to nose, with Chet's car. Barney and Mosely get out. I'm ducking down in the backseat, because I don't want Chet to see me. I hear some arguing, and then there's a single shot. I stick my head up and I can see Barney and Mosely, but I can't see Chet. Then I see Barney wipe off the gun with a handkerchief and throw it over the fence into the woods beside the road.

"I'm petrified, you know? We're on a public highway, and they've just shot the chief of police. Then I see Barney looking inside Chet's car, and he goes to the trunk, too. Then he and Mosely get back in the car and we drive off. Mosely's at the wheel, and Barney's giving him instructions. He doesn't say where we're going, but a few minutes later we arrive at Hank Doherty's place. Barney tells me to stay in the car. He and Mosely get out, and I can see that Barney has a shotgun. They go inside, and I can hear the dog going crazy—the dog never liked Mosely—but a minute later that stops. I guess Hank put her in the kitchen. Then, half a minute after that, I hear the shotgun, just once. A few minutes later, Barney and Mosely come out of the house. I start to ask questions, and Barney tells me to shut up. They take me back to where my car was. Barney gives me a thousand dollars in cash and makes me sign a receipt for it, then they drive off." Hurst stopped talking.

"Who shot Chet Marley?" Holly asked.

"It must have been Barney. I gave him the gun, and I saw him throw it away."

"Who shot Hank Doherty?"

"Barney had the shotgun when they went in; he didn't have it when they came out."

"What's going on out at Palmetto Gardens, Bob?"

"I don't have the slightest fucking idea, and that's the truth. Barney never told me anything, and I sure wasn't going to start asking questions, after seeing what happened to the accountant and Chet and Hank."

"Who else was giving Barney information about Chet and the department?"

"I don't know, I swear it. I'd tell you if I knew."

"And that's all of it?"

"That's everything I know from day one, I swear to God. I mean, shit, Holly, what could I have done? I didn't know he was going to kill Chet."

"You could have arrested him as soon as you heard the shot," Holly said. "If you'd done that, Hank Doherty would still be alive."

Holly switched off the recorder. Bob Hurst began to cry.

57

Holly, Daisy, Hurd, Jackson, and Ham all arrived at the Community College gymnasium as the sun set. There were at least forty vehicles in the parking lot, mostly plain sedans and vans, some of them towing boats. Holly could see why Harry had wanted a quiet place to assemble.

The gym was a hive of activity. Piles of duffel bags lay around the polished wood floor, and weapons were everywhere. Men were checking assault rifles and small submachine guns. Everyone was dressed in black.

Harry waved Holly's group over to a folding table that had been set up on the gym floor. "Everybody have a seat," he said. He had a sheet of paper in his hand. "I've just heard from the National Security Agency," he said. "They've decoded the microbursts on the transmissions from the Palmetto Gardens com center."

Holly leaned forward in anticipation. "Do they shed any light on what's going on out there?"

Harry looked at the sheet of paper in his hand. "Apparently, they're having a golf tournament."

Nobody said a word.

"This is a list of the entrants," Harry said, and started to read. "Ben Hogan, Bobby Jones, Gene Sarazen, Walter Hagen, Harvey Pennick . . ." He read off another fifteen names. "Anybody got any ideas about this?"

Ham spoke up. "Harry, are you a golfer?"

"No."

"You know anything at all about the game?"

"No."

"Then you don't know that all the people whose names you just read out are either dead or very, very old?"

"Oh," Harry said. "Anybody got any ideas?"

"Harry," Holly said, "why would they go to the trouble to encode into microbursts the names of twenty dead golfers? Is this some kind of cryptographic joke?"

"Is there anything else in the microbursts?" someone asked.

"Just stuff about the golf tournament," Harry said. "'Exciting news: Bobby Jones will be playing.' That's one. Here's another. 'Players will be glad to hear that the prize money has been increased.'" Harry looked around the table. "Any ideas? *Anybody?*"

"Let me get this straight," Holly said. "All the microbursts are about more golfers signing up and the prize money being increased?"

"That's it. None of it makes any sense."

"Maybe the names are a kind of code, too," Hurd Wallace said. "Maybe they're just substitutions for real names. You can't crack that kind of code, can you? When one name is simply substituted for another?"

"I guess not," Harry said. "But why would they encode the names of players in a golf tournament?"

Holly's eyebrows went up. "Appalachin!" she said.

"The mountains?" Harry asked.

"Maybe the FBI would like to forget Appalachin, New York," Holly said, laughing. "After all, it was a New York state police bust."

"Appalachin, New York?" Harry said. "Why does that sound familiar?"

"Because it was the biggest Mafia meeting of all time—back in the fifties. The commission—the heads of all the families—had a big meeting at a country house in Appalachin, New York, somewhere upstate. The New York state police got wind of it and raided the place. There were guys in silk suits running through the woods like deer, with state patrolmen chasing them. It was a huge embarrassment for the mafiosi and a major coup for the New York cops. I think J. Edgar Hoover was still denying there was a Mafia at the time."

"Palmetto Gardens isn't Mafia," Harry said. "This is way too slick for those guys—too classy and too rich, as well. The Mafia could never muster the kind of money it took to build that place."

"It's got to be a meeting," Holly said. "So, it's not Mafia—it's whoever is behind Palmetto Gardens. They're getting together."

Harry turned to one of his men. "Ed, call Miami Center and find out what flights have been coming into Palmetto Gardens, starting a week ago and going right up to now."

The man disappeared to find a phone.

"Okay, Holly, we'll check that out. Now, before I start spouting off, I'd like to hear from you, Ham. You're the only one we've got who's been inside with any kind of effect. I've read your military record, and I want you in on this. There are some U.S. marshals here, and they can deputize you. You game?"

"I'm game," Ham replied. He turned to Holly. "And don't you say a word."

Holly looked at the ceiling.

"Okay, Ham," Harry said, "here's the situation: we've got a large, residential community spread over hundreds of acres, set down among lots of other residential communities, so we don't want stray rounds flying around the barrier island. How would you take this place with the least fuss, the fewest casualties and the fewest rounds expended?"

Ham stood up, leaned over the table and pointed. "They're vulnerable here, at the marsh north of the marina, where I went in; otherwise, I wouldn't have gotten in. I think what we've got to do is first, put a team in through the marsh to knock out their backup electrical generator, then cut their outside power supply. There's also a battery backup wired to the Jungle Trail back gate, and that should be taken out, because that would alert the security center if the back gate were opened. Once the power's out, we hit the main and service gates, break down the Jungle Trail gate, and we're in. Then, pretty much simultaneously, we've got to hit ten or eleven spots all at the same time. Those spots are: the security station, the com center, the airfield, the six camouflaged gun emplacements and the other two gates." He pointed them out.

"Thanks, Ham," Harry said. "That makes perfect sense to me. Will you lead the team in through the marsh?"

"Glad to."

"How many men you want?"

Ham did some counting. "Two each for the generator, the back gate battery backup and the back gate; four men right here to lay down covering fire, if we're detected. That's ten, plus me, in three boats. You'll want flat-bottomed boats, like Boston Whalers, either paddled the last half-mile or with trolling motors."

"We can do that. I'll pick some men, and you can brief them."

"Good."

"How many men to take the gun emplacements?" Harry asked.

"There was only one man in the one I checked out, but I think I'd count on two in each emplacement. However many feds you reckon it takes to deal with two men in each one."

"I think two each will do it."

"I wouldn't send in any choppers until the gun emplacements are out."

"Of course not."

"Maybe on the other two gates you could do this: You're going to need power to open the gates and lower the tire barriers, so after you get word that the preliminary infiltration is complete, cut the main power. Then, during the five seconds before the generator comes on, take the two guards. Say thirty seconds later, after the two gates are open, kill the generator. Then you can run as many vehicles as you want into the place."

"What about the marina?" Harry asked.

"Jesus, I forgot about that. You don't want people escaping by boat, do you? I think I'd take it from the shore side; the guards won't be expecting that. Do it first thing, along with the airfield."

"All right. Ham, do you think you could take the com center with your group? I'd be very surprised if the man on duty there didn't have some way to wreck the computers in the event of a raid."

"I bet he doesn't have the authority to do that without orders," Ham said, "and if there's no power, he's not going to get any orders."

"There's radio, but we can jam all the frequencies they use. Still, I'd like him taken out first thing after the power goes."

"We can do that. I'll give you odds that when the power goes and his radio doesn't work, he'll walk outside for a look around, to see what's going on."

"I hope it's that easy."

"If it isn't, we can do it the hard way."

"Use your own judgment, but take him alive, if you can. I want all the witnesses I can get."

"Right. You got stun grenades?"

"Yep."

"That should do it, in a pinch."

Harry turned to Bill, who was standing behind him. "Pick twelve men and assign them to Ham. Make sure they understand that he's in complete charge, then have them to get the necessary equipment together. Ham can brief them on what he wants to do."

Bill left the group.

Ed returned, clutching a sheet of paper. "Harry, Miami Center said six international flights came in the day before yesterday, eleven yesterday, and thirty-three more today. They're from all over everywhere—Europe, the Caymans, Mexico, the Dutch Antilles— you name it."

"Appalachin," Holly said.

Harry turned to Holly. "Where do you want to be in all this?"

"At the security station," Holly replied. "I want Barney, Harry. He killed Chet Marley and Hank Doherty. I can prove it, and I want him for that before you get your crack at him."

"He probably killed Rita Morales, too," Harry said.

"You might not be able to make that stick, but I've got a witness who can put Barney in the electric chair."

"I'll talk to the U.S. attorney about it," Harry said.

"I want him in *my* custody from the moment he's arrested," Holly said. "In *my* jail."

"Okay, done."

"Then if the U.S. attorney wants him, he'll have to sue me."

Harry grinned. "I can live with that. We'll want to interrogate him at some length, though."

"In my jail," Holly said.

"All right."

"Something we've got to consider," Holly said. "Whatever security people are on duty in the middle of the night are going to be patrolling, so they'll be loose on the landscape and will have to be dealt with accordingly. I doubt if there will be more than one or two men at the security station, and Barney won't be one of them. He'll be at home in bed, and we don't know where home is, yet."

"Good point," Harry said.

"I reckon we'll find out at the security station where Barney lives, and then I want to go after him. If we're lucky, if this goes well, he won't know we're on the grounds until we're cuffing him."

"And if we're not lucky?"

"Then he may elect to shoot at us. I'm ready for that, I think."

"Right," Harry said. He turned to Jackson. "You can hang out at the command post with me."

"Sounds fine," Jackson said.

"What about me?" Hurd Wallace said.

"I'd like you with me," Holly replied.

"Good. I'd like a crack at Barney Noble, too."

"Okay," Harry said. "Have some coffee and doughnuts, everybody. In a few minutes we'll meet with the team that's assigned to the security station, and you can be privy to all their planning."

Holly and Hurd wandered over to the coffee urn and helped themselves.

"Jesus," Hurd said, "this is really going to be something, isn't it?"

"Yeah," Holly agreed. "I just hope it goes the way Harry wants it to."

58

At two A.M., after nearly eight hours of briefings and planning, Holly, with Daisy by her side, sat sweating in the front seat of an FBI van, half a mile north of the main gate of Palmetto Gardens. She was armed with a silenced pistol, four stun grenades, a truncheon and pepper spray, and she was wearing a black jumpsuit with FBI stamped on the back, full body armor and a black Kevlar helmet. Behind her were a dozen more vehicles filled with men and equipment, and half a mile south of the main gate sat another dozen vehicles, their engines idling. Another group waited on Jungle Trail, near the back gate. Holly had pulled all her OBPD patrol cars off the north end of the island, to avoid any confusion. She knew that two men had worked their way on foot to within yards of the front-gate guard shack, and similar preparations had been made at the rear service gate.

At the same hour, Harry Crisp sat at a table in the gymnasium, a radio operator and Jackson Oxenhandler seated on either side of him. Jackson held a telephone in his hand, with an open line to the power company, which was standing by to cut the electricity supply to the whole of Palmetto Gardens.

"Don't tell them until I tell you," Harry said to Jackson.

Jackson nodded.

In the Indian River, half a mile north of the entrance to the Palmetto Gardens marina, Ham sat in the bottom of a Boston Whaler, paddling steadily. He led his little flotilla into the creek that meandered through the salt marsh, and they proceeded steadily toward the riverbank until the shallow-draft boats began to touch bottom. Ham held up a hand, a signal to sit still and be quiet. He waited several minutes, listening, and then, with his silenced pistol in hand, he stepped out of the whaler and waded slowly toward dry ground. It took him only a minute or so to find the break in the thick underbrush that he had used before, and a minute after that he was through to Palmetto Gardens. He stopped and listened for a time while he slipped on a pair of night goggles and looked around. Seeing nothing, he spoke into a handheld radio.

"One," he said, then held the radio to his ear.

"One," he heard Harry Crisp repeat.

"Ham's ashore," Harry said to the people in the gym.

The men waiting in the whalers heard the same transmission and began leaving the boats and wading toward shore.

Ham stood and counted the men as they emerged from the brush. When he was sure they were all with him, he spoke into the radio again.

"Two," he said, then listened for Harry's repetition of the number. He held up one finger, and two men stepped forward. He pointed in the direction of the Jungle Trail gate, and they trotted silently off in that direction. He held up two fingers, and two more men stepped forward. He started them toward the standby generator.

Holly, in her van, heard the number two spoken. "They're in," she said. "We've got four to six minutes to wait."

The man at the wheel nodded and heaved a deep sigh.

. . .

His men dispersed on their various errands, Ham beckoned for the two remaining to follow him. They set off toward the com center, following the deer trail Ham had used last time. When they reached the building's parking lot, Ham pointed at the front door. His two men skirted the parking lot and approached the building from both sides, taking up positions on either side of the front door. Only the one desk light inside seemed to be burning, as had been the case the last time Ham had visited. When his two men were in position, Ham circled the building, found the big live oak and climbed onto the roof of the building. He located the metal box and inspected it carefully with his hooded flashlight. When he had found the wires he wanted, he took a set of short bolt cutters from his backpack and cut both wires, then he went back down the tree. By the time he had skirted the parking lot again, there were two men on either side of the building's entrance.

Ham looked at his watch, counting the minutes, as more of his men joined him. Two remained at the back gate, ready to cut the padlocks, and two were at the generator. He was waiting for only one more radio signal, from those two. He pressed the handheld to his ear. The silence continued.

"Three," a voice said, finally.

"Three," Harry repeated.

"We're ready," Harry said to the command group. "Anybody got a reason not to proceed?" He looked around the group, but nobody said anything. Harry nodded at Jackson.

"Cut the power," Jackson said into the phone.

After a moment, the answer came back. "All power cut."

"Here we go," Harry said. No further commands were necessary.

Holly watched the main-gate guardhouse through binoculars. Suddenly, the light inside the little structure went off. "Go!" she said to her driver. The man slammed the vehicle into gear and accelerated down A1A. Holly kept the binoculars to her eyes, counting, ". . . three, four, five." The light in the guard shack flickered, then came on again. She could see a figure, dressed in black, waving both hands over his head. The guard was down, and the gates were opening. "We're in," Holly said.

Ham watched as the desk lamp inside the main entrance of the com center went off, then, five seconds later, came back on. "Thirty seconds," he whispered. He watched the seconds tick away on his wrist, and when the lights went out a second time, he stood up and sprinted for the front door. Just as he had predicted, the guard inside unlocked the door and stepped outside, looking around him. Immediately, two men were on his back, cuffing and gagging him.

Ham raced through the front door and stopped for a moment, listening to the handheld radio on the desk. A shrill whistle came from it. "Their radio frequencies are jammed," he said. He waved his men ahead of him; they were the experts in breaking into buildings, after all. He followed four of them upstairs, while others searched the ground-floor offices. They burst into the second-floor computer room, illuminating it with powerful flashlights while each office along the wall was searched.

"Nobody here!" an agent crowed.

Ham picked up his radio. "Four," he said.

"The com center is ours!" Harry Crisp yelled, and everybody yelled with him.

Holly's van roared through the open front gate of Palmetto Gardens and hung a right. "It's less than a mile," she said to the driver. Then she saw something ahead and to her left that nearly made her heart stop. The country club building was ablaze with light. She rolled down her window, and as they passed, she could hear the bass thump of incredibly loud music coming from the building. "Stop right here," she said to the driver.

"We're supposed to go straight to the security station," the driver said.

"Godammnit, stop right here!" she yelled.

The man stopped, and Holly got out of the van with Daisy. "Wait here," she said.

"You're going to get us in a lot of trouble," the driver said.

"I'll take the responsibility," Holly replied. "You just wait here." She ran up the driveway toward the clubhouse, keeping to the grass verge of the roadway, ready to jump into the bushes, if necessary. Ahead, she could see the parking lot, and it was full. A man with an automatic weapon stood guard at a corner of the building; she couldn't go farther without engaging him, and she couldn't see into the clubhouse from where she stood. She ran to an oak tree, holstered her weapon and began climbing. "Daisy, stay and guard," she said to the dog.

Daisy sat down at the base of the tree and stared into the darkness.

Holly stopped when she was twenty feet up. She had a clear view of the dining room, and what she saw appalled her. The huge room was jammed with people in evening dress, dancing to a rock band. This was no staff party, she thought. She climbed back down the tree, dropping the last six feet, then ran back to the van with Daisy and got in. She picked up the radio. "Harry," she said.

"No transmissions, except as planned," Harry's voice said irritably.

"Listen to me," she said. "Emergency."

"Go," Harry replied.

"There's a huge party going on at building CC. You read me? There must be three hundred people in there, you understand?"

Harry slammed his fist on the table. "Holy shit, we're in trouble!"

"What is she talking about?" Jackson asked.

"The country club! They're all at the fucking country club, and our people are going to be hitting empty houses!"

"Can't you change the orders?"

"I guess I don't have a choice," Harry said, looking at the team lists on the table before him. He pressed the transmit button. "Attention all parties," he said, his voice cracking with tension. "Emergency change of plans. Teams one, two, three, continue as planned and hold your objectives. All other teams—*everybody else*—mass two hundred yards from the clubhouse building. I say again: all other teams except one, two, and three, mass two hundred yards from the clubhouse building and wait for further instructions. Employ maximum concealment possible, maximum concealment. Team four, immediately on securing your objective, penetrate and neutralize security at clubhouse. Use extreme caution and any necessary prejudice. Team four, report when original objective secured."

"Team four, wilco," Holly said into the radio. "New assignment, guys," she said to the other men in the van. "We take out clubhouse security, then go in on Harry's command. And remember, a lot of the staff at the clubhouse is going to be packing."

Harry pressed the transmit button again. "Attention all personnel: clubhouse staff is likely to be armed."

Holly's van had reached the darkened village. "About the fourth or fifth building on your right," she said. "Slow down . . . stop!" She leapt out of the van and ran through the unlocked front door of the security office. "Daisy! Stay with me!" She followed a hallway and came into a large room with a bank of radios along one wall. A shrill shriek seemed to come from all of them, and a uniformed man was trying to use the telephone.

"Freeze! Police and FBI!" she shouted, and the man stood up, his hands in the air. An agent took the pistol from his belt and started to handcuff him. "Not yet!" Holly commanded. She grabbed the security man by his necktie and dragged him to a large wall map of Palmetto Gardens. "Where does Barney Noble live?" she said.

The man looked at her as if she were insane. "What?" he said.

Someone cuffed him across the back of his head. "Talk to the lady!" the agent said.

"Where does Barney Noble live?" she repeated.

The agent pointed to a house not far from the rear service gate. "Right there," he said.

"Handcuff him to something, and follow me," Holly said. She grabbed her radio. "Five," she said. "Team four to clubhouse." Then she ran for the van.

59

Harry Crisp jumped out of his seat. "There's five!" he yelled. "We've secured all the main objectives, now let's get over to that clubhouse." He grabbed a handheld radio, and he and his command people sprinted for their cars.

Holly's van pulled out of the village. They drove along the perimeter of the golf course.

"Pull over," Holly commanded. "We go from here on foot." She got out of the van, put Daisy on a short leash and closed the door quietly. "Now listen," she said to her men. "This wasn't part of the plan, so we're going to have to wing it. Our job is to take out any security people outside the building without alerting anybody inside." She divided her group into two teams. "Bill, your team goes counterclockwise, and watch out for the front door; there could be extra men there. Gag anybody you detain. The rest of you will come with me, clockwise. We'll meet on the opposite side of the building. I think the kitchen door is over there, and when we get the order to move in, we'll go through the kitchen. Expect armed resistance at all times. When we get inside, there are going to be more people than we have cuffs or ties for. Cuff the staff first, then the male guests. Cuff the women only if we have ties left. Now, go!"

Holly started up the driveway to the clubhouse at a trot, Daisy moving easily beside her, her men following. Keeping to her right, moving silently through the grass, she came to the pro shop entrance. A man was standing at the door, fumbling with a set of keys. She let him lock it, then she pulled her baton and struck him sharply across the back of the neck with it. He emitted a small grunt and collapsed. One of her men used a plastic tie to secure his hands behind him, gagged him, then they went on their way. They made it nearly to the other end of the building before Holly saw someone else, and he saw her at the same time. She raised her silenced pistol and hissed, "Freeze!" His hand went under his jacket, and she fired once. He flew backward, his pistol striking the side of the clubhouse.

Holly ran up to him. His eyes were open, staring, and his breath was rattling from his body. After a moment, he was still. "First time," she whispered to herself. "No need to tie or gag him," she said. She ran on, the tempo of the booming music keeping time with her feet.

She came to the rear corner of the clubhouse and peeked around the corner. Two men in white cooks' clothing stood beside some garbage cans, smoking, twenty yards from the kitchen door. She dropped Daisy's leash, stepped out from behind the building and held the pistol out before her. "Freeze!" she commanded. Her men stepped out, their weapons ready. The two men looked at them: one threw his hands into the air; the other bolted for the kitchen door.

"Daisy!" She pointed at the running man. "Stop and guard!" Daisy took as if fired from a cannon. Six feet from the kitchen door she sank her teeth into a running leg, dumping the man onto the ground. Then she stood over him, snarling quietly. The man did not move a muscle.

Holly secured the other cook, then went to the man lying on the ground.

"That dog bit me!" the man complained.

"Shut up, or I'll let her tear your head off!" Holly whispered. She tied and gagged him. When she looked up, the remainder of the team appeared, dragging three men, all tied and gagged.

"All clear," one of them said.

Holly picked up the radio. "Team four, objective accomplished. At the kitchen door, awaiting further instructions."

The music was louder than ever. Holly thanked God for it.

Harry heard Holly's transmissions. "All teams move to clubhouse. Cover all entrances and exits. Wait for my order before entering." He turned to Jackson. "How much longer before we're there?"

"Maybe thirty seconds," Jackson said. "Look, there's the main gate."

The van turned in, and, following his map, the driver headed for the country club.

"There it is," Jackson said, pointing. "All lit up."

"Jackson, you're to stay in this van, do you hear me?" Harry commanded. "You're unarmed, unofficial, and that armor isn't enough to protect you. Don't you get out unless I say so!"

"All right, all right," Jackson said.

Holly stood at the kitchen door and peeked inside. A dozen cooks and dishwashers were working like beavers inside. She held her radio to her ear.

"Team four," Harry said. "Take the kitchen, but go no farther. Confirm your objective."

"Let's go," Holly said. She and her team ran into the kitchen, weapons up. Nobody said a word. The cooks and their helpers stood like statues. Suddenly a door swung open, and a uniformed waiter strode in, sweating, carrying a tray of dirty plates.

Holly swung her pistol toward him. "Freeze! Armed man!" she said. An agent stepped forward and yanked the man's gun from under his arm. "Everybody lie down on the floor," she commanded, "and maybe you won't get shot." She pointed at the door to the dining room. "You two men, over there. Take anybody who comes in." She raised her radio to her ear and listened. Other teams were reporting that they were in position.

Harry Crisp's voice rang out. "All teams! Go, Go, Go!"

"Daisy!" Holly yelled, pointing around the room. "Guard!" She looked at the men on the floor. "Anybody moves, the dog will kill him!" She turned to the rest of her team. "All right, let's go!" As one man, they rushed the dining room door, Holly out front.

A wave of incredibly loud music struck them as they burst into the large room. Holly ran for the bandstand, knocking a guitarist out of the way, and grabbed the microphone. The music trailed off. She could see men in black pouring into the room through every door. "Everybody stand still! Nobody move! Police and FBI! You are all under arrest." She gazed out over the elegantly dressed, completely astonished crowd, the men in tuxedoes, the women in long, glittering dresses. Then all hell broke loose.

Everybody ran in all directions, trying to get out of the building. Tables were knocked over; people fought with FBI agents; waiters pulled guns; agents shot waiters.

Harry Crisp burst through the main dining room door, appalled at what he saw. "You!" he said to a man standing beside him holding a Mac 10 machine gun. "Take the suppressor off that thing."

The man did as he was told.

"Now fire a clip into the ceiling!"

The man pointed the weapon up and pulled the trigger. Forty-five-caliber rounds sprayed the ceiling, and the noise was incredible in the enclosed room. Ceiling tiles and glass fell onto the panicked crowd.

Holly yelled into the microphone again. "On the floor! Everybody lie down on the floor!" This time it worked. People—men and women alike—dropped like slain cattle, shielding their heads from falling debris. Only FBI men were left standing.

Hurd Wallace stepped up onto the stage beside Holly. "I guess we've got them all," he said.

"Do you see Barney Noble?" she asked.

"No, and I've been looking for him."

"Then we haven't got them."

Harry Crisp stepped up onto the stage and grabbed the microphone from Holly, but she cupped her hand over it.

"Harry, Barney isn't here; I'm taking my team and going to his house."

"Go," Harry said, then he addressed his supine audience. "I am Special Agent Harry Crisp of the Federal Bureau of Investigation. You are all under arrest. You will form a line at the rear of the room and give your names and your passports to the agents who ask for them. Do it now!!!" he yelled.

An agent ran up to the stage. "Holly, your dog won't let us into the kitchen."

Holly ran for the kitchen.

Holly and her team were back in the van. "Take your next right," she said, consulting her map. "It's the first house on the left. Switch off your lights now, and don't turn into the driveway."

The driver did as he was told. The van glided to a halt on the street, a few yards from the driveway.

Holly looked at the house. It was handsomely designed, but not large; no lights were burning. "Everybody out of the van, but don't slam any doors," she said. "I think Barney might still be asleep, and I don't want to wake him until we're ready." She led the group up the driveway. Near the front door she stopped them. "There may be an easy way to do this," she said, taking off her helmet and body armor and slipping out of the FBI jumpsuit.

"What the hell are you doing?" an agent asked.

"I'm going to ring the doorbell," she said. "If Barney's in bed, he'll come down to answer it, and a familiar face will be standing outside." She took off her gun belt and dropped it, then, with the Beretta in her hand, she went up the front walk, gesturing to the others to take positions out of sight. She looked through a glass side panel into the house, but the interior was dark. She rang the doorbell and stood, the pistol behind her, and waited for Barney Noble to walk into her hands.

Ham walked around the com center, looking into offices. "We got it clean," he said to his men. "Let's check out downstairs." He ran down the steps, went to the end of the corridor and turned the corner. Before him sat the large steel door with its security features. "I wonder what's behind that," he said.

"Whatever it is," an agent replied, "it's what we came for. I hope to Christ it's illegal."

Harry Crisp's car arrived at the airfield. Four FBI vehicles were parked on the runway, and agents surrounded the tower. Harry got out of his car and approached them. "How did it go?" he asked.

"Only one man in the tower," the agent said. "We took it clean."

"Is there any aircraft here that could take off?"

"A dozen or so, but there are no pilots here."

"Put their man back in the tower, under guard, and get those vans off the runway. If any aircraft wants to land, let it, and detain everybody aboard. Got that?"

"Yes, sir," the man said.

Harry got back into his car. "Let's go see the com center," he said. "Have we heard anything from the gun emplacements?"

"We got a report while you were out of the car," an agent said. "Everything is secure."

Harry turned to Jackson. "I guess you can get out of that armor," he said. "You look pretty silly in it."

Holly rang the doorbell again. No one came. She turned to the nearest agent, flattened against the side of the house. "I guess we're going to have to go in," she said.

"Not until you get back into that gear," the man said, pointing at the jumpsuit and heap of armor. Holly got back into it and stood away from the door. Two men with a ram tore the jamb off with a single thrust, and the group flooded into the house, flashlights and guns out in front of them.

"Daisy, stay with me," Holly said, then headed upstairs, followed by two men. She stopped at every corner, gun at the ready, safety off. A moment later she was in the master bedroom. Suddenly the bedside lamp came on.

"Power's back," somebody called from downstairs.

The bed had been slept in, but the room was empty. "Search the house," Holly said.

Two minutes later, an agent entered the bedroom, pushing a beautiful young woman ahead of him. She was wearing a lacy negligee.

"Where's Barney Noble?" Holly demanded.

"I don't know," she said. "He left when the lights went out the second time. He told me to stay here. When I heard you break down
the door, I hid in the guest room."

"He may have gotten out of the house, but he won't get out of
Palmetto Gardens," an agent pointed out.

Holly picked up her radio. "Marina," she said. "This is Holly."

"Marina," a voice replied.

"Is your location secured?"

"Roger. We were a couple of minutes late, but it's secured."

Holly picked up her map and looked. "Jesus, we're less than a
hundred yards from the marina. Barney's gone."

"What now?" an agent asked.

"You guys can join the house searches," she said, "but first, drop
me off at the com center. I want to see that."

On the way, Holly took out her cell phone and called her station.

"Orchid Beach Police Department," a woman's voice said.

"It's Chief Barker. I want a statewide APB on one Barney Noble,
white male, late fifties, six-one, two hundred pounds, short, gray hair,
armed and dangerous. The charge is murder of a police officer."

"Got it, Chief."

"And call the coast guard and ask them to stop anything moving
on the river. Check every boat for Noble."

"I'm on it."

Holly broke the connection. She had a sick feeling in the pit of
her stomach. Barney Noble was gone, and the chances of catching
him were growing slimmer by the minute.

Harry Crisp toured the entire com center building, once the lights
had come back on, and he finished up at the huge steel door. "Anybody got an opinion on how to deal with that?"

Bill stood next to him and examined the door. "We could blow it, but God knows what it would do to the computer equipment in the building. I think what we need here is a first-rate criminal."

"Everything here is electronic," Harry said. "The keypad and the palm reader. Get a couple of our electronics people in here and see if they can jump-start that thing."

Holly got out of the van at the com center, and it drove away. Teams of agents were conducting a house-to-house search, armed with warrants, and the agents in her group went off to join them. She met Harry Crisp on his way out the door.

"How did it go?" she asked.

"Perfectly. But there's a steel door in there that we've got to deal with before we can find out what's downstairs. I've got two men on it, and I'll have a report soon."

"Where's Ham?"

"He's around here somewhere. He and his group did brilliantly. I don't know what we'd have done without him."

Jackson stepped up. "Did you arrest Barney Noble?"

Holly shook her head. "He got out, probably by way of the marina."

"Shit," Jackson said.

A man came out of the com center. "Harry," he said, "The steel door is open. It was a piece of cake."

Harry rushed back inside, followed closely by Holly and Jackson. The door was, indeed, open. A stairway led down from it.

"Let me clear the area, first, Harry," a man called out. Two men with automatic weapons went down the well-lighted stairs. "Okay," one of them called out, "all clear."

Harry and his entourage walked down the stairs and emerged into a large room containing only a desk and a huge steel door.

Holly's mouth dropped open. "Holy shit," she said under her breath.

"What the hell is that?" Harry asked.

Jackson spoke up. "Looks like a bank vault, Harry."

"I know that, but what the hell is it doing down here?"

"Looks like these people don't want you to know what's behind it," Jackson said. "Looks like there's a time lock, too," he said, pointing, "set for nine A.M. Even with the combination, you wouldn't get it open until then."

"It's a Friedrich," an agent said. "German. I think they've got an office in New York. Maybe Miami, too."

"Call them first thing in the morning and get an expert down here to open it," Harry said. "Jesus, I hate waiting."

Ham joined them and slipped an arm around Holly. "Wasn't this fun?" he said.

60

Holly sat in the dining room of the Palmetto Gardens Country Club at seven A.M. and finished a large breakfast. Harry had ordered the staff to work as usual, except the dining room was full of federal agents instead of members. The staff had cleaned up the mess from the ruined ceiling. Harry Crisp sat down beside her with a cup of coffee.

"So, who have we got here, Harry?"

Harry grinned. "It's sort of an international Appalachin," he said. "They've all got good passports, but in fake names, and nobody will say anything, but it looks like we've got the number two man in the Cali Cartel and the number one man in the Mexican organization. And that's just for starters. We're running prints now, and a courier is bringing mug books from Miami. I'd be willing to bet a year's pay that we've got the biggest bust ever."

"Except for Barney Noble," she said.

"I'm sorry my guys were late to the party at the marina," he said, "but Barney will turn up. He can run, but he can't hide—not for long."

"I hope you're right," Holly said. "I want him bad."

Harry waved an arm at the view of the golf course out the window. "How do you like my country club?" he asked. "This is all *mine,* now, this and whatever's in the vault at the com center. We'll confiscate it all, nice and legal-like."

"It looks good on you, Harry."

"It's a relief, I tell you," Harry said. "My career was on the line here."

"Mine, too," Holly said. "I've just busted into the property of the biggest taxpayers in town. If it came to nothing, my plan was to blame the FBI."

Harry laughed. "I was going to blame you."

Holly looked at her watch. "Well, there's nothing else for me to do here, so I think I'll go home and grab a shower and a change of clothes and go to work. Keep me posted, will you? I'll be anxious for news. Is this going to make morning television?"

Harry shook his head. "We're keeping it locked down until we've got some more information. We should be able to delay any kind of statement until the end of the day."

Holly got up and went to find a ride out of Palmetto Gardens. She found a car and driver and asked to be taken to the station; she wanted to know what was going on there.

She was dropped off in the parking lot and went inside. All was quiet. "Anything going on?" she asked the dispatcher.

"Not a thing," the young man replied. "We haven't had a call of any kind all night, except for your APB on Barney Noble."

"Anything at all on that?"

"Not a peep."

"Is Jane in yet?"

"No, she's not due for another hour."

Holly went back to her office to check her messages and found nothing of consequence. She looked into Jane Grey's empty office, and that reminded her that she had something unpleasant to do, and she might as well get it over with.

She put Daisy in the chief's car and, following a map, drove out to Jane's house. It was an attractive, if modest place, in a good neighborhood. A lawn sprinkler system was at work, and the grass was green. Holly pulled into the driveway behind Jane's station wagon, which was sitting there with its tailgate open, half filled with boxes and luggage. It looked as though Jane was planning to go somewhere. Holly got out of the car, went to the front door and rang the bell.

Jane came to the door, dressed, but looking frazzled. "Holly," she said. "What are you doing here at this hour? Is anything wrong?"

"We have to talk, Jane. Can I come in?"

"Why, uh, yes, of course. Come in and sit down." She showed Holly to a chair. "There's some coffee on. Can I get you some?"

"No, thanks. Sit down, Jane."

Jane perched on the edge of a chair facing Holly.

"Are you going somewhere?" Holly asked. "I see you're loading your car."

"Oh, ah, just a brief trip. My mother is ill. She lives in Miami. I was going to call you as soon as you got to the station."

"Your mother is dead, Jane," Holly said. "I read that in your personnel record, along with some other very interesting information about you."

Jane looked at her oddly. "What information do you mean?"

"Your original employment application gave your name as Jane Grey Noble, divorced. You were married to Barney Noble, weren't you?"

Jane flushed. "Yes, I was, for a little more than fifteen years."

"So when you were divorced, you left Miami and came up here?"

"Yes, I read about the job in a police journal. I had had a clerical job with the Miami department."

"And that's when you met Barney?"

"In Miami, yes. He had a security firm."

"And then Barney turned up here, in Orchid Beach, didn't he?"

"So I heard." Jane was increasingly nervous.

"And you began seeing him again."

"Not really."

"And when did you start giving him information about the Orchid Beach Police Department?"

"I don't know what you mean," Jane said, flustered.

"Sure you do, Jane. You kept tabs on Chet Marley for Barney, didn't you?"

Jane said nothing but looked at her feet.

"It was you who told Barney about Chet's conversations with the accountant from Palmetto Gardens."

Jane still said nothing.

"Chet confided in you, didn't he? He told you everything, and you reported everything to Barney."

"I didn't do anything wrong," Jane said.

"You got Chet Marley killed, that's all," Holly said. "You're an accessory to his murder."

"I had nothing to do with his murder," Jane said.

"Sure you did, Jane. What you told Barney convinced him that Chet had to be killed. And after I arrived and went to work, you reported all my actions to Barney, didn't you? At least, those you knew about."

Jane shrugged. "All right, Barney and I are . . . close," she said.

"Oh, really? Funny, I was at Barney's house last night. There was a very beautiful young girl there, Jane."

Jane looked horrified, but her gaze was not at Holly, but over her shoulder. Holly heard a door squeak. Daisy stood up and looked at the door.

"Good morning," a male voice said.

Holly turned to find Barney Noble standing in the kitchen doorway, a gun in his hand. "Morning, Barney," she replied.

"Looks like you've discovered our little love nest," he said. "What have you two been talking about?"

"I was just telling Jane about the young woman I found in your house last night."

"And exactly what were you doing at my house last night, Holly?" Barney asked.

"I was in the company of three hundred federal agents who went into Palmetto Gardens in the middle of the night and shut it down."

Barney didn't look very surprised. "I figured something was up when the lights went out and the backup generator failed, too."

"So you went out through the marina and called Jane."

"Something like that."

"And that's why you and Jane are packing, isn't it?"

"Could be."

"The feds are out there right now combing the computer files at the com center. The vault will be open soon, too."

"Funny, I don't even know what's in the vault, or on the computers, either," Barney said. "I just ran a security force, that's all. The feds have got nothing on me."

"It doesn't really matter," Holly said. "The feds aren't all that interested in you, Barney. You're mine now."

"What the hell are you talking about?" Barney asked.

"Well, let's start with the state charges," Holly replied. "There's falsification of state records, perjured weapons applications, that sort of thing. But most of all there are two counts of murder in the first degree. Bob Hurst spilled everything, Barney, and I've got it all on tape."

"Stand up," Barney said, raising his gun.

Holly got slowly to her feet. "I hope you don't think you're going anywhere, Barney. There's a local and statewide APB out on you already. You won't get far."

"I'll use your police car," Noble said, "and I'll get as far as the Orchid Beach Airport. There's a plane coming for me. I'll be out of the country in two hours."

"Barney, you didn't say anything about a plane," Jane said.

"I was just making the arrangements on the kitchen phone, honey," Barney replied. Noble reached over and pulled Holly's Beretta from her holster.

"Well, hadn't we better get going, then?" Jane asked.

"Sure, honey, in just a minute."

"You don't get it, do you, Jane?" Holly said. "You're not going anywhere; you never were. Barney was leaving here alone."

"You shut up, damn you!" Jane spat.

Barney flipped off the safety on Holly's pistol.

Holly knew that before another half a minute had passed, both she and Jane would be dead, and Barney would be on his way. "Think about it, Barney," she said, and her heart was in her mouth.

"I already thought about it," Barney replied, "but I didn't know I was going to be lucky enough to get you, too, bitch." He raised Holly's weapon and fired two shots into Jane's chest. She was thrown against the wall and collapsed on the floor.

As the second shot was being fired Holly moved. She ran at him and hit him low, driving her shoulder into a kidney and taking him down. Daisy got hold of an ankle.

Barney dropped one of the guns and used his free hand to take Holly by the hair, pulling her head back. But Holly had hold of his other wrist and was able to keep the gun pointed away from her.

Barney had size and strength on Holly, but she was younger and no weakling, and she had the advantage of desperation, not to mention Daisy's help. His face was close to hers, and she managed to drive an elbow into his eye, hurting him enough that he let go of her hair. She tried to pin him to the floor, but he rolled over and dragged her to her feet, snaking an arm around her waist and taking her weight off the floor.

Daisy still clung to his ankle, resisting all attempts by Noble to kick her away. Holly jammed a thumb into his uninjured eye and twisted it, hanging on to his wrist for dear life. The gun went off once, then again, shattering a display of crockery with the first shot and putting the second dead center through the picture window. Holly could see a car in the street slow down for some rubbernecking.

Holly got some traction again and sank a punch into Barney's solar plexus. Then, with all her strength, she drove him backward. The two smashed through the punctured picture window together, landing in the azaleas outside the window, taking Daisy with them, Holly on top. Barney was now virtually blind and very winded, and when Holly sank her teeth into his thumb he let go of the pistol. She rolled them both away from it and began punching him with both fists wherever she could—face, neck, belly. The sprinklers were soaking them both, and they were making the lawn muddy. Finally she got him turned over, facedown, with his wrist between his shoulder blades. She got that wrist cuffed and used the leverage to cause him enough pain that he stopped resisting. She cuffed both hands behind his back. "Release, Daisy," she said to the dog, and Daisy backed off, still growling.

Holly got Barney up on his toes and marched him toward her police car. She shoved him into the backseat and slammed the door. He was as good as in a jail cell now, with the wire barrier between the front and rear seats, and rear doors that wouldn't open from the inside. She went into the house and checked on Jane. She was dead. Then she went back to the car and grabbed the radio microphone.

"Base, this is the chief," she said.

"This is base, Chief, go ahead."

"Get an ambulance and a coroner out to Jane Grey's address; she's dead of a gunshot wound. Find Hurd Wallace and tell him to get out here, too, to secure the scene. I have Barney Noble in custody. I want a paramedic to treat him for superficial wounds at the station, when I get him there."

"Roger, Chief," the man said. "I'm on it."

Holly put the microphone back in its cradle and turned to look at Barney Noble, who had struggled into a sitting position. One eye was already closed, and he was squinting at her with the other.

"Bitch," he said.

"Barney," she replied, "coming from you, that's the highest praise I've ever had."

61

Holly waited for Hurd Wallace to arrive and take over the scene, then she drove Barney Noble to the station and booked him on three counts of homicide. Jane Grey was dead, and Holly was the eyewitness to her murder. She had never cared much for the death penalty, but now, in the case of Barney Noble, she had become enthusiastic.

When her work was done, she drove home, showered and tried to go to sleep. It couldn't be done. She dressed in a fresh uniform and drove out to Palmetto Gardens. An FBI agent was manning the front gate.

"Where's Harry Crisp?" she asked the man.

"At the com center, I think. I just let in some guy from the safe company."

Holly drove into the compound and out to the com center. Federal agents, still in their black clothes and heavily armed, stood around the front door, looking bored.

"Harry inside?" she asked a man she knew.

"Yeah, Holly, go on in."

Holly went into the building and downstairs to the vault room.

Harry and a group of agents stood around watching a middle-aged man in a nerd outfit—polyester trousers, short-sleeved dress shirt, tie, pocket protector—open a briefcase, take out a sheet of paper and start to turn the dial on the door of the vault. He turned a large wheel, and the door swung open a few inches.

"Jesus," Harry said, "how'd you do that so fast?"

"It was easy," the man replied. "I had the combination."

"Oh."

"We keep the combinations of all our safes, just in case."

Harry stepped forward, took hold of the door and swung it slowly open. "Okay," he said, "let's see what we've got here."

Holly followed him inside the vault room, which was, she reckoned, about eighteen by twenty-four feet. She stopped and stared. The room was filled with steel shelving and crisscrossed by aisles. On many of the shelves, stacked from floor to ceiling, were shrink-wrapped blocks of currency.

Harry took a block off a shelf and cut through the plastic wrapping. "Twenties, fifties and hundreds," he said. He read a label. "There's half a million dollars in this one package."

There were some whistles, then silence, as the group toured the room.

"Bearer bonds," Harry said, thumbing through a stack of certificates. "Hundreds, thousands of them."

At the rear of the room were two steel cabinets with shallow drawers. Harry opened them to reveal trays of cut diamonds. In other drawers were rows of gold coins, mostly Krugerrands.

Holly finally managed to speak. "This is breathtaking," she said. "Is there this much cash anywhere else in the world?"

"Maybe at the Federal Reserve Bank in New York," Harry said. "Hardly anyplace else."

"Why is it here?" she asked.

"I don't know, but I expect the computer data will tell us." He turned to his men. "All right, I want an inventory, and I want it fast. The currency will be easy, since the packages are labeled. Count the Krugerrands and the diamonds; estimate the weight of each stone. There are gold bars over there. I want this done pronto!"

Holly followed Harry out of the vault and upstairs.

"Let's go up another floor and see how our guys are doing with the computers," he said.

Holly followed him to the top floor, where she was introduced to the head computer man.

"What have you got so far?" Harry asked.

"What we seem to have here is two things: one, a scheduling operation for drug shipments all over the world, from the poppy fields and jungles to the streets of American cities; and two, a collection point for cash from every corner of the United States."

"We found a hell of a lot of that downstairs in the vault," Harry said.

"They were shipping it out of here to points in South America and Europe," the computer man said.

"How?"

"Apparently, in the corporate jets that brought people into the complex. Customs did their usual searches when the planes came in, but nobody searches departing aircraft. They brought in passengers and took out passengers and money."

"We've already found half a dozen drug lords in residence," Harry said. "They come here for R and R and to collect their revenues and take them home. We're doing an analysis of the flight plans in and out of here that isn't complete yet, but when we're finished, we'll know where the money was going."

"Any idea how much money is down there?" the computer man asked.

"Not yet. Soon."

Holly sat in the Palmetto Gardens Country Club dining room over lunch with Harry Crisp and some of his men. An FBI agent came into the room, walking fast, looking around. He spied Harry, came over to the table and handed him a sheet of paper.

Harry looked at it for about a minute, while everyone else waited to find out what was going on. Finally, he spoke. "The estimated value of the contents of the vault is a little over *two billion dollars*," he said.

There was the sound of people sucking in breath, then a long silence.

"Harry," Holly asked, "since you're confiscating all this money on what is, after all, *my* turf, do you think I might be able to get a helicopter for my department?"

"Holly, I'll get you a squadron of jet fighters, if you like, and anything else your little heart desires."

"The helicopter will do for starters," Holly said. "Then I'll see what else I can think of."

62

The evening was growing cool. Holly and Jackson sat on the beach, warmed by a driftwood fire. Daisy lay between them, her head in Holly's lap, having her ears stroked. Eight months had passed since the Palmetto Gardens Bust, as it had become known across the country. Barney Noble was due to go on trial the following month; more than a hundred other people had taken plea bargains or been convicted of various federal and state crimes. Harry Crisp had netted eight major drug lords and more than a hundred of their underlings. Various federal law-enforcement agencies had been using Palmetto Gardens for training and recreational purposes, and a huge auction of the property would take place in another few months.

Harry Crisp was now the agent in charge of the Miami office of the Bureau, and there was talk in the papers of his being promoted to deputy director of the FBI, in a reshuffle at the Bureau. He and Holly had both been decorated by the director.

Jackson stroked Holly's cheek. "You think you might have everything under control, now?"

"Just about," Holly said. "But it won't be over for me until Barney Noble has been convicted."

"I can understand that," Jackson said. "I was just wondering if you might be able to take two or three weeks off between now and the trial."

"I've got the vacation time coming," she said. "What did you have in mind?"

"I don't know, where would you like to go on your honeymoon?"

Holly held his hand still. "Am I getting married?"

"Yep."

"Anybody I know?"

"Yep."

"When?"

"The sooner, the better. I know a judge who will perform the ceremony on short notice."

"Wow," Holly said.

"Wow, what?"

"I never really thought I'd get married."

"Life is full surprises," he said, kissing her. "You didn't answer my question."

"You didn't really ask me, did you?"

"I asked you where you'd like to go on your honeymoon."

"Oh, that," Holly said.

"Hawaii? Europe? The Caribbean?"

Holly hugged Daisy and smiled at her fiancé. "Anyplace that takes bitches," she said.

"I figured," Jackson replied.

Acknowledgments

I would like to thank my editor, HarperCollins Vice President and Associate Publisher Gladys Justin Carr, and her assistants, Elissa Altman and Deirdre O'Brien, for their hard work on and on behalf of this book. I would also like to thank Laura Leonard for her efforts in publicizing this and previous books.

I would also like to thank my agents, Morton L. Janklow and Anne Sibbald, as well as everyone else at Janklow & Nesbit for their continuing fine work in furthering my career.

I must also express my gratitude to my wife, Chris, who is always the first to read a manuscript. Her keen eye and sharp tongue help keep me out of trouble.

Finally, I would like to thank those people in a certain Florida town (which Orchid Beach may, in some ways, but not others, resemble) who have so quickly made us feel at home.